HOW

MEGAN
MITCHAM

Published by MM Publishing LLC
Edited by Jenny Sims
Proofread by Tina Rucci & Lynn Mullan
Cover Design by Shayne Leighton of Shayne Leighton Designs

HOW

To Dirty D, my ride or die. I don't know how I made it thirty-some-odd years without you in my life. Our friendship makes Larkin, Libby, Marlis, and Gen's look downright elementary. Here's to many-many-many more!

ONE

AGAIN? SHE'D BEEN FIVE TIMES IN THE PAST HOUR. Libby Irish snapped her boots together and clenched her legs. No room to cross them. The tactical response vehicle traded its consistent jitter for an all-out lurch. An expletive popped like a flash bang from the front, and Joel toppled as though a sniper's bullet had cut him down. She wasn't that lucky. A terrible thought. There it was all the same.

Travis, the FBI SWAT team leader, stayed him with a single massive hand. He nodded toward the top of the rig. "Handle, before you end up with your face in someone's barrel."

Laughs and whoops reverberated around the 8 x 4 footprint. Out of twelve federal agents cramped in the tin can, she was the only woman, and the only one who kept her snicker to herself.

"Hell, if Irish had found us a decent point of entry, we

wouldn't be tossed around like a bunch of pinballs." Joel grabbed the handle with both of his shaking fists.

She wished Travis had let Joel take a barrel to the nose but showed no outward reaction to the man's ignorant words. At least she was the only one who knew she had to pee. Her hands were as sure as the big guy's next to her, and she took solace in that.

"You should be kissing Irish's ass." Travis hitched an elbow toward her. "She found this route when none of us did. Dodging potholes in a rig is a fuckload better than dodging bullets in Kevlar."

The men answered with nods, grunts, and hell yeses.

Libby schooled her features as though she hadn't heard a thing. The attagirl spun in the vortex of her mind, bringing fresh air to a space caught in the vacuum of office politics. With a boss who hated her based solely on her gender—covertly, of course—this was a banner day in so many ways. Ross Quinn, her boss, knew how to play the game, which was why Joel was here at all. The dummy had his chance at this case for the past three years and had turned up squat. Had she been given a choice of who to bring on the op, she'd have chosen Alec. Someone—hell, the only one—who watched her back at the Bureau. Until Travis.

"Sixty seconds till contact." Travis pointed at Libby, the lead on the op, the lead on the case against the single citizen with the greatest cache of weapons ever known.

Libby hugged the assault rifle to her chest. She was all for the Second Amendment. However, stockpiling to start a rebellion from a tyrannical government that didn't exist, except inside the schizophrenic's mind? Nope. Not even a little. His illness didn't stop the few hundred followers he'd amassed from joining his cause. That put everyday citizens in harm's way and infringed on everyone's civil rights.

"Ten, nine, and Joel secure shipping containers on the west side of compound," she barked. The elite team members offered two fast checks while Joel groaned his. Before he was finished, she continued. "Eight, seven, six rear entrance breach." They confirmed quickly. They knew this. Everyone on the mission knew it. They'd been over it no less than a dozen times. But this was no conference room. This was no warehouse. This was go-time.

"Five, west side of the house and four, the east side." The men nearest her clipped their confirmations. "Three, two, with me at the front." The two standing in front of her bumped fists and offered her nods. "There's one known occupant in the house, our target, Darrell Hegarty. Haul ass to your posts. We move together at Travis's command."

She didn't have to pee anymore. Her blood churned, and her muscles ached to move.

Travis stood. "You heard the lady. I'm in your ear. If anything goes sideways, keep moving. Probability of bombs and traps are low, but two, six, and nine are checking and clearing before entry."

Libby and every other man in the vehicle gave the all-set signal except for Joel, who seemed to be in the midst of a panic attack.

"Ornby, you gonna puke?" Travis hollered.

"No, sir." Joel gagged.

"Good. You puke in my rig, you lick it up." Travis gave the signal, and everyone stood. A beat later, the tactical response vehicle rolled to a stop.

Excitement sizzled through Libby's veins.

"Let's move," Travis barked.

Libby pulled the lever, swung the door wide, and leaped out onto the final curve of the dirt road before it bypassed the rear of Hegarty's property. A thicket of evergreens shielded them from the view of the house. Travis and her breach team joined her.

Commotion drew their attention back to the truck. Joel shoved his way through the group, clung to the door, and spewed. The chunks of burger he'd eaten back at the warehouse they'd set up as base were as appetizing as every word that had ever come from his foul mouth. Bile and barely masticated food nearly hit the rear wheel. Travis rolled his eyes. A few of the guys laughed, but most were too anxious to care. They were in go-mode with their minds on the task at hand. He heaved once more and then spat before straightening and joining their group.

"You're with ten and nine," Travis growled. He pointed at the two men who leaped from the truck to avoid Joel's mess and gathered on the far side of the tree line.

The rest of the group hit the ground, splitting into their assigned teams.

Two and three, Travers and Knoles, flanked her, and they moved toward the property line, leading the group. At the east edge, she found the old, broken-down eighteen-wheeler. They used the rusted-out frame for cover and pushed to within two hundred yards of the house. Her heartbeat throbbed inside the tips of her fingers, but her breathing was slow and steady. She checked back, saw that everyone was together, and then gave the signal.

By the end of the hour, her career would be made or broken.

A grin set her mouth, and she ran for the northeast corner of the one-story house. Cut and crinkled wiring hung from a metal pipe protruding from the ceiling. Yellow paint curled up from the siding, revealing worn brown underneath. The sound of static found Libby's ears. It was as if the house itself was a static channel on an old bubble front television. Operable but no longer functional.

Most of the skirting had long ago fallen from around the structure. It littered the ground along with shards of glass from cracked windows that had been boarded up.

She signaled Travers and Knoles. They nodded, and the group pushed carefully forward, dodging slats and rusty nails as they made their way to the front porch.

"C team, in place and ready," they said through her earpiece.

The sound of static grew louder still.

Movement of a white curtain froze her to the ground just an inch past the front edge of the house. Travers' barrel jerked high, toward the center of mass through the wall. Knoles swiveled toward the rear of the house, centering his weapon at the window in the middle of the long wall.

Libby held her breath. She eased to the slats one centimeter at a time, reached for a mirror in her vest, and lifted the telescoping lens around the corner. Indeed, a white curtain had moved at the front of the house but not because a person moved it. Wind tickled her skin and ruffled the light fabric. She stowed the device and turned to her teammates.

"The window is open," she mouthed. "The curtain is moving." She pointed at her ear, emphasizing silence.

She climbed onto the porch and crawled on knees and one hand under the window to the far side of the door. Both men followed suit, except Knoles stayed on the opposite side of the door.

Travers remained crouched. He let the M4 Carbine slip to his side, held in place by a strap, and then produced a tiny camera on a bendable housing from his pocket and slipped it under the door near the corner. He pulled a phone from his pocket and watched as a video of the cluttered room beyond filled the screen.

Hegarty sat in a recliner ten feet from the front door. A laptop balanced on his hoisted legs. The dirty bottoms of his swollen, bare feet rested on a threadbare footrest. His fingers pecked at the keys. Libby expected to see guns of every shape and size littering the tabletops, countertops, end tables, and even leaned against walls, but there were none. Well, not zero, but not near the count she had expected.

Her stomach bottomed out. The nausea Joel had been battling minutes ago caught up with her. Maybe there had been something in the burgers. If only! This was her guy, no question. She'd followed up on the deliveries, his web traffic, and the satellite images. The guns had to be in the shipping containers. They had to be.

Travers directed her attention to the end table next to the recliner. There was a gun.

One freaking gun. A single gun. Woohoo.

She only cared about that one gun because it was really close to her suspect.

Knoles hugged his rifle a little closer to his chest. Travers nodded. They were all thinking the same things.

Is this the guy? How do we get him without getting shot?

Libby signaled Knoles, pointed at her flash grenade, then to his, and then at the open window. He nodded.

The camera panned up and around. There were no traps, no bombs. None that they could see anyway. Travers stashed the equipment and then nodded.

Libby covered her mouth. "A team in place and ready," she whispered into the coms.

Then they waited.

The more time that passed, the larger and more terrifying doubt's shadows became. Sure, Joel hadn't found any leads on the case. In the year that she'd had the case, she'd found leads. Three dead ends. And this one. What if this one, the one that utilized hundreds of man-hours, SWAT, and base support, was another dead end?

If it was, she hoped Hegarty was a good shot and went for her first.

"B team in place and ready," they whispered.

Knoles pulled the flash bang from his vest. Libby

pulled hers. Travers pulled the battering ram from his pack.

"On my mark," Travers breathed ever so quietly into the coms. "Three. Two. One."

The old wood splintered. Knoles launched his grenade through the open window. The door flew wide. Libby chunked hers into the house.

Boom! Boom!

They moved as a unit through the door and into the house in seconds. Hegarty's laptop lay on the ground. He screamed and lunged for his gun.

"No!" Libby screamed and trained the barrel of her Glock on his chest. She did not want to shoot him, but she would.

Hegarty's watering eyes found her gaze and stalled for a beat. It was all the time Knoles needed to secure Hegarty's pistol and continue through the house, clearing as he went.

The team poured in from the rear and split off in their respective directions.

Libby stared at the scraggly kept, bearded man who tested the stability of the oversized chair. "Darrell Hegarty?"

He glared at her.

"Federal Bureau of Investigation. We have reason to believe you have illegally amassed a significant cache of weapons."

Travers moved in with cuffs, grabbed the man's left hand and placed the binding around his meaty wrist.

In a flash, Hegarty plunged his right hand between the chair's cushion and his big thigh. The bright silver of a long-barreled handgun gleamed as he drew it from the chair.

"Gun!" Libby fired a single round.

It tore through the first two knuckles of his right hand.

The Desert Eagle 50 AE clattered to the ground. Darrell Hegarty shrieked as though he'd never seen blood.

Knoles skidded to a halt in the center of the room.

"Fuck me."

"Fuck you?" Travers squealed. "Fuck me. I thought I was shot."

"Would've been." Knoles rushed forward and helped him cuff Hegarty. The two agents hauled the man across the small living room and through the splintered front door, away from any other stashed weapons.

"I need medical attention for Hegarty and a report on those shipping containers," Libby demanded into the coms.

"Critical?" someone asked.

"Negative," she assured. Though, the guy crying wouldn't believe it.

"Joel? Containers?" Libby barked.

"I don't know how to tell you this," Joel wheezed.

Libby's heart sank.

"This is ten, they're loaded! Stuffed so full, you'll be here cataloguing for days. Hell, weeks. I've never seen so many guns ... and I'm from Alabama."

TWO

"YOU SHOULD TAKE THE DAY OFF." Larkin's voice filtered through the speaker of Libby's cell phone and echoed off the mirror and tile.

"Says the woman who works so much she built a condo directly above and adjoining her office." Libby wrestled with the back of her earring.

"Okay, but I built that so I could get more than two hours of sleep."

She muffled a curse as the tiny piece of metal slipped through her fingers and landed on the floor. It bounced several times before coming to rest near the tip of her black pump. When she crouched low, the muscles across her lower back tensed and burned. Nearly forty hours spent scooping rifles off a dirty floor and hunching over the computer cataloguing them into the database had taken its toll.

"We didn't leave Elk State Forest until midnight. The plane didn't land until two thirty a.m." Libby squeezed the fastener between her thumb and index finger, secured it to the back of her simple pearl earring, stood, and assessed her reflection.

Puffy eyelids. Dark circles below her eyes matched her extra flat dark hair. There wasn't time for makeup. And really, what did it matter? At the office, she wanted to impress everyone with her work ethic and drive. Makeup only attracted the wrong kind of attention. She'd learned that on day one.

Libby offered herself a grin. At least she had her smile. With her big lips, it distracted from her obvious lack of sleep. Over the years, she'd learned it put people at ease. It also made them underestimate her.

"By the time I got home, I was too amped to sleep." She snagged her phone from the counter and hit the light on her way out of the bathroom. Scooping the hulking computer backpack off the bedroom floor, she slung it over her shoulder, crushing the air from her lungs.

"Because you got him," Larkin squealed.

"I did." Libby headed for the kitchen but paused in the short corridor. Her fists double punched the air above her head. "I finally did." Joy she hadn't gotten the chance to fully embrace wrapped its arms around her and squeezed, lifting with it all the doubt and worry she'd shouldered for the past year.

"Now, we celebrate."

"Hell yes, we do." She hurried to the fridge and pulled a pre-prepped meal from the cold, shoved it in her pack along with an apple and a cashew bar, and headed for the door.

"We'll have to do it in Gen's hospital room," Larkin whispered.

Libby paused with her hand on the knob of the back

door. "Of course. I'm totally fine with that. I feel guilty for leaving during her ICU stay." She plucked her car keys from the counter. "I'm just glad she's in a real room now."

"Real hospital room," Larkin corrected. "She's ready for her real bedroom."

"I bet she is." Libby unlocked the door, opened it, and released a truly bloodcurdling scream.

"Libby? Libby, what's wrong? Are you okay? Libby!"

"Shit!" Libby shivered and gagged a little. "Yes, I'm fine." She backed into her house several steps, staring at the bloody carcass at the center of her threshold.

"What the hell happened? A snake?"

"No, Larkin. Why are you so obsessed with snakes? I've lived here for two years and have never seen a snake. Wait, I know why. I learned it in Psych 101. Freud taught me." She laughed, thankful to have something besides the dead rat to think about.

"Laugh it up. But you were the one bursting my eardrum two seconds ago."

"Sorry! I'm trying to leave for work, and my neighbor's cat left a dead rat on my porch ... again."

It was Larkin's turn to gag.

"Yeah, vomit." She didn't mention that she shot someone's knuckles off two days ago without flinching. Larkin would want to know why, and then she'd tell the girls, and then they'd worry more than they already did about her chosen profession.

"Wait. I thought the cat was yours. Didn't you rescue it from the Brooklyn shelter last year?"

"Yes, I did." Libby sighed. "I've gotta go. Text me later with the time."

"I will. Good luck with the rat."

"Thanks." Libby ended the call, shoved the phone in her pack, and set it and the keys on her small breakfast table in the kitchen. She placed one foot in the doorframe and eased her cheek around it as though she was clearing a building full of hostiles.

The killer, aptly named Killer, lounged on Libby's padded outdoor chair, licking one of his white paws and rubbing it over his black face. Sure, he looked cute and peaceful, but she knew better. She pulled the end of her right pant leg up and eyed the pattern of scars his teeth had left just above her ankle.

"Asshole." She glared at the cat from the relative safety of her home. He wouldn't come in here, not since the day he attacked her and escaped. His orange ears bobbed like little devil's horns. Yep, she knew better.

Libby stepped over the rat and out onto the screened-in porch. It was her favorite place. The cat stood and rounded his back. His lips curled and white teeth flashed.

"Damn, am I that repulsive?" She threw her hands wide. "All I wanted was for you to love me. But no." Her thumb hiked toward her neighbor's house only six or seven yards from the edge of hers. "You love him. I hate to tell you. He's hot, but he's weird as hell."

She says as she argues with a cat about the state of their relationship.

"Forget it. Thanks for the present." She pointed at the furry rodent. "Now, if you would, take a hike. I have to get to work." Libby pulled open the screen door and waited. And waited. The woman at the shelter had warned he'd had a rough life. She'd been willing to give him all the time he needed to acclimate. He'd tried her on for two days before bolting.

Killer plopped his bottom on the cushion.

"Drawing clear battle lines, huh?"

Libby hypothesized that her presence inside the porch kept the cat from leaving. She walked down the three short steps and rounded to the far side of the concrete block. It wasn't easy or comfortable, but she shoved the screen and pushed the door wide from the ground. If it swung the other way, he wouldn't be able to get inside.

Killer stretched out his front feet and slowly relaxed himself in the chair.

"Jerk."

Her watch read 7:38 a.m. She didn't have time for this. Her gaze slid to the right toward her neighbor's house. There were no lights on. There hadn't been any on when she'd arrived home in the early morning. He usually kept odd hours. It was nothing for her to see him awake in the middle of the night or early morning. Then again, she could go days at a time without seeing him at all. In the past six months, they'd both worked crazy hours. She didn't want to bother him, so she marched back up her stairs. As she looked at the cat and his sharp claws, her nerves faltered. Her steps eased to a tiptoe toward Killer.

"Can you go outside, buddy? If I leave you here, you'll be stuck until who knows when." There was so much work to be done.

The cat ignored her. She eased closer, cast her gaze to the ceiling as though she didn't care a thing about him, and reached for the arm of the chair. Killer hissed and swatted at her hand. She jerked away at the last instant, saving her own knuckles. She hooked the toe of her shoe around the leg of the chair and pulled it toward the door. The little devil lunged and spat.

"Fine." Libby stomped into her house, slung on her bag, grabbed her keys, slammed the door, and locked it. All the while, she dodged the rat carcass. "Stay! See if I care." She yanked open the screen door and let it crash closed behind her. "You're going to starve, you know." Her parting joust stabbed her in the back because she immediately thought of the cat eating on the rat. Her stomach gave way.

She stomped in the opposite direction from her car to

the left, hooking a right through the yard to her neighbor's back door. He didn't have a screened porch only squatted concrete steps, which meant his backyard was bigger.

Libby knocked. "Hello?" She knocked again, louder. "Hello?"

7:43 a.m.

Cupping both hands to her face, Libby pressed them to the glass. Her gaze searched the interior. Their homes, it seemed, were mirror images of one another. She stared into a kitchen as tidy as her own. Tidier even. There wasn't a stack of mail on his breakfast table. Ah, but there was a wok and base on his stovetop. They were even. Her study shifted from the kitchen into a small living room. An open book sat on the coffee table. She hadn't known he could read. He certainly couldn't speak. Not a word in the more than a year that he'd lived next to her.

A small couch sat on the wall nearest her house. Above it hung a huge world map. It looked old and expensive, housed in a sturdy frame. On either side perched what seemed to be authentic traditional African masks. Not the kind you'd pick up in a Pier One or World Market. The closest one looked to be an expressive dark face carved out of an animal hide of some sort. The far one was wood. It seemed etched from the body of a tree.

On the far wall, closest to the road, hung a collection of ancient and highly lethal weapons. A tomahawk. A mace. A spear. The most jarring of the arsenal was a nearly foot long and four inch wide tapering silver dagger on an H-shaped gold handle. A gold goddess adorned the hilt of the blade. She could imagine the crossbar being the place where the warrior held the small dagger just above the knuckles and jabbing it—

A deep cough jerked her from the window. She spun on unstable heels, and her long, high ponytail smacked her cheek.

Her neighbor stood in the grass and was nearly eye level with her in heels and on the steps. His wide frame filled a leather jacket. He wore ass-stomping boots, threadbare jeans, and a disinterested scowl. He was a hell of a lot stealthier than when he'd first moved in. His limp had gotten so much better, and she hadn't noticed it in several months. So much better that the huge man had snuck up on her without a sound.

Libby's body heated twenty degrees. Her nipples plumped, and her lower lips bloomed in outrageous invitation. Thank heavens she wore her dull black suit, and she had a ton of practice at acting like she didn't want to rip his clothes from his body, climb him, and fuck him where he stood.

"Your cat is on my porch again."

His dark gaze slid from her to her porch. She noticed the way the muscles in his neck contracted and bulged. The clean lines of his face pulled her in. He had a hint of dimples, but his jaw, lips, and cheekbones were too pronounced to allow any more features. His gaze slid back.

She swallowed the saliva pooling in her mouth and staved off the urge to lick her lips. "He brought me a rat."

He bowed his head, flopping the dark curls of his unruly hair forward. After a beat, he straightened.

Could he not speak, or did he not want to speak to her? She gave him several moments in which to say something, anything, but nothing came. Maybe the same accident that had given him the limp had taken his voice. Maybe he was a monk, forbidden to speak. Maybe he thought her not worth the effort of speaking.

Libby offered him one of her biggest smiles. "Okay." She sidestepped and then descended the stairs. His nearly black eyes tracked her movement. This close on the same level, he seemed a giant. He wasn't all that tall or all that wide. Maybe he reached six feet four, two hundred and twenty pounds of muscle. His persona, silent and mysterious, was imposing as hell.

"Have a great day." She waved.

One foot in front of the other, Libby made it past him, her porch, and the demon cat to the corner of her house. She told herself not to look back, but like every other time, she stole every opportunity she could to look at him. He hadn't moved from the bottom of his steps, and he still watched her.

She offered him a sarcastic bow and rounded the corner to her car. Cheeks flushed and breaths racing, she depressed the key fob and slid into her two-year-old Honda Civic Hybrid. She should feel creeped out by her weird neighbor, but damn if she wasn't ready to come on her leather seat.

THREE

LIBBY STUFFED HERSELF ONTO the elevator full of other people in dark-colored suits. This was where the fifteen minutes she'd lost dealing with the feral cat and his equally wild handler would have come in handy. Fifteen minutes sooner and she'd have been sharing the space with a handful of people. Instead, she reconciled herself to the cramped corner with the edge of someone's briefcase jabbing her ass cheek. At least she hoped it was a briefcase.

Finally, the double doors neared her floor.

"This is me." Libby wormed her way to the front, and the moment they opened, she poured out the double doors.

Two seconds out of the tin can and Libby noticed the significant murmur among the cubicles in the middle of the floor. Usually the early morning was quieter than a funeral parlor. The murmur reached a low roar by the time she made it past two rows of cubicles. A slow clap started when she hit the center of the large room. It rumbled louder and louder until she stopped and turned in a tight circle, desperately searching for the cause of the upheaval.

People stood behind their desks. Others slipped from their offices along the wall. Still more crept in from the locker rooms and break room. They began to whoop and holler. Some clapped. All of them directed their mania on her.

She ran a hand down the buttons on her blouse as terror gripped her. Had one of them come undone? Had more? It'd happened more times than she cared to remember but never quite so publicly. Each secured button bumped against the edges of her fingers.

Then Libby remembered that she'd caught Darrell Hegarty, the man with revolution in his heart and the means and followers with which to carry it out on a relatively small but terribly bloody scale. The news would have been dispensed in their daily department email on Monday. Hadn't people forgotten by now? It was midweek, for goodness' sake. Surely other important things had happened since then.

A grin stretched her mouth so wide she covered it with her hand. She stared wide-eyed at people she passed every day, people she spoke to only in polite greeting, and people she looked up to. These people were celebrating her success. She'd been on the other side many times before, and now it was her turn. As much as she hated the spectacle, it filled her every hole and salved every scar self-doubt had made through the years. After she'd invested so much time and effort in her work, she'd finally made a difference. She'd finally be looked at not for the size of her bra cup or the length of her legs, but for the effort she gave and the skills she possessed.

Patricia, a young agent who now worked in her old

cubicle, rushed up so quickly Libby thought she might try to hug her. The woman stopped with a hop at arms' length and extended her hand. "I am so happy for you."

"Thank you." Libby shook her offered hand.

"What a big win."

"It was a hard fight to get the assignment and even harder to track Hegarty."

"But you were given the opportunity." Patricia pointed at her, which consequently meant she stabbed a finger toward Libby's boobs.

"Yes, and it took four years before they considered giving me any assignment of substance." This chick had been in the FBI for less than six months and in the Civil Rights department less than that. "You'll get your chance. Just keep your head down and plow through what they give you."

"Yeah, thanks." Patricia smiled and nodded so hard Libby worried the clip holding her hair back would fall. The woman waved and turned toward her cubicle.

As quickly as the uproar began, it waned. Most people returned to their work. A few took the opportunity to split off in conversations. Two younger male recruits hurried forward, offering their hands. She shook them, knowing with Ross Quinn as their senior management, they'd get a shot at the good assignments—human trafficking, hate crimes, international human rights violation—long before Patricia ever would. They grinned expectantly. She didn't know what they wanted, but she had a guess. And they could go fuck themselves.

Libby stepped backward to retreat to her office.

The sharp point of her stiletto found a raised and uneven surface. A grunt filled her ears, and she whipped around to see Ross Quinn's stern face. His ruddy complexion was redder than normal. He doubled over and gripped the top of the cubicle next to them. He had been so damn close. Hell, he still was.

She looked over her shoulder. The two agents had taken off. No worrying about stepping on their toes. She moved back, offering herself room, more so than Quinn.

"Sir, I apologize for stepping on your toe. I had no idea you were right behind me." She tried not to emphasize the word right, but she was only human.

He straightened and wheezed a breath. Of all the senior staff on their floor, Ross Quinn was the most fit. Having started his career in the Explosive Ordinance Disposal division, he maintained an almost military precision fitness regimen. It paired perfectly with the cool way he handled his subordinates.

Quinn snapped together the breast of his suit. The redness filtered from his creased forehead but hung in his slim cheeks.

"I was coming to congratulate you on a job well done on the hoarder assignment."

Hegarty was much more than a collector of guns, and Quinn knew that. The special wording was his covert way of belittling her achievement.

"Thank you, sir." Libby nodded.

Her boss turned on his heels and hobbled away, using the cubicle tops to steady himself. She bit her lip to keep from laughing. The hotter than hell man who lived next to her hadn't limped as much when he'd first moved in. She knew just by the crazy character of the man that his injury had been a bit more serious than a hurt toe. In fact, she'd guessed his trauma had been life threatening.

She followed Quinn slowly, moving out of the theatre of the floor. He peeled right, and she continued straight to the bustling little hallway that housed her office plus a few others, the break room, and the locker rooms at the end of the corridor.

A crowd spilled out the break room door and congealed in the hallway, stopping her progress. The only time that happened was when someone brought in goodies for a birthday or a retirement, but that sort of thing never interested her. The crowded sharing of food actually made her stomach shiver. All the germs.

"No!" The anger-brimming tone grabbed her attention by the collar. "Give me that!"

Libby knew the voice that bled out from the room. Though she'd never heard it in quite a demanding state.

Alec?

In the two years they'd been across the hall from one another, she hadn't known the mild-mannered guy capable of raising his voice.

Libby shoved through the crowd. Her pack did the job of spreading the masses.

"It's her," someone whisper-screamed from over her shoulder.

A guy she recognized from one hallway over looked at her, and his eyes bugged out of his face. He backpedaled, skirted the doorframe, and practically ran away. Why was the biggest brownnoser on the staff running from her?

When his large, should-be-decaying nose moved from in front of the door, Libby saw it hanging from eye level by a one-inch piece of clear tape.

If only the picture wasn't so clear.

But it was.

As pictures went, it was a pretty damn good one. The way she'd been captured walking from the goat path in the shipping container with one foot in front of the other accentuated the curve of her hips. Long rifles in each hand and the ones in the crook of her arm elongated her waist. The black shirt tucked into her jeans drew attention to her full breasts. The FBI hat shielded her gaze, giving her the appearance of bedroom eyes. Her long ponytail cascaded over her left shoulder just so.

As pictures went, it would have been a nice one to press into a photo album and look back at twenty years down the road.

As pictures went, it would have been awesome to have proof that she'd taken down an anarchist for the FBI to protect the innocent people of this amazing country.

As pictures went, it was not the one you wanted printed off and hung on the break room door. You especially didn't want the words scribbled on each page in black permanent marker displayed for your co-workers to see.

THE BIG BUST

Even as she stood on the threshold of the meanest prank anyone had ever pulled on her, a group of men shouldered Alec out of the circle while they pointed and laughed at her figure like schoolyard bullies.

Alec held a stack in his hand and tried his best to wedge between them and get to the humiliating display.

Libby reeled in the instinct to pull her weapon and shoot off every knuckle in the room, save for Alec's. She blocked the even greater one that had her running from the room and hiding under her desk inside her office for the rest of her life.

"Raise your hand if you'd like a sexual harassment lawsuit brought against you by my attorney? For better or worse, she never loses." Libby let her voice fill the room.

One by one, the horrified gazes found hers. One by one, the crowd filtered past her out of the break room.

She shifted, blocking the exit for the trio of pig-headed assholes who'd been bullying her friend, the one man standing up for her.

"Chill out," the tallest one demanded.

"Yeah, it was a joke," his slightly shorter friend added.

The other one had the presence of mind to keep his damn mouth shut.

"Chill?" Libby smiled at the tall one. "I'm as chilled

as the bottle of vodka you keep in your mini-fridge, David." She turned her sweet expression on the next one and pointed at the remaining pictures Alec had hurriedly tore from the cabinets. "This joke is as hilarious as your attempt to date Larkin Ashford last year."

Both men gritted their teeth.

"Now, fellas, if you wouldn't mind doing the world a favor. Choke on your breakfast." She stepped out of the way and ushered them out of the now empty room with a flourish of her hand. "Goodbye."

They left, pressing their heads together and chattering like angry schoolgirls.

Alec pulled the last two pictures from the refrigerator and then the entrance. His head shook and his chest puffed, not in posture but in pure anger. It poured off him in waves.

"Are you okay?" Libby asked.

"Me?" His mouth dropped open, and his brows shot high, which seemed to take the edge off his quiet rage. He punched the thick stack of pictures he held. "Are you okay? Those guys—"

"Fuck those guys. And fuck whoever did this." Libby pulled the stack of pictures from his hand and tossed them into the large trash receptacle. Then she yanked open the fridge, grabbed a soda, and popped the top. She poured half the contents atop the pictures and then replaced the lid. "Want a drink?"

"Whose was that?" Alec's Adam's apple worked.

"No idea."

"Shouldn't we replace it?"

The irritation that swelled inside her chest burst into a full laugh. She swung the flavored drink she knew he enjoyed in front of him. "Live on the edge, Alec."

"I was." He pointed at the place where he'd had the minor run-in with guys. "Did you see me? I shoved those guys."

"Nudged."

"It was a shove," he protested.

"Whatever you say." She grinned and motioned him forward. "Come on. We've wasted too much time on stupidity this morning. I have a ton of work to do."

He followed her down the hallway toward their respective offices.

"Thank you for sticking up for me." Libby knocked his shoulder with hers.

"You'd do the same for me."

"I would actually shove someone for you." She offered him a wink.

He gave her a small laugh.

"So, you want this drink or not?" She held the soda in front of him.

Alec snatched it and disappeared into his office with a grin. Libby shoved inside hers, closed the door, and collapsed onto her chair without turning on the light. She pressed her face into her hands.

Her smile disintegrated. The breaths flowing between her fingers shuddered. She bit her lip and shook her head. Hot tears hit her palms, despite her best efforts to stave them off. She gave over to the rage and embarrassment, thankful she had an actual office.

Thirty-ish seconds later, she straightened, dried her cheeks with the back of her hand, and blotted her eyes with the end of her suit sleeve. The sharpest edge of her anger had dissipated, but she hated that she'd let someone else dictate her emotions, even if she was the only one who knew about it.

She had too much work to do before dinner with the girls to give any more time or mental effort to envious assholes.

Libby pulled the apple from her pack, shoved it into

her mouth, and set up her computer while she ate it. For the next eight hours, she catalogued and categorized the weapons and munitions found on the property. Most of them couldn't be tracked because the serial numbers had been filed off. She had ten more pages left to go through when her calendar alerted.

She packed up and snuck out of her office. Alec's door was closed, and his light was off. The stairs at the end of the hall offered the seclusion she desired. After traipsing down too many flights, she crawled into her car and drove from Federal Plaza to the hospital. Exhausted feet and half-lidded eyes got her from the parking space she'd snagged to the main elevator. She pressed the call button, and then realized she had no idea where to go.

When the door opened, she stepped inside all the same and looked around for a directory. She found it on the wall above the operator panel. The doors closed, but she still hadn't a clue. She shot a text to the group.

Libby: Room number?

The car hadn't moved, but the doors opened to a white-headed little lady who shuffled forward one inch per minute.

"Oh, let me—" She stepped forward to offer a hand, but a big one already steadied the woman. The helper's face cleared the corner, and Libby's mouth fell open.

Her neighbor's feet stopped in their tracks, halting the old lady's progress. He caught himself before causing the woman too much trouble and slowly guided her onto the elevator.

Libby sank back into the corner. Her jaw scraped across the floor, dragging behind her. Of all the people in all the places, she'd never expected to see him in a hospital. The ultimate in male virility seemed inordinately out of place in a building whose sole purpose was fixing people. He was perfectly formed. What the hell was there to fix?

His vocal cords.

His manners.

His large thumb hovered over the buttons, and he looked in question at the lady. Though from the way he helped the small woman, his manners to others seemed to be intact.

"Two, please, doll." Her voice was well worn and sugar sweet.

He looked at her with the same question.

"Five." She blurted the number.

He pressed it and stepped back to the lady's side.

They rode up in silence. Imagine that. The elevator dinged, and the door opened on two. A nurse with an empty wheelchair stood in the opening and shook her head. "Miss Melba, you're not supposed to leave the floor, especially not without a wheelchair."

The little lady chuckled. "You're not supposed to eat sugar, but I don't tell the other nurses that you're cheating on your diet, do I?"

"What a piece of work," the nurse huffed. She rolled the chair into the elevator and secured the wheels. Libby's neighbor placed his arms under the older woman's and around her back and slowly lowered her into the chair.

"You're a good, man." The lady patted his cheek.

He offered her a smile.

The nurse visibly swooned. "Thank you for taking care of Miss Melba. Who knows what would have happened to her if you hadn't come along."

Libby couldn't blame her. She'd been fighting the losing battle for too long.

He waved them off with a rigid hand.

When the nurse and older woman retreated onto the second floor, the doors closed, and Libby was stuck inside the tiny space with ... an enigma. A highly fuckable and apparently sweet to old ladies mystery.

The elevator car rose. Her stomach stayed on the second floor.

He stared straight ahead as though he knew any sudden movement would incite her to rip his clothes from his body.

"I'm not stalking you. My friend is here," she offered.

Why are you talking?

He didn't say a word.

Shocker.

They passed the fourth floor. An overwhelming sense of sass inflated her posture.

"She's fine. Thanks for asking." Libby offered the parting shot as the door opened, and she stepped from the elevator.

Her neighbor followed.

Everything inside her shriveled like a flailing, dying balloon. She looked left and right but had no idea where to go.

Her phone dinged. She snatched it to eye level.

Genevieve: 726

Libby lunged for the closing elevator. Another second later and she'd have missed it. She skirted through the doors, stabbed the seven with her middle finger, and didn't dare to look at the man who disappeared behind the closing doors, the man who lived next to her, the man she wanted more than she'd ever wanted a man before.

She hurried to 726 and shoved through the door without knocking. Flaming red hair and her equally fiery friend's wide grin greeted her.

"Lib!" Gen's arms shot wide.

"It's so good to see your smile." Libby sat on the bed and wrapped her friend in a bear hug. She'd been too scared to give this level of affection the last time she'd seen her.

"Ladies?" Larkin's voice filled the room.

They both turned to see their friends Larkin and Marlis shove through the door with bags of takeout and who knew what else.

"Who's ready to party?" Larkin slipped a bottle of champagne from her oversized purse.

Gen raised her hand. "Oh, me. Me!"

"Tough stuff, missy." Libby shook her finger at her. "Ladies with brain injuries don't get bubbly."

"I thought we were friends." Gen shoved her toward the edge of the bed.

"We are." She grinned.

"Just one glass?" Her stunning redheaded friend batted her lashes.

"Nope." Libby kissed her cheek and stood. Grabbing a bag from Marlis's hand, she helped her set it on the skinny table meant for horrible hospital food.

"Lib." Marlis grabbed her arm. "I swear I just saw a man who looks exactly like your neighbor help an old lady off a bench out front and walk with her inside. My ovaries melted on Larkin's back seat."

"What about melting ovaries?" Gen asked.

"Oooh!" Larkin pointed at Marlis but spoke to Gen. "She saw a guy who looked like Libby's hot neighbor help a little old lady into the hospital. I only saw him from the back, which was mighty nice."

"Hot damn." Gen circled a finger in the air. She slid her legs off the side of the bed. "Field trip."

"No, you don't." Larkin grabbed their friend's ankles and swung them back onto the bed.

"It didn't just look like my neighbor. It was my neighbor," Libby grumbled.

"Field trip!" Gen thrust her fist into the air as though it were her battle cry.

"He got off on the fifth floor," Libby admitted.

"No reason you can't too." Gen waggled her brows.

They shared a laugh. It seemed as though it'd been a long time since they joined in such innocent banter. Libby released the bag, grabbed Marlis's hand in her right one, and pulled her toward the hospital bed. She grabbed Gen's hand in her left one, and Larkin connected the circle on the other side.

"I am so thankful for each and every one of you." Gen looked from one to the other.

"Wait, I was about to say that," Libby scoffed.

"No, I was," Larkin interjected.

"Well, I was about to say let's pop open the bubbly." Mar laughed.

"I second that," Gen agreed.

"Second it all you want, but you can't have any." Libby smiled and pulled her friends, her life, into a big hug. "I'll have your glass because it's been that kind of day."

"Let's hear it," Gen cheered as though starved for gossip not pertaining to her own life.

FOUR

Libby shoved through the screen door. Movement to the right pulled her heart through her chest and snapped it back into place like an oddly shaped rubber band. Her heavy backpack shifted, and she nearly crashed, though not at all in the way she planned. A quick grip on the doorframe stabilized her enough to see the bold black and white creature who'd scared a year off her life. The damn thing extended its front paws to the chair's arm and stretched his mouth even wider with a yawn. His full set of sharp white teeth flashed in the dim moonlight. She unlocked the house, tossed her pack inside, and then stared at the cat.

"No, sir!" She snapped a palm in the cat's general direction. "Not tonight. I'm windblown, probably sunburnt, and I've been yelled at by dock workers all day. And"—

she jabbed a finger at him—"I had to drive to Staten Island." Her head shook ferociously. "No!"

She stormed out of the porch, down the steps, and across the yard. She'd reined herself in a little before she shuffled up his steps and lifted her hand to knock.

Her balled fist froze midair.

The blinds were drawn over the glass.

Hot, heavy moans drifted from behind the door and caressed her ears. They drifted over her neck, then slipped lower, grazing the suddenly heavy swells of her breasts. Grunts assaulted her clit. The rhythmic banging of a headboard or sofa cooked her from the inside out.

She exhaled a breath.

Embarrassment stained her cheeks.

Turning, Libby fled past the cat and entered her house. She slammed the door and placed her hands on her hips. Her heart raced as though she'd run a hundred miles. Sure, she'd heard people fucking before. Those two people, actually. She'd just never been so close. If she wasn't mistaken, she'd heard the suctioning sounds of their bodies connecting.

"Aaagh!" Irritation had her ripping her own clothes off and tossing them every which way but in the hamper. Men had never provided much of an obstacle for her. They either liked her or they didn't and vice versa. But this man … His heated gazes made it look as though he wanted to mount her, to devour her whole, while his actions said he hated her stinking guts. For the life of her, she couldn't understand why his body was the only one she seemed to want. Sure, she flirted and dated right up until he moved in.

Then mayhem corrupted her insides, overthrowing her better judgment.

She fumed through a shower, through the cleanup of her clothes, through a mini-moisturizing routine and dressing for bed, then through the prep and cook of her dinner.

The rumbling of a motor, make cat and model Killer, vibrated so loudly it coaxed a laugh. Libby opened the back door wide. Killer sat like a proper little guy with his vicious claws hidden away, and his tiny paws tucked together in front of his soft belly.

"Oh, I have fish, and now you wanna be my friend?"

He, like his human, didn't answer.

"Okay." After tying the loose pajama shorts around her waist and adjusting the spaghetti straps of her camisole, she grabbed her plate and glass of water, and headed for the porch. Killer didn't take a hint. He sat squarely in the center of the doorway. "Excuse me." Still, he didn't budge.

Libby wedged the glass between her arm and boob, broke off a piece of fish, and tossed it toward the screen door. Killer turned on a dime, crouched, and darted atop the flaky morsel while she rushed for the chair in the corner. Wetness slipped down her arm, but she managed to sit before the cat. She placed the glass on the tightly packed wooden slats that created the surface of her porch, crossed her legs, then breathed in the cool night as she ate. She slowly savored the asparagus, baby potatoes, and trout. Spending the day organizing the shipments of guns at the docks had weighed her down, but this, this was nice.

A soft noise that she didn't recognize hit her ears. She looked left and right but didn't see anything. The drip, drip of liquid pulled her gaze to her glass, and Killer, who was lapping up water.

"By all means, help yourself."

He did for several more gulps. When he was finished, he sauntered to the tips of her toes of the foot he'd nearly taken off at the ankle and sat. His expectant gaze pinned her to the seat.

"Okay. Okay." Libby pinched off another piece of her

fish. She drew a deep breath, drawing on all the courage she possessed, and lowered it toward that precious pink nose and those sharp, able teeth. "Please, don't eat my fingers."

Killer peeled back his lips. His white teeth gleamed.

Libby held her breath.

As sweet as he could, he ate the trout one nibble at a time. When he finished, his sandpaper tongue scraped across the pads of her index finger and thumb. She grinned as wide as she ever had.

"Fish is the key to your heart. Got it."

He left her fingers and returned to her glass for a palette cleanser.

"You're quite sophisticated when you're not trying to rip my limbs off." Libby sat back and laughed. It had been a shitty day. Joel was supposed to oversee the transfer of the weapons at the docks. But no. Just when he might prove slightly useful, Quinn had pulled him from the assignment.

"I should have stomped harder on his toe yesterday." She grabbed the last piece of her fish and fed Killer. "So what brings you here?" she asked the cat. Her gaze lifted to the house next door and the blazing lights inside. "Did you know I was going to cook fish, or was it too loud over there?"

After he cleaned her fingers, Libby stretched high and set the plate on the wide windowsill. Up until a few days ago, the spot had hosted a plant that after six years together had up and died.

"Too loud, huh." She yawned and spread her arms wide. The long days and short nights compounded. Her legs might have weighed a thousand pounds. Or maybe that was the weight of her will to move them.

Libby reclined in the cushy chair and stared out the screen at the hint of stars that peeked out between the trees.

Two small stars and a larger one flickered and danced against the dark backdrop. Most days, they weren't visible. The city lights blotted them from the sky, but tonight, they revealed themselves to her. Her limbs, muscle by muscle, relaxed. Her breathing slowed.

The loud bang of a car door jerked her from sleep, snapping her head to attention. Sharp needles punctured her stomach as a heavy weight shifted, punching her in the belly.

Killer bounded from her onto the floor with an unhappy hiss.

Her mouth dropped open in pain and wonder. He'd been curled up on her. She dropped a hand to her belly. Sure enough, a circle of warmth slowly dissipated from the thin material. It might have faded in the now chilly night air, but it also traveled inward, warming her heart. He'd snuggled with her, and she'd rudely woken him.

"I'm sorry."

The cat turned his head and gave her an irritated snarl. She'd woken him because something had startled her awake. Libby stood in time to see the girlfriend stroll down the narrow driveway between their two houses.

"I'm surprised she can walk," Libby grumbled.

She didn't walk. That was too plain a term for the sexy saunter that conveyed her to and from her lover's house. Her hair, as always, was pulled into a sleek ponytail as though she hadn't just been nice and screwed. A pang of jealousy lashed at her chest.

"What a useless emotion." Libby brushed a hand down her face, shuffled to the screen door, and pulled it open.

"Ready to go home?" she asked Killer.

Obstinately, the cat cruised to her chair, hopped up, and curled himself on the warm cushion.

She released the door and folded her arms. Her neighbor was done screwing for the night, so she could go get

HOW

him, or she could leave Killer out here. He'd been fed. It wouldn't be a problem to leave her water glass out for the night. The cat knew how to use it.

Quiet steps drew her gaze to the bottom of the stairs. *Not even close to fair.*

Libby wanted to tell the universe to go fuck itself because this was more than she could handle. She swallowed and stared at her half-naked neighbor. Sleek and sinuous traps sloped from his neck and spread wide to shoulders she could make a meal of, and dessert too. Large slabs of muscle covered his chest like lean shields. His stomach.

Whew!

She could ride his abs to orgasm in less than eight seconds. Libby licked her lips and let her gaze drop. Black sweatpants hung low, revealing every godlike arch and groove of his hips. Even his feet were hot, bare and sexy. Never before had she thought of feet as sexy. Especially not on a man.

He stood there on her bottom step, looking good enough to eat and not saying a damn word.

His gaze raked up her bare legs to her shorty shorts. Those dark angel eyes narrowed on the points of her nipples that tented her spaghetti strap top. He studied her shoulders, neck, and face, taking his time and looking his fill of her.

Her heartbeat spiked. Heat flooded her chest and poured lower still.

They stood staring for moments too long. If she opened the screen, would he come inside? If she walked into her house, would he follow? Would she screw a man who'd just finished with another woman?

Libby knew if the first two answers were yes, then the third one would be the same.

His gaze finally broke, shifting toward the cat.

"Oh, yeah." She was a horny moron. A hot breath blew

between her lips as she turned and headed for Killer.

She reached for the cat before her brain engaged.

Killer swiped without warning. Libby jerked back but not before his nails dragged across the inside of her wrist.

The screen door creaked.

"Son of a …" Libby stepped back and clamped her hand over it. "I thought we were friends now." She gawked at the cat who hadn't moved more than was necessary to murder her with one well-placed swipe. When she removed her hand, blood seeped from the long, angry cut, pooling at one jagged end.

Libby backed toward her door. She needed a towel or something. Her shoulder blades hit solid heat, causing her to jump forward and spin.

Her neighbor stood inside her porch, so close. His gaze zeroed in on her arm.

She pulled it to her body. No way did she want him to touch her. If he did, she'd make a bigger ass of herself. The scent of sex and sweat wafted off him. She should be revolted, but holy hell. Her nostrils flared.

"It's … fine." She promised.

His brow hiked.

"Seriously, it's just a scratch." Libby nodded to the cat.

He stared at her.

Libby's breath caught.

Then he turned and scooped Killer off the chair with one hand. The damn cat hung like a long clump of putty. Her neighbor pressed the cat to his chest, and the wild thing nuzzled him as though he were the tamest creature on Earth.

She couldn't blame the cat.

Her neighbor's gaze raked her one more sultry time, and then he turned to leave. A white, raised scar ran damn near the length of his spine. It was well hidden between the two slabs of his back strap, but it was there all the same.

Libby lifted her hand from her scratch. Suddenly, the diagonal slash that ran from one side of her wrist to the other didn't seem like anything at all.

FIVE

A KNOCK SOUNDED ON HER OFFICE DOOR. and Libby froze. Everything in her body constricted, bracing for the dick sure to walk into her office and say something disparaging about her breast or brain size.

"Come in."

The door opened, and Alec's puppy dog face popped around the corner.

"Oh, thank goodness." Libby sighed. "I thought you were going to be Quinn or Joel or one of the other hundred assholes we work with."

"It's just me." The top of Alec's shoulder bobbed.

"Not just." She waved him in and shoved a picture and magnifying glass into his hands. "Third letter from the right. What is it?"

Alec's long arms stretched out in front of him. He popped the picture to make it stiff. His soft blue gaze assessed the image for no more than a second.

"Zero."

"I was fifty / fifty on eight or zero."

"I don't even know how you managed the first two." He handed back the items.

"Yeah, over half of the serial numbers are scratched off the guns, so they are untraceable. It seems he got distracted on this one." She set the picture atop the stack of two hundred more and placed the magnifying glass beside it. "Thank you."

"Not a problem." Alec braced his feet apart, crossed his arms, and studied her.

"What?"

He tilted his head and shifted one sandy blond brow.

"You heard?" She winced.

"How bad was it?"

"Bad enough that I'm taking the stairs tomorrow."

"Tomorrow's Saturday."

"Yep." She grinned so wide it hurt. "I'll be taking them Monday too and possibly all of next week."

"Damn. That'll hurt." He grimaced.

"Yeah." There were hundreds of steps between the ground floor and her office. Going down them was one thing, but up? "It'll hurt, but my pride will remain intact."

"Unless you miss a step." His lips pursed.

She crumpled a piece of trash paper from her desk and threw it at him.

"Come on." He stepped toward the door. "I need food, and you need a break. You'll end up going cross-eyed."

"I'll keep my crooked eyes. I don't wanna go out there." Libby threw her hand up to ward off the idea. "Wednesday, I'm lauded, and Friday, I'm shunned."

"You were not shunned."

"Were you there? Did you hear them?" She let her eyes narrow on him.

"No."

"Well, this time the pictures were plastered through the halls and on the cubicles. And all those assholes pointed and whooped." She stabbed a finger toward the general assembly of humans outside the door. "They jeered and laughed like I was some sideshow on the pier."

"Surely, an agent who'll storm a house and capture an anarchist by force isn't going to let a bunch of middle-aged ass-kissers bully her."

"Uuuugh!" Libby stood, stuffed her cell into her pocket, and trudged after Alec. "I'm not your friend anymore."

Alec stalled in the doorway and craned his neck toward her. "Were we friends?"

"You're the only human in this building I'll voluntarily hold a conversation with, so yeah, we were."

"But not anymore?"

"Nope." She gently pushed him through the doorway and pulled her office door closed.

They walked side by side toward the break room. A place she'd been avoiding at all costs.

"What are we now?"

The subtle swing of his arm and the sway of his hips all portrayed a casualness to the question, but his tone was different. She sensed a seriousness, almost hopeful spirit in the soft timbre.

"Enemies, of course." Libby made a joke. The last thing in the world she wanted to do was hurt Alec.

He'd been obsessed with a woman by the name of Kate Archer. For the past two years, every conversation, in some form or fashion, had the word Kate. It was the sweetest thing to hear about two people madly in love with one another. She and the girls had known nothing of love. Hell, she still didn't. Six months ago, every mention of the woman had stopped him cold. After a few weeks, Libby had asked what had happened to Kate. She'd dumped him to marry her high school sweetheart, with whom she'd been rekindling a romance for nearly half of her relationship with Alec.

The joke was selfish also. She didn't want to alienate her only ally in the office.

"After you." She paused outside the break room and ushered him in with a flourish of her hand.

Alec entered and tossed, "All clear," over his shoulder. He grabbed his lunch out of the microwave and set it on the table she'd strategically chosen nearest the door for a quick escape.

"You checked it before you came and got me." Libby leaned back and toyed with the edge of a napkin someone had left on the table.

"Maybe." He grabbed two waters from the refrigerator and slid into the chair opposite her with his back to the door.

"Were there any pictures?"

"Only one."

"Where?"

"It doesn't matter. I threw it away."

Libby pressed her elbows against the tabletop, rested her chin on her hands, and waited.

"Inside the refrigerator. On top of your lunch."

The hits just kept coming. Her job was great. The people in this office sucked. All except for Alec. She bit the inside of her cheek and nodded.

"The picture originated from the intra-office email." Alec pulled open the lid on a perfectly cubed chicken breast and precisely halved broccoli and baby carrots.

"I know, which'll make it harder to figure out who's responsible."

"You could go to Quinn and file a report. He can pull the security footage and find out in five minutes." He paused with his fork over his food.

"Eat," she insisted.

He sat straight and took one clean bite and chewed.

"I thought about that already."

"And?"

"And …" Libby checked the doorway. "Quinn's a dick. If I file the report, his supervisor will have to sign off on it, and I'll never see another good assignment as long as I'm in the New York office."

"Shitty, but true." He ate another hunk of chicken and veggies.

Libby uncapped both waters and set Alec's in front of him.

"Thank you."

"No problem." She took a long pull on hers and then drew a deep breath. Joel trotted down the hallway from the direction of the locker rooms. "Besides, I have an idea about who's behind it."

"You do?"

She nodded long and lowly.

"Are you going to make me ask?"

Her grin grew into an all-out cheese.

"Who?" He threw his hand up, but her gaze was focused on the dick in question.

"The person who took the picture in the first place. Joel Ornby."

"No shit?"

"Oh, a big bag of it." A shit who waltzed toward the break room with a shit-eating grin on his face.

"True again." Alec drank half of the water in his bottle in one swig. "You can put Joel in his place."

"Yes, I can." Libby lifted her chin toward the door.

Alec's gaze followed her gesture, and he nearly choked on his water.

Joel sailed through the door, red-faced with a small white towel hanging around his neck.

"Alec." Joel nodded a hello. "Big Bust, good morning." He continued on to the refrigerator, pulled out a water bottle, and turned to leave.

Libby stood and blocked his path. She let her gaze drop to accommodate his slightly shorter stature. "Don't be a dick just because I'm wrapping an assignment you couldn't get off the ground. We all have our strengths. Mine is completing assignments. Yours is kissing ass."

"Don't take office politics for granted." Joel's upturned nose flared. The far edges of his wide mouth shifted toward the florescent lights.

"Politics might get you a leg up, Joel, but your complete lack of skill and follow-through will ensure you screw it up. And when you do, I'll be there to take your place." She grinned and stepped out of his way.

He fled the break room like the bitch he was.

Alec snorted.

Libby collapsed into her chair. "You laugh, but he's right. He'll get the first crack at the good cases."

"You're right too," Alec assured her.

She guzzled her water. "Let's hope so."

Her phone vibrated in her pocket. She plucked it out and looked at the screen. Not Gen. Just a bill's auto-pay notice.

Libby swirled the remainder of her water around the bottom of the bottle.

"Why don't you let me take you out for a drink this evening?" Alec's voice pulled her attention from the water and the mire in her mind. She replayed the words in her head to be sure she'd heard them correctly. "A real one," he added.

Oh, no.

Alec was tall and sinuous. His face was nice to look at, beautiful even. He had a kind and generous personality, if not a little quirky.

But aren't we all?

They had a great repartee, but there had never been a spark. Not even a flicker. And the way he'd worshiped Kate? Well, she wasn't the kind of girl who could handle that sort of blind devotion.

Libby didn't want a "bad boy." She demanded to be treated well, but she needed a man tough enough to take her shit and stern enough to tell her when enough was enough.

Poor Alec. She'd mow him over.

The phone between them jiggled and danced across the table. When Libby plucked it up and saw Gen's picture brighten the screen, joy overrode all dread and worry.

"Alec, I have to take this. It's my friend Gen. She's supposed to get out of the hospital today, so I'll be with her this evening." She snatched her phone.

"Of course." Alec motioned for her to go ahead.

"Thank you." Libby stood. "And thank you for the break. I needed it." She skirted out the door and hurried to her office.

"Hi," she answered the phone just as she closed her office door. "What time is Owen busting you out?"

"Forget about me." The fun and flamboyant friend she was so accustomed to wasn't on the line. The lawyer and successful career woman was front and center.

"What's wrong?" Libby wasn't the type to panic. Neither was Gen.

"You've gone viral," her friend squealed.

Libby looked at the sky, searching for the actual meaning of those words, but she found none. "I'm pretty sure I took a test to ensure I didn't have that after I broke up with that asshole."

"This isn't the time to joke, Libby," Gen huffed. "You know the picture of you at the crime scene surrounded by the guns?"

"Yes." She knew it too damn well. How did Gen know about it?

"Well, it's an internet sensation. Viral."

"No," Libby wheezed. "I knew it was bad in the office, but ..."

"Yes!" Gen shrieked.

"Like Sandra Bullock and the Bird Box memes big?"

"Bigger than."

"What are you talking about?" None of this made sense. It was a stupid picture of her and some guns.

"Victor Juliet said he wants to give you a role in his next blockbuster film."

Words flowed through her brain, but none of them made their way across her nervous system to her mouth.

"I heard it on *E! News*," Gen explained. "You're at over a million views, and it's just a picture. You're set to break records for a static image."

"Oh, no." Libby sank to the floor and stared at her phone as though it were a foreign object. The news it delivered certainly was foreign.

SIX

LIBBY DIDN'T USUALLY WORK on Saturdays, but she managed to leave her house at six a.m. for the office. Even so, early parking across from the New York field office was near to full. She wedged into a parking spot between two vans on the west side of Foley Square that wouldn't leave her guessing whether her car would be towed by the end of the day. After a long night of staring at her ceiling, worrying about the ramifications of that stupid picture—despite the girls' best effort to assure her otherwise—things were looking up. She'd make it in before the rush, and with any luck at all, she'd have her initial report submitted to Quinn's inbox by lunch. Then maybe he'd see how integral she was to the field office's Civil Rights department. Just maybe the picture wouldn't matter at all.

Large antennas atop the vans caught her attention. It wasn't unusual to see news station vans on Federal Plaza or Centre Street. Between the Supreme Court, the NYPD, The Thurgood Marshal Courthouse, and FBI, there was usually something newsworthy happening.

She shrugged on her pack, locked up, crossed the street, and worked her way around to the Worth Street entrance. With the current threat level and them sitting ducks for any crazy with pipe dreams and pipe bombs, they funneled and filtered all foot and vehicle traffic there. The parking garage had gotten to be such a headache that she preferred to park on the street. It gave her a twenty-minute head start on her co-workers. Not that many of them would be in today. Only those with ops ramping up or ending. Or the brownnosers—there to be seen and do no more than play the game.

A heap of reporters and cameramen cluttered the stairs that led nowhere. They literally butted up to guardrails that gave a pretty view of the spacious rear entrance and curved greenery that no one utilized.

The hairs on the back of Libby's neck stood on end.

There was no reason for them to be there.

Every so often, the Bureau made statements to the press, but they were always scheduled and announced ahead of time in the weekly email brief. A brief she'd missed Monday because of the weekend raid. She should've read the entire thing when she'd gotten back. But no. She'd only read through the short snippet about her Hegarty bust and stared at the picture.

Relief washed over her. Surely, there was an upcoming announcement. With her being out of the office for the first half of the week, she just hadn't heard about it. Alec probably hadn't mentioned it because it was on Saturday, and they rarely worked in the office on the weekends.

"Libby Irish?" A woman with perfectly appointed eyebrows, overflowing lashes, and a pink power suit that contrasted with her long blonde hair stepped from behind one of the half-dozen vans lining this side of the street.

Her stomach hit the sidewalk while the woman cut off her path.

"I'm Trisha Moyer, legal correspondent for—"

"I know who you are." Libby straightened despite the weight of her backpack and worry.

"Of course, you do. You are friends with Genevieve Holst, the lawyer who set a murderer free." Trisha revealed a full set of blinding white veneers.

Libby's fist itched to knock them out of her head.

"That's not why I'm here." Trisha lifted the microphone she'd been holding discreetly by her side. A massive camera with a man attached rounded the van. The light above the lens shifted red to green. "Social media is abuzz with the snapshot heard 'round the world. Your image has over twelve million views and counting. Celebrities from Leonardo to Ellen have liked and shared your picture. They're calling you a real-life superhero. What do you have to say about all the fuss?"

She longed to tell Trashy Trish exactly what she thought about her and the entire situation, but they were recording.

"With hate crimes on the rise after decades of decline, women's rights still struggling to make it to the forefront of legislative changes, and our environment on the brink, I say we have much more important issues to which we should give our attention."

Libby turned away and strode toward the entrance.

Her breaths kicked in and out of her lungs like fire. Blood churned through her veins. It wasn't that cold, and she hadn't exercised this morning even though it sure did feel like it. Rage would do that to a person.

Miracle of miracles, the horde of reporters hadn't noticed Trisha accosting her. Libby kept her head down and walked as quickly as she could without running.

"There she is." The high-pitched feminine voice came from behind her. Fuck Trisha Moyer. Now Libby no longer hated the woman out of solidarity with Gen. She hated her for her own acute reasons. Mainly, she was a bigmouthed bitch.

The mass of media descended the steps and formed a military-style phalanx across the sidewalk. Her steps slowed. If she turned around, she'd have to confront Trisha again, and based on her current mood, it wouldn't go near as smoothly as it had the first time. Even then, she should have kept her mouth shut. They were ordered not to comment to the outlets on ongoing investigations. This wasn't about one, but the powers-that-be probably wouldn't see it that way. They wouldn't like her giving her opinion on political issues, though Libby saw them more as humanity issues.

Libby's hand shook. She tightened it on the strap of her pack, drew a deep breath, and let it out slowly. As much as she hated to speak to the media, to provide any fuel to this outrageous wildfire, she hated even more for Trisha to have the only soundbite.

Their voices attacked from all sides. Their questions ran the gamut from her sexual orientation to her thoughts on how this type of attention set women back in the workplace. The verbal assaults congealed into the most unpleasant sound she'd ever been forced to endure. There was only one way to silence them.

She opened her mouth to speak.

Their mouths closed. The group lurched forward, every man for himself. Microphones and handheld recorders thrust toward her face. The group jostled among themselves.

"With hate crimes on the rise after decades of decline, women's rights still struggling to make it to the forefront of legislative changes, and our environment on the brink,

I say we have much more important issues to which we should give our attention." She offered them a sedate smile and plowed through their failing center.

She refused to run to the entrance. Her curvaceous backside would certainly make the ten o'clock news. Since the scavengers would run over people for a good story, they made short work of catching her and swarmed her at the corner.

Why the hell hadn't she parked in the garage today? How many people would've come into the office on a Saturday anyway?

"Agent Irish, what do you think about Victor Juliet's offer to hire you in his next film?" one reporter hollered.

"You're going to accept Juliet's offer, aren't you?"

On a frosty day in hell.

"Miss Irish, do you think this will affect your ability to do your job?" another shouted.

Were they serious? This wasn't news. She wasn't news. Stopping Darrell Hegarty was.

The off-white guard shack was in her sights. Libby gritted her teeth. She kept her head high and marched on even when a reporter's wingtip scuffed her black pump and a camera knocked her shoulder.

When the guard nodded, offering her safe passage, and scurried from his booth to ward off the media, a huge weight—the approximate size and weight of all twenty in the mob—lifted from her shoulders. The moment she rounded the corner, she ran for the elevators. Only a handful of people speckled the main floor and not one of them whooped or clapped for her today. They stared as though they'd witnessed her humiliation of only a few seconds ago. *Impossible.* They stared as though she'd disgraced the badge or some shit. *Not even close, even if they'd seen the stupid picture.* She ignored them and pushed ahead to her office. She sagged against the door and caught a scream in her hands.

"Assholes!" Now those assholes didn't matter. Another, bigger one did. Darrell Hegarty. The case against him needed to be solid.

Libby shoved the picture and stupid reporters from her mind and got to work. She submerged herself in guns and Hegarty's associates. By the time she moved on to the list of possible targets they'd found in his home, she'd nearly drowned in numbers and names. Breathing was becoming more and more difficult ... probably because her shoulder hunched like Quasimodo's. Still she persisted.

The phone on her desk rang.

She jumped quite literally out of her seat and glared at it. "Shit!"

Surely, it wasn't a reporter. It might be a return call. She'd made three this morning to local authorities concerning the Hegarty case. After waffling too damn long, Libby snatched the phone up from the receiver. "Federal Bureau of Inv—?"

"Irish?" She recognized her boss's voice. Her brief relief was traded for dread.

"Yes, sir."

"The conference room in two."

"Yes, sir."

The line went dead. Libby gaped. What the hell? She assessed the clock on her computer. 10:43 a.m.

After unplugging her laptop, she grabbed her notebook and files on the case, gathering them all to her chest, and shoved out the door. Each step brought her closer to the unknown. The unknown had never scared her. It brought excitement. It brought growth. It brought progress.

Libby grinned and walked into the unknown, armed and ready to defend her work.

She rounded the corner to the conference room. The

long wall of glass revealed an empty space, save for the long black-top table and chairs. Uncertainty tickled the backs of her arms.

"Irish, go on in."

When she turned toward the voice, Ross Quinn headed the charge on a four-man group. He shooed her toward the room with thick fingers and an expression that gave away nothing.

If he wanted to play like that, no problem. Libby rammed a shoulder into the door, opening it wide. She stood near the wall, holding the door open for the entourage right up until the end. Joel's smug mug brought up the end of the line. She sidestepped and let the heavy glass careen toward his face. He caught it with a grunt that took the edge off his grin.

"Irish, please have a seat." Quinn indicated for her to sit across the table from him and the other two men she'd never seen before.

No, that wasn't entirely true. One of them looked vaguely familiar.

Joel sat at Quinn's right hand. It took everything she had not to say something about the stain on his brown, brown nose. She sat and opened her laptop.

"I suppose you want an update on the Hegarty case." Libby shifted her mouse to the setting on her computer and looked for the correct Bluetooth selection to connect with the room's projection system.

"That won't be necessary. Special Agent Ornby will be taking it from here." Quinn's words met her ears, but her brain refused to compute their meaning.

Libby straightened. Her gaze pinned Quinn to his seat. She wouldn't waste a second on Joel. "Do you have another of Special Agent Ornby's assignments you need me to crack, sir?"

The corner of Quinn's mouth quirked. "No, Irish."

She was Special Agent Irish just like Joel was a special agent, the only difference between them was she completed every task the son of a bitch Quinn had ever put in front of her and Joel had not. Oh, and she had a vagina, and Joel was supposed to have a penis. Though she'd yet to be inspired to believe in its existence. Yet Quinn never referred to her with any amount of respect.

Libby pressed record on her laptop's audio.

"Just to be clear, you're giving Agent Joel Ornby the case he had for two years and made zero headway on after I tracked down Hegarty, his weapons, and his network of associates?"

"If that's the way you'd like to spin it, yes." Quinn's jaw twitched.

"There's no spin on it. Those are the facts." Libby smiled. "I can provide you with a list of Joel's cast-offs I've been handed down and closed out."

"That won't be necessary. At the end of this meeting, you'll collect your things from the office and be on a leave of absence until further notice." Quinn shattered her world with a vacant countenance.

"Why?" She had no idea how her voice operated in such a mellow tone.

"Surely, you're aware of the snapshot heard 'round the world."

The men to his left and right nodded. Joel smirked.

"It's causing quite the uproar in the Bureau. Therefore, you'll be put on leave until further notice."

"No." Libby stood with both hands fisted at her sides. Her chair rolled farther away than she expected and hit the wall and bounced sideways. "If it were a male agent in that picture, getting all the attention for the Bureau, you'd pat him on the back and tell him good job."

"If it were a male agent, this wouldn't have happened." Her boss's muddy eyes narrowed on her. They didn't match his light hair, thinning at the close-cropped center. "You were dressed provocatively."

"False." Libby kept her tone even. "I was dressed like every other agent raiding Hegarty's compound, your golden boy Joel included."

Quinn's cheeks burned pink. His gaze slid to the left to the two men in high dollar suits that spoke of more money than the Bureau had to offer. "It's disrupting the work environment."

"I'm at the center of this ridiculous media storm and can still do my job." Libby pressed her hand to her heart and was shocked to find it hammering against her palm.

"Not until this dies down, you can't." Quinn lifted his hand as though he was done with the conversion. "You can bring Special Agent Ornby up to speed on the Hegarty case before you leave."

I'd sooner shoot you both between the eyes.

Her boss—used-to-be boss—stood, and his minions followed suit.

"You're setting an incredibly sexist precedent, sir. I would hate to bring a suit against you and the Bureau." Libby pulled the pin on the veiled threat. She was desperate.

"Our decision is made. And our lawyers are ready." Quinn pointed at the two men who'd accompanied him.

Rage turned her blood to steam. She beat the men to the door and blocked Quinn's escape. "You can't make me leave for having boobs."

"No, but I can fire you for insubordination." His teeth flashed inches from her face. "Or would you like to offer your two weeks?"

Libby drew a deep breath and let it out in his face. "No." She returned to her computer and ended the recording.

Quinn left with his lawyer and the Bureau's. Joel sat

with his smirk across the table. "So you finish the initial report yet?"

"Fuck a barbed-wire fence." Libby snatched up her belongings and tore to her office.

She grabbed her cell and scrolled to Genevieve's number. Gen would support her in whatever kind of suit she wanted to bring.

What good would that do? None.

It'd create more media scrutiny, and neither of them needed that kind of attention.

Libby slammed the phone on the desk and yanked up the file box of Hegarty's organized inventory. She turned it on its end and scattered it across the floor. The box made a great backstop for the heaps of personal bullshit she chucked into it. She slung the pack onto her back and groaned.

What if the reporters were outside?

A string of silent curses strained her mouth. She grabbed her phone again and placed a different call.

When she left her office for who knew how long, she held her head high and offered those looking a get-wrecked expression that dared them to say a word. By the time she made it to the parking garage, she only had to wait a couple of minutes before the sleek black Infinity prowled into the concrete structure, made the loop, and stopped in front of her. When the trunk popped open, Libby placed her belongings in the center of the pristine space, closed the lid, and hurried into the passenger seat.

"I can't thank you enough." Libby settled herself onto the leather, closed the door, and offered Alec the biggest smile she could muster.

"Please." He waved her off. "I was staring at my phone thinking about calling you."

"You were? Why?" Had he known about the leave of absence.

"I saw Trisha Moyer's breaking news report."

"Breaking news, my ass," Libby growled. "I'm sorry. You don't deserve my shitty mood. Thank you for doing this."

"Don't worry about it." Alec put the car in gear. "You might want to put these on." He handed over a pair of oversized feminine sunglasses. "They're camped out by the guard shack."

"Great." Libby slid the glasses on her face. "Better?"

"The dark tint should be enough to hide you." He drove to the exit with a confidence she didn't often see from him in the workplace. He slowed before the turn. "Take your hair down, just in case."

Libby unraveled the ponytail holder from her locks and situated it around her face.

"How's that?"

"Wild." He chuckled. "I can't believe Quinn is doing this."

"I can't believe he thought I was going to give Joel everything I worked my ass off for." She wrung her hands together and breathed deeply, trying to stave off the emotions battering her insides. "If you hear him cussing in my office Monday, let me know, okay?"

"You bet." Alec pulled out onto the street. Sure enough, a gaggle of reporters were posted up near the gate she'd run through hours ago.

"There are less than this morning. Rat bastards."

Alec turned away from them and weaved through the traffic, making the block. "Have you had lunch?"

Oh, no. She was in no mood for food. Nor company.

This was why she'd hesitated to call him. But she hadn't wanted the girls involved with her drama. They each had enough of their own.

"No, but the thought of food makes me queasy."

"Yeah." He nodded. "Sorry. It still hasn't set in that Quinn put you on leave."

"I know what you mean." She feared the moment it did. All she ever wanted to be was an agent for the FBI.

The streets passed by outside the window. People continued about their lives completely unaffected by her dramatic morning. She envied them.

"What are you going to do, Libby?"

She plastered on a smile and turned toward her friend. "Take a few days off until this blows over." Then she'd put in for a transfer. Quinn would never be her boss again.

"Tonight?" he pushed.

"I'm going to drown my sorrows in the magnum of wine that's been rolling around my trunk for the past few months." Hell, nearly six months. Larkin had given it to her for her birthday.

Alec pulled up right alongside her car.

"Thank you." Libby opened the door and swung both legs out.

His hand caught her shoulder. "If you need a life raft, call me."

Libby blinked back her tears and nodded.

SEVEN

DAY HAD TURNED TO NIGHT. and she'd been through several different music streaming stations. She'd started on an up-beat, girl-power note with the likes of Halsey and Demi. Then the power turned to hard-core rage with some Slip-knot and Disturbed. From there, it took a detour into de-pression land with Lana Del Ray.

The dark red wine level on the magnum flagged at midway. She realized she needed food to blot up a little bit of the alcohol in her system, so she popped in a frozen piz-za, then sat in front of the oven and watched it cook while one dreary song after another played in the background. The cheese turned from icy to melty to the verge of crispy before she pulled it out and stared at the thing as though she had no idea what to do next.

"You don't," she whispered.

The porch door slammed. Libby jumped so high her

full glass sloshed over her hand and up her arm. She grabbed a dishtowel and patted up her mess while she eased toward the back door.

A robust meow created a new mess for her to clean.

"Damn cat!" Libby jerked the door wide. Sure enough, the damn cat sat at the center of her threshold, talking smack to her. "I don't need your lip today." She pointed the towel at him. He just sat and stared. "Whatever."

Libby left him at the open door and returned to her pizza. It took extra concentration to cut it into equal pieces, but she managed.

Killer slowly eased his fluffy self over the threshold. He skirted the wall and shuffled between the curtains and the breakfast table. Libby looked through the window over her kitchen sink. The girlfriend's car wasn't in the driveway, but neither was the neighbor's motorcycle, though he kept it in the basement garage most of the time. The house was dark.

"Come to maim my other limbs, have you?" Libby snorted. "Sorry to say you don't hold a candle to my co-workers, buddy." She gobbled down a piece of pizza.

Killer meowed.

"You hungry?" She looked at the large pie. "Can cats eat pizza?"

There was a leftover fish in the fridge, so Libby plated a piece and set it on the floor.

She scarfed a slice of cheesy goodness and then decided to salvage her mood with Australian songbird, Vera Blue. After the first chorus, Killer made his way to the plate and pawed at the fish. "What, you don't like leftovers?"

She laughed so hard she snorted. Her drunk ass danced around the room like she hadn't just lost her job.

"You haven't," she reminded herself. "Just a leave of absence."

"... free on my own. Unattached and ready to bone.

Now I'm alone, dancing because nobody is home. I don't need anybody much. Wouldn't mind a regular touch!" Vera's lyrics were good, but she liked to add her own little flair.

Libby danced through several more songs with her discordant steps and didn't give a damn. Then the cat complained.

"What now?" He sat and stared at her. "Wanna dance?" She bobbed and wiggled. He protested once more. With one last large swig of wine, she polished off her glass and approached the counter for a refill. "Don't bite or scratch me."

She poured him a small cup of water and set it next to the fish, and then poured another generous serving of wine and slid down the cabinets to sit on the floor next to him.

"Living on the edge," she breathed into her glass.

Killer drank his fill. Libby did too since there was nothing else to do. She leaned her back on the cabinets and swayed to the music. The cat must have liked Vera or maybe he was just tired and looking for a comfortable spot. He walked onto her lap and curled himself into a precious little ball on her belly.

"Best day ever," she whispered. "I mean, shittiest, but this is … pretty amazing." He cut his eyes at her, and she filled her mouth with some wine to keep from talking. Over the next few songs, the cat fell asleep as did her left leg and ass cheek.

Her favorite song, "Hold," played, and everything in her relaxed.

The song filled her up and melted the world away. She sang about opening her heart too many times. Libby never had. She never would. The idea of love, devotion, and forever after was an interesting thought, though not at all practical. While not for her, it was nice. She couldn't even get a cat to love her. Though, said cat was currently purr-ing away on her belly. One step in the right direction.

A soft knock brushed the open door.

Her neighbor stood in her doorway wearing low-slung jeans, a well-worn T-shirt, and his ass-stomping boots. He looked good enough to eat.

Killer perked up in her lap but didn't do more than assess the man he'd chosen to live with head to toe as she had.

"At least he has on clothes this time," she told the cat.

Libby waved her neighbor in and motioned him to get the cat off her. Lessons learned. Always the hard way.

He stepped into the house almost as wary as the cat. His gaze slid left and right, cataloguing everything. Her frozen pizza. Her near empty magnum of wine. Her home.

"I won't bite. Can't say the same for the cat." She stuck her tongue out at Killer. "I'm going to invest in sign lan-guage classes and catnip since you both keep showing up." Libby drank to that.

Her neighbor stopped and assessed her.

"Yes, I'm drunk," she huffed. "I'm drunk, and I'm fired. Don't judge me. That's apparently the world's job now." Libby threw her free hand into the air. "I have bib tits. Big," she corrected, "must not be good at FBI-ing. No matter that I finished top in my class at Quantico. Who cares about the year of work I put into tracking down the biggest case? No cache? Yes, a cache of weapons. The larg-est cache a single civilian has ever amassed No. No. No. They're only interested in the Big Bust." She patted her boobs.

"What the hell are they good for? Not getting me laid. Not the job I've sacrificed a life for."

Libby put the glass to her lips to keep from saying an-other damn word. She knew how dumb and pathetic she sounded, but she couldn't stop. She could pour out her anger and frustration on her neighbor, and it wouldn't matter. Not one bit.

She rubbed Killer's scruff and gulped again.

The cat hissed and jumped higher than her head. His back legs jackknifed toward her face, slamming into her glass. It hit the cabinet by her head and shattered. Glass and wine rained. She leaned back quickly and smacked her head on the cabinet.

Her eyes closed. Pain radiated through her skull. Hot, embarrassed breaths hissed from between her lips.

"Please get the cat before he cuts himself."

Something hot and solid grazed her inner thigh.

Libby's eyes popped open to see her neighbor's large fingers caress the skin where her thighs touched. Her cheeks burned. On a leaner woman, the area would be a gap. What a shame it would be for that woman to miss his touch. She bit her lip to keep from moaning. While he dutifully gathered a long sliver of jagged glass from her leg, she entertained a thousand fantasies about where it would lead, despite the throbbing at the back of her skull.

He plucked another larger shard from just above her knee and lifted another from the crook of her arm. She couldn't hold back a giggle. It tickled. Behind him, the cat sat at the screen door ready to go. Her gaze found her neighbor's, narrow and resolute. No sign of even one fantasy in his eyes.

"What a pity."

Deep brown irises flecked with amber and circled by a thick black border shifted toward her.

Her breath caught in anticipation. Would he grace her with a word? If he did, what would he say?

His gaze studied her for seconds that stretched near a minute, and then his stunning gaze shifted down. He tossed the pieces onto the floor with the other shattered remnants of her glass. One warm hand slipped under her right arm and threaded behind her back while the other looped under her knees. He plucked her from the floor as though she weighed way less than her 145-ish. Instead of cradling her to his chest, he held her out away from him. Her mouth gaped. It was a feat of strength in itself. A feat that chapped her ass more than wooed her.

What, she wasn't good enough to touch him?

He walked her into the living room, set her on her feet, and straightened. Only then did she realize the tank and itty-bitty cotton shorts she wore were soaked with wine. They suctioned to her right boob and thigh. The outline of her areola darkened the fabric and her nipple protruded against the wet material. Her neighbor didn't seem to notice or care because he turned away and stalked to the kitchen. He found a rag lying on the sink partition. His massive frame squatted low, and he moved the cloth around the floor, gathering the broken pieces of glass. The T-shirt he wore clung to his muscles, exploiting every shift and bunch of his well-developed lats and shoulders. He stowed the shards in the trash can he found under her sink in only two tries. Next, he wet the rag, wiped down the floor, rinsed it, returned the rag to its spot on the sink, and then he left … without saying a word.

EIGHT

WITH THE OPEN DRAWERS VOMITING half their contents onto the floor, the sheets hanging off her bed, and the red-stained pajamas clumped in the doorway, her bedroom looked like a crime scene.

Libby shuffled through the mess, dragging her comforter behind her. It'd been her only company in the bathroom, where she'd spent the majority of the early morning hours. She climbed onto the bed and heaved the fluffy cover atop her. It helped block out the midday light that seeped in from her blinds. If only it could mute the pounding in her head.

Every breath jolted pain through her abdomen. Her throat burned, no matter that she'd brushed her teeth four different times, gagging all the while.

Her phone vibrated so loudly it might have been a shuttle about to take flight.

"No!" She pulled the covers more tightly around her head, waiting for the incessant noise to stop. When it did, she relaxed … for the two seconds it took for the person to call again.

She poked a hand out from her cocoon, felt around the cold surface of her nightstand, and grabbed the shaking thing. The worst of the noise died down. If she shoved it under her pillow, it would mute the rest. But her pillow was lost. Somewhere on the floor probably. Peeling half an eyelid back, she saw Gen's name lit on the screen.

If she was lucky, it would be her friend calling about her own problems. Lord knew she had them. But knowing Gen as well as she did, she knew exactly what answering the call would get her. She also knew what not answering would get her. An irate lady knocking on her door in less than forty minutes.

Libby answered, pressed the speakerphone feature, and turned the volume down before groaning her hello.

"How are you holding up?" Gen asked without pre-amble.

"Piece by piece." Libby sighed.

"That well, huh?"

"How'd you find out?" Libby thought it'd take longer for the news of her leave to spread.

"Mar saw the news. I should storm Trisha Moyer's office and slap her with a harassment lawsuit."

"Can't you just slap her?"

"I can."

The last thing she needed was Mar leading the charge for her. It would only put her—significantly more high profile, at least before this picture bullshit—friend in the spotlight. Their little group had been in the news more than enough lately.

"That won't be necessary. It'd be awesome, but unnecessary."

"I'd love to do it for you."

"You didn't do it for yourself." Moyer had slandered Gen's name far worse.

"I know," Gen agreed.

"Thank you."

There was a beat of silence. "Wait, you had to know one of us would see the reporter outside your office on some regurgitation of the newscast."

"Please don't say regurgitation." She drew a deep breath in through her nose and let it out slowly.

"Back up. What are you talking about? How did I find out about what?"

Her friend should have been a detective or an FBI agent.

"The reporters?" she tried.

"Libby, don't make me drug my guard and come over there."

"Don't give Owen a hard time. He doesn't deserve it. Besides, you need to take it easy."

"Then tell me what's going on," Gen warned.

"Quinn placed me on a leave of absence yesterday."

"That rat bastard."

"Yep."

"Why? You just landed the crazy guy with all those guns."

"Yes, I did. He gave the case to Joel and—"

"That worthless little piece of shit?" Gen shrieked.

"You're not supposed to get worked up, brain swelling and all." Christ, she should have kept that to herself. All the girls hated Joel, and most of their hatred was earned. He'd treated her like shit her first year with the Bureau. Once he'd realized he couldn't outwork or outwit her, he'd resolved himself to playing the game. Something she wanted no part in.

"Okay, mom," Gen huffed. "Why would he do that?

Joel is an idiot."

"He put Joel on the case because he knew it'd piss me off. He put me on leave because of the interruption caused by the media circus surrounding that picture."

"Like hell." Gen scoffed.

"I know that's not the real reason."

"We can bring suit against Quinn's sexist ass and the Bureau for backing his sexist move."

"And throw more shit into the storm?"

"I'm clearly not afraid of that, now am I?"

"No, you're not." Libby smiled through the pain because she had people who loved her. "I appreciate the thought, more than you know, but I don't want to do that to you or me or the Bureau."

"Drinks tonight at a dive bar. My treat," Gen commanded.

"No. I did too much of that at home last night."

"Without me?"

"I would have been terrible company."

"Woman, don't ever deprive me of cheap wine, your bad company, and the opportunity to trash talk power-abusive assholes."

"I'll try to remember that the next time I'm put on leave."

"Don't joke like that."

"Fine. Also, the wine wasn't cheap. It was the magnum from Larkin."

"Oh shit, Lib. Is your face still attached to your head?"

"Mostly."

"Do you want me to keep the news close to the chest?"

Secrets between them never lasted long. It worked best that way. "You can tell the girls, but let them know I need some time before the invasion."

"I'll try my best."

"I love you, Gen."

"I love you, Lib. Drink a Bloody Mary. It'll help."

"Not a chance." Anything added to her body right now would send her and her comforter back to the bathroom floor.

They ended the call, and Libby poked her head out from the covers for a fresh breath. Killer's loud meow seeped in from under her back door, down the hallway, and into her bedroom.

"Fuck you!" She looked around for something to throw in the beast's general direction, but when she found nothing she was willing to break, it irritated her all the more. Her legs thrashed for a few seconds.

The fit drained what little energy she possessed, and her limbs collapsed. She dragged in breaths, causing her bare breasts to heave against the comforter. The image of her neighbor's large hand on her inner thigh whipped up heat at the very juncture.

What kind of ass had she made of herself last night? All because of that damn cat. That cat and her asshole neighbor. Though he hadn't been any kind of an ass. Weird, but not an ass at all.

"Ass!"

NINE

WATER DRIPPED FROM LIBBY'S HAIR when a knock sounded on the back door.

"Christ, it's not even daylight yet."

She'd managed to avoid her neighbor and the damn cat yesterday. Not too hard when you didn't leave your bedroom.

Libby toweled off her hair and body, wrapped a robe around her, and tiptoed to the end of the hallway. Marlis's long blonde hair and sweet smile greeted her through the thin pane of glass in the back door. She padded through the kitchen and held her breath, waiting for a missed shard from the wine glass to end up in her foot. None did. She unlocked the door, and Mar's sweet lilac scent preceded her into the house.

"When will you girls learn to spill the beans before things get so bad?" Marlis grabbed the back of Libby's neck and yanked her in for a hug.

She wrapped her arms around her rail-thin friend and squeezed. "Never, I'm fairly certain."

"I'm sure you're right." Mar planted a kiss on her cheek and then rushed to the table. A large plastic bag was clutched to her chest while a smaller paper bag hung from her fingertips. She dumped the big bag onto the table and set the other one beside it.

"What is all that?"

"That's"—Mar's hands swooped wide, drawing a bulging circle around the huge bag—"your mail." A single hand swung toward the other bag as though it were an afterthought. "And that's your breakfast."

It was super sweet that Marlis had brought her breakfast, but Libby couldn't get over the lump on her table. "That's from my mailbox?"

"No, it was on your porch. There's another bag out there too. I just couldn't carry it all in at once."

"Holy shit."

"I know. What do you think it is?"

"Oh, no." Libby's shoulders slumped. "Pervs with nothing better to do than comment on the size of my breasts."

Mar patted her beautifully trim chest. "Would it help if I said I was envious of your boobs?"

"No. But breakfast will help." Libby skirted the mail-bag and opened the package to find a veggie and bacon omelet from her favorite breakfast place near Mar's house. "Oh my gosh, this looks so good. Thank you."

"It's the least I could do."

"You already ate?"

Mar nodded. "You know I get up at four a.m."

Libby placed her hands over her ears and shook her head. "The only four o'clock I'm familiar with is p.m." She let her hands fall to her sides. "But yes, I know you're one of those crazy people who do more by eight a.m. than most do all day."

"It really helps me tackle the day."

"I prefer to slow dance with the day." Libby picked off the edge of the omelet and tossed it into her mouth. "It's still warm." She chewed and hummed her appreciation.

Mar leaned against the counter, very near where Libby had made an ass of herself two days ago, and smiled.

"I'm surprised you showed up alone."

"Larkin is out of town, and Gen is under Detective Owen's supervision at Beena Carter's house."

"What?" Libby gaped. Beena was the sleazy mother of Perry Carter, Gen's boss who'd killed his family and gotten away with it thanks to her friend's unwitting help.

"You remember Roderick, Beena's young lover? Her kept boy?"

"How could I forget? Number one, he's beautiful. Number two, I thought he was a decade older than he was. Number three, Gen talked about avenging his trampled rights as much as she did landing Perry in jail."

"I think she knew they were going to bury him under the jail by the time Owen finished his case against him."

"She shouldn't have stopped Owen." As the story went, Gen's lover had been ready to beat the life from Perry one solid punch at a time. "I know why she did, but I don't think I would have stopped him." Gen was all about justice and serving the time for the crime. Libby was too, but she wasn't opposed to the death penalty. "Hell, I don't think anyone could've stopped me from bashing in his skull."

"Well, they're digging up Beena's yard, looking for Roderick's mother."

"Shit."

"Yeah." Mar nodded and smoothed a hand down the front of her dress. "Did you get a cat?"

"No. It's my neighbor's."

"How did I forget about him?" Whipping around, she lifted up to her tippy toes and craned her neck toward the window.

"Is he home?"

"I don't know." Libby shoved another hunk of omelet into her mouth and then another.

A full minute later, Mar turned back with a huff. "I can't tell."

Libby bobbed her shoulders and ate another bite.

"So you want to talk about it?"

She exaggerated her chewing.

"Well, if you change your mind, call me. I'll be here in no time." Mar assessed the face on the pretty gold watch on her wrist that cost more than Libby's monthly mortgage payment. "I have a meeting to get to, but after that, I'm flexible." She stepped forward and kissed Libby's cheek. "I'm serious."

Mar turned and headed for the door.

"Thank you, Mar. I love you."

"I love you." Her friend kissed her fingers and waved them over her shoulder before closing Libby inside her home.

Through the window, the sun shone brightly through the few trees in her and her neighbors' yards. She turned toward her breakfast and snagged the last bites.

When her gaze shifted to the lumpy mail bag, the eggs turned sour in her mouth. She could make a fire in her backyard tonight. It wasn't like she expected there to be legitimate correspondence in the thing. Still, she ripped into the sack and then the first letter.

Dear Special Agent Irish,

I am Kara McKenna. I am eight years old. I want to be a Special Agent just like you when I grow up. That was a lot of guns. Good job catching the bad guys.

Sincerely,
Kara

A silly smile spread across Libby's mouth. She checked the envelope to be sure she hadn't destroyed the girl's return address, and then placed it on the far-right side of the small table. She opened the next letter more carefully, slipped the tri-folded white page from the envelope, and flipped open the two sides. A 4x6 inch picture fluttered to the floor.

Libby crouched low and scooped up the print. She turned it over. Molten rage had her crumpling the image and wishing she could do the same to the pictured appendage. Her white-knuckled grip released the trash to the floor. She didn't bother with the letter, just balled it up and dropped it next to its mate's mate.

From there, she turned off her emotions and created a quick system. Dick pics crumpled on the floor. Letters from agents, lawyers, and production companies joined them, along with any communication vaguely mentioning her looks or a proposed relationship of any sort. She was left with three piles on the table and just as many paper cuts.

A short stack of letters from kids brought a hint of joy to an otherwise soul-crushing job. The largest stack were wackos, threatening retaliation against the government as a whole, while the last and smallest of the stacks hit closer to home. They were a few people her work had affected in some way. Whether they were family members of the criminals she'd caught or the people themselves varied from letter to letter. Each promised reprisal for her actions and took zero responsibility for their own.

Libby washed her hands thoroughly and dressed in running clothes. She threw a baggy sweater on over top, pulled her hair back, and shoved out of her house for the first time since she'd been put on leave. The second bag of mail sat beside her door. It scared her more that the freaking cat did. Using the side of her shoe, she shoved it inside, locked the door, and pushed the key in her mini pocket.

Thankfully, the temperature had jumped with the sunshine. The sweatshirt was hardly necessary, and she hadn't even begun. No way was she taking it off and drawing any more attention to her boobs. In a sports bra, they'd set off the next atomic bomb.

She started at a reasonable pace, turning away from her neighbor's house. The sun warmed her face. With each stride down the sidewalk, activity warmed her limbs. A small group of moms hovered close to their toddlers at Underwood Park. They prattled on about whether the farmers' market organically labeled produce were in truth chemical free. Something about runoff from neighboring farms. The gothic, gray stone front of St. Luke Academy had her picking up the tempo. It reminded her of the first act of a horror film. Creepy, but no one's head spun a 360.

Timing the intersections took a few moments of jogging in place. By the time she crossed Atlantic Avenue, sweat ran down her neck. The barest scent of alcohol bled from her pores. She made the turn into the Brooklyn Botanic Garden and hit her stride. It was the cheapest yearly gym membership she'd ever found and the most stunning. Something was magical and grounding about witnessing the changes of every season. Terry, a guard Libby had known for the last decade, sat in a high-backed stool just inside the gate.

"Morning, Mr. Terry."

He lifted a hand from his slowly expanding belly and shot her a fast thumb and forefinger gun wave. "Not catching bad guys today?"

"Not today." If she showed up every day this week for a run, she might have to tell him she was having some work troubles. The thought sucked a bit of the joy from her favorite place in the city.

"I suppose even superheroes need a day off." He'd always been so proud of her and excited to know an FBI agent.

She smiled. "Forever my favorite, Terry."

He saluted her, and she continued through the withering green canopies of Osborne Garden. To her left, the large fountains still sprinkled. She skipped out on the narrow footpath of the small birch forest. Not like she had to hurry to anything … like work. Not today. The path took her through the Cherry Esplanade, a true marvel in the springtime, and then around the Chinese Hill and the Pond Garden. At the end of the loop, she stopped at a split in the lane. Right would take her back home, back to her problems.

"Left it is." Libby dragged the back of her sleeve over her face and took off past the Reinhardt Conservatory toward the very back of the complex, a place she hadn't been in years, a place not many people had the stamina or time to reach. No matter running or walking.

Her lungs burned. Her body ached. Her mind quieted, and the world fell away.

That Zen of oblivion was the reason she ran.

Stride after stride, she embraced it … until a familiar figure brought it all crashing down. Her push sputtered, and slowly, her legs ground to a halt. Her chest heaved, and her pulse thumped. Her mouth unhinged, and her eyes bulged.

On the split from her path at a quaint little rest spot nearest the pond, her neighbor sat on a stone bench next to another man. His companion was a foot shorter and a few decades older, judging by the gray creeping up his sideburns, but he was no less compelling. Something in his presence made the hair on the back of her neck stand on end. His dead eyes said killer, more than her—not her—cat.

Even more unsettling were the perfectly formed words shared between the two men. She couldn't make them out, but HER NEIGHBOR COULD SPEAK.

She took a slow step back, shielding herself from their view with a short hill covered in lush foliage. Both men stared at the water. From any farther distance, she wouldn't have noticed them engaging at all. Actually, they sat at opposite ends of the stone bench. From a distance, they looked like two strangers.

Libby peered through a small gap in the bushes. The older man stood, crossed in front of her neighbor, and headed down the path away from her. Had she not been looking so closely, she would have missed the tiny package he passed to her neighbor.

Drugs?

If it was, she'd just witnessed the most unlikely deal in the history of drug deals.

Her neighbor slid the small envelope into the pocket of his tweed jacket. In all the time he'd lived next to her, she'd never seen him so put together. Wingtips. Crisp slacks. Pointed collar. It didn't suit him, yet her body still responded to the sight. Despite the clandestine interaction she'd witnessed, she swallowed the saliva pooling in her mouth.

In one instantaneous movement, his face snapped in her direction.

Instinct screamed for her to run, yet training forced her to remain. Movement drew the eye. She was far enough back and hidden that he couldn't see her. Could he? Sweat slicked her palms. Shivers rolled over her head to toe.

Slowly, he turned back to the pond.

Libby stepped from the asphalt lane to the grass and sprinted in the straightest route for the exit.

What had she just witnessed? Who was her neighbor? Why hadn't she just kept pace and ignored him, just as he ignored her?

The barrage of questions followed her through the different parts of the gardens.

"Woo, girl, you're going to burn the soles off those shoes." Terry's dark mouth widened into a great smile. "Someone after you?" He laughed.

God, she hoped not.

"See you later, Mr. Terry."

"Later, Libby." He waved her out of the gardens.

She kept the burning soles pace until she rounded the first high-rise and then eased off. If not, she'd collapse before making it back.

Images of his mouth forming perfectly intelligible words tormented her all the way to the mommies and toddlers now sharing a too-fucking-cute picnic on the most picture-perfect quilt. Irritation mounted her as though she were a brood animal. What was wrong with her that he couldn't speak?

"Not a damn thing."

Libby dug in and charged to her driveway. Her rubbery legs slowed to a stop in the sliver of no-man's land between their two houses. She placed her hands on her head and sucked wind. Blood throbbed and pulsed through her limbs. Muscles in her core tightened.

The clack of a gate had her spinning. Her neighbor's large hands grasped the rod iron arrows at the top of the chest-height gate. His dark gaze narrowed on her.

She wanted to scream at him or at the very least flip him off.

I know you can talk.

His constant scowl morphed into a full-blown lip purse. His head shook.

It was all she could take.

"What?" Her hands and arms opened wide as though challenging him to a fight. And she was. More than anything right now, she wanted something from him. Some acknowledgment of her humanity. She wanted to know that he saw her even though he looked at her unlike anyone else. Deeper, yet more dismissive because nothing ever followed the intense expressions.

"Enjoy the garden?" His voice was deep and rich like expensive chocolate. It wasn't loud, but she heard it clearly over the bustle of the cars and pedestrians.

Her lips parted. No sounds came out.

He fastened the padlock on the bars' latch and disappeared down the narrow driveway that led to a basement garage before she could compute the words. He'd seen her by the pond.

She stared at the empty space where he'd been for too long, trying to make sense of what she'd seen and the fact that he'd actually spoken. The words had done nothing more than put her in her place, exposed and idiotic all at the same time. She stomped down the sidewalk to her driveway. Her sweat left a trail down the concrete. When she turned the corner to the steppingstones leading to her door, she averted her gaze. If he rounded and entered the backyard, she didn't want to see him.

Libby pushed through the screen door and rushed for the back door but fell back against the porch frame.

The picture that started the madness stared back.

Her neck craned left and right. Looking for what? She didn't know. Whoever the fuck had wedged the print in her doorjamb would be a start. No one lurked in the bushes. Not that she could see. No one was bold enough to stand in the open and take credit.

No way would the girls trick her. Not this way.

Had Joel done this?

Work was one thing, but this was her house, her sanctuary. Rage cuddled close. She plucked the picture from the frame, grabbing unnaturally deep onto the print, let herself in, locked the door, and headed straight for her closet. On the far wall, sitting crooked on her floor right where she'd thrown it, sat her pack. She reached inside and pulled out her florescent powder, brush, and the UV light.

Ten minutes later, she threw the useless light across the room, more aggravated than when Quinn had told her to go pack her shit and leave. Not a damn print or speck of possible body fluid. She ripped the sweat-soaked clothes from her body and thrashed each article to the floor on her way to the bathroom.

Where the shower curtain was closed.

The blood drained to Libby's little toe. Thoughts wouldn't come fast enough.

Your gun! Where is your gun?

She lunged from the bathroom, threw herself at her night-

MEGAN MITCHAM

stand, and yanked the drawer so hard the base teetered. Relief soothed the most jagged of her edges. Her personal Browning 1911-380. Quinn had requested she relinquish her standard issue Glock. Gripping the matte black gun, she checked the chamber and flicked off the safety, then leveled the barrel at the bathroom. Slowly, she moved into the room as though in hostile territory. Inside her chest, her heart jittered and jibbed. Her hands remained steady. She drew a deep breath and wrenched the curtain wide.

A loofah, hair care bottles, and a benign razor sat in a neat row on her shelf. That was it.

Overreact much?

No, she really didn't. She never closed that frilly white curtain unless company was coming, and the girls didn't count as company. Therefore, she hadn't had company in more than a year. Sure, it looked better closed, but she could never sleep with it that way. She always wondered who was hiding behind it, so she always kept it open.

Libby cleared the rest of her house and resigned herself to a shower. She scrubbed at the irritation that clung to her skin like an infection. Maybe the magnum had messed her up more than she'd realized, but she didn't think so.

To get her mind off the unsettling feelings, she made a mental grocery list. Later, she could worry about how long she'd have a paycheck with which to buy them, pay her rent, and her insurance. Screw that damn picture.

TEN

Libby stood in front of the produce cooler in the same spot where she'd been for the entirety of her phone conversation with Larkin. She held two bunches of bananas. One in each hand. The difference came in their displays. Organic: $0.88 per lb. Regular: $0.79 per lb. Not a big price jump. Maybe it was worth it. Maybe not.

"I know you are. You're always fine."

Yeah, until she was pulling her gun inside her house, clearing her home, and sleeping with it under her pillow.

"I feel a *but* coming on." Libby returned the bananas to their spots. The simple decision seemed insurmountable. Instead, she grabbed a handful of kiwis and dumped them into the basket.

"But I've been running errands this morning. It wouldn't hurt anything for me to stop by before I head to the office."

"I'm not even home." Libby grabbed a bag of carrots and two containers of hummus instead of the usual one. Now that she was home all day, snack time was in full effect.

"Oh, where are you?"

"The grocery store. I didn't go before heading out of town, so the situation was dire I was down to my last almond."

"It's so quiet. I thought you were home."

Libby's gaze shifted around the small market. A young guy puzzled over which bag of chips to choose. Two workers argued about whose responsibility it was to take out the garbage. She had snagged a prime parking spot in front of the store and had not been forced to elbow her way through reporters.

"It is quiet. All the upstanding citizens are at work on a Tuesday morning." For better or worse, she hadn't been able to drag herself out of the house after the unsettling neighbor, picture, curtain situation yesterday.

"You'll be back and bitching about the next assignment before you know it."

"I know." She hoped so. Downtime was doing terrible things to her psyche. It had already inflamed her natural paranoia to dangerous levels. "I'll talk to you later."

"Promise to call me if you need anything?"

"I promise." Libby grabbed a container of black bean salsa. "Love you."

"Love you, girl." Larkin ended the call.

Libby sensed a presence behind her and turned, expecting no one to be there.

Wrong.

"Heeey." The young guy had chosen cool ranch flavored chips to go with his straight-leg jeans and FUCK T-shirt. Literally, his white tee boasted a bold font with the

letters F-U-C-K across the chest followed by the definition.
- Verb [Faak] -ing -er -s Fuck can be used in many ways and is probably the only fucking word that can be put every-fuck-ing-where and still make fucking sense. Fuckers.

His face was pretty. Childlike.

"You're that chick." He smiled and pointed at her as though he'd solved a difficult puzzle. His gaze slid down her body, and the grin grew. His light brown baby eyes narrowed on the swell of her boobs in her baggy sweatshirt and then widened when they reached her hips wrapped in this morning's workout pants. "Yeah, you're definitely her. Daayuum." He elongated the word.

"Good talk, kid." Libby turned away, looped her cart around the island of fruit, and pushed deeper into the store, hoping the guy would go on about his business.

"I love you," the guy hollered from the front.

Libby ignored the obnoxious declaration and studied the options of edible greenery in front of her. Spinach, kale (gag), and romaine were coming home with her. When she shifted to the pasta section, she allowed herself one glance toward the front of the store. The kid had forgotten her in favor of his phone. His thumbs were going a thousand taps per second while the guy behind the counter rang up his chips, soft drink, and candy bar.

"Oh, to be young again." She yanked a package of veggie-derived faux pasta from the shelf, chucked it into her basket, and went on about her gathering.

Twenty minutes and a hundred and forty-six dollars later, Libby pushed out of the store into a crowd. Terror stepped on her throat. Reporters? She assessed the situation in a fraction of a second. Not reporters. She'd stepped into the middle of a five-year high school sidewalk reunion. Dudes only.

"FBI!" One of the guys—a tall, gangly one—pointed at her with one hand. In the other, he kept her in the frame of a camera. Living in Brooklyn, she saw about a dozen You-Tubers and bloggers a day wandering the streets talking to the bulky things.

Five men restricted her movement in a tightening semi-circle.

"I told you." Her Fuck T-shirt friend brought up the end of the little crescent. The youthful innocence she'd seen inside the store was gone, and in its place, in the presence of his pack, mania turned his pretty grin devious. "Didn't I? Look at that rack." He gave a full laugh that crawled into her mouth, down her throat, and expanded.

The biggest not in height, but breadth stepped forward, taking the position of alpha in the group. He stood too close. His smile was too big.

"FBI! You know what the F stands for?" Alpha waited a beat and then grabbed the crotch of his pants. "Fuck."

How original.

Fight and flight went to war inside her body. Fear flamed her outrage. How dare these little shits gang up on her? How dare she let them make her feel vulnerable? But she was, in fact, quite vulnerable ... unless she wanted to pull her weapon on a bunch of kids. Yet no matter how angry or intimidated she became, she wouldn't go there. This wasn't a life or death situation. This was a display of male dominance. These were boys who didn't dominate in any aspect of their life putting someone in their place. Under them.

Libby depressed the trunk latch on the key fob in her hand and dodged left. Saying anything would only escalate the situation. A situation that was being recorded. She glared at the asshole on the end until he moved out of her way and stepped off the sidewalk. Her trunk gaped. The bags on her arm no longer weighed an ounce as she heaved them into the space atop her riot gear.

"Hey, Fuck-BI." Alpha stepped off the curb.

He was killing it with originality. She kept her head down, but her eyes rolled high. She unhooked her wrists from her reusable bags.

Fingers bit into the flesh of Libby's right ass cheek. The grip was so hard her thin fabric pants provided little defense. His punishing hold shook up and down, throwing her forward into the trunk.

The group's laughter swelled into fevered whoops and whistles.

Her attacker's other hand threaded up along the left side of her abdomen, aiming for her breast.

Libby intercepted his hand. She ran her right thumb up his palm to the base of his thumb and wrapped it tight. Her left arm hooked around his elbow. She used her weight and position to help pin his arm in place. Then she wrenched his thumb back toward his elbow.

An unsettling scream sliced through the revelry.

The biting grip on her ass released, and his weight lifted off her. He shifted to her left, trying his best to relieve the pressure on his thumb.

She moved with him, keeping close to his body while she levered up from the trunk. The group moved closer, their faces drawn with concern.

"What the—?"

Libby released her hold and thrust her right elbow into the guy's jaw.

The whack of flesh bone on bone echoed off the metal and concrete surrounding them. His bravado was reduced to a guttural, "Umph."

Alpha fell back against the side of her car and slid toward the ground. His feet tried in vain to counteract gravity, but he landed on his side, staring up at her.

"The F stands for federal, motherfucker." Libby grabbed her keys and slammed her trunk. She swung her gaze toward the group, daring any one of them to step forward.

"Ohh, that's police brutality." The tall one's index finger pointed once more. "Caught on camera." He swung his digit toward the device that, judging by the amount he was swaying and bouncing, could have used a stabilizer.

"That was called sexual assault and defense." She turned away from the group, stepped over the asshole on his side, got into her car, and tore away down the street.

Libby pulled her phone from her pocket and found the app she used for meditation and linked into her Bluetooth. The soothing sounds filled the interior. She turned it high and did as the gently commanding voice told her.

"Deep breath in. One. Two. Three. Four. Five. Six. Seven. Eight. Exhale. One. Two. Three. Four. Five. Six. Seven. Eight. Deep breath in, allow renewing, rejuvenating oxygen to fill your lungs. Exhale. Release the pollution of noise, negativity, and worry."

In and out. Inhaling and releasing, her muscles quivered. Her fists clenched. If only she could have punched the tall guy and broken his camera. If only she could elbow that asshole again and again and again.

Libby arrived home so quickly that she'd hardly had a chance to decompress. At least she hadn't earned herself a ticket. It took her several minutes of sitting in the driveway to compose herself before she grabbed her groceries out of the trunk and headed for the porch. She drew a deep breath and approached.

No picture. No cat. No neighbor.

Her exhale took away the last of her jitters.

She worked her way inside and set her haul on the table. The lumpy mailbag she'd added to the other one after her run this morning hadn't moved. No way in hell was she going through it.

No way was she touching her groceries to unload them before she washed that creep's germs off her hands. Her ass still stung from his brutal grip.

Libby kicked the bag and headed for the sink. She shoved the lever. The water rushed, but it was the tiny cactus on the windowsill that drew her attention.

A precise cut down the center separated the prickly, spherical plant in two.

ELEVEN

THE VELCRO RIPPED. Libby spit the strap from her mouth and slung the boxing glove off her hand to answer Gen's call. She pressed the speakerphone. "Yes, I know I fucked up."

"Excuse me?" Gen's indignant voice filtered out through the screened porch and disseminated among the trees. She wasn't worried about her neighbor hearing. He was too busy banging his phone-a-fuck. The neighbors on the other side had never set foot in the backyard, always used the front door, and their building started the connected brownstones on her side of the street. And the cat curled up in her favorite chair didn't give a damn what she said.

"Uh ..." She sucked in a breath. "Are you not calling to bitch about my latest viral bullshit?" Sweat dripped into her eyes. She used the back of her arm to wipe her brow.

"Hell, no. I'm calling to congratulate the hell out of you."

A bit of relief eased the cramp forming between her shoulder blades.

"I pressed replay on that video too many times. You beat his ass." Gen chuckled.

"Made that big boy cry," Owen's deep voice called from a distance. "Way to go, Lib."

"Did you hear, Owen?"

"Yes. Tell him I need no encouragement."

"Libby says thanks," she hollered. "Now, tell me what he did to earn your wrath. The video was edited and only showed you lighting into him. But I know he had it coming."

"Thank you, Gen." Libby wiped at a tear threatening to escape. "Larkin and Mar, they meant well, but they were so focused on the blowback." Quinn had been worried about the blowback too. So worried, that she was to be brought in front of the review board later this week for possible termination.

Her stomach knotted, and it had nothing to do with muscle fatigue.

She'd gone viral twice in one week. This doctored video showed her going off on the guy. It failed to show what he had done to incite her. Not that Quinn cared to know the whole story.

"It's the lawyer in me."

"He grabbed my ass and was going for my breasts." She had the beginnings of a series of bruises on the right buttock.

"That bastard deserves to be in jail."

"Probably so, but I just want all this to go away."

"I know you do. Owen promised he'd look into the group and get them on something."

"You and Owen both have plenty enough to keep you

busy. You don't need to worry about me."

"We don't need to, but we do."

"You're a we, huh?" Libby kicked the boxing glove.

"Crazy, right?"

"Nah, it's good. I'm happy for you … both."

"You know Larkin or Marlis would be more than happy to have you stay with them for a while. I would, too, if I had the room."

Libby knew it because both the girls had invited her to stay already, but if the anomalies in her house weren't a product of a chemical imbalance in her brain, then someone was fucking with her. There was no way she'd bring the girls into this. She wouldn't be able to live with herself if one of them got hurt. Besides, the last thing any of them needed was more media attention. Marlis and Larkin garnered enough on their own, being billionaire CEOs and all.

"I'm fine. With today's round-the-clock newsreels, my fifteen minutes of fame will soon be over."

"Owen found human remains in Beena Carter's backyard. So that should blow up tomorrow and knock you out of the mainstream limelight."

"Thank you?" She winced. "That's awful. Is it Roderick's mother?"

"Won't know for a few weeks … but all the markers indicate that it was. And …"

"What?"

"She was pregnant at the time of her death."

"Oh, no." Libby's head shook, and a lump formed in her throat.

"Yeah, a rough day all the way around."

"Go hug your man. I'll talk to you later." Libby leaned her forehead on the heavy bag she hadn't pulled out of the hall closet and hung in a few weeks.

"Who are you going to hug?" Gen sighed.

"My punching bag. Good night, Gen."

"Night, Lib."

Libby ended the call, set the phone on the windowsill, and then remembered the other dead plant. There were too many things out of kilter for it to be a coincidence, yet she couldn't make herself believe that anyone would give two cares to spend their time screwing with her.

A heady moan wafted from her neighbor's open windows. It turned into a pitched cry.

She snatched the glove from under the chair, keeping as far away from the cat as possible. He didn't stir. Her hand shoved inside the steamy compartment. She grabbed the strap with her teeth, wrapped it around her wrist, and started with a jab, jab, cross. The longer she hit, the more her rage seeped through her pores. Droplets of it spattered onto the bag while others fell to the floor.

Her neighbor's girl was working toward a crescendo.

Libby was just working. Working up a fury.

Since she was twelve, she'd been employed. Her mother cleaned houses for a living—still did—and at the tender age of twelve, the woman had put her to task. For two hours every weeknight and all day on Saturdays, Libby had dusted, wiped down counters, mopped floors, and scrubbed toilets. Though she hadn't seen any actual money from the job, she'd learned what it meant to earn her keep.

At sixteen, she'd gotten a job in an accountant's office. The woman had lived just a street over from Libby and her mother and was keen to bring up a young girl to know and love numbers. It had started her unlikely career path. Numbers made more sense than people. Numbers created patterns that could be followed. Patterns that helped her catch criminals. She'd worked for the woman through college and even after she'd earned her degree in accounting and minor in finance while she waited for the Bureau to accept her.

They had accepted her. Now they'd abandoned her.

For the first time in her life, she wasn't actively working. For the first time in her life, she might get fired. Then what?

She wouldn't sue the Bureau. No matter what Quinn did, she wouldn't bring shame upon their name because of that awful man. She wouldn't go back to cleaning anything. The prospect of becoming an accountant, dealing with no more than balancing accounts, made her want to cry. With the Bureau, the balancing of numbers led to criminals. It led to action and excitement.

The neighbor's back door clicked open, and two sets of footsteps exited.

Libby kept her head down, torqued her hips, drove with her legs, extended her shoulders, and beat the bag in a full-out melee. The chains jerked and clanked above. She thrust a knee at the bag and followed it with a few elbows. His booty call's car started and drove away. Backhand. Backhand hook. Her shoulder sagged against the rough material, and she pounded short strokes of her fists into the imaginary man's belly, exposing too much. Her back. Her head. Exhaustion pulled her toward the ground. Still, she pummeled back the demons.

The screen door slammed against its frame.

She rounded on the intruder.

Of course, he'd come to get the cat. She hadn't expected him to come when she was out here, especially after the park incident. If that wasn't enough to keep him away, there was the wine incident. Then there was her mouth always rambling and running.

Then there was his body.

The clothes were gone. So gone. So good, God. Only a pair of shorts hung off his hips. Sweat clung to his skin. The massive width of his chest expanded and contracted on steady breaths, as though he'd landed his ten-point dismount from the woman, bowed, and then rushed her out the door. He was too gorgeous. Not pretty in any way. He was too big and brooding for all that. His facial features struck a chord. Hell, they struck every one she possessed and some she hadn't known about. Thick brows hooded that intense gaze. A strong nose was there, leading the eye to his full lips. His jaw looked like it could deflect the elbow she'd given the guy outside the grocery store.

Her neighbor stood inside between both doors, hemming her in and blocking any escape she hoped to make. An escape she should be hoping to make. Though, the last thing on her mind was running. Her fingers itched for the feel of his heated skin. She curled her hand tighter inside the gloves and lifted her chin.

If he thought he could intimidate her with his physicality—

He stepped forward.

Libby straightened her shoulders. He didn't strike her as a drug dealer. No, he was something much more dangerous.

"The garden was nice. Did you enjoy it?"

He kept coming. Closer and closer.

Her chin lifted in preparation.

For what?

Anything. Everything.

He stopped inches away. Too close. It put her eye level with his collarbone. She shifted her gaze to meet his. Heat scorched her inner thighs, and her clit twitched.

The amber flecks in his eyes sparked in the light that shone from inside her house. Thick scruff covered his impressive jawline. His thick lips were pressed into a grimace. As though, for the first time, he wanted to speak and was struggling not to.

Her imagination, surely.

His gaze roamed her sweat slicked shoulders. While most men's eyes went directly to the crests of her breasts, especially when cinched tight inside her sports bra, his shifted down her arm. Of all the men she might have invited to look their fill, he didn't. Figured. Nope, it stalled on half of the jagged red tattoo Killer had given her. He grabbed her forearm and lifted it to the light.

"It's fine," she whispered.

He peeled the Velcro strap and eased the glove off the tips of her fingers. The cool air hit her wet hand. Heat encompassed her arm and traveled through her veins like nuclear radiation, dismissing the wind. After he set the glove on the windowsill, his touch slid to her wrist.

Libby trapped a moan between her lips. After examining the healing scratch the cat had given her days ago, he lowered it to her side but didn't release her. His grip pulled her forward. His nostrils flared. He bit the inside of his lips, compressing them. With every breath, the scent of sex wafted off him. Sex with another woman. With her every breath, she banked the need to extend her tongue and flick it over his chest. A shiver of desire quaked through her.

She wanted him more than she remembered wanting anything. Her lips parted.

His hand opened, releasing her.

He rounded her, grabbed the cat, and left. Killer hung over the back of her neighbor's shoulder. Could cats flip the bird? His amused expression communicated the same message as a middle finger.

On the bright side, tomorrow she didn't have to go to work, so she could buy a damn hook for the screen door.

TWELVE

"HA!" LIBBY THRUST HER DRILL into the air as though it was a sword. After all, she'd won a battle. The hole she'd drilled into the screen door and frame lined up perfectly. The shiny silver hook fit neatly into the small eye bolt, both of which she'd installed. She gave the trigger three quick pulls, and the tool whizzed and whined. "Take that, cat!"

A sense of accomplishment washed over her, cleansing the crippling feeling of utter defeat. She'd taken control of a small aspect of her life. It was time to wield the reins on the rest of it and get her job back. Not that Quinn would be receptive to the thought, especially after the grocery store incident. Sure, the full video had been released, thanks to an eyewitness who'd filmed the drama from the moment she'd exited the building, but it wouldn't matter to her boss. Hell, if she wasn't on leave already, Quinn would have completely severed her from the FBI after the initial report without a sliver of input from her.

She clung to the small win, gathered the measuring tape and pencil from the floor, and carried everything to the kitchen table. One by one, she replaced her tools in the small toolbox. The small plastic packaging and bag she'd gotten from the hardware store this morning—without incident—she placed into the recycling bucket.

"Three hours of this long day down. Now what?" She shoved the toolbox under the sink and turned in a circle around her home. Two garbage bags of mail sat by her back door. Before her run to the hardware store this morning, she'd dropped off the handful of letters she'd responded to at the post office. She planned to throw the bags away but hadn't gotten around to it. Like she had so much to do. Hilarious.

Libby marched to the front door, determined to check and sort her mail, and then toss all the trash mail where it belonged.

A picture on the mantel drew her up short. Two frames adorned the skinny shelf above her sealed-up fireplace. The picture on the left of her parents in a hospital room with a baby swaddled in white held lovingly between them was per usual, a pretty image and nothing like the life she had after leaving that hospital. The picture to the right of her, Marlis, Larkin, and Genevieve taken on their first ever girls' night out … was face down.

Her first thought darted to the closed shower curtain two days ago and her fantastic overreaction. She huffed out a breath, lifted the frame, and then threw it onto the floor as though it had cursed her.

Metal collided with the wood floor. A thud echoed through the house followed by the crack of glass.

"Goddammit!" Libby's hands clenched. Her fists shook. Anger, she could deal with, but the fear … It crowded her with high walls. It sucked the oxygen from the room. It liquified her cells.

The shattered red heart stared up at her. In its center, her green eyes stared back.

Her shower curtain fit hadn't been an overreaction. This wasn't an overreaction. Libby sprinted for the kitchen table. When she reached her purse, she pulled the sidearm from it. For the first time since the academy, her hands trembled.

Rightly so. Someone had drawn a heart on the glass around her face and placed the picture face down.

Someone had been in her house without her consent or knowledge.

Twice. That you know of.

Tears blurred Libby's vision. Gooseflesh crept down her arm.

But who?

Her gaze snapped through the kitchen window to her neighbor's house. He was weird as hell. He was close as hell. She was screwed as hell.

She blinked furiously, looped her purse over her shoulder, and reached the back door. Thought of the screen's new hook stopped her. To keep the cat out, she'd have to use the front door. Right now, though, the damn cat was the least of her worries. Cats couldn't perform B&Es or draw hearts.

Still, she flipped the lock on the back door. She eased forward, cleared the hallway with the barrel of her Browning, and sprinted for the front, jumping over the picture like a scared child as she went. With a flick, she turned on the front porch and living room lights and flew out the door. Warm sunlight and frigid, gusting wind greeted her on the front stoop.

Despite its apparent inadequacies, Libby locked the front padlock as well. Her gaze slid to the neighbor's house. The lights were off. No music poured through his paper-thin walls. He appeared to be gone but looks could be deceiving.

Libby shoved her pistol into her purse and rushed to her car. She got in and drove. No meditation this time. She drew deep breaths and drove. She focused on action and drove.

Soon enough, the front of her car wheeled into the entrance parking garage, and Libby stopped at the small guard shack. She offered the familiar man sitting on the high stool the best smile she could muster and then swiped her magnetic access card across the panel. Her breath locked inside her lungs for the second it took the light above the sensor to blink red. No access. The guard hopped down from his stool. Libby tried again, dragging the card across the panel. Full contact. She'd never had to do that before. A blacked-out government-issued SUV pulled into the lane behind her. Again, the light blinked red.

Fucking Quinn.

"What's the trouble, Special Agent Irish?"

The sweet gentleman knew her name. Too damn bad she didn't know his.

"I don't know," she lied. "My card is acting up. I think it knows it's Wednesday, and that it's been a horrible one at that."

"They always know, don't they?"

"It seems so."

The guard held out his hand. "Let me see what I can do."

"Thank you." She sighed.

Then he did the most infuriating thing all people trying to help do; the same thing that she did that got her exactly nowhere. Like he could hold it better than her. Like he could wave it in the air better than her. Magically, the light blinked RED.

"Worth a try, right?" He offered her a smile and turned into the booth with her card.

"I suppose." Her skin itched. If he figured out that she was on leave, there's no way he'd let her inside. It wouldn't matter that she was blocking the entrance and now backing up traffic on the road.

The guard's laptop screen brightened, and he began typing. Then he typed some more.

A horn blasted from a few cars back.

"Man." The guard did the awe shucks swing of the arm and snap of the fingers.

Libby's itch turned into full-blown hives as heat flared around her neck. It was nothing like the kind of heat she felt near her neighbor, a neighbor who was in all likelihood stalking her. But that didn't add up. He didn't talk to her. He hardly looked in her direction. When he did, though, he looked deeper and more intensely than most.

Motion inside the booth refocused her attention. The guard lifted the phone to his ear.

"Great." Libby rubbed her neck.

He spoked into the phone, but she couldn't make out the words. Not for lack of trying. A moment later, he groaned.

"Are you serious?" He moved the receiver from his mouth, exhaled, and then returned it. "All right."

Her hives spread to her chest.

Again the car honked. Another joined in.

"Well, Agent Irish …" The guard exited the booth and offered her back the card.

Her heart sank to the area of her belly button.

"I'm sorry about all that. They're updating the computer." He stepped backward into the booth and felt for something. The arm lifted and the metal barrier lowered. "I'll note your entry in the log. You have a nice day."

Her smile was genuine this time. "Thank you so much.

I hope you have a great day too."

A horn blasted once more. Libby raised her window and quickly guided her car into the parking garage before he changed his mind, or the computers came back up. The thick concrete structure blocked the sunlight and suited her mood much better. She found a coveted spot near the main entrance, parked, and hurried out of her car before she lost her nerve.

High-waisted jeans, a high-cropped cream sweater, and pointy suede booties screamed, "I don't belong here." She hadn't taken the time to change, under threat and all. Truthfully, she'd had so much on her mind that it hadn't occurred to her. Now she was a walking neon sign, but it didn't stop her from marching for the double doors. Breaths whooshed in and out of her lungs as though she were pushing the tempo in a run. She was running from something, someone.

Libby lifted her card to the panel. A second later, the stupid little light blinked red once more.

"Perfect." She walked several feet away from the doors and pulled her cell from her pocket.

The screen unlocked with one glimpse of her annoyed scowl. She shifted to call log and scrolled through her recent calls. Genevieve. Larkin. Marlis. Larkin. Genevieve. Alec. Her finger hovered over the screen. Only one of them could get her in this building. She stalled because if he agreed to it, he'd get in trouble, and it would be her fault.

Voices from a small group in the parking garage met her ear.

Libby locked the phone, made certain it was on vibrate, and held it to her ear. She turned her back to the group and hoped like hell they didn't recognize her. It helped that she looked nothing like the buttoned-up agent in the first viral image, nor like the slouchy woman outside the grocery store in the viral video.

"That's the one." Out of her periphery, one of the men rounding the corner gestured in her general direction.

"Yes, I'm still here," she said into the phone.

"The one?" another guy asked.

Her shoulders straightened ready to deflect their jibes.

"Who stole your parking spot," the first said.

"Must be a source."

"Must be."

A smile threatened her lips. She was a source … of irritation for Ross Quinn. Of this terrible ordeal that was the enduring bright spot. They continued to the door, swiped, and in they went. Libby ran for the door and caught it just before it hit the locking frame. After waiting ten seconds, she strode through the entrance as though she belonged. Not so long ago, she had.

The lobby was crowded with people coming and going. With social media what it was, they were all amateur reporters, ready to call her out to the world. She turned to avoid them and shoved inside the stairwell. One set of shoes clopped their way down the staircase. With any luck, they'd get off on another floor before they came face-to-face.

Libby started the climb. Her legs burned immediately. The soreness from her recent sprint and heavy-bag marathon set in to nearly every muscle down to the bone. She took it slowly, hoping with every flight that the footsteps growing ever nearer would exit. They didn't. Sure, she could exit onto a floor, but then she'd have to deal with who knew how many people. Since she was only on the second floor, there would be a lot. She tucked her chin and increased her cadence.

"Libby?"

The man hadn't called her Big Bust, so that was a start. She lifted her chin.

"Alec." Stopping, she stared, and relief eased the tight muscles in her neck. Her friend trundled down the flight with a thick manilla envelope in his hand. "Hi."

His blue gaze bulged, shifted up the stairwell, and then back to her. He closed the space between them with his lanky legs. "I saw the video. Are you okay?"

"Is there a person in this building who hasn't see the video?"

"I'm sorry, Lib." He winced. "If there is, I haven't met them."

"No need for you to be sorry." She kicked the step in front of her with the heel of her boot. "I figured as much."

"Then why are you here?" There was no judgment in his tone, just concern.

"I need to talk to someone in Violent Crimes."

"Are you hurt?" His cheeks paled. He stepped onto the same step with her, his gaze searching.

"No." She stalled him with both hands. "I have a stalker."

"A stalker? Like inappropriate calls and emails?"

"Someone's been in my house."

Alec jerked back as though she'd hit him with the words. His hands went wide, the envelope too. "Shoot them."

"Believe me, I will if I see them. So far, it's only when I'm not home."

He plowed a hand through his shaggy blond hair. His shoulders bobbed, and his gaze shot this way and that for several seconds. "You have to go to the police. Violent Crimes won't do anything. It's not a gang or serial related, is it?"

"I don't think so."

"Before your leave, they might have put someone on it, but with the current situation ..." His head shook.

If she was one of them, they'd help, but thanks to

Quinn, she'd been put on the outside. Libby gripped the railing and squeezed hard to keep from punching the wall.

"Walk with me." He headed down the steps. She shoved off the railing and followed. "If you report it to the police, especially with your current status, they can at the very least increase their presence in your area." When they reached the first floor, he opened the door to the side lobby, but then used his body to block her from view of the handful of people. They rushed to the exit, and he opened the door.

"So will you report it, please?"

Libby skirted out the door, and he followed close behind, heading for the parking garage. "I don't have any evidence."

"How do you know?"

"I dusted for prints on the things that'd been moved."

"But things have been moved!" The manilla envelope in his hand flopped with his expressive gesture.

"That's not enough to take to the police and have them take it seriously."

"Then get some evidence." He hurried their pace into the dank garage. "Get a camera and a security system. Hell, Libby, get a big ass dog."

"No animals," Libby interjected.

"Call me anytime, for anything. You hear a crazy noise, or you get a funny feeling, you grab your gun and call me." They rounded the corner. "Where'd you park?"

"Why are we walking so fast?" She pointed at the prime spot and her utilitarian car.

"I don't want Quinn to see you. He doesn't need another reason to make your severance official."

"Another reason?" Libby unlocked her car.

"He was hot after the video."

Somewhere in the distance, a car door slammed.

"Me too. That little twerp left a bruise on my butt." It

hurt every time she sat.

"He touched you?" Alec's voice dropped an octave.

She stopped at the back of her car and assessed her friend. The color in his face turned a Quinn-like hue. "Manhandled is the word."

"I'm glad you broke his thumb." Alec rounded the trunk and opened her door for her.

"I didn't break it." Libby walked to the back door and leaned her hip on the car. She wouldn't wedge herself between Alec and the car, and she wasn't ready to get in.

"Are you going to get a camera? A security system?" One of his full brows lifted.

"I need to get my job back."

"That's not an answer." Alec rested his forearm on the top of her door and pinned her with a look.

"I'm serious," Libby threatened.

"So am I." He pursed his lips. "Quinn has made it pretty clear that's not going to happen."

"He's not the director of the FBI," she protested.

"No, but I'm having lunch with him tomorrow."

Alec jumped at the unexpected voice that thrust into their conversation. Libby didn't budge. Quinn trundled up from the long row of government-issue SUVs. She'd forgotten about the car door she'd heard. That was what she got for losing awareness. At a time like this, she couldn't afford it.

Quinn smiled his hideous smile, nodded at her, and continued walking. "I'll be sure to say, 'Hi,' to him for you. I'm sure he'll be giving you a call."

A call to tell her she was fired.

Rage boiled in her veins, and her skin bubbled. But what could she do?

THIRTEEN

What the hell else was she supposed to do on a Thursday when work wasn't a possibility?

Libby flipped the page on the booklet of instructions. Not that it was much of a stakeout. She'd been lucky to get her crappy parking spot. Every thirty seconds or so for the last hour, her gaze shifted up the street. She catalogued the front of her house as well as her neighbor's, the driveway between the two, and the cars on the street immediately in front of them. No change. The front porch and living room lights blazed through the dimming night. Her neighbor's house hadn't changed in the last two hours. No lights. No motorcycle. No fuck buddy.

Her pitiful stakeout beat driving around aimlessly. She'd done that for several hours after she left Best Buy. There wasn't much of anything more embarrassing than being scared to go home. Though eating old crackers from the glovebox when she had a house full of real, delicious food just yards away? Well, that came close.

She grabbed the last of the round crackers and popped it into her mouth. Peanut butter stuffed between two didn't age well. The diagram on the page seemed out of whack. An associate had told her that the tiny camera was Bluetooth. "Place, plug, connect, and go," the salesman had said. So why were there wires—positive, negative, and ground—shown on the diagram and in the instructions? She could build simple furniture, hang pictures, and install faucets, but electrical was out of her league.

"Ridiculous." This whole situation was ridiculous, and she could hardly say the word because the peanut butter crackers had sucked all the moisture from her body.

Water was only a minute away. Less, maybe. She choked down the bite, tossed the instruction booklet atop the camera and packaging, cranked the engine, and zipped down the street and up her driveway.

The backyard was dark as death. Why hadn't she left the back porch light on as well?

Because you were running scared.

She cut the engine and grabbed her keys. Her insides quaked.

"Still scared." Libby checked the Browning she'd placed in its holster on her hip. One in the chamber with a full magazine. "Time to quit running."

A chill in the evening air crawled inside her cropped sweater and whispered across her midriff. Bustling filtered in from the street, but the backyard was quiet and so dark she couldn't see the steppingstones that led across the yard to the back door. She closed the door quietly and left the bag in the car for now. Before she installed anything, she had to clear the house and be sure no one was inside.

Libby cleared the first few stone pavers by memory more than sight before she remembered the hook on the screen door.

Shit.

It would take her a while to change that routine.

She stopped.

"Where have you been?" a feminine voice sprang out from the darkness.

Every cell in Libby's body jolted, and a scream sprang up from her chest. She reached for her sidearm, wrapped her fingers around the stock, and tensed to draw. Then her mind caught up with her actions. She trapped the scream inside her mouth and slacked her hold on the gun because she recognized that voice.

"Fucking Christ, Mar! Are you trying to get yourself shot?" Libby doubled over, braced her hands on her knees, and drew a deep breath. "Shit!"

"What do you mean? I was just waiting for you. You weren't answering your phone. With all the media attention and everything going on, I just wanted to make sure you were okay."

Okay? She most certainly was not okay. Someone was stalking her. They were close and Marlis's presence only placed her in harm's way.

"How long have you been here?" Libby fumbled for her phone. She hadn't heard any calls come through. Then she remembered that she'd turned it off after two calls from reporters, or people claiming to be reporters, earlier in the day. "Where's your driver?"

Mar's phone screen lit her sweet face and the stoop she sat upon. "Thirty-two minutes." She pointed toward the front of the house. "In the car across the street."

How had she missed the car and Marlis crossing the street? Some stakeout.

"You can't just hang out on my stoop. It's not safe, especially at night." Libby shoved her phone back into her pocket and stepped closer to Mar.

"If this place isn't safe, then you shouldn't live here." Marlis turned on her phone's light, illuminating their immediate surroundings.

Huge evergreen bushes lined either side of her house. They provided too much cover for anyone willing to get a little dirty. In fact, her stalker could be hiding from sight at this very moment. She should invite Mar in, but he could be hiding inside her house.

Though no woman should be wandering around at nighttime in any area of any city, state, or country alone, the area in which she lived wasn't unsafe. Actually, it was usually safer than many parts of the city. But things weren't usual right now.

Libby didn't want to tell Marlis about her stalker. She didn't want to tell any of the girls about it. More than anything, she didn't want them hurt. In the past few months, she'd seen Larkin and Gen in the hospital. Even Douglas had been hurt. No, she wouldn't involve them. Not in this. She had to keep them away. She had to keep them safe.

"Move into the city."

Not a chance. She couldn't afford a shoebox apartment in the city. Out here, she had a yard and a house with two bedrooms and an attic … that she was scared to go inside.

"I'm fine." Libby patted the 1911 on her hip.

"If it's not safe for me, it's not safe for you." Marlis flicked her long blonde hair behind her shoulders and crossed her arms over her chest. The light wobbled with her hand.

"I'm fine," Libby reiterated. Mar was only trying to protect her, which was what Libby was trying to do for her friend.

Mar stood. Her arms fell to her sides. The small phone light spotlighted a patch of ryegrass. "You could move in with me." Mar's lips quirked. "I've always wanted a roommate."

"Only because you've never had one. Trust me, it's not all it's cracked up to be." Libby shook her head. She'd shared a room with up to three kids at a time while in her mom's home. Half siblings and new boyfriend's kids rotated in and out through the years. At sixteen, she'd moved out with three other mates, and they shared a one-bedroom apartment until she'd gotten into the academy. No way was she ever sharing her space again.

"Thank you, really Mar, but no. I attract negative publicity these days. If anything happened to you because of me, I'd never forgive myself." Libby shook her head and stood her ground.

"You think I could?" Mar's mouth screwed up tight.

"Marlis, go home." She raised her voice higher than Mar had likely ever heard it. "Don't come back unless I invite you over. Do you hear me?"

Her friend's chin lifted. She would not be cowed. Of course she wouldn't. That was why they were all friends. They stood up for what was right. No matter what.

"Just because I'm not a badass like the rest of you doesn't mean I'm worthless." Marlis bolted from the steps.

"Mar." Libby reached for her friend, but she moved faster than Libby expected. She'd never actually seen Mar run or do anything active, but she was actually quite agile. "Of course you're not worthless. Mar!"

Marlis turned down the driveway, and her footsteps didn't falter.

"Dammit." Libby kicked the dirt. She braced her hands on her forehead and stared up through the tree limbs at the sky. Sure, she'd achieved the goal of getting Marlis out of danger. Great. But what damage had she done to their relationship in the process?

A simple, "Mew," drew her attention from the one star

she could see through the clouds. Killer stood on the top step in the exact spot where Mar had just sat. He shoved at the screen with the top of his head, but the door didn't budge. Killer sat back on his haunches and stared at the door. His head canted left and right, as though he were trying to make sense of the development. He stood once more and dragged the full length of his body across the bottom of the door, turned on a dime, and did the same with his other side.

"Huh." At least she'd done one thing right tonight.

Her gaze slipped past the cat to her neighbor's house. His cat tormented her. He tormented her libido. Was he her stalker? His proximity would make it easy for him to keep tabs on her, to know when she came and went so he could come and go. She expected eerie chills to follow, but they didn't. Only the long, lasting simmer he incited heated her chest. It was better than fear.

She drew her sidearm and set about clearing her house outside and in.

FOURTEEN

LIBBY JERKED AWAKE Her eyes snapped open to the familiar white ceiling and the tops of lavender curtains. The soft caress of well-worn sheets tangled around her legs. Where was her pillow? Not under her head, that was for certain.

An awkward weight shifted on the center of her chest. Her hands shifted for it. Cool metal rested under her hand.

She scrambled to sitting. The weight slipped down her chest. Her hand cradled the weight while harried breaths rocked her woozy senses.

Libby stared, completely confounded, at her gun.

After spending the previous day in a coffee shop, watching the feed from the nanny cam, that had, in fact, been easy to set up, and seeing no one enter her home, she'd gone to sleep with her weapon close.

Had there been a noise or had the horrible string of nightmares she'd endured urged her to seek protection?

Either way, if she didn't remember grabbing it, maybe she didn't need to keep it on her nightstand. Inside the drawer would be close enough, wouldn't it?

She set the Browning pistol on the nightstand, where she'd placed it before going to sleep, and stared at it for a long moment before taking in the room. Her light pink comforter was on the floor, as were the patterned pink and purple flower pillows. The far corner of the fitted sheet had slipped its hold, exposing part of the creamy white mattress.

"Wow." Usually Libby didn't move much when she slept.

It looked like she'd had amazing sex. Too bad she hadn't had that in months and months. Scratch that. That sex had been decent, but nowhere close to amazing. Amazing had been years and years ago.

"How depressing." She shoved off the mattress and shuffled to the bathroom where she handled her business with an open shower curtain as nature intended.

Libby grabbed the edges of the sink and assessed her reflection.

The linen spaghetti strap pajamas and shorts she wore looked like they'd been wadded into a ball and ironed. Her hair had fallen from the bun she'd fixed it in before going to bed. It hung on the side above her ear like a lone, shabby Princess Leia bun. The eyes staring back at her were bloodshot and toted around puffy little bags.

"Oh, well." She pulled the ponytail holder from her hair, set it on the counter, and headed for the coffeemaker. Though she'd slept a full nine hours, her body felt heavy and groggy as if she hadn't gotten one bit.

As she prepped the machine, her hair slowly uncoiled and fell to her shoulder. She pressed start and leaned on the counter. Everything inside her shook slightly, like it did at the end of a really hard workout. Only she hadn't done more than sit yesterday, sit and stare at her living room and kitchen from twenty blocks away. Not true. She'd also consumed four cups of coffee and two muffins.

She stared at the dark liquid slowly dripping into the carafe. Maybe she didn't need this one today.

Too late.

Today, she should go see Marlis and explain at least a little bit more about her situation. Not enough to freak her out, but enough so that Mar would know that none of what she'd said was meant to hurt her. But she didn't want to leave her house. If she didn't leave, then she wouldn't have to clear it again and feel like a huge fool. Also, based on the number of unanswered calls to Marlis yesterday, her friend was not yet ready to hear what she had to say.

Maybe a punching bag session was in order, then she could go from there. Libby walked to the back door and peered out the window. Once again, no Killer on the porch. She unlocked the door and eased her arm out. A nice breeze fluttered across her fingers. Not too cold. Sleeping late had its perks. Warmer temps. The edges of her mouth kicked up until she saw her shirtless neighbor in his backyard, picking up fallen limbs from the grass. She jumped back, eased the door to its frame and herself to the cabinets. The number of limbs in the yard were as though a storm had blown through, but she hadn't heard a thing.

Libby absently pulled a mug from the cabinet above the coffeemaker and shuffled to the fridge. She'd bought hazelnut creamer at the grocery store the other day and had yet to use it. Her mouth watered.

She pulled the refrigerator open, but the image hitting the back of her retinas didn't compute. It short-circuited her synapses.

No!

She looked left and right. There was no boogeyman. There was nothing except the house she'd known for years and loved.

But inside the refrigerator …

The snapshot seen round the world, her viral photo sat inside her refrigerator on top of …

No! No!

Her head shook furiously. Breaths wheezed in and out of her lungs.

His black fur was matted. The orange tips of his ears, his little devil horns had been …

No! No! No!

Tears filed her eyes. The white of his paws were red with blood, and his head arched at an unnatural angle. A gaping wound stretched from one side of his throat to the other.

"Killer?" she sucked in the word on a sob.

"No!" Libby thrust the refrigerator door closed and backed away, wrapping her arms around herself. A scream worked itself into a heavy force inside her chest. She clamped one hand over her mouth while tears streamed over her fingers.

Her hip hit something hard. The table. She stumbled right. Her arms flailed wide in search of balance. There was none. There was no justice. There was no right. Only wrong. Her foot caught the leg of the chair, and she canted toward the floor.

Libby hardly felt the thud of her hip on the old wood floor. The fall released every jammed-up emotion she'd been hoarding since Hegarty's in a window-shattering shriek. It was a howl that stole all the oxygen from her lungs and continued to rage. A wail that might never end.

She shoved up to sit on the floor and then doubled over. Her head hung between her quaking hands.

In all her years with the FBI, she'd seen dead bodies in all grades of decomposition and methods of murder. It had never been in her home, though. It had never been meant as a threat to her. It had never been someone she cared for.

Something in her throat cracked, and then the high-pitched cry shattered into a hundred tiny sobs. They bounced around her chest and aching throat. Each one bruised and mangled as the realization that Killer would never torment her again hit harder and harder still. They would never become friends—mostly because he'd been an awesome asshole—but now they wouldn't because someone had murdered him.

The screen door screeched, and a moment later, the back door burst wide open. Her shirtless neighbor bar-reled inside her home, crouched low, as though ready to pounce. His eyes were narrow and searching.

Libby scrambled back. Her hand slicked with tears slipped. She backpedaled with both heels and warded him off with both hands. The wall met her back. There was no place to go.

Where was her gun?

He came forward so fast there was no way she could get to it in time. Even if it was on her hip, he'd close the distance before she could draw. Her sobs continued, de-spite the danger.

Her neighbor reached for her with both hands.

She lunged for his thumb with her left hand while she aimed the right for his nose.

In one smooth move, he dipped and evaded her grip on his thumb and manacled her left wrist. With an easy shift of his shoulder, he missed the palm she intended to crush his nose with. He hooked her upper arm under his left bicep. The weight of his thighs pinned her legs to the floor while his left hand doubled back under her arm and slipped up behind her neck. His fingers threaded through her hair. He grabbed a handful, and just like that, in a splinter of a second, she was outmaneuvered and completely at his mercy.

She whimpered and hiccupped in the prison of his embrace.

"Are you hurt?" His voice was quietly demanding.

Her head shook.

"What's wrong?" Again he spoke calmly, commandingly.

"Your cat," she hiccupped.

His head shook, and locks of sweaty, dark hair fell forward, shielding his dark gaze. It didn't dampen its intensity one bit.

"Crazy Broad, if my cat bothers you that much, all you had to do was say so. What's he done now?"

Libby choked on a cry.

How could she have thought for a minute that he was the one secretly torturing her? At every turn, he'd been kind, quiet, and withdrawn, but above all, he'd been compassionate to that cat, to his cat. He'd called Killer his, and by all that was right, the cat thought of himself as belonging to her neighbor, no matter who had signed the papers to bail him out of animal jail.

"Where is he?" His gaze lifted toward the street. The muscles in his jaw clenched. It was as if he knew something wasn't right. It wasn't. Not at all.

"I'm so sorry." Emotion shook her like a tambourine. Even in his grip she clattered.

"Where?" he gritted the word.

She let her gaze slide past him to the refrigerator. Tears filled the frame. When she blinked, they rolled in waves down her cheeks.

His head jerked toward the fridge and then back to her. A deep swallow worked his throat. It was the first hint of emotion she'd ever seen from him. She hated what he was about to see, but she needed to see his reaction to know for sure.

He released his grip on her, and she sagged against the wall. Had it not been there, she'd have fallen over, completely gutted. The damn cat had hated her, and she'd loved him. Her neighbor stayed crouched over her for several seconds. His gaze searched her, as if trying to make sense of the situation, but there was none to be had. None.

There were no words to express the hollowness inside her, so she pulled a page from his book and said nothing.

Soon, his weight lifted, and he reached the refrigerator in one stride and opened it.

Libby lifted her gaze to spare herself another look at the image that would haunt her dreams for years to come. His sinuous shoulders tensed. The muscles in his jaw worked, and his teeth ground audibly.

He closed the refrigerator door and turned to her. There were no tears. No expression. Not that she'd expected any.

"Who did this?" He barked the question so ferociously she jumped.

She hated showing fear and emotion, and since he'd stormed through the door, that was all she'd given him. Stubborn pride shoved her upright. It wasn't enough to pull her off the floor. Wetness coated the backs of her hands. At least, she'd gotten the bulk of her tears off her cheek.

"What makes you think I didn't?" Her voice was shaky and not her own.

Her neighbor just stared at her.

"I don't know." She chewed her entire bottom lip. "If I did …" Her hands clenched. If she knew who it was, she'd shoot more than their knuckles off. "Someone has been coming into my house while I'm away. They've moved things around, not enough to be blatant just enough to screw with my head. Until now." She pointed at the refrigerator. "He wasn't in there last night, and I checked every inch of this place before I went to bed. Which means that the perpetrator came in during the night, while I was here, and I didn't hear a thing."

"You're FBI," he growled. "Why didn't your people set up a sting to catch the bastard before my cat got caught in the crossfire?"

There was real anger and sadness in his tone. It cut deep because he wasn't a man who readily showed anything other than a raw sexuality that he'd never focused on her.

"I used to be. I'm on forced leave, and on Monday, I expect the call that they've made it permanent. Fired."

"I thought you were just being dramatic the other night." His jaw hitched to the side.

"Dramatic?" Libby stared at him for a couple of beats but didn't bother elaborating on how offensive the suggestion was. "I've fingerprinted everything that's been moved or left behind. There's been no evidence, which is why I haven't been to the police. I tried my friend at the FBI, but he's hemmed in by our boss."

"This person knows exactly what they're doing because I haven't seen anyone around here who isn't supposed to be, except your friend that you got into a fight with the other night."

"I thought you weren't home."

He shrugged. "I thought you were spying on me."

"I was, kind of."

"Your stakeout skills need work."

She pushed to her feet. Ready to fight or rip her hair out or crawl into his arms. He crossed those big arms over his chest and took a small step back.

"Why are they firing you?" He cleared his throat.

"That picture." She cocked her head toward the fridge. "And the fact that my boss is a sexist prick." Her throat ached. "It's a long story."

He drew a deep breath and let it out slowly.

"I want to hear it all, but first, I need to tend to Cat." His arms dropped to his side. "I'll have someone over to set up a security system by this afternoon."

"Uh, I appreciate that, but I can't afford an extensive security system. Fired and all." Not that she could have afforded one anyway.

"Don't worry about it." He made a half gesture with his hand that struck her as too cute and incongruent with his blatant masculinity. "He owes me."

"Then that will mean I'll owe you. I don't do owing people, especially people who only speak to me in emergency situations."

"Someone killed my cat. The only thing you owe me is their identity."

He said it with such absolution that she wouldn't be surprised if he finished the sentence with, "… and I'll erase them from the Earth."

"To get that, you need security that they can't take with them when they leave." He pointed at the bookshelf where she'd wedged the camera. All the books were askew, and her camera was nowhere to be found.

"How'd you know about the camera?" Libby took a step back.

"Still don't trust me?"

Libby shrugged.

"Good." He offered a nod of approval. It eased the tightest of the knots in her shoulders.

"I heard you cussing at it when you were trying to set it up Friday."

"Oh." Again, she shrugged. "Who is he?"

"His name is Slade. If you want, you can call him." He shifted to her counter, took a pen from a cupful on the top of the refrigerator, pulled the blank 'grocery list' pad magnetized to the side of it, and wrote something on it.

Presumably, Slade's phone number. "Give him your name and tell him your silent neighbor sent you. He'll know."

"How will he know?"

He just stared silently.

"So it's not just me that you don't talk to?"

Her silent neighbor dropped the pen atop the pad and gave a halfhearted half of a grin.

"Or…" Libby dragged out the word. "Did you talk to this Slade about me?"

"I'm not going anywhere today. If you need to go out, I'll watch the place."

Avoidance. Fine.

"What do you do?"

He stared. She stared. He was stunning to look at and fun to talk to, now that he actually spoke. Even though the topic was horrifying.

"You know, you don't say a word to me for a year, and then you call me a crazy broad. I have someone coming into my home, threatening me, killing my cat." She hitched a thumb at her chest. "I adopted him, and yes, he adopted you. I loved that damn wild animal, despite him. The least you can do is give me some sort of confidence that you aren't the one behind this. Who are you?"

Her neighbor turned to the refrigerator, picked up the platter the psycho had set Killer on, and walked out through the back door.

This could easily be a trap, an easy way to get eyes all over her house. The only thing she had to base her decision on was her gut. It said he was weird as hell, but it didn't send her running … away from him.

FIFTEEN

IF HE WANTED HER DEAD, she'd given him a myriad of opportunities over the past week. Judging by the way he effortlessly subdued her, an FBI agent with a rusty black belt in Krav Maga, he would have no trouble in the execution of her death, yet he hadn't killed her. So while he traded limb picking for hole digging, Libby dragged herself to the shower. After all, it was daylight, and he was right outside … shirtless … preparing to bury their murdered cat.

Libby shoved her face into the hot spray and willed the panic away. She'd toyed with the idea of bringing her pistol inside the shower with her. Instead, it sat just outside the curtain under her towel on the counter. Not that it had done her any good being that close last night.

After scrubbing and drying, she clutched the gun and headed to the bedroom. The covers dripped off the bed in knots as she'd left them, only she never slept like that.

Where she started was usually where she found herself in the morning. No crazy sheets. No lost pillows. This morning was no different, save for the mess. She'd gone to sleep in one spot and woken up in it. A shiver dug its nails into the flesh at the back of her arms and scampered down to her toes. Had the perpetrator staged her bed as well as the refrigerator?

"Oh God."

She dressed in her favorite tattered jeans and a pale pink sweater because she needed comfort. She chose red suede boots because she also needed to project power, the thing she lacked now more than ever before in her adult life. And she'd become an adult at a very early age.

With the Browning stuffed into the jeans at the small of her back, Libby walked cautiously toward the back door. Her gaze hit every nook and cranny between the two points. The drum of blood increased its tempo, awaiting a jump scare from her tormentor. If it ended at a jump scare, it might not be so bad, but she suspected whoever was doing this had a much bloodier ending in mind. She hadn't a single clue why.

Libby peeked out the window at the back door. Thin curls of smoke lifted toward the sky from three, six, or more spots on the ground. Incense lay in small piles, surrounding a hole in the dirt. Other trinkets were scattered about the ground. One looked to be a strand of red beads. Another was a miniature gold statue of some sort. A series of shallow bowls were spread out to the side.

Her neighbor knelt in front of the hole. His butt rested on his bare heels while one arm hung loosely in his lap. The other bent at a small angle. That hand seemed to have all its fingers extended, pointing at his heart. He didn't move, not a muscle.

She'd never seen anything like it.

Her parents hadn't raised her in a church, but she'd

attended enough funerals to know this wasn't the norm. Not in Western culture, at least. She thought back to the African masks and weapons hanging on his wall and the map. He'd clearly been all over the world. Had he picked this up along the way?

For minutes that turned into an hour, Libby leaned on the doorframe and watched from the non-comfort of her home as nothing happened, aside from the burning of incense. When she was about to give up and begin pacing, he brought both palms together and bowed before pulling a split log from a pile to his right and laying it across the hole. He laid several in succession, and then started another layer that ran perpendicular to the first over the hole.

The man created two more crisscrossed layers before striking a small knife across a flint. Sparks cascaded into the hole. Slowly, the glow of flame whipped up from inside. It swelled and grew into fiery tongues of red and orange. They licked the logs, turning the bottoms black.

Her neighbor grabbed something from just in front of his knees. Knees that had to be beyond numb. She hadn't seen it before. His large body had blocked her view. He lifted Killer to eye level, and the man's lips moved.

Realization struck Libby like a physical blow, and her breath fled. She jerked the door wide and barreled through the screen porch. It kicked back against the house. The hook hadn't been latched. She forgot it for now and charged for her neighbor, ready to jerk Killer's body from him and bolt. He couldn't burn the cat's poor body.

Libby reached his yard in a manner of seconds.

He lifted his gaze to her. The somber expression on his handsome face stopped her several feet away. This was his cat. This was his ritual. This was his sorrow.

Without a word, he turned back to Killer, bowed his head to the cat, and laid him atop the burning logs.

Her insides squirmed.

He placed a piece of greenery over the body and bent low. Words she'd never heard, not even in a movie, seeped quietly from his lips. They sounded loving and peaceful even in his deep timbre.

Libby swallowed so many regrets that she nearly choked. Respect forced her back slowly. The retreat stopped when she reached the back steps. She sat on the stoop and watched him pray over the cat. She sat for a long time watching the ceremony, the flames, and the enigmatic man in front of them.

SIXTEEN

her house and filtered through the open back door.

Libby jumped to her feet on her back stoop. Her gaze jerked back through her open back door to the front door. It loomed like a monster on the other side of the house. There were no windows in the door through which she could see the person knocking, and she'd drawn the curtains across the large picture window in the front of the house. Her gaze shifted back to her neighbor. The fire had died, and all the ashes had fallen, and still, he sat motionless. It utterly amazed her that such a large man could fold in such a way for so long.

Again, a hefty knock sounded.

She filled her right hand with the butt of the 1911, opened the screen, and cautiously entered her own home. Using the toe of her boot, she pushed the back door until it hit the wall. If she needed an escape route, it was the best option.

Slowly, she approached the front door. Sweat slicked her palms, forcing her to re-grip the gun at her side.

"Who is it?" Her voice sounded as though it were a chunky bowl that'd been dropped and glued back together.

"Slade." No last name. No added descriptors. Nada.

Libby hadn't called him. She'd been too wrapped up in the spectacle of an unfamiliar ritual ceremony and her neighbor.

Why hadn't she installed the peephole that'd sat in the top of her closet for the last two years?

"Why are you here?" she demanded.

"Security assessment and system installation." Concise and accurate.

She reached for the door but stopped with her hand on the lock. "Who sent you?"

"Your neighbor." His voice had lost its power and was wane and monotoned, as though he was supremely bored with the back and forth.

He could have given her a name. Not that she'd have known it for recognition. Her neighbor, well, she knew that moniker quite well. She could just use that. First name: Her. Last name: Neighbor.

Libby flipped the lock and opened the door a couple of inches. A brown-headed man in his mid-twenties patiently waited on her front porch. His chin was covered in a close-cropped beard, and he wore head-to-toe black. Even a black beanie covered the top of his head. He was tall but not too tall. Not like her neighbor. He was sinuous but not thickly muscled. Not like her neighbor. He was handsome, but he didn't singe her insides. Not like that crazy man who she knew only as her neighbor.

Slade carried a large black duffel bag with a confident

stance. It didn't persuade her to open the door just yet. Just in case he tried to rush the door, she braced her foot against the back at the base.

"Who do you work for?"

"Myself." His facial expression remained indifferent.

"What's in the bag?" she pressed.

"Tools and supplies."

Tools and supplies for dismembering a body?

"Open it." Libby's hand tightened on the 1911.

"Lady—"

"Please." She wanted to trust her neighbor, and in turn this man, but she couldn't. Not yet.

Slade eyed her through the crack, then his gaze shot toward her neighbor's house before he gently set the duffel onto the stoop. He crouched low and unzipped the bag. The two sides gaped, revealing a loaded tool belt, spools of wire, and unopened boxes of electrical and tech equipment.

"Thank you." Libby shoved the pistol back into her waistband, pulled the door wide, and waved him inside.

"Sure you don't want to scan my passport too?" He grabbed the duffel, and for the first time, an expression broke his blasé façade. The sarcastic crook of a smile turned up his lips.

"Actually, that's a great idea." She stepped into his path and held out her hand.

Slade stopped mid-stride. His smile fell, along with his shoulders.

Libby let her smile spread wide.

"Smartass."

She shrugged and backed up near the fireplace, giving him room to get himself and the bag inside. He closed the door behind him. His light brown gaze assessed the living room and kitchen in a slow, steady sweep.

His head shook in a firm back and forth.

"What?" Her voice cracked.

"Please tell me you don't leave your doors and windows open."

"I don't."

He pointed at the open back door.

"I needed an escape route."

"No, you didn't. You point and shoot with that cannon at the small of your back."

Her bottom lip rolled into her mouth, and she gnawed. He had her there.

"Anyone who had a mind to get in here could." He jabbed a finger at various directions around the air. "Your hedges are overgrown all around the place, giving anyone all the cover they'd need. Your windows are so old that I could break the paint layers with a knife and use it to slip the latch in seconds. Your doors are solid, at least."

Finally something wasn't totally horrible about her home.

"Except for the big ass panes of glass." He used his whole hand to gesture toward the back door.

"Anything else?" she asked sarcastically.

"Your locks suck."

Libby glared at him. He spoke more than her neighbor, but she didn't like much that came out of his mouth.

He looked at his watch and then stared at her, measuring her.

She continued to glare.

"Your neighbor isn't the type to get involved."

Understatement of the century.

"He's not involved."

"I'm here, which means he's more than involved." Slade smiled as he crouched down, unzipped the bag, and lifted the tool belt from it.

Her head shook even before he reached for the duffel. "He's only helping because of a personal vendetta."

"Uh-huh." He clipped the belt around his narrow waist. A hammer and screwdrivers dangled from their various holders. His hand rested on the measuring tape clipped to the center, which hung low at his right hip.

"Seriously," she protested, "they killed his cat."

His gaze narrowed. "He said it was your cat."

"It's complicated." She sighed.

"Sounds pretty simple to me." He turned to the front door and opened it.

"Meaning?"

Slade pulled a small drill from a pocket and removed the screws holding in the latch in a fraction of a second. His gaze met hers.

"The person who's stalking you is dead. They just don't know it yet." He returned to the task of removing the latch and deadbolt without so much as a chuckle or a tacked on, "just kidding."

A lump formed in Libby's throat, and she edged toward the couch. When her calves contacted the base, she collapsed onto the cushy seat. The seriousness and casualness with which he'd made the statement left no doubt in her mind that he wasn't joking. It also spoke of something else. These two were men who dealt with death on a regular basis. They were up close and personal with it. Judging by the scar on her neighbor's back, they sometimes came too close to it.

Slade exited the front door without a word. Half a minute later, he returned with a long metal plate with a rectangle cut out of the middle. He affixed it to the face of the doorframe with long, thick screws.

Maybe they were soldiers. Though neither had the close-cropped do for that, nor the "Sir, yes sir," attitude. Perhaps they had at one point. They weren't cops or feds. Too independent for all that. Maybe CIA. Private securities? Mercenaries?

By the time Libby gave up trying to figure them out, Slade had removed the latch and deadbolt and was installing a lock with a pad unlike any she'd ever seen.

"Is that a coded entry?"

"Fingerprint entry with a double failsafe for temperature range and tampering."

Her mouth screwed into a purse. She hadn't a clue what that meant.

He tightened the mechanism into place, snapped on the sleek metal panel, and straightened. "Come here."

Libby stood and walked slowly over.

"Place your thumb on the scanner." He hurried to the bag, pulled out a laptop, and opened it on the coffee table. "What's your email address?"

Her gaze scanned the street outside through the open front door. She saw nothing out of the ordinary.

"Libby_Irish@gotmail.com."

"Scanner." He paused from his maddening tempo of typing and pointed.

She placed her thumb on the small glass scanner. The surface chilled her finger.

"Keep it there until it beeps."

The beep sounded before he finished his sentence.

Libby withdrew her finger and crossed her arms over her chest.

"Is there anyone else you want to have access?"

"No." She shook her head.

"Okay." He typed some more. "I reinforced the frame and exchanged the century-old screws in the hinges with three-inch screws. When I'm finished with the back door, the cameras, and window locks, I'll send you an email that will give you access to the security system. You'll be able to monitor it for any alerts and make changes as you see fit."

"You aren't going to persuade me to register my neighbor's fingerprint into the system?"

"No."

Good. She nodded.

Slade didn't expand, only grabbed a new box from the bag and headed for the back door.

Libby closed the front door, and a thick deadbolt automatically slid into the frame.

"Damn," she whispered.

"Pretty sweet, huh?"

"Very." She turned to find him about five feet behind her. He'd already dropped the box off on the kitchen table.

"I need to go out."

"Oh." Libby opened the door.

"Close it behind me."

"Okay."

He hurried out, and she did as he'd instructed. Again, the bolt slid into place. She peeked out the curtain and saw him pull another long metal piece from the back of a truck that didn't belong on the city streets. It was desert brown and jacked up on tires that looked like they were made for climbing mountains.

Before he turned around, she let the curtain drop. Seconds later, a shrill sound filtered through from the other side of the door. He knocked.

"Who is it?"

"Seriously?" Slade huffed.

Libby opened the door with a grin. "No."

His head shook.

"He's got his hands full with you." Slade traipsed through, metal in tow and a smile balling his cheeks.

"He does not." Libby closed the door a little harder than she had to and resumed her arms folded stance.

"When you get into the program, you'll see that you have one unverified scan. Me." He ignored her indignation completely and got to work on outfitting the back door.

"Okay."

His quiet laughter met her ears.

She rolled her eyes, but they stuttered mid-roll. Her neighbor pulled open the screen door and climbed the stairs. He'd found a shirt. It was gray and clung to his chest and stretched a little over his shoulders and biceps.

"Ronin." Slade holstered his drill, straightened, and stretched his arms wide.

Her neighbor pulled Slade to his wide frame and wrapped his arms around the man. Both smacked heavy fists on the other's back several times before they separated.

Libby's jaw shattered on the floor and scattered in every direction. His name was Ronin. First or last? It didn't much matter. It was more than she'd known. Equally shocking was the evidence of his capability to show emotion. It was subtle but there, in his admiration for Slade.

"Took you long enough to even things up." The younger man smacked Ronin playfully on the shoulder.

"Even?" Her neighbor, Ronin, laughed. "It'll take a hell of a lot more than this to get us to the universe of even."

Slade bobbed a shoulder. "It was worth a shot."

"Yeah, a killshot." Ronin placed his hand over Slade's face and pushed him toward the tools. "Get to work."

The younger man batted at Ronin's hands, and then caught one in his. When Slade clapped his other hand over her neighbor's, something deep passed between them. Just as quickly, Slade released his hand, and Ronin turned his heavy gaze on her.

She wasn't prepared for it. So she hedged.

"How do you two know each other?" Libby stepped toward the counter and eased herself in the space between the two men.

Slade stared at her blankly. It was an expression she

knew well.

Libby cocked a hand on her hip and hiked a brow, but neither of the men said a word.

"If you tell me you'll have to kill me?" She braced her cheeks in her hands and chuckled.

"Yes," Slade whispered.

A chill sledded down her spine and caught air.

Ronin sliced his gaze at Slade and then grabbed her wrist. He pulled her off the counter, the only thing that'd kept her upright. She followed in his wake, propelled by his determination and strength. His grip was powerful and commanding but not painful. He towed her down the short hallway and left into her bedroom.

The sheets still hung off the sides of the bed. Pillows still littered the floor.

He stopped a foot from the near naked bed and turned on her.

Libby put on the brakes. She stopped too close to him, inches from his chest. So close heat radiated from it and seeped into her pores. His eyes were dark, completely intense. He worked his jaw. His lips were inches away. As close as they'd ever been.

She wanted him to stop the madness and kiss her. She wanted him to release her wrist and let her run away screaming.

Conflicts piled upon conflicts.

Libby licked her lips and did the only thing she could.

"Who are you?"

SEVENTEEN

Libby stared at him as though he had three faces, and all were as compelling as the first. She waited for him to say more.

Moron.

She waited a second more.

Nothing.

"That's it?"

"That's all I can give you." He was unapologetic, completely aloof. Nothing like the other night when desire had raked off him in waves. He was in business mode.

"So, you're a black ops guy or something." She threw the declaration out there, just waiting for a massive denial or a secret sign that she was on the right track.

His dark eyes rolled toward his thick brows. "A few

hours ago, you thought I was your stalker."

"And a few days ago, I thought your vocal cords were broken. I've reevaluated." She grinned. "So, are you going to tell me?"

"It's better off you don't ask." He released her wrist but kept his hands by his sides. "Tell me about your stalker?"

"Not much to tell, really." Libby gnawed on her lip. "It started after that picture was taken."

"Right after?"

"No." She thought back through the last two weeks and the mess that had become her life. "The day after I was put on leave ... two days after. I didn't get out of bed the first day. I went for a run and—"

"I remember."

Of course he did. That was the day she'd seen him in the garden, the first time she'd known for sure he could speak. "When I came back, there was a copy of that picture wedged in the back door at eye level. There was no missing it."

"Where is the picture?" He braced his hands on his hips. She averted her gaze from the delicious bulge of his traps.

"In my closet." She pointed at the left one of two shallow closets. "I dusted it for fingerprints but got nothing."

"I'd like to see it."

Libby opened the closet she rarely used. Heels in every color and texture filled the skinny shelves on either end. Sequins, lace, and tulle bulged at the center. She reached high for an old sturdy boot box on the top shelf. No dice. She pushed up onto tiptoes. Her fingers hit only air. She'd used a chair to place it there, so of course she'd need one to get it down.

"Just a second." She adjusted her sweater that'd hiked up and passed him heading for the kitchen.

"Here." He stepped up to the closet, extended an arm, and pulled the box from the shelf.

A swath of light pink feathers slid with it and tumbled onto Jake Ronin's head. It slipped to the side and nestled on his wide left shoulder. He turned slowly and offered her the box.

Libby pressed her lips between her teeth to keep from smiling. This wasn't the time for jokes. He'd just buried Killer's ashes. She took the box and placed it on the jumbled bedding.

Jake dumped the boa from his shoulder into his hands and studied the heap of feathers. He pulled it into a long feathery pouf and hooked it behind his neck. "Does it go with my outfit?"

A man she thought incapable of humor seemed to know she needed it. Just when she thought he couldn't surprise her more … Her heart swelled. She offered him the most sincere smile she possessed.

"It's a little much for the casual attire, but it'd set off a gray suit." She nodded. "You can borrow it anytime."

His gaze dropped to his jeans and boots, and then it lifted to her.

"What'd you wear it with?" His voice was thick as honey.

Libby swallowed. "Nothing."

His gaze narrowed.

"Oh, no." Libby shook her head. "I didn't mean with nothing." She gestured to her body. Her cheeks heated. "I meant, I've never worn it. My friend Gen wore it one night when she crashed here. Actually, all the girls crashed here. It was before you moved in. And I'm rambling."

A smile quirked his lips.

"And you're enjoying this." She pressed her hands to her cheeks, and sure enough, they were hot to the touch.

His smile faded, as though he'd realized he was enjoying it and didn't want to. She didn't understand him. Not one little bit. He slipped the boa from his neck, wrapped it up, placed it back inside the closet, and joined her at the foot of the bed.

Libby pinned her gaze on the box and pulled open the lid. The picture that had changed her life stared up from a pile of other pictures, newspaper clippings, and certificates she'd kept over the years. She hardly ever took out the box, but she figured she would one day when her skin was wrinkled, her bones frail, and her life lived.

She'd closed the picture in an evidence bag, just in case.

Jake lifted it from the box and drew it close. His head bowed, and he catalogued the composition. The clipping at the top of the box was a New York Times article about the gun hoarder and the FBI's seizure of the collection. He lifted it from the box and read. The Times had left out many important details because they weren't public knowledge, but the journalist had done a fine job of covering the basics.

"Who took the picture?"

"An FBI agent in charge of cataloguing the scene."

"You're not part of the scene."

"I know," Libby grumbled. "I didn't know he'd taken a picture with me in it until I got back to the office, and they were plastered all over the break room with the words Big Bust written in Sharpie over each one."

"The agent's name?"

"Joel Ornby. He's a worthless jerk, hardly capable of tying his own shoes. I have no idea how he made it into the Bureau. He had the Hegarty case before me and added almost nothing to the file in two years." Her upper lip curled. "I don't know how he made it there, but Ross Quinn, our boss, takes care of him. No matter that I solved the case in less than a year."

Libby drew a deep breath and let it out slowly.

"What happened when you were put on leave?"

"I packed my shit and left."

Jake's head tilted ever so slightly, and his mouth pursed just a touch, but he didn't say a word.

"How do you say so much without saying a damn thing?" She threw up her hands and let them slap her jeans-covered thighs. "I got into it with Quinn. He was sidelining me over a picture that I didn't take and certainly didn't share. His excuse was that its popularity inhibited my ability to do my job. Reporters were camped outside the building, but reporters are always there for one reason or another. It was just an excuse to get rid of me. Then he gave Joel the Hegarty case to close out. That little bastard will get credit for work he never thought about doing."

She drew another deep breath and then another.

"After that?" He sat on the edge of her bed and looked up at her, but barely.

"I drank too much. I slept too much. Then the mail started rolling in. Dick pics mostly. Some marriage proposals."

"Romantic."

"Completely," she copied the dryness in his tone.

"Any wackos?"

"A couple." She shrugged. "I didn't go through all of it."

"Do you still have it?"

She nodded. "Those garbage bags by the kitchen table."

"I'll have someone go through them. They'll narrow down any serious crazies."

"Who?" Did this guy have a team behind him?

"What else?"

"Fine," she snipped. "The day of the run, after the picture, I found my shower curtain pulled closed. I pulled my gun and cleared the house. The entire time I thought I was overreacting. When I found nothing else out of place and no one, I knew I was. But I never close the shower curtain. Never."

"So they were in here as early as Monday."

Libby choked back the bile that crept up her throat. "There were other things. I had a cactus on the windowsill at the kitchen sink. It was cut in half. If wasn't until that happened that I realized the plant I'd had on the back porch, one that I'd kept alive for years died suddenly. That happened before anything else. Days before. It might be a coincidence."

The muscles in his neck flexed, and his shoulder rolled. "Not a chance."

"Yeah." She knew he was right, but she didn't want him to be. "A picture of the girls and me was laid on its face. Whoever is doing this had drawn a red heart around my face."

"That made you get the camera?" He dropped the picture into the box.

"Yes."

"He's escalating."

"The perpetrator could be a female. I don't think we should assign a label. It limits the scope."

His gaze pinned hers. "Do you think it's a woman?"

"No."

"Then he's escalating."

Libby rubbed a hand over the healing scratch on her wrist. Moisture gathered, blurring her vision, and she bit the inside of her cheek. "I know."

Jake's warm hand cradled the back of her wrist. His thumb rubbed the skin above her hand and the scratch.

"I really loved that scrappy little bastard," she sniffled.

"I know." He stood and ushered a little more, then dragged her back down the hallway.

Slade was just outside the back door standing atop a chair, drilling. Shavings of wood fell like snowflakes. Jake's hand left her wrist, and both of them braced her hips. The intimate contact robbed her gaze from the work being done and squared in directly on her neighbor. He walked her back to a chair.

"Sit."

She did as he commanded without a fight, and she loved a good fight. She liked a good fuck too.

He released her too quickly and put the distance of the kitchen between them. One by one, he opened her cabinets until he found the ones she used as a pantry. He pulled a handful of potatoes and an onion from the baskets in which she kept them and set them on the counter. Next, he grabbed broth, and then he shifted to the refrigerator.

"Wait!" Libby hollered. He turned to her and did as she asked. "Are you hungry?"

"No, not particularly."

"Then what are you doing?"

"You need to eat before you pass out. You look paler than snow."

"Gee, thanks." She offered him a grand eye roll. "I've kind of lost my appetite, though."

"You need a new memory in this room." Jake shoved a thumb into his belt loop and leaned against the counter. "I do too." He motioned her forward.

Libby's insides quivered, but she stood and walked to him a little too boldly. She was a little too eager for another memory in this room that had nothing to do with potatoes and everything to do with his arms around her and his lips on hers. She stopped when the tips of her boots nearly touched his. Head high, she looked him square in the mouth, ready.

Jake straightened, bringing them so close his scent toyed with the tip of her nose. He turned and patted the counter near the vegetables. "Cut these. I'll get the carrots."

She stared into open space. Again, her cheeks heated, only this time he wasn't playing with her. He opened the cursed refrigerator and pulled out butter, milk, and the carrots.

"Want broccoli in it?" he asked over his shoulder.

"No." She didn't want anything from this kitchen. Well, not nothing, but clearly, he was only interested in … soup.

He straightened and assessed her.

She just stared.

"Well, get to chopping." He gestured to the vegetables.

As if she hadn't known what he meant by chopping. She turned away from him, yanked open a cabinet, jerked a cutting board from inside, and slammed it closed.

Slade's head swung in at the top corner of the door, and he looked around. Libby offered him a glare too. He wisely smiled and retreated to his drilling.

Libby grabbed a knife from the block, placed the onion on the board, and whacked off the ends with two well-placed slashes.

"Maybe you should work on the stock." He clutched a medium-sized pot in his hands.

She ignored him and lopped the onion in half.

"All right." Her neighbor, Jake—it was still so odd to think of him with a real name, as if he were a real person, instead of a heartless robot—set the pot on the stove, turned it on, and dropped a hunk of butter into the center.

Her eyes burned. She blinked and peeled the skin from the two halves. While she shifted to the garbage can, she breathed the fresh air filtering through the open door. When she got back, she ignored Jake and cut up the onion. The moment she finished, he reached across her with his big, hairy, hot arm. His arm grazed hers in the task of stealing most of the onions with one swoop of his hand.

Libby's breath stalled.

The onions hit the butter with a series of sizzles and pops. Just like every time he touched her. It wasn't fair. She chopped potatoes to dull the ache that made no sense.

Minutes passed. He opened the cabinet above the stove and poured various seasonings into the pot.

"Wine?"

Several bottles filled a small wine rack inside the spice cabinet.

"Probably never again," she admitted.

"Why not?" His strong hand held her favorite cooking spoon and gently stirred the pot's contents.

"I made an ass of myself the other night." She chopped the last of the potatoes.

"Nah, you were just speaking your mind."

"I don't have trouble doing that anyway." Libby shoved the cutting board full of potato bits toward him.

He looked her in the eyes. "No, you don't." A smile hitched his lips. "I like it."

She wanted to say, "I don't care," but it would've been a bold lie. Instead, she returned to her seat at the table. Jake combined her work with his own and stirred. Whenever he finished with a supply, he put it back where it belonged.

On the back porch Slade shimmied his chair to another section and continued drilling holes into the wood.

Jake placed a lid on the pot and turned to her.

"Let it simmer for forty-five minutes. Stir it occasionally. Turn it off and let it rest for fifteen with the lid off, and then you'll have enough for lunch and dinner. Don't feed him." He pointed at Slade. "He can afford to have his own food delivered." Jake stepped toward the door. "I'll be around. Holler if you need anything."

He turned to leave.

Libby jumped to her feet. "You're not going to eat?" God, have mercy. The reedy desperation in her voice thickened the air.

Jake Ronin turned and looked her up and down as though she'd offered herself up on the menu.

She melted from the inside out.

"No." His mouth said no, but his eyes said yes.

Libby nodded.

"I have some work to do."

Again, she nodded.

He stepped onto the porch. "Lock it down tight. No one in or out without her knowing."

Libby hurried to the door.

"You've got it." Slade saluted with his drill.

She clung to its frame for support. "Thank you, Jake."

As though he'd become mute once more, he offered a flash of his steely gaze and left.

EIGHTEEN

from 2:23 a.m. to 2:24 a.m.

Libby flipped it off. She grabbed her phone for the first time that hour and considered it a win. From midnight to 1:00 a.m. she'd stared at the camera feed near constantly. Slade had run her through the basic use of the app before he'd left at 10:00 p.m. That man had put in a full day's work and then some without complaining at all. In fact, he left seeming ready to tackle the next problem. She was ready to do the same, only she didn't know who it was or where they were. If only they'd come out and face her. It was nearly impossible to fight what you couldn't see.

She put the phone down without opening the security application, rolled onto her stomach, and punched her pillow one time too many. Her eyes closed, and she breathed in and out, forcing each one to last as long as she could. One by one, the muscles in her shoulders relaxed.

Sleep evaded her still, but she found a middle ground between wake and sleep and hung there for a time.

A cry jerked her upright.

Libby's gaze searched wide. She'd left a light on in every room. Every corner came clearly into view. No one was in her bedroom. Her ears strained, trying to reach any sound, but there was none. Her heart raced. Something had woken her, if she'd even been asleep. Her gaze shot to her phone. She pressed the home screen. Nothing had changed since the last time she'd looked at it.

Maybe she'd gone to sleep. Maybe the noise had been in a dream. Maybe she'd woken herself up screaming.

Another cry split the night. It seemed to be coming from right outside her window. And it wasn't a cry; it was a cat. It was a cat meowing.

She threw the covers back and jumped to her feet but stayed put. Again, the mewing filled the early morning. It wasn't a normal cry, but an animal, a cat in distress. The cells in her body vibrated, willing her to take action. Still, she stayed.

It could be a trap. A man had used the recording of a crying baby to lure women from their homes and rape them. Why not a cat?

The cries continued, sharp and shrill.

Libby lunged for the curtains covering the window and shoved them to the side. Her gaze searched left and right along the driveway. The lights Slade had installed along the sides of her home lit every crack and imperfection in the aging concrete. She saw nothing else. No cat. No person.

Heart-wrenching calls for help continued.

What if it wasn't Killer in the refrigerator?

Like there were two cats with the same devil's orange ears. Her head shook. She ran to the spare room for a better look but saw nothing. Her steps brought her to the kitchen. She looked out the window over the sink. Her neighbor's lights were out. He hadn't left a phone number. Surprise, surprise.

The call to action rang in her ears. It contracted her muscles and stretched her patience to the breaking point.

Libby assessed the backyard. Darkness. Was it good or bad? Slade had installed a motion sensor and pointed the light toward the backyard, so that meant nothing had tripped it. She blew out a breath and flipped the switch, illuminating the yard. She saw no cat. Nor a would-be intruder.

The cries grew more and more frantic as though the poor thing was stuck.

That was no recording. She was no pussy. By fucking God, she was an FBI agent, and she'd lived on her own for more than a decade. She didn't need a man to handle her shit.

Libby pulled the 1911 from the holster she'd strapped to her thigh before climbing into bed. Silk teddies and handguns created the best ensembles. Her head shook as she unlocked the back door. Doubt crept up her spine as she stepped onto the back porch. The concrete had absorbed the sunlight during the day. It soothed the edges of her concern, as did the firepower in her hand. Cool night air coaxed gooseflesh across her arms.

Outside, the cries still reached her ears. The house, the steady breeze, and the quiet drone of the blower from the heater she'd turned on earlier in the day all buffered the sound. She moved cautiously to the screen door, unhooked the latch that Slade had actually liked as a minor security measure, and hurried down the steps.

Instead of walking on the steppingstones, Libby stuck close to the house, covering her back as she eased along the rear of the house. Dew, bits of grass, and leaves clung to her feet. Her eyes scanned the nicely lit driveway. Slade had replaced a single old light she never remembered to turn on with motion detecting lights along the eaves as well. The house was a little too well lit. It brought attention to several spots where a green film tinged the white siding.

When she rounded the corner, the cries amplified to the fever and pitch she'd heard through her bedroom window. Libby lifted the pistol into a tactical position and sidestepped along the house.

Searing pain radiated up her foot and slammed into her groin. She jumped back. Her gazed searched frantically for an attacker, but she found none. Her left hand went to her leg and held it near her thigh while breaths hissed through her teeth. Strings of curses paraded through her mind. Somehow, they managed not to overflow from her lips. Her gaze dropped to her foot. The blood she expected to see gushing didn't even trickle. She looked lower still and found the culprit. A pointy stump protruded from the ground. Before Slade had taken trimmers to her property, it'd been a beautiful luscious bush. Now every other one had been lopped at the base, while those that remained had been pared to half their usual size.

Libby cursed several more silent times, stepped away from the stump, and continued with only a slight limp. The wind and pain in her foot combined to create a miserable situation, yet still the animal called to her. Since she could clearly see no one was lurking behind any bushes, she hurried to the spot under her bedroom window where she heard the noise the loudest.

The cries seeped out from under her house.

"Shit." White boards bridged the gaps between the brick pillared foundation. Most of them. There were two places that'd fallen over the years, but the bushes had kept her from monkeying under there to replace them. They'd also hidden them so well that she'd forgotten about them until now.

She stared at the black abyss. Why hadn't she brought a flashlight out with her or her damn phone? Her gaze scanned the driveway. She hadn't brought one because it was bright as day outside and she never expected to have to look under the house. Not like she couldn't go get one.

"Cat," she coaxed. "Here. Cat. Cat. Cat."

The cries turned more frantic.

Is this Killer? No, it couldn't be.

Libby's heart lodged in her throat. If it was, he'd maul her to death. The prospect dropped her to her hands and knees. Her pupils strained for any sliver of light in the murky space.

"Cat. Cat. Cat."

She scooted forward, braced her left hand on the side of the house, and eased her head inside the hole. Cool, pine-scented air that hadn't been stirred by a breeze in over half a century clung to her face.

"Cat?" she whispered. She closed her eyes for several beats, and then opened them in an effort to see something.

The animal seemed to know she was there to help. Its cries ratcheted so high the time between them melded into one long keen.

"It's okay, buddy." Libby used her calm and in control voice even though her ass was flapping in the breeze, her knees were covered in dirt, and she couldn't see a damn thing. She sensed it, though. The animal was close.

Her legs and shoulders strained, counterbalancing her weight as she ducked deeper into the darkness. It was no use. She planted her right hand with the gun on the ground and slipped her left arm into the abyss.

"I'm right here, buddy. Where are you?" She gently waved her hand through the inky black, searching.

The cries stopped instantly. Libby's gaze narrowed, though she still couldn't see a thing.

A cold hand wrapped around her wrist.

Her scream knotted in the back of her throat. She shifted to lift her right hand up, to aim into nothingness and fire.

The hand jerked.

She tumbled forward. Her face met compact dirt. The gun was gone. She grasped for it even with her face in the dirt.

The hand, now two hands, gripped her waist and heaved again.

Libby lurched, desperate to sit upright. The side of her forehead smacked something hard and immovable. A foundation beam? The first light she'd seen since she looked under the house shimmered in bright silver spears behind her lids. She hit the ground with a thud.

The hand worked hard and fast, jerking her lower half under the house. Her legs bent in an uncomfortable angle, almost doubled over on themselves and pinned by her own weight.

Libby grappled for orientation as her head floated in a choppy sea. It all happened so fast. He had her ankles.

The hands crawled up her torso. One grabbed a breast. Another clutched the back of her neck.

A wet, cold cloth covered her mouth.

Chloroform.

Libby gridlocked her burning lungs. At that moment, the consequences of her action met her in a full frontal. Her friends would never know what happened to her. They would never find her body. She would be erased from the world.

She extended her free arm, grabbed cold air in her fist, and rammed her elbow back as hard as she could.

A decidedly masculine grunt filled her ears, and the

cloth slipped from her lips.

Elbows on the hard ground, Libby kept her head low and churned her arms and legs for the glimmer of the newly installed floodlights that gave her a heading.

Too soon, the hands were back, crawling up her body.

"No! No!" She screamed and grappled with the ground, trying to make headway.

His weight slowed her crawl and pinned her legs to the earth. She threw an elbow. He deflected it and threw the weight of his torso onto her right arm. A hand tangled in her hair and arched her head. The cloth clapped over her mouth once more.

Libby held her breath and bucked.

The cloth didn't move. Strands of hair ripped from her head.

The ink black of her gun taunted her in the flooding light. She reached for it with her left hand.

Her lungs boiled, demanding air. She jerked her head left and right, but the hand and cloth stayed firmly in place.

A figure blotted the light from her only escape. She lost sight of the gun. Warmth gripped her searching hand and slid to her wrist.

Two of them!

She dug her fingernails into the arm and used the rest of her strength to shoot her hips high in a final effort to dislodge the cloth.

"Fuck, Libby! It's me," Jake bellowed from the light.

Though she hadn't heard his voice often, she recognized her neighbor's voice straight away. She disengaged her nails from his skin and gripped his wrist with what little strength she had left.

Jake pulled.

The cloth slipped from her mouth. The weight pinning her to the ground eased.

Libby gasped and gagged for breath.

A biting grip latched around her waist. The man under her house pulled too.

Libby was caught in a game of tug-of-war.

"Jake." She reached for him with her right hand.

He grabbed her other wrist and pulled harder.

Her shoulders and middle stretched to the point of tearing.

Libby lifted her knee toward her chest and fired her heel hard into flesh and bone. The grip around her waist lessened. She cocked and fired again in the same direction.

A crunch and a grunt filled the space which before had only contained fear, her fear. His grip loosened, and Jake yanked her into the light. She curled onto her side. Words refused to form between the hacking and gasping.

Her neighbor hulked over her in jeans and no shirt. His brow was knitted and jaw set. He grabbed her gun from the edge of the house and slapped it into her hand. Before she could form a thought, he dived head first under the house.

No!

If he got hurt because of her, she'd never forgive herself. The guy under the house was strong and knew what he was doing. He'd prepared for this. He'd prepared too well. Slade had made her house impenetrable and this psycho had known how to circumvent the problem. He'd known exactly how to get her outside.

Libby focused on breathing and not dropping her gun, though her hand lay on the cold ground. No matter. Her hand shook like an addict's at rehab.

Moments later, the sound of tires leaving half their rubber on the city street screamed in the night.

Her gaze jerked toward the street, hoping to get a look at the bastard's car. The noise of the revving engine faded away, as did her hope of identifying him. She could review the camera footage. It might show something.

She looked left and then back at the hole. No sign of her neighbor.

There hadn't been a gunshot.

What if he'd been stabbed?

"Jake?" her voice quivered.

No answer.

The thought of him hurt ceased her coughing and minimized her shakes. If he was hurt, could she get him out from under the house without help? Where was her phone? Should she call the police or Slade? He'd left his number.

Using her leg, hip, and elbow, she edged toward the house, toward the hole. That dark space would haunt her for years to come if she lived that long. Her stalker seemed intent on not letting that happen.

"Jake?" she whispered into the nothingness.

No answer.

Libby's heartbeat slowed. Her body temperature dropped five degrees.

"Jake!"

"What?" He shouldered his way out of the hole, crawling on his elbows and dragging his legs behind him.

"Are you okay?"

He stared at her with a confused expression distorting the angle of his brows. "I'm fine."

She released the breath that'd been burning her lungs.

Jake stood, brushed at the dirt on his pants, and held out his hand.

Libby reached up to take his hand, but he stepped closer and snatched her gun from her weak hand.

"Hey!"

She watched indignantly as he shoved the thing into the waistband at the small of his back, crouched down, looped his arm under her back, another under her legs, and lifted her off the ground.

He held her firmly to his chest. His naked chest. Heat came off him in waves. Heat and anger. His forearm nestled in the crease of her legs and his open hand securing her to him spread intimately across her bare thigh. The contact was too much. It made her head swim more than the blunt impact under the house.

"I can walk."

"Judging by the size of the knot on your head, I'm not willing to risk it."

Libby lifted her hand to her forehead and immediately regretted it. She felt skin before she should have. The contact made her eyes water, and she winced.

He walked quickly around the back corner of her home.

"I need my gun."

"Why?" His jaw tightened. "It's not like you're going to shoot anyone with it."

She opened her mouth to protest but realized he was moving quickly past her house and toward his own.

"Wait—"

"No." He hustled up the stairs and through his open back door.

A single lamp illuminated the living room she'd spied through the window, but she'd never been inside. The house smelled of cleanliness and a hint of cologne. Dior's Savage? Maybe a note of Paco Rabanne's 1 Million. Either way, her mouth watered. The décor and textures gave the place a comfortable yet stated feel.

It was, by far, the best bachelor pad she'd ever seen.

Jake carried her through the kitchen into the living room and laid her on the couch. When she looked down, horror struck. Blood and dirt marred her blue silk gown. The blood would never come out … of her gown … or his fabric cushion.

"Oh no." Libby tried to sit up. "I'll get your cou—"

"Fuck the couch. Be still." He stayed her with a finger to her sternum.

She gulped and stilled.

He held his finger in the valley between her breasts for an eight count and then disappeared into the kitchen. The refrigerator opened. She'd bet no one was dumb enough to stick a cat in his. Then the faucet ran full blast for a few seconds. A minute later, he returned with an ice pack wrapped in a damp towel.

Her shakes had returned full force.

Jake pulled a blanket from the back of the couch and laid it across her shoulders.

"I've been in fights before." Her teeth chattered. "I've never reacted like this."

"It'll pass. Give it time. Now breathe." He settled the ice pack onto her forehead. She wanted to scream. Instead, she followed his direction.

"It'll pass whenever I catch this bastard," Libby hissed.

"He's mine."

"Chauvinist."

Jake shrugged one dirty shoulder, completely unapologetic. He hurried down the hall and came back with a long-sleeve shirt pulled over his head and one arm. Slowly, deliciously he worked it the rest of the way down his torso before turning his gaze on her.

"There's no need for me to mess up your things. I can go to my house."

"Not now, you can't." Jake turned away from her and pulled a deep drawer wide. He pulled a small pack from it, closed it, and then moved to another.

"Why not?"

From this drawer, he extricated a flashlight and a long knife, which he strapped to his thick thigh.

"He left us another treat, which is the only reason he got away." Jake pulled the blade from the sheath, checked it, then sank it back in its home without even looking. As though he'd done it a time or a thousand.

"Oh God," she breathed.

Her stomach dropped from her pelvic floor, where it had been for the last ten minutes. It split in two and fell in equal parts to each of her big toes.

"Stay there and don't touch anything." His sharp gaze said he meant business.

"Where are you going?" Libby hiked up on an elbow.

He turned and left, closing the door behind him. Like hers, a deadbolt slid automatically into place.

NINETEEN

SHE COULDN'T HANDLE MORE than twenty minutes of the ice pack. She couldn't handle more than twenty minutes staying, "there." She couldn't handle more than twenty minutes not touching anything.

Where the hell was he anyway?

Libby dropped the pack and cloth onto the blanket she'd stripped, then used the arm of the couch and levered herself up to stand. Her legs quivered, but they didn't all-out shake as they had for the first ten minutes. The grandfather clock on the far wall helped her keep time. And she'd given him all she could. Unstable steps got her to the hallway. She walked slowly down the short corridor that mirrored her own. The first door she came to was equipped with a lock similar to that on her front door, but there was another on the frame, higher up. It looked like a scanner too but not for fingerprints.

"Eye scans?"

Hers widened in disbelief.

Not only had the wood frame been exchanged for metal, but the door had been as well. No one was getting inside that room, except Jake.

The second door she came to was the bathroom. She flicked on the light and waited for an alarm to sound. When none did, she shuffled to the sink, braced herself on the vanity, and faced her reflection.

Dirt smudged across her right cheek. A small abrasion accompanied it. That was nothing compared to the half-dollar goose egg above her left eye. Dried blood crusted under her left nostril. Her attacker had hit her nose when trying to knock her out with the chloroform, but she hadn't realized how hard.

Libby carefully washed her face with soap and water, and then grabbed the hand towel to blot away the droplets. She stalled. A custom holster had been attached to the wall just under the towel hook. When a towel hung there, the weapon was perfectly hidden from view. She drew a deep breath, dried her face, and then carefully replaced the hand towel. Her gaze swung to the large, neatly folded towels near the shower. She stepped close and eased up the edge. Sure enough, another holster had been attached to the wall nearest the shower.

"Paranoid?" She didn't think so. Those guns were there for a reason. "Nope."

She turned off the light and eased into the hallway. The last door was surely his bedroom. The desire to go inside tugged at her, but she turned away and headed for the kitchen. She needed water. Her throat ached.

After assessing the situation, she opted to scoop water into her mouth from the sink. He'd told her not to touch anything. She'd bet anything there were other guns stashed throughout the house. The edge of one peeked out from under the small island, when she'd crouched low. For all she knew, he had boobytraps set up around the house. She didn't want to be murdered by her stalker. She didn't want to accidentally die either.

Libby dried her mouth, sat back on the couch, and checked the clock.

"Thirty-six minutes," she huffed.

Two minutes of staring at the map later, the back door beeped and then opened. Jake stepped inside. His pants and shirt were covered with dirt. It clung to the stubble on his chin and to his knuckles. The dirt didn't matter one damn bit.

He clutched a fluffy gray kitten to his wide chest.

Her ovaries exploded.

She shot to her feet and cleared the distance between them in seconds. It was almost worth getting attacked to see this. Almost.

"I knew it wasn't a recording." Libby reached a tentative hand toward the kitten. It smelled her fingers with its tiny black nose. "Oh, hi buddy." His little whiskers grazed her knuckles.

"And you were willing to give your life for this little wimp?"

"Don't talk about him like that." She rubbed under the cat's jaw. The quivering in her legs ceased. "That's not how I thought about it."

"You didn't think at all," he snapped.

Jake turned his back on her and slammed the door closed. The lock slid into place. He slammed the small pack onto the counter, his back still to her.

Libby sidestepped and put herself in his face.

"You don't have to be a jerk." She pressed a hand to her chest. "I made a mistake."

He stared at her for a minute. "Me too."

His declaration surprised her. What mistake had he made? Helping her? Letting her inside his fortress?

"Thank you." She offered him a weak smile. "Thank you for saving my ass tonight."

Jake shoved the kitten at her chest. She took it readily and held it with one arm under its tiny bottom and the other securing it to her body. Her neighbor reached the hem on his shirt and tugged it up over his arms and head. His hair fell forward around his eyes. Thoughts of running her fingers through it filled her mind. She took a shuddered breath and petted the kitten, hoping for a distraction. He toed off boots she hadn't seen him put on.

Libby moved back a step.

"I'll get out of your hair."

"Not tonight, you won't." He unzipped his jeans.

Her clit twitched.

"Excuse me?" Her voice cracked, yet she watched transfixed as his thumbs hooked into the waist of his pants. Everything inside her begged him to make a move, to warm her with his body and take away the bone-deep cold that wouldn't go away.

The straps of his knife sang under his grip. He pulled the sheath from his thigh and set it on the counter next to the pack.

Before she could think another thought, Jake dropped his pants right there at the back door. Her heart shot out of her chest and cleared the Earth's atmosphere. She became an instant ghost. She was dead, and this was heaven. The abdomen she'd seen several times, but not nearly enough, guided her eyes to a tuft of hair and a cock so thick and firm and fully erect that her mouth watered. She licked her lips.

He bent forward, obstructing her view when he grabbed his clothes, and sidestepped her.

"Stay put," he demanded.

Libby turned to watch his perfectly formed backside round the corner and leave her view down the hallway.

"Fuck me," she whispered to the kitten.

A moment later, a door closed and the spray of a shower joined the raising beat of her heart. Finally, her gaze dropped from the spot where his firm ass had been to the kitten.

"What did that horrible man do to you?" She lifted him into the air and examined every inch of him by sight and feel. The little one made no whimpers or cries. "Does anything hurt?"

The kitten didn't respond. Something she'd grown quite accustomed to.

She walked to the sink, ran some water in her hand, and held it to the kitten's mouth. He sniffed tentatively, and then lapped at the water, creating ripples in the surface.

"Good boy ... or girl." She had no way of knowing. The kitten was no more than, well, she didn't know kitten ages all that well. It wasn't small enough to need nursing from its mother. At the same time, it wasn't big either.

Libby offered him some more water. He took another lap and was done. She turned off the water and headed to the couch. Her legs were shaky once more.

When she crossed the hallway, she heard it.

Her cheeks flamed instantly. Her belly warmed. Her breasts grew heavy.

The unmistakable grunt of self-pleasure ricocheted off her bones, making her knees weaker than they were from her ordeal. She sat on the edge of the couch and covered the kitten's ears. Her ears perked to every nuanced sound. The rise of his tempo. The grunts that morphed into groans. The pain that turned into exquisite pleasure.

Not fair. Not at all.

Libby sank back into the cushion and focused on slowing her breathing. If he saw her sitting there panting, he'd know she heard him.

A few minutes later, Jake came out from the back of the house. Near black, damp hair hung almost to the edge of his jaw. He wore jeans and a T-shirt.

Was he wearing boxers?

He walked to the kitchen as confidently as ever and fixed himself coffee as though he hadn't just masturbated within her earshot and tormented her to the edge of sanity.

"Want some?"

Fuck yes, but you're not offering that.

"No, thanks." She rubbed the kitten who'd fallen asleep nestled between her boobs.

His bare feet entered her line of sight a second before he sat directly in front of her on the coffee table. He set his mug down next to him, reached for her head, and pulled her close to his face. Too close. His palms heated both sides of her face.

Which hand had he used in the shower? Had he been thinking about her?

Libby couldn't handle all the unknowns. She pushed his hands away.

"I need to check your pupils, and the knot growing on your forehead."

Great! He certainly had not been thinking about her in the shower. She sat opposite the man of her most erotic dreams in a tattered nightie with the whopper of all whoppers on her head and her hair a damn mess.

He coolly, medically examined her eyes, and then used his thumbs to press the boundaries of her knot.

"Goddamn." She pulled away. "It'll go down on its own. You're not supposed to try and pop it."

"I wasn't." He reached for her head.

"Could've fooled me." She swatted his hand.

Finally, he gave up, straightening, then bracing his

MEGAN MITCHAM

—

fists on his thighs. A great big breath hissed out of his lips.

"What?"

"You're stubborn."

"Says the jackass to the mule." She smirked.

His laughter filled the room, rich and just as inciting as his grunts and groans.

Slowly, he rubbed the smile away. His gaze locked on hers. "Tomorrow, I'll gather the evidence for analysis."

"What evidence?" This was serious. He was back in business mode. "The kitten wasn't the surprise?"

"Nope."

"What was it?" She hugged the kitten close, wanting to know and afraid of the answer at the same time.

"A bomb."

Libby nearly choked on her tongue. Her mouth fell open, and she gaped.

"What?" Jake leaned forward to the edge of the coffee table. "What is it?"

"My boss, the one I fought with after being told I was on leave, he was on the FBI's bomb squad."

Jake looked at her as though the bombshell atop the bomb was somehow insignificant.

"Don't you see?" She grabbed his forearm, well, half of his forearm. Her fingers couldn't reach around his whole arm. Not even at the wrist. "He's our guy."

His gaze lowered to her hand.

Libby released her hold.

"Could be." He covered the spot she'd touched with his other hand.

"Of course he is." She flipped her only free hand over and shook it at the sky. The kitten shifted its paws and nuzzled deeper into her.

"He's worth a look, but it was a crappy setup." He met her gaze. "A combo of batteries, gas, and a shitty timer. It screams amateur."

"That could be a diversion." Quinn hated her. He always had. Even when he wasn't shitting directly on her career, he'd made it as unpleasant as possible. "He's a smart guy. He'd know that he's the first person in my life they'd connect it to." She drew a breath and rattled on. "He's always reliving his glory days, talking about this exploits with the guy in the office.

"The kiss asses," she added.

"I'll look at him," he assured her.

Libby remembered a particular story she'd walked in on nearly eight months ago, where Quinn was talking about bomb placement. He'd said a bomb in a house was nothing compared to the carnage of a bomb under a house. The chills returned with a vengeance. Her shoulder shook, and she clung to the kitten for warmth.

Jake leaned across her. His neck was so close, so exposed that she could press her lips to it without much movement.

The realization struck her like a subway car rolling at full speed.

He straightened and pulled the blanket over her shoulders.

"Wait," Libby gasped.

He offered her his hands in surrender.

"No, I just ... There was a bomb. A bomb under my house. And you ... What did you do?" If there was ever a time to call the cops, it was now. The cops. The FBI. The bomb squad. It was time to call everyone.

"I disarmed it."

She pressed a hand over her mouth for an eight count, and then let it slip away. "You say that as though it's no big deal."

"It's not."

"Yes, it is."

He did the no-talk staring thing.

"Fuck." All the air went out of her lungs, and she could do nothing else but stare right back. This guy was next level. A level she vaguely knew existed.

"Yeah." He rubbed a hand down his face, and then pointed at the couch. "I'd give you my bed, but you're smaller."

"I have a perfectly good bed just over there." She hitched a thumb in the direction of her house.

"No." His voice shook in its deep baritone.

She huffed.

"You may not value your life, but for some insane reason, I do." He pointed at the couch again. "You'll stay here."

All her fear and sadness melted away, and in its place, a joy she never expected to find in this place sprouted deep. It rankled. It wasn't her joy to have.

"How would your girlfriend feel about that?"

Again, he just stared.

"She's not your girlfriend?"

More staring.

Libby gnawed at her lip and laughed near hysterically. "Of course she's not your girlfriend. Having a girlfriend would require talking. You know, communicating, offering up an inner thought or personal opinion more than once a year."

He moved so quickly she didn't realize what was coming until it was upon her. Until he was upon her. One of his hands slipped under the blanket and braced low on her back. Her mouth fell open. His hot fingers spread wide and pulled her to the edge of the cushion. That dark, mysterious gaze leveled on her parted mouth. He leaned close and captured her mind, body, and spirit.

His lips were insistent but soft, warming her to the idea she'd been obsessing over for twelve long months. She arched forward, opening herself and inviting him in.

He read it and accepted. He nudged her mouth wide. His tongue invaded her in seductive sweeps and coiling rolls.

A soft moan rumbled in her throat.

Jake scooped the kitten from her chest and set it to the side without leaving her mouth. His hand returned, cupping the side of her neck. He shifted their angle. It brought them closer still. He nibbled on her lips. He sucked on her tongue. His knuckles grazed her collarbone and whispered across the top of her breasts. Need pulsed deep, roaring through her veins.

He tasted like the best dessert she'd never had. Illicit. Delectable. Fatal. He'd ruin her for sure. She was fine with that.

His hand left her chest. She was ready to beg for it back when he gripped her bare thigh. A groan vibrated his chest. He spread her leg wide. Like the wanton woman she was, Libby spread the other in equal measure. She wanted his hands all over her, inside her. She wanted more than his hands. She wanted it all.

He leaned forward, pressing her back into the couch, pressing his hips into the gap between her thighs. The bulge she'd seen only a half hour ago nestled perfectly atop her clit, causing her to shiver. Her palms itched to grab his ass and move him exactly where she wanted him most. She squeezed her fists; sure that if she touched him, the spell would be broken and the dream would end with her drooling on her pillow alone.

Jake grabbed her ass, held her in place, and rocked his hips.

Libby lost all control and keened into his mouth. She gripped the back of his neck and rolled her body against him.

"Dammit, Libby." He levered back a few inches. His eyes were narrowed, intense.

She stilled, terrified she'd crossed his invisible boundary. He'd said her name, but she couldn't even enjoy the novelty of it.

"I'm sorry. I—"

He ate her words. He hugged her waist and pulled her flush with his body. He went wild, arching and thrusting their bodies together.

His heartbeat pounded against her thumb.

A ring split them apart like a bomb.

Libby sprawled in front of him, her legs wide, her chest heaving.

Jake knelt. His chest puffed and constricted, nearly as much as hers. His gaze scanned their surroundings like a bristled back dog.

The ring filled the spaces again.

"Christ." Jake's head hung for half a second before he jumped to his feet and crossed to the kitchen.

The chill he'd chased away doubled down on her exposed skin. She straightened and tugged down the edges of her ruined nightgown.

Jake grabbed a cell phone from the counter near the black, apparent, bomb disarming kit. He pressed a button and put it to his ear.

"Yeah?" After a second of listening, he adjusted the front of his pants.

Libby would've smirked, but her breaths were coming too fast. She pressed a hand to her mouth in an effort to regulate them.

"The system's working fine, but it didn't do a damn bit of good. He lured her out of the house with a cat," Jake growled. He kept his back to her.

Self-consciousness reared its ugly head. Libby grabbed the blanket and pulled it around her. The kitten had snuggled up to a decorative pillow and was fast asleep.

"Damn cats." He was quiet for a few seconds, and then added, "Hell yes, I'm keeping it."

Libby gently scooped the kitten into her hand and pulled it against her chest under the cover with her. Like hell was he keeping the kitten. He'd stollen Killer. No way she was giving up this sweetie. Not that she was shaping up to be a good cat mom. Her heart lurched.

Poor Killer.

"No." Jake's voice drew her attention back to him. He'd

turned and was looking her up and down. "We're good here, battened down for the night." He nodded. "Sure will. Thanks, man." He ended the call, held tight to the phone, and walked to the intersection of the kitchen, living room, and hallway.

He was bailing.

Libby stood, letting the blanket fall off her shoulders onto the couch, and faced him head-on. He couldn't deny what had just happened between them. She wouldn't let him. She'd liked it too damn much.

"If anyone steps foot on my property, I'll know."

He was erecting a wall between them. A natural reaction for a loner. She took a page out of his book and just stared at him, letting the hunger in her eyes speak for her.

"Get some sleep."

"Right."

He turned and stalked down the hallway. She looked down at her dirty teddy.

"Can I get a shirt?" she called out after him.

Silence was her answer.

"Okay." Libby tapped a foot and then remembered that she'd jabbed the hell out of it. It hurt but not enough to ease her irritation. She toyed with the edge of her gown. She could sleep naked. That'd show him.

Before giving it much more thought, Libby set the kitten back near the pillow he'd claimed and pulled the nightie over her head. She dropped it on the coffee table. It would be her only way out of here tomorrow.

The clearing of a deeply masculine voice startled her. Jake stood at the end of the hallway, holding a folded T-shirt in his white-knuckled grip.

Libby lifted her chin. "I thought you were ignoring me."

"Impossible," he grumbled and launched the shirt across the room.

She snagged it on its downward arch. "Thanks."

"Good night." He was already gone. His usually silent footfalls thudding with every retreating step. The firm slam of his door stalled any retort.

She smiled, proud of herself for throwing him off his cool, calm, collected game. No one could have it together all the damn time. She'd learned that the hard way.

A yawn caught her off guard, and her shivers returned. She looked at the shirt and then the couch. Her head throbbed. Maybe this wasn't the best time to jump his bones.

TWENTY

SUNSHINE PIERCED HER FITFUL SLUMBER. Had she forgotten to close the curtains or something? Libby threw her arm over her face and rolled onto her belly, and nearly fell off the bed. She steadied herself and blinked in an unfamiliar world. Not a bed. Not her bed. Not her house.

In a flash flood, everything crashed into her. No job. The attack. The near fuck on the couch. Her cheeks burned. She would have loved nothing more than to bury her face under the covers and hide there forever, but her bladder had another, more pressing agenda. She pushed off the couch, yanked the bottom of his shirt to cover her under-booty, and crept toward the kitchen. No sign of Jake. At some point when she'd been unconscious, he'd put away the bomb kit and flashlight from the counter.

Libby tiptoed to the bathroom and eased the door

closed. She peed. While washing her hands, she nearly screamed at her reflection. Her hair frizzed toward the ceiling. Couch creases lined her cheek. The goose egg had deflated. However, the dark bruise it left behind was worse.

She eyed the shower.

As a rule, it was always better to ask for forgiveness than permission. Besides, she doubted he'd even let her go shower in her own home until the bomb was taken away. She'd planned to jump in for a quick wash, but the warm water and fancy jet spray massaged her stiff muscles. His soap was manly but natural and smelled like a fresh sky. She indulged, scrubbing every inch of her body. Specially delicate attention was paid to the bruise at the arch of her left foot and her forehead.

Twenty-five minutes later, Libby stepped onto the pedestrian rug, pulled one of the two towels from the rack, and blotted herself dry. She wrung out her hair and finger brushed her teeth. It hadn't done much to change her look, but she felt a thousand times better.

Her gaze skipped from the rumpled shirt on the floor to the towel. Then back and forth again. Her thoughts jumped from that wrinkled shirt, to her wrinkled teddy, to the kiss, to the kitten. When she'd gotten off the couch, it hadn't been in sight.

She wrapped the towel securely around her body, tucked the loose end between her boobs, and opened the door, expecting him to be standing there fuming at the liberties she'd taken in his home. Nope. She peered into the kitchen and living room. They were both empty. Unless he'd snuck out without telling her. Not likely. Her gaze slid toward his open bedroom door.

Libby padded to Jake's bedroom.

Huge mistake.

Her heart did a stupid flutter, dip thing.

He slept on his back with one hand tucked under his head. His bicep bulged and a brazenly male tuft of dark hair flared from his armpit. The other arm cradled the kitten to his chest. A dark gray sheet clung to his waist. He lay arrogantly spread in the center of his bed.

She couldn't say that she blamed the cat one damn bit for abandoning her.

Jake's eyes opened.

Had her sigh been audible?

His gaze crashed into hers. It roved her from head to toe, heating her from the inside out. He didn't say a word.

Shocker.

"I'll leave you two alone." She offered an awkward wave.

His head tilted ever so slightly. "You could join us."

A bulge formed at the V of his hips. It stirred the sheet and whipped her nerves into a frenzy.

"I'm not into threesomes with cats or otherwise."

Jake lifted the kitten to his face. He nuzzled his chin against its head, waking it from a deep sleep, and then set it on the floor. His knowing gaze found hers and stilled in challenge.

Libby had wanted this for a year. Who cared if he didn't communicate? It wasn't like she was looking for a relationship.

Her heart thundered inside her chest, creating a flood of emotion. Something she hadn't experienced while considering the option of a purely physical interlude. It was only perplexing because Jake didn't act like she'd expected him to. He was complex and interesting and what she wanted.

Just for today?

She wanted him today, and she could have him.

Her finger hooked into the terrycloth overlap. She tugged and let the towel fall to the floor. His gaze lingered on her face for several beats before raking the length of her body. This was no false invitation. Intent heated his gaze. Whatever ghosts had stopped him last night had evaporated in the bright morning. His blatant desire doubled her own. She walked to the end of the bed and then crawled onto the mattress.

Jake's gaze catalogued her deliberately unhurried progress. He'd made her wait. Turnabout was only fair.

Libby stopped near his calves and sat back on her heels. Damp hair hung down her back and over her chest. The ruby tips of her nipples peeked out, evidence of her want. Though her throbbing, swollen clit was doing its best to make itself known. She grabbed a handful of the sheet and pulled. The shift in position pinched her thighs together. Lust radiated from her center and warmed every part of her. A moan quaked up her throat.

Slowly, the retreating covers revealed her prize. Delight and anticipation lifted the weight of worry from her shoulders. The newfound buoyancy intoxicated like a double shot of whiskey. It emboldened her to tiptoe all ten fingers up his bare legs and over his thighs. She stroked the notch of the glorious V he'd displayed more than once in the last week, the V that robbed her of mental function every time. It didn't matter. Right now, she operated on carnal instinct.

The indomitable man opposite her arched into her touch. Sinew corrugated his skin from the boarders of the bulging veins in his neck all the way to his toes.

"Nice," Libby murmured.

She toyed with his delineated abdomen, adding pressure to her touch, and then taking it away to a whisper. With each caress, his heavy cock lengthened and swelled. Her mouth watered. She bent low and dragged the flat of her tongue from base to the dewy tip.

A hiss sailed through Jake's teeth. Dimples formed in

the sides of his ass.

Libby grabbed his sizable length and a girth that made the walls of her vagina clench. She gathered the moisture from his head, spread her thighs, and slicked it across the erect nub at her center. Her mouth descended, and she sucked him in one maddening inch at a time.

"Fuck, Libby," Jake barked.

His hands fisted in the sheet.

She hummed her approval and pushed him deeper. Her fingers worked the silk of his pre-cum against her clit while she popped off his dick just to plunge him to the back of her throat once more. His gaze narrowed but remained fixed on her. He gritted his teeth as though trying his best not to give himself over too completely.

Libby teetered on the same dangerously thin line. Her breaths rushed in and out her nose. Heat gathered at her center. Her climax was a stroke away. She released her last tether to control and smiled all the way down. The crash came hard and fast, clamping every muscle in her lower half. Barely human sounds careened from her chest. They edged out between his smooth, hard cock and her mouth.

"Dammit." Jake gripped her shoulders, heaved her up off his cock, and flipped her onto her back.

She panted. He looked dark and devilish. He stared down without a single move. For a second, Libby worried he'd leave her barely hinged and more desperate for him than ever before. She licked her lips and tasted him around her mouth.

"Have a problem with the female orgasm?" she breathed.

His gaze was intent; his mouth narrowed. "Only that I didn't give it to you."

"Haven't you ever heard of a team effort?" Libby rubbed the side of her leg against Jake's. His coarse hair abraded her skin.

"I work best alone." The kiss he pressed to her lips was savage. She took it—every bite, every lick and suck—and yearned for more. When her lips ached, he moved down her neck to her collarbone.

"Yeah, I heard that last night," she purred.

Jake levered back and shifted a brow at her, trying to make the connection.

"But I wouldn't say it's best alone." Libby smiled, grabbed a handful of his balls, and tugged ever so gently. She arched her breasts against his chest and slid her hand up his length.

His teeth clamped, and he groaned, rubbing himself into her touch. He allowed himself only a moment of abandon before he grabbed her wrist. She released him, and he pulled both her hands wide. He blew heated, moist breath across her breasts. The long strands of her hair furled in the breeze he created. His breath exposed her nipples, and his mouth took full advantage. Full lips clamped over her reddened tip. His tongue lapped at it. He suckled her until she panted and writhed.

Slowly, he worked down her body, kissing and licking every inch of her. Libby watched him catalogue her as though she were a unique find, as though he would never see her again. When worry clouded her horizon, Jake's mouth found her core. His hands molded her ass and spread her sex wide.

It only took three strikes of his tongue, and she felt her edges fraying.

"Wait," she gasped. "I'm not ready." She didn't want to come again without him inside her. She'd never been good for more than two orgasms with herself or anyone else. Hell, with anyone else involved, she was lucky—or determined—to have one.

"What are you waiting for?" Jake spoke, but he didn't back away far enough. He caressed her engorged clit with his lips.

"For you to be inside me," she panted.

"I will be." His timbre, his promise, his touch catapulted her.

Space was dark, but it sparkled with wonder. She hung there in the void of blissful oblivion convulsion after convulsion of her inner muscles. Then she glided back to her body, to his bed, under Jake.

He nibbled her inner thigh and worked his way down her legs. Most men went straight for the kill. Not this one. He took his time, flipping her onto her stomach and caressing the backs of her legs, her butt, and her back.

Libby shifted her hips up to find him still fully erect and drenched. She maneuvered the head of his cock between her legs, over her needy slit and pulsing clit. His hips bumped into her ass cheeks. He grunted.

Jake buried his face in her hair and breathed deeply. He whispered her name. It seemed more intimate than he'd intended.

Surely.

It crawled into the center of her chest and burrowed deep. She clamped her eyes shut and breathed to hold back a wave of emotion sure to drown her. That didn't make sense. She wasn't an emotional lover. He wasn't hers. More than anything, she knew this would end with no strings attached. And that was fine.

He brushed the hair from her face and pressed his lips to her cheek.

Her chest constricted.

With one hand, he flipped her onto her back.

"Eyes open, Libby."

She snapped him into focus. He was gorgeous in a dark and painful way. She smiled.

"That's better." He reached over to the nightstand, pulled a condom from it, and sheathed himself.

Libby was so close to what she'd wanted for so long, and the desire to run rode her like a derby winner. She filled her hands with Jake's traps and shut down all analysis. Her legs hooked around his waist, and she opened for him. Fuck the aftermath.

Jake grabbed her in his arms and pulled them up with him kneeling in the center of the bed. It brought them face-to-face, eye to eye. He pressed into her. Stretching and pressure she hadn't expected robbed her of breath.

"Relax." He gripped the back of her neck and smashed their mouths together.

His tongue coerced her attention from the near embarrassing pain, drawing it to the unfed desire still clawing at her insides.

In the distance, a phone rang. His. Not hers. She didn't care, unless he stopped stretching her.

Don't stop. Kiss me more. Kiss me forever. Fuck me.

The rings shifted further and further into the background as he filled her to the point of bursting. She'd taken him completely. The joy of it emboldened her. His arm clamped around her hips, barring their restless sway. He drew full breaths and released them against her neck.

"Jake," she begged.

"Wait."

"You didn't wait for me," she protested.

"I've waited," he growled.

He threw her onto the bed and climbed atop her. His waiting was done.

Jake plunged deep and then pulled out to the tip. He drove home again and again. His hand knotted in her hair at her nape. Libby arched into him, rubbing her swollen, aching flesh against him with every thrust. She held tight to his shoulders and matched his manic rhythm.

She came apart piece by piece. Every neat and tidy edge inside her tattered. Her moans morphed into cries and shouts. Feeding off her energy, Jake tensed and shook. A moment later, he collapsed onto the bed and pulled her with him.

They stayed engaged, interlocked for several quiet minutes.

Libby focused on breathing instead of enjoying the feel of his body against hers and his arms around her too much.

He pulled his still full cock from her body, rolled away, and left the room.

She would not cry. She would not feel abandoned. She'd feel well fucked.

When her legs rubbed together, she swore she could come again if she put a little effort into it. A smile quirked her lips.

Jake came back without his brimming condom. He handed her a warm, damp cloth.

"Thank you." She took it and set about cleaning herself.

He looked at his phone while he dressed in boxers, jeans, and a T-shirt. Libby crumpled the cloth into her hand and sat in the center of the bed they'd warmed together.

She would not care.

"Slade is at your house." He slipped boots onto his socked feet and snapped a sexy 1911 and holster onto his belt.

"Oh." She refused to cover herself with the sheet.

"I'm going to head over and get you some clothes. What would you like?"

For starters, she'd like more of what she'd just had.

"Unless you'd like to make the walk of shame in one of my T-shirts." He winked.

"I'm not ashamed." She lifted her chin in defiance.

"Good." He offered her a sweet smile. His thumb grazed her chin, then he turned and walked out the door.

"So, are you bringing me clothes, or am I using one of your T-shirts?" she called after him. The kitten mewed from the floor. She leaned over and eyed the tiny thing. "Did you catch an answer?" He mewed again. "Me neither."

Libby pulled the small cat onto her chest and collapsed back against the bed. Eventually, he'd bring her clothes, or she'd walk over in one of his shirts. First, she'd marvel because she knew what it was like to be at the center of Jake Ronin's unwavering focus.

And it was fucking amazing.

TWENTY-ONE

"ARE THESE ASSHOLES SERIOUS?" Slade bellowed from the kitchen. He held a letter in his hand. For a second at least. The next, he slammed it down into one of the three piles on the table in front of him. That letter had landed in the sexual deviant heap.

"Now do you see why I quit going through them?" Libby asked. They'd given her a hard time for not assessing each letter for a threat level.

"No. It helps to know what you're dealing with." Jake typed on his laptop, seemingly able to multitask without worry.

"You say that, but you're not reading them." Slade grabbed another envelope from the bag of mail. "I could give you one that'd make you spit and go hunting in a heartbeat."

"Hunting?" Libby asked.

Slade winced, but Mr. Multitasker didn't flinch while he clicked his mouse like a professional researcher.

"Probably best you don't show him any." Libby grabbed the mug of coffee from the coffee table they sat picnic style at on the floor in her living room. Jake had made the dark brew and eggs by the time she'd dressed in the clothes he'd brought her. He'd set the pile of clothes on the end of the bed and left without a word. It'd hurt until she found the bra and panties he'd chosen for her. Black. Lace.

Slade offered her a sideways salute.

"Look at these and tell me who besides Ross Quinn stands out." Jake turned his screen toward her. He'd blacked out everything on it except a white sheet.

She squinted at the words in front of her, not because she couldn't see them, but because she saw things she shouldn't be looking at.

Ross Quinn Jr. 1540 Albany Circle Apartment D4 Jersey City, New Jersey.

Her boss's name and address were followed by his phone number, his social security number, his driver's license number, and his vehicle's VIN number. After the numbers were the names of his known associates and his immediate family. Libby scrolled. There were names and information for ten or more individuals per sheet.

Alec Keith. Libby Irish. Joel Ornby.

The list went on and on.

Each of them worked in her office.

Libby's gaze lifted to Jake's.

"How do you have all this information?"

She waited for an answer. And waited some more. Jake stretched his legs out and leaned against her couch. Luckily, it backed to the wall. Otherwise, the light thing would have shot across the floor.

"It's more guarded than most. I don't even think I could access this information. Not even before," she clarified.

"Who stands out?" He completely ignored her question.

Imagine that.

"Quinn, Ornby, MacInerny," she offered and scrolled.

"Quinn is obvious. Ornby is the picture source. What's up with MacInerny?"

"He's Ornby's lackey. He's quiet and creepy as hell."

Jake crossed his arms over his wide chest. He settled her with an amused look. "Quiet and creepy? I was both until yesterday."

"You still are." She grinned.

He grabbed a handwritten list she'd started working on before he'd pulled out the ten-digit code and retinal scan-encrypted laptop and crumpled it. The small note fit in the center of his big hand, and he launched it at her. The paper bull's-eyed her left breast, striking her sensitive nipple.

Libby couldn't tame the stupid smile that stretched her abraded lips. She'd certainly never seen this side of him. Actually, she would have bet her measly life savings that he didn't possess any side remotely capable of any type of humor.

"Anyone else on that list look good?" He pointed at the computer.

Libby nibbled on the edge of her smile and scrolled down the list of everyone who worked in the building. Many were people she'd never met and never would. "No."

"Have you had a relationship with anyone in the FBI?"

It was her turn to cross her arms over her chest. That smile she'd been banking faded away completely. What business was it of his?

"We're trying to catch someone pretty intent on harming you," he reminded.

"No." She glared.

"Anyone show unreciprocated interest?"

"No." Libby shook her head.

"Outside of the office?" he pressed.

"No one of note."

"Last serious relationship?"

"Never."

His head recoiled as though she'd aimed for his nose. Not that she'd ever land a punch on the man. "Never?" His deep voice rose an octave.

"Nope."

"Why not?"

"Is this a therapy session, doctor, or are we going to stay on point?"

He kept quiet, so Libby pressed her lips together. She studied the mantel and the picture she'd wiped clean after Jake had scanned it for prints. Nada. That fucking red heart still gave her chills. Slade read through and catalogued three letters. Jake stretched his arms above his head, and then nestled his head in the fold of his hands. He looked like an old-timey sheriff, ready to wait her out until the last little doggies came home.

Jerk.

"Didn't seem worth the trouble," she huffed.

"I can second that." Slade raised a fist into the air in solidarity.

He could second that because he was listening to their conversation, no matter how preoccupied with the letters he appeared.

Great.

Jake made a noise that was somewhere between a scoff and a snort.

Libby rotated the computer back to him, hoping to

derail this line of questioning. If she wanted to answer uncomfortable questions, she could just call the police. Something she probably should have done last night, instead of staying with her hot neighbor.

"How long since"—he dropped his voice—"you've had sex with a man or woman?"

Libby looked at her wrist, pretending she wore a watch. "About an hour ago and never," she bellowed.

Slade covered his mouth. A wise move.

Jake's hands dropped from his head and clapped on his chest. He cleared his throat. Libby didn't let her irritated gaze waver. He uncrossed his feet position on the floor and straightened. After drawing a long breath, he said, "Before that?"

Was he trying to make her hate him?

She jabbed her tongue at the roof of her mouth to keep from screaming.

A serious thought exploded behind Jake's eyes. Libby watched the usually cryptic man's features catalogue shock and horror. He leaned forward so close she expected him to lay one on her. His gaze narrowed.

"Were you a virgin?" he croaked.

Libby slapped her hand over her mouth and released the most obnoxious and deeply felt laugh. Her sides cramped, and she doubled over. Moisture gathered in her eyes. She fanned at it and struggled to gather a full breath.

"The … look of … panic," she gasped and cackled. "Oh." A stitch in her side wrenched tight. "It was …" She collapsed the rest of the way to the floor and rolled. "Oh God." She sighed. "That was the best."

Slade backed away from the mail all the way to the counter to look at her flailing on the floor. He bit back a smile and then eased back to the kitchen table.

She wiped at the tears that'd fallen onto her cheeks and pulled in a shaky breath. The cramp in her side eased one tangled fiber at a time. She stared up at the ceiling for several seconds and then canted her head toward Jake.

His head shook, but the slightest glint brightened his gaze. "I'm glad my unease could give you a laugh."

"Serves you right with all your questions." Her hands flatted across her belly.

"This is private stuff, but they're things we need to think about." His tone was soft and serious, almost intimate.

"Yeah, I know. It's just"—she jabbed her fingers at the air—"a little invasive."

"More or less invasive than an hour ago." His full mouth pursed.

"Match point." Libby shoved off the floor and found herself sitting closer to Jake than when they'd started. "I am most certainly not a virgin," she whispered. "But it had been a year and seven months since I'd been with anyone."

"Was that regular?"

"For a few months, but it was easy come, easy go. No hurt feelings. No feelings at all. Just convenient."

"Did he want more from the relationship?"

"He wanted more relationships. I didn't want complications. Jealous women are the worst."

"And you're not a jealous woman?" His knowing gaze pinned her.

"I know my worth. Another person's doesn't change mine."

He studied her and then nodded. "What do you do outside of work, besides run and beat on that heavy bag?"

"Go to the grocery store." Libby shrugged. She spent time with the girls, but they weren't behind this, so she saw no reason to bring them into it. The farther they stayed away, the better for them and her peace of mind.

"Have a favorite restaurant or bar?"

"I like to cook." When he toppled against the couch, she lifted both hands palm up. "It's healthier."

"Jesus. I thought my life was stagnant." Jake chuckled.

"I'm career oriented."

He made a face that said "so the hell what?"

"I work out at the office. I eat at the office. I work ridiculous hours, plus some weekends."

"It certainly narrows the playing field." His head shook in a slow, sad swing. Like her life.

"Unless it's some random wacko," she interjected.

"No." His head stopped shaking, and all traces of playfulness fled. "This is personal. It's someone you know."

Air caught in her throat and soured.

"Slade," Jake called. "When you're finished, I want a look at the stack of serious threats."

"Sure, boss." Slade added another letter to the perv stack. It was now twelve times as big as the stack claiming she'd inspired someone in some way. And the serious stack was near to nonexistent.

"I'm not your boss," Jake snapped.

"Yes, boss." Slade saluted Jake and offered a smile.

Jake's gaze rolled toward the sky. "I'm going to cross-reference the parts of this shitty excuse for a firebomb first."

"You say shitty excuse, but if he had abducted Libby and set it off like he planned, the house would have gone up like kindling." Slade snapped his fingers. "No one would have known she was missing for at least six hours, but more likely a day. Maybe two."

The worry she'd lost while in the throes of passion rained on her head, matting her hair and soaking her shoes.

Jake's gaze found hers, and they shared an unspoken thought.

What would the madman have done to her?

"Gather some clothes." Jake tilted his head toward her bedroom. "You'll stay with me until we get this guy nailed down."

"No, I won't." Libby laughed at the absurd suggestion. "You live right next door. It's not like whoever is doing this wouldn't know I was there."

"Your family is out of state." Jake stated something she knew but had no idea how he'd found out. "You could go stay with them until I find this guy."

Libby sucked in a lungful to tell him exactly what she thought about his idea, but he continued.

"I don't peg you as the type to run from danger." His big hand slapped the coffee table. He sighed. "You won't want to put your high society friends in danger either."

"How do you know about the girls?"

"I live next door."

"So you know all this stuff about me." Libby's words rushed from her lips. She sat up, pulling her knees under her. "You know about my comings and goings, my friends, my family, yet you haven't seen whoever is doing this?"

"No. He hasn't paraded himself around the house or sat on the porch drinking wine, waiting for me to come out of the house with my shirt off so he could get a look." Jake's cheeks turned a light shade of pink, and it wasn't from embarrassment.

Libby opened her mouth to speak.

"And if I knew who it was, they'd be dead."

She stared at him. He stared back.

How many times had Libby threatened to kill someone who was driving crazy on the road? 1,000. Easily. She was 1,000 times certain that Jake meant what he said.

"So you'll stay with me." Jake closed his laptop.

Libby worked on a decent rebuttal.

"Two is better than one." He stood.

Whew, was it! She catalogued his thick frame through

his clothes, remembering what went where and how it felt. Yep, that was exactly what she was worried about, two being better than one again, and again.

"And I count as four on my own." He winked, grabbed his laptop, and headed for the back door.

TWENTY-TWO

LIBBY STOOD IN JAKE'S LIVING ROOM with her bag of clothes, her laptop, and no idea where to put them or herself. She turned in a tight circle, looking at all the intricate pieces on the walls she had seen from the door and not paid much attention to the night before. He'd traveled the world and seen a lot. Much of it terrible, she'd guess.

Slade had left, grumbling about needing a drink and not to see Foster, to whom he owed money for something. She hadn't a clue who the hell they were talking about. Libby and Slade had gone through letters until their eyes crossed. In the end, there were three worth a serious look. All three had prints, and they were running them through AFIS. She didn't know how they had access to the Automated Fingerprint Identification System, but she was glad to know they might have some questions answered by the end of the night.

Jake pushed through the door, set the bags of groceries she'd convinced him to take from her kitchen onto his counter, and turned to her.

"I'd say you can put them in my guest room, but I don't have one."

"Not one for overnight company, huh?" She knew that from watching his comings and goings. The thing she'd yelled at him about earlier.

"Not usually." Jake's gaze warmed. It scraped her up one side and down the other. "Waking up to you wasn't half bad." His voice dropped. "Not half bad, crazy broad."

"Wow, the compliments just keep coming." Libby slapped her free hand to her pants. "I think I liked it better when you didn't talk." She dropped her bag next to the couch and put her laptop on the coffee table. The same table where he'd kissed her the night before. Sure, she'd sleep there for the next few nights. The problem was staying out of his room in the mornings.

She didn't want to marry Jake. Hell, she didn't even like him. A blatant lie. She liked his reverence, his calm, and his surprising sense of humor. Even more, she liked his body on hers, in hers, over hers. However, she refused to be his cheap call girl.

Libby picked up the kitten nuzzling her ankles. The little guy had clearly missed them during the long day sifting through clues. It'd been contented with food, water, an assortment of well-worn cat toys that'd belonged to Killer, and a litter box so well hidden she hadn't known he had one until she'd asked that morning.

Jake moved efficiently through his kitchen, placing everything neatly in cabinets and a refrigerator that hadn't hosted a murdered cat. After everything was put away, he grabbed a casserole dish she didn't recognize from the fridge and popped it in the microwave.

He gathered plates, cutlery, cups, and napkins and set them on a small table inside the kitchen.

Like an idiot, she stood, holding fast to the kitten, feeling more and more as though she was infringing on his solitude.

"Cat food?" Libby asked, desperate for something helpful to do.

"Under the cabinet by the door. A fourth of a scoop."

He didn't look in her direction as he situated the place settings for two. Maybe his girlfriend, non-girlfriend was on her way over. Libby's skin crawled away without her. She wasn't jealous, but she was self-respecting. Dammit. She grabbed the cat's food and set the kitten and the bowl next to the water bowl near the back door. Now her hands were completely empty, and she was completely out of her element.

The microwave dinged. She would've welcomed the opportunity to get whatever smelled pretty damn delicious from it, but Jake walked past her without a glance. He yanked two mittens from a drawer and shoved his hands inside. A smile tickled the edges of Libby's mouth. The large blue mittens were so incompatible with the large man. Still, he used them as though he knew exactly what he was doing. He set the dish in the center of the small table, chucked the mittens into the drawer, grabbed tongs from it, and closed it.

He motioned for her to sit.

Which chair was the one he preferred? Libby looked from one to the other.

"It doesn't matter," he said.

She wasn't going to ask. Though she'd thought about it. Of course, he read her like a flashing highway sign. From a mile off.

Her bottom smacked into the closest chair, facing the door. Through the window, the sun turned what little bit she could see of the sky into pink cotton candy. He removed the lid, and she stared down at chicken, asparagus, and potatoes.

"Wow." Her mouth watered.

"Help yourself." He walked into the living room and turned on the television. Instead of keeping it on the sports channel, he pressed a button on the remote, and the screen filled with six boxes. All were security feeds from outside his home.

The edge of Libby's rear stoop was visible in one of the shots.

She paused with her hand halfway to the tongs he'd set on the table and pointed at the screen. "That's my—"

"I know. I reviewed all the tapes while you slept last night. Early this morning," he amended.

"And?"

"A brown boot and a jeans-covered leg."

Her gaze dropped to his brown boots and jeans.

"Considerably smaller than mine." He sat across from her with a smug look on his face.

"How do you know?" she challenged.

"The security software measures. It's a size ten and a half men's shoe."

"What's yours?" She didn't really care but wanted to be snooty. He'd kept this from her.

"Thirteen." He plucked a chicken breast from the container and placed it on her plate and then added a bunch of asparagus and a few cuts of potato.

"Why didn't you tell me?"

He loaded his plate with food, forked a piece of chicken, and consumed half of it with one bite. While he chewed, Libby waited. Her stomach growled since they'd skipped lunch. Finally, he swallowed.

"There's nothing to tell. When I have something more concrete, I'll let you know."

"A men's ten and a half brown boot is concrete."

"No, not until it has a foot attached to it."

Libby stabbed a potato and shoved it in her mouth. Outwardly, she consumed the rest of her meal in relative silence. Inwardly, she cursed him for acting so misogynistic. She could use that information to garner a lead. He knew it, yet he wanted her on the sidelines.

She'd show him.

When Libby chewed the last bite of her chicken, she grabbed their plates and took them to the sink. He sat at the table, studying her.

"I know you have a job." She wet and soaped a sponge. "I don't expect you to babysit me all day, every day. You can go do whatever you need to do." They'd nearly licked the plates and utensils clean, yet she still scrubbed. "I won't break into your dungeon or snoop through your stuff."

His laughter was rich and full. It settled in her ears and warmed a path down her neck. He stood, collected the now empty container and tongs, and carried them to the counter. The heavy container slid into place right next to her.

"My dungeon, huh?" He rumbled the words into her ear. His breath whispered across her skin. "You think I'm a hard-core Dom?"

There was laughter in his voice.

She looked toward the hallway. Big mistake. His lips brushed her temple.

"That first room is locked up tight." Her voice quaked.

"I'll just have to show you once again how I like it." His presence was larger than life and so close she could fall back into his embrace. "No gimmicks. No restraint. Just you and me."

Her knees went slack, and she braced a soapy hand on the counter to steady herself.

"I actually don't have a job."

It took Libby more than a beat to catch up to the conversation. She didn't want to. It was nice and hot back where they were.

Just you and me.

Libby shuddered a breath. "That makes two of us," she quipped.

Jake plucked the clean plate from her hand and used a dish towel to dry it. "You're on a leave of absense. I'm retired." He stowed it in the cabinet behind his head.

She couldn't help but look at him as though he was the craziest person she'd ever met. He was far from it, but he made her the craziest. "You're what, thirty?"

"Twenty-nine."

"How does a twenty-nine-year-old retire?"

He grabbed another plate from her and got to work. "It's like a professional football player. A broken back takes you out of the game, no matter how well you recover."

Libby left the soapy forks in the sink and turned to him. She'd known something had been up with him when he'd first moved in. There was the limp. Then the scar. A broken back turned her insides to goo. It was a miracle he was alive, much less standing in front of her more capable than every other person she knew, and she knew some insanely capable people. As much as she wanted to pull him into her arms and hug him tight, she couldn't show him an ounce of the sorrow she felt for what he'd been through.

She cocked a wet hand on her hip. "Then why have you been gone most weekdays and on short business trips over the past few months?"

His smile was big. It startled her.

"They figured out I wasn't as useless as they thought." He shrugged.

"They?"

He stared at her. His smile remained but not a word

slipped from it.

"Right." She turned back to the dishes. "So you're not retired."

"I'm mostly retired."

"Whatever you need to tell yourself." She handed over the forks they'd used and then pulled the casserole dish into the sink. Never before had she had this much fun washing dishes or talking to a man. Neither of them were accustomed to sharing. He far less than she.

"I have something I need to do. It won't take long. Someone will be watching the house, so you can sleep or watch TV."

"You get more channels? Security feed isn't exactly a riveting program."

"Input two." He pulled out the drawer closest to the door. It was an ordinary kitchen drawer. A metal plate covered the contents and guarded it with a fingerprint scanner and keypad. After unlocking the mechanism, he flipped open the lid and swiped a set of keys from the small safe.

The keys were the least interesting thing inside the well-placed security feature. A stack of passports took top billing in her mind. They were followed closely by stacks of hundred-dollar bills that barely fit in the five-inch gap between the bottom and top. A small pistol and ankle holster, a knife, a flashlight, and two other sets of keys filled the rest of the space.

Jake closed the lid and met her curious gaze. "Stay here. Keep the doors locked. Don't open them for anyone, whether you know them or not. If necessary, use any of the guns you've already found in here to protect yourself." He rubbed his knuckles across the kitten's head and then reached for the back door.

"Have fun at work." Libby had no idea what he did, legal or not, but she suspected he was off to complete a task in his mysterious line of work.

His head shook as he closed the door behind him. The lock engaged, and she was alone inside his home.

Where the hell was he going?

What the hell was she going to do while he was gone? She finished up the dishes, dried them, and left them on the counter. No way was she going through his cabinets. Who knew what she'd find. An unusual turn for Libby. Her typical inclination was to scavenge for clues, but for whatever reason, she wanted Jake to give her the answers freely. Stealing them would feel wrong.

The kitten busied himself batting a small mouse toy around the living room. She curled up on the couch, pulled the blanket over her legs, and realized that she was the mouse. Someone was batting her around on their whim. Anger boiled beneath her sedate surface.

Without thought, her fingers reached for her phone.

She dialed Marlis. It'd been four of the longest days of her life since she'd sent her friend packing. There was tension and unsettled business between them, but it was worth it to shield Mar from this madness. Fear prickled at the nape of her neck. If her friend had gotten caught up … She blocked the evil thoughts and listened to the line ring and ring and ring. Then the message played. Dejected, she still waited for the beep.

"Mar. No, you're not a badass, but that's what makes you so special. You're the heart of our group. You keep us from burning it all to the ground. You remind us that love is what keeps the world turning. I don't want anything to happen to our center point. Can you understand that? I hope so. I love you. Call me back."

By the time she clicked off, tears blurred her vision. She wiped them away, drew a deep breath, and called Genevieve. On the second ring, her friend's warm, sultry tone filled the line.

"Lib, how's your hot neighbor?" It was the way she'd answered nearly every one of Libby's phone calls since their wine-fueled neighbor stakeout nearly eight months ago.

"Hot as ever." It wasn't a lie, but she didn't want to talk about the man whose couch she snuggled into, nor the reason she was there. "How are you feeling?"

"Like a million bucks … that's been heavily laundered and hung out to dry." Gen snorted. "It's not that bad. Owen is mother henning me, making me take breaks, drink water, and stop everything to eat three meals a day."

"What are you doing? Or do I not want to know?"

"You definitely want to know." Gen chuckled. "We've had to be on good behavior."

"Because of your traumatic brain injury?" Libby let a hint of sarcasm lace her tone, but it had been serious. She, Larkin, and Marlis had all camped out in the hospital for the first twelve hours Gen had been in the ICU.

"No." Her friend scoffed. "Because public fornication is illegal. We've been camped inside the station, wrapping loose ends and awaiting test results."

"On the body they found in Beena Carter's yard?"

"The bodies, yes," Gen reminded.

"It was her husband's child, no question." Libby pulled the edge of the cover over her shoulder to ward off a chill.

"I know. Roderick gave his DNA for the lab to cross-check," Gen explained.

The dead woman in the ground was most likely Roderick's mother who had been Beena Carter's cleaning lady and Beena's husband's lover. Roderick had been fathered by the man, no question. The DNA test was a mere formality.

"Do you think there will be enough evidence to charge Beena with both murders?"

"You mean all three murders," Gen corrected.

"Good Lord, what a monster."

"Yep. We have her signed, sealed, and delivered on Perry Senior's murder. I'll know in the next week whether we have her for the mother and baby. I'm hopeful."

"You deserve a win." Libby winced. "Bad choice of words. Sorry."

"Don't be. I'm not that fragile. Yes, I'm pissed Perry fooled me." Perry Carter Jr. had been Gen's mentor and a devoted family man, or so everyone had thought, when he'd been arrested for the murder of his wife and two children. "But that's what narcissistic psychopaths do. They mimic human emotion, show you what you need to see, and stab you in the forehead before you can blink."

Libby swallowed the lump that'd formed in her throat. "How are things going with you?"

Her gaze scanned the room. What kind of life had she been living before all this started? Work. Work. Work. Jake had been right. She'd been stagnant. "I'm just ready to get my life back, but then you know all about that."

"Media vultures. Listen, with the twenty-four-hour news cycle as it is, you and I will be forgotten as soon as the next starlet overdoses."

"Would it be wrong to send Camille Newsome some cocaine?"

Gen's chuckle filtered through the line. "Wrong is such an abstract concept."

"Hey." Libby strived for nonchalance. "Have you talked to Mar lately?"

"No, I've been caught up with this circus. Why?"

"She hasn't answered or returned my calls in a few days."

"Did you two fight?"

How the hell did Gen always know?

"It wasn't a fight, really. She showed up on my doorstep in the late evening. I hadn't been home and freaked out on her for waiting alone at night."

"And she inferred that she couldn't take care of herself?"

"Something like that," Libby admitted.

"She's the most sensitive of us. Just give her some time. She'll come around."

TWENTY-THREE

BY THE TIME JAKE CAME BACK, Libby had long since figured out the security system and was reviewing the last of the feeds from the cameras that caught any portion of her house. She didn't look in his direction, afraid of the censure she'd find in his eyes. He replaced the keys in the drawer safe and stalked into the room.

His weight caved the cushion. He spread his arms along the back of the couch and his legs wide. One leg anyway. The other was hemmed in by the coffee table. Well, it had been until he lifted it onto the small table's top. He crowded her and still she didn't look at him. She'd never been a coward, but something about having him close scrambled her brain more than the current dramas in her life.

"I had to take a long, boring class to learn how to operate that thing," he admitted.

Relenting, Libby turned to him. The feed ran, but she was certain it wouldn't reveal any more than what he'd told her, which matched what she'd seen for herself.

"I'm not afraid to press buttons until I figure things out."

"Don't I know it."

The backs of his knuckles grazed the edge of her forehead and pulled the hair back from her eyes. He released a long, heavy breath.

She wanted to ask him where he'd been and what he'd been doing, but she knew he wouldn't answer and it would only make her angry. Based on what she knew of the world, she shouldn't trust him, yet she did. He'd shown her only kindness between bouts of extreme reserve. Those bouts were getting fewer and farther between.

Libby met his intelligent gaze. "I'm sorry about Killer."

"Killer?"

"Your cat. I called him Killer."

"I'm sorry too." He nodded. For a minute, he was silent. She expected him to stand and beg off for the night, but he didn't move.

"When he showed up, I didn't know where he'd come from. I didn't try to steal him away. I ignored him for a long time, guessing he'd move on. He never did. So I installed a cat door in the garage where he could come and go as he pleased. I left food out and waited. It took him a week to make it into the garage and another few days to eat all the food in the bowl."

Jake pinched his left thumb and forefingers together and plucked the air. "He'd grab one piece and bolt outside to eat it."

"He didn't want to be trapped."

"No, and I could appreciate that." He patted his chest with his left hand but left his right so close it nearly touched her once more. "As soon as he figured out that I wouldn't contain him, he settled in like he owned the joint. And he did.

"The first time he snuggled with me, I ended up with cat pee all over me, and he nearly ended up dead. It was the middle of the night. I was sleeping, and then I felt a weight on my chest." He blew out a breath and chuckled. "Neither of us reacted well."

Libby didn't know Jake contained this many words, but she hung on to every one. He was so animated and unguarded. Her insides warmed.

"He was a loner, a fighter."

Jake could have been talking about himself. Not once over those first few months Jake had moved into the house had anyone been with him, helping him recover from a life-altering injury. Where the fuck was his family? Had he pushed them away, or did he not have any?

"I didn't know you'd rescued him until he brought you that first lizard."

That'd been a few months ago. Just like last week, she'd been headed to work and had found Killer on the porch with a present for her.

He laughed. "I thought you were being robbed or something. It was the loudest shriek I've ever heard. Hell, you didn't even yell that loud when you were being attacked." His jaw tightened.

She didn't want him thinking about the bad. Not right now. This lightness in him, the openness fed her soul. And maybe his too. She hoped it did.

"He had a live lizard flopping around in his mouth." She used both hands and flapped her fingers on each side of her mouth to demonstrate. The image of that thing flailing about the cat's whiskers flashed in her mind. "Ugh."

"I think it was his first attempt at a peace offering."

Libby harrumphed. "I'd prefer a plant or a small box

of chocolates."

Jake smiled for several beats, and then his expression turned serious. "Even after he treated you so terribly, you still liked him?"

She didn't know if they were still talking about the cat or him, so she answered honestly. "I always liked him way more than I should. Something about him got under my skin and stuck."

"He hurt you." His thumb slid over the now faint scar that Killer had left on her arm. Now she had a well-camouflaged bruise on her forehead that took precedence.

"He'd been hurt," she whispered. "It was the only way he knew how to be."

"Not the only way." Jake dragged both of his hands into his lap and looked down at them. He rubbed his fingers together as though trying to remove something only he could see. "He never hurt me."

Libby covered his hands with her own. "I think he knew you'd been hurt too."

"Huh." His head shook even as he moved closer, closing the gap between them.

"Huh, what?" She looked into his eyes.

His warm finger cupped her chin and pulled her to within inches of his mouth. He pressed his lips into a hard line. His nostrils flared.

"I should take you to your friend, Larkin Ashford, and disappear." He pressed his forehead to hers and hissed a breath. "It'd be safe for you. She has a top-notch security team. It'd be safe for me to be away from you."

Libby closed her eyes. He wasn't referring to her deranged stalker. She knew without a doubt Jake could disappear in an instant. The thought of never seeing him again slammed a fist into the center of her heart. It stole her breath and all logic along with it.

"I won't hurt you," she promised.

"What if I hurt you?"

He could. More than anyone before him, this man could leave her in pieces, and she hardly knew him. What she knew was she wanted more. She wanted everything he could give for tonight or as long as it lasted.

"I'm not easily hurt," she promised.

"No, you're not."

Jake lifted her chin and covered her mouth with his own. The kiss was unhurried and thorough. It was kind and exploratory. It built slowly, one thin layer of need stacked atop the last until there were a hundred thousand, and she could take no more.

Libby pressed him back against the couch and swung a jeans-clad leg over his lap. She braced his face in her hands. Stubble tickled her fingers and pricked her palms. Gently, she shoved his head back and assailed his neck with languid kisses. His scent shot up her nose like a drug. Less than one day in and she was a full-blown addict.

His fingers looped into the bottom of her shirt and lifted. She stopped kissing him only for him to pull the shirt over her head, but the look of sheer admiration as he took her in stopped her. She'd seen lust a thousand different times. Desire too. But this was something new. It pushed beyond the physical to a place she'd never gone before. It scared her stiff. It was too much, too good, and at any moment, he'd take it and run.

Slowly, his touch skimmed up her sides. He skimmed the sides of her breasts and traced the outline of her neck. His fingertips tickled a line down her throat and over her collarbones to the crest of her shoulders. He dragged each strap of her bra until it fell from her shoulders. Libby's insides clenched. She arched, pressing her erect nipples to him. Bit by bit, he scraped the lace over her heavy breasts. When he gently traced the fullness and throbbing tip, she moaned his name.

Jake unfastened the clasp, and the bra fell away. He wrapped his arms around her and stood. He walked them down the hallway and into his bedroom. His gaze never wavered from hers. He laid her on the covers as though she were breakable, special, and then stepped back and studied her.

Stupid tears threatened. She bit her lips.

"You are stunning, Libby."

He leaned over and hooked a hand behind her calf. As though he were unwrapping a precious artifact, he removed her shoes. His hand moved to the fastener on her jeans and worked it open. He pulled her zipper down one maddening notch at a time and then spread the flaps wide. The tip of his nose and the crest of his mouth slid along the boundary of her panties, not kissing, but loving the exposed skin as he worked the pants down her thighs. His hands worked the jeans and panties—the ones he'd chosen for her to wear—lower, and his mouth followed over her thighs and across her knees to the tops of her feet.

"Jake," she whispered his name, unsure of what she wanted but acknowledging her vulnerability.

"I said I should disappear." Jake stood at the end of the bed and peeled the shirt from his chest. His gaze disappeared for half a second. He tossed the fabric onto the floor, toed off his boots, and then dropped his pants. "I'm not."

There wasn't an ounce of misplaced muscle or excess fat on his large frame. He was a well-honed machine. His use? Covert operations, she was sure. It was the degree to which she was unsure of. Were they so covert his own government didn't avow them or even know about them? There was no way she could see a body like his sitting behind a desk. Even injured, he was so commanding and capable, but that wasn't what drew her to him at this moment. His openness to the depth of this experience drew her in and held her captive.

Jake climbed onto the bed, running his hands up her thighs and bracing them on her hips. He pressed his face into her belly and breathed deeply before he kissed a line to the valley between her breasts. His fingers dug into her backside, angling her hips up, and he pressed the slick head of his cock at the center of her opening. Libby grabbed two handfuls of his hair and held his gaze while he stretched and entered her. His heavy weight pushed into her.

A moan rippled through her body and sang through her lips. Jake offered the perfect mixture of pleasure and pain. What a precise representation of their entanglement.

His tongue laved at her nipples. He bit and sucked. Need melted her inside and opened her to him.

Jake filled her completely.

He pressed his wet mouth to hers. Libby suckled his tongue and ate at his lips. Her name whispered across his lips and filtered into her mouth. His arms climbed higher, wrapped around her, and held her to his chest. More than a sexual position, it tingled like a hug. He pulled out and eased deep, strumming her insides with his silky, hard ridges.

Euphoria clawed at Libby's insides. Heat churned through her veins.

Libby whimpered against his mouth. Her hand slid around his neck and down his back. She coiled her legs around his waist. With all her strength, she held him close. He felt so good it made her want to scream and sob and rejoice at the same time.

His mouth trailed kisses up her cheek to her temple. He threaded a hand into her hair and tilted her head. His stubbly chin rested in the crook of her neck. Hot, weighty breaths cascaded over her shoulder. His tempo climbed as did her need for him on her, in her, all around her.

Every thrust pushed her higher. It had never been like this. So heavy and so freeing. She arched into him. Her clit pulsed and throbbed. Pants filled the air and burned her chest. With the next crash of their bodies, she catapulted. Each muscle contracted and held. For an eight count, she floated in the ether before every muscle convulsed. Pleasure sang. She sighed and moaned, milking the crest of her orgasm.

"Fuck." Jake groaned the word but jerked from her body.

For an instant, confusion and the delicious haze of completion disoriented her. Then the liquid heat of his pleasure painted her belly. His muscles strained, and his face arched toward the sky.

"Oh." Libby stared down at the evidence of her carelessness. No wonder it had felt so decadent. It had been. There had been nothing between them but deep desire and something she couldn't and wouldn't dare to name.

He collapsed next to her. His chest, hip, and thigh still pressed against her. He shifted his arm to cradle her head. His pecs rose and fell in rapid succession. His gaze remained on the ceiling while his breaths slowed. He seemed to be grappling with something.

The cum cooled on Libby's belly. She hadn't thought about a condom once while they were entangled.

Jake rolled onto his side toward her. She found herself scared for the first time to meet his gaze, but like a magnetic pull, she found his intelligent eyes. His thumb caressed her raw lips.

"I never forget." His head shook. "Not ever."

Libby offered him her best expression of shock. "I took your virginity?"

He gave her a crooked grin, grabbed her chin, and planted a kiss on her lips. Her fingers slipped gently through his hair. He purred, sank deeper into the kiss for a second, and then pulled back.

"I'm serious, Libby. I never forget."

"Well, you took mine too."

Jake huffed and pressed their foreheads together. Libby closed her eyes and took in the headiness of the moment. When he straightened, she let it go.

"I'm on birth control. I haven't missed an appointment, and I was tested after my last—" His thick finger pressed over her mouth.

"I don't regret it." Before she could say anything else, he left the bed and room. He came back with a wet rag. Gently, he cleaned between her legs and then her belly.

From the other room, an alarm of two simple shrill alerts sounded.

Libby bolted upright. Her heart kicked into her throat.

"It's okay." Jake grabbed a loose wave of her hair and rubbed it between his thumb and forefinger. "I know who it is. Stay here." He pulled the covers from under her body and covered her to the waist in the sheet and well-worn comforter. "Get some sleep." After retrieving his clothes from the floor, he pulled them on. "You'll be safe. I have someone on guard."

"Slade?"

"No. Someone just as capable."

"I can take care of myself."

"Not when you're asleep, and you need sleep." He walked to the edge of the bed and leaned down.

"So do you," she countered.

"No. When I need to be, I'm good until the seventy-five-hour mark."

She stored that tidbit of information in the file backing up her assumption that he was some sort of soldier or covert operative.

"Where are you going?"

"To find out who killed my cat." Jake's full lips sealed off her rebuttal. Too soon, he straightened and left the room, pulling the door closed behind him.

She stared at the door for several seconds and then let her gaze travel to her breasts. The tops were rubbed red from the connection of their bodies. She dragged a hand over them and then her belly in awe of what they'd done. It had been more than sex, more than anything she'd ever experienced.

The back door beeped and then opened.

Jake's deep timbre rumbled. Though she couldn't make out a single word, he went on for a minute. Then a higher, decidedly feminine voice said, "As long as you need."

Libby's entire body flashed incinerator hot. At the same time the bottom of her stomach opened a trapdoor. Cold sweat clung to her skin.

She scrambled from the bed, ripped the sheet from it, wrapped it around her, and stormed out the door and down the hallway. At the mouth of the corridor, she stopped dead. The sleek, sexy woman Jake had been fucking every once in a while, for the last six months, leaned against his counter with one stiletto boot crossed atop the other. A large pistol hung in the holster on her hip and a larger knife was strapped to her thigh.

Libby clamped back a sob. Though her heart cracked inside her chest, she told herself that there was nothing between her and Jake. She'd known that, and this proved it. Still, he didn't have to lie to her about his relationship with the woman. They were obviously close. He stood only a foot away from her, his hands on his hips.

Both their gazes found her naked, except for the haphazardly wrapped sheet.

No one spoke.

An odd silence stretched as the woman's gaze jumped from her to Jake and back. His held on Libby, but hers refused to focus on either of them for too long.

She finally focused on the woman. "Look, we slept together. He said you weren't his girlfriend, but obviously, you two are close. I'm not getting in the middle of this." She pointed from one to the other. "No matter how much ..."

Libby clamped a hand over her mouth to keep from saying another word.

The woman banked a smile.

Jake just stared at her.

Rage pounded fast fists against Libby's temple.

"We're not together." The woman's head straightened.

"We have been, but it's not because of some deep-seated love on either of our parts."

"Foster," Jake warned.

Libby walked on wobbly legs to the nearest kitchen chair and dropped into it. "It's because you both look amazing naked." She offered an empty smile. The kitten trundled across the floor and batted around the end of her sheet. Lord, oh Lord, she was making an ass out of herself, and she couldn't make herself care. She picked up the kitten and pulled it to her chest. "I'm guessing," she added. "I haven't seen you naked."

The woman, Foster, laughed. Jake's stony façade cracked, not quite revealing a smile, but it was something. Foster took several sultry strides past Jake and extended her hand. "I'm Reece Foster."

"Look." Libby held up her palm in surrender. "He knows this already, but I'm not into threesomes."

"It's not like that either." Reece Foster shook her head and let her hand fall to her side for a beat before gesturing between her and Jake. "We both—"

"Will you close your mouth?" Jake begged.

The woman continued as though he'd never spoken. "We both want people we can't have." Foster's gaze slid to Jake's. "Or people we think we can't have." Her gaze returned to Libby. "We were just releasing angst and passing the time."

She stared one to the other and back again. They made a stunning, deadly couple. It was in the way they moved, the way their gazes never settled for too long. The way they could look at you and still be aware of everything around them.

"I can't imagine either of you wanting someone and not being able to have them," Libby said almost to herself.

Jake stepped around Foster and pulled her attention. "I asked you here to protect her. Not gossip."

The lethal woman offered him a smile. "After all that's happened, I love that you still think you can control everything."

His gaze jumped to Libby and held, and then he turned and stalked out the door.

TWENTY-FOUR

LARKIN: REALLY?!

Libby: No, I'm interrupting your morning staff meeting as a prank. Yes!

Larkin: I've never known Mar to hold a grudge that long.

Libby: Me either.

Larkin: I'll give her a call and let you know.

Libby: Thank you!

While she waited for Larkin to text her back, Libby applied a tinted moisturizer, a swipe of mascara, and some gloss. It was the first time in too many days that she felt human. Sleeping on the couch hadn't helped. The shower and hair dryer had. She pushed out of the bathroom. The scent of coffee and bacon filled her nostrils. Excitement and dread warred. They hadn't said more than good morning before she'd bailed into the bathroom.

Now, just as he had the other night, he'd set two place settings and filled plates with food.

Oh, Foster's coming for breakfast?

The ugly question tickled the tip of her tongue, but she bit it back. She wasn't a jealous woman. Not normally.

Libby carried the cosmetic bag into the living room and shoved it inside her small suitcase. She checked her phone. When there was still no message, she shoved it into the back pocket of her jeans and finally lifted her gaze.

Jake leaned against the counter in the kitchen where Foster had the night before. His legs weren't crossed, but his thick arms were knotted across his chest. A scowl pulled at his lips. His head canted toward the food. "It's probably cold."

"Is that for me?" She expected it was, but she couldn't stop the barb. Hell, it could be for Foster, her, or the woman he thought he couldn't have. Because unless the chick was dead, there wasn't one on earth he couldn't make his. Her reaction last night made no sense, yet she couldn't bring herself to feel remorse for it.

"Don't recall ever cooking for another woman."

Her mouth fell open. Served her right for being ugly. She tongued her tooth, slunk to the table, and sat. "I don't mind if it's cold."

Why had she expected any other response? Hadn't she seen the relationship between Jake and Foster. Screw ya, see ya. Not once had the woman stayed the night or any longer than it took them to orgasm.

He sat across from her and dug into pancakes, eggs, and bacon.

She took a sip of coffee. "Did you get any sleep?"

"A few hours." He shoved a hunk of pancake into his mouth and stared past her at the kitten playing with the string that adjusted the blinds in the front window.

Libby set down the mug and waited for him to look at

her. He didn't.

"I'm sorry," she breathed. His gaze found hers and she swallowed. "I acted …" Her head shook. "I reacted."

"I thought you weren't a jealous woman."

"It's a new development." She grimaced.

"Eat."

She shoved a piece of bacon into her mouth and chewed. Next, she enjoyed a double stack of pancakes, and then she finished off her bacon. He cleared everything but his second pancake off his plate.

"Why didn't you go back to the bed?"

His question startled her. After their exchange, she hadn't expected another word out of him.

"I didn't know if you'd want me there after last night." She forked some eggs and shoved them into her mouth.

He measured her. The right side of his mouth tilted into a smirk.

"What?"

His head shook in a single side to side. She wasn't getting it out of him. Not right now.

"Did you find any leads last night?"

Libby's phone beeped. She pulled it out of her back pocket. "I'm sorry, but I have to …" Her eyes started reading before she finished the sentence.

Larkin: I texted and called twice each. Nothing.

Libby: I'm going to check on her.

Libby finished texting, pinned Jake with an expression that meant business, and used her official FBI tone. "I have to go check on my friend." She jumped to her feet, grabbed her phone off the table, then hurried to the living room for her coat and keys. Her fingers patted the kitten on the head. "Bye, kitten."

When she turned around, he stood by the door with his jacket on, his keys in his hand, and a gun bulging the leather holster at his side. "Are you going to name him?"

She shrugged. "Are you?"

Jake opened the door and ushered her out. "I'm not so good at that. I mean, I called Cat, Cat."

"True."

"So we have to go check on a grown woman?"

"We don't. I do."

"I'll never understand your sex." He closed it behind them and guided her down the driveway to the garage.

"Likewise." She smiled. "I can drive."

"I'm aware." His thumb pressed to a seamless scanner, and then the thick metal door lifted. The black motorcycle sat in the center of a workshop filled with tools, supplies, and a bank-grade vault big enough to fit a party inside.

"Rob any banks lately?" she jabbed.

"Nope."

"Not ever or not lately?"

Jake strode into the garage, and the light turned on in response to the motion. A blacked-out full-face helmet hung from the bike's handle. He pulled another from a far shelf and threw it. "Who are we going to check on?"

"Marlis." Libby took a step into the garage and caught the awkward object against her belly. She banked a groan. "She's the woman you saw at my house several nights ago."

"The woman you fought with?"

She nodded. "I was trying to protect her."

"Did you tell her about—?"

"No. If she knew, if any of the girls knew, they'd insist on helping, and helping puts them in danger."

He kicked a leg over the beast and grabbed the helmet from the handle. "Why are we checking on her?"

"I've called, texted, and left several messages with her since that night, and I haven't heard back from her. I found out this morning that none of the girls have heard from her."

"Maybe she just needs some time to cool off."

"That's not how friendships work. You don't block each other out."

"Says the woman keeping a massive secret from her friends."

Libby rolled her eyes and shoved the helmet on her head, blocking him out because he was right. She walked to him, threw her leg over the machine, and adjusted herself on the seat. The gap she left between them was for her own sanity.

"Where to?" He flipped up the kickstand, braced the bike, and then looked at her.

She flipped open the shield. "I'll show you. Just head across the bridge."

"An address?"

Her answer was the flip of the shield. It was her way of maintaining control. Though, Foster's words echoed in her mind.

After all that's happened, I love that you still think you can control everything.

He shoved the helmet onto his head. Moments later, the machine roared to life. Even through the padding and plastic, the engine sounded as though it could bring the whole house down on top of them. He shifted the bike to center. Libby lifted her boots onto the back pegs and gripped the small chrome handle low behind her back. He walked the motorcycle outside the garage and waited for the door to meet the concrete, and then he poured on the gas. The bike responded instantly, shooting down the driveway and nearly pitching Libby off the back.

Her arms shot forward. She hooked them both around Jake's middle and held on as he whipped the motorcycle onto the street. Her hold for dear life pressed her hips against his backside and warmed her thighs against his. His breadth blocked the bulk of the wind, but cool morning air frosted her fingers and curled around her back.

Jake guided them through traffic and to the bridge with smooth efficiency. No wonder he'd wanted to drive. The precision machine cut minutes off the first half of her regular commute. She'd crossed this bridge twice daily for nearly her entire life. Its tresses, bricks, and pointy archways excited people from all over the world. To her, it was mundane at best. Today, though, she found herself breathing deeper across the open sky and cataloguing things she'd never cared about, like the texture of the metal cables and the way the light glinted through the bracings.

The temperature across the water dropped noticeably, and she shivered. Jake unzipped the top fourth of his jacket, grabbed her hands and shoved them inside the supple warmth. She sagged against him and savored the feel. Once they left the motorcycle for the day, she wouldn't touch him again if she could help it. Because as dangerous as he was to those who wronged him, he was even more dangerous to her. He made her feel things. He made her want things.

Off the bridge, Libby used tactical hand signals to guide him to The Ashford Building. They parked in a special space Larkin reserved for her on a side street, climbed off, and he locked their helmets to the bike. They headed toward the main entrance in step with each other with effort on her part. Libby took a step and a half to Jake's one.

At the opulent entrance, Jake stepped around her, opened the door wide, and waited for her to enter. Inside, they hurried across the marble foyer toward the security desk blocking access to the bank of elevators. The Silverback Gorilla-sized security guard waved her through with a smile. When his gaze hit Jake, who was hot on her heels, he stood and moved to the end of the counter.

"He's with me, Rick."

"Yes, Ms. Libby." The guard stopped but didn't remove his wary gaze from Jake.

They rounded the corner and hopped on the first available elevator to the seventh floor. The doors opened, and Marlis's Babybook logo hung in sculpted metal on a glass wall. To the left was a simply yet beautifully appointed sitting area. She turned right, and Jake followed her past a receptionist's desk.

"Mar's office is this way." She pointed toward the end of a long marble hallway.

"Your friends are loaded," Jake whispered.

"Yep, they all are. Gen not quite as much as Mar and Larkin, but she does well for herself."

"And that doesn't cause problems?"

Libby hiked her confused expression over her shoulder at him.

"I'll never understand you women."

"You're not supposed to. We're the eighth wonder of the world."

She grabbed his hand because she wanted to touch him and pulled him along to Mar's assistant's desk. The blonde looked up from her computer screen. The phone to her mouth sagged. Her mouth formed a surprised O.

"Yes, Mr. Engle, I'll connect you with our PR team. Please hold." The assistant pressed a series of button before dropping the receiver into the cradle, then standing and rounding the desk. May opened her arms. Libby dropped Jake's hand and walked into them, hugging the woman who'd taken care of Mar since she was a sprite. She smelled of coffee, J'adore Dior, and a hint of cigarette smoke.

"I thought you quit," Libby growled into the forty-something woman's ear.

"I did." May eased her to arm's length and smiled. "And then I did again."

"It's time to do it for good."

"I will." May fanned away her concern. "Now, when did you two get back, and why didn't I know you were getting in early?"

Libby quirked a brow at May and looked from the woman to Jake and back. "What? Us?" She gestured between Jake and herself, thoroughly confused.

"No, you and Mar. She texted me several days ago that you two were headed to Vegas," May said.

"Vegas?" Libby wasn't a gambler and had no love for the flashy city. She'd only gone there with the girls years ago, but they hadn't talked about going back.

"Yes, she said she was accompanying you to an FBI conference."

"No." Libby covered her mouth. Her head shook, and her heart skittered across the floor.

"When was the last time you saw Ms. McCain?" Jake's deep timbre broke into the conversation.

May's gaze bloated on Jake. "Who are you?"

"A friend," Libby hedged.

"I, uh … Thursday. Yes, it was after our big meeting on the revamp. She left here to check on you." May pointed at Libby.

Dread tore at Libby's insides, and an inhuman sound exited her throat.

Jake's strong hand braced her shoulders. "Maybe she was pissed, maybe overwhelmed with this revamp. It's possible she just needed to get away."

"No." May shook her head. "She was excited about the overhaul, and Mar would never lie to me, not about where she was going."

"Get on the phone. Call everyone who has daily contact with her and see if they've heard from her by voice. Texts and emails don't count," Jake clarified.

May rushed to her desk, jerked the phone to her ear, and dialed while Libby's brain spun in sickening circles. Each lap was more terrifying than the last. They whipped around so quickly her stomach gurgled and clenched.

"Libby." Jake's voice commanded her attention. She hadn't

realized he'd turned her to face him.

"What?" she choked.

"Where does she live?"

"Leonard Street."

"What's it like? Security? Traffic?" He held her tight in his grip, and his voice was even and calm, nothing like the mania shooting from every angle inside her skull.

"It's a condo. The building looks like a stack of glass boxes. Security is the usual, but Miller Watts is her head of security." Libby stumbled over the words.

"Miller handles more of the business and tech security," May interjected. "His men provide personal protection for events and conferences, which was why I was surprised she hadn't brought any of his guys to this conference, but then it wasn't social media related. It was out of the blue. It hadn't been on her schedule."

"Any word?" Jake asked the older woman.

"Miller drove her home from Libby's house Thursday evening, and that's the last time he saw her. He received a similar text to the one I received. None of us have seen her since Thursday." May drew a deep breath. "Miller has a guy scouring security tapes from The Ashford for the last six days. He's focusing on the digital footprint and pings from her cell. I can't get an answer at her home." May clung to her well-manicured composure, but her fists clenched. "Where is Marlis?"

"I don't know." Libby bit back a sob.

"We're going to her home." Jake grabbed Libby's hand and tugged her along behind him. "Keep calling around," he hollered to May.

TWENTY-FIVE

LIBBY'S QUAKING FINGERS FLUBBED the call log twice before she found Douglas's number and dialed. He answered on the second ring. "Libby, how can I help you?"

She stopped in the middle of The Ashford's foyer. "Marlis is missing. She has been since Thursday, but no one knew it. A text was sent from her phone, but we don't think she sent it. I need you to do whatever you can to find her."

"I'm on it." Douglas clicked off the line with no further question.

"Who's Douglas?" Jake asked.

"Ex-CIA and Larkin's biological father."

"Every bit helps." Jake placed his hand on her back and urged her toward the exit. On the street, people rushed like rodents, filling and flowing down the sidewalk. No one seemed to notice her distress, her panic, her pain. No one but Jake.

"We'll find her."

"More than 600,000 missing person records are added to the National Crime Information Center every year. That's the population of Baltimore. Of those, less than a thousand are removed from the NCIC each year."

Jake interlaced their fingers and pulled her to the motorcycle. He placed the helmet on her head, climbed onto the bike, and pulled her on behind him. In seconds, they were on their way, clipping through standstill traffic, and flying through lights that were more orange than yellow.

She should call Larkin, but she didn't want to frighten her, not until they knew what they were dealing with.

It only took a few hand signals, and they roared up to Marlis's building. The stack of glass boxes was offset so that they looked like one gust of wind would topple them all. Jake pulled the bike onto the condo's plaza. They jumped off, left the helmets on the seat, and ran for the entrance.

Through the sliding door, they nearly ran into a Ken doll dressed in a suit with a secret service-style wire looping over one ear. His hand shot out flat against Jake's chest. "Sir, you cannot park there."

Without a single thought, Libby stroked her elbow high into the man's forearm, jarring the security guard's hand from Jake. "Don't touch him." She was scared and coiled for a fight. This wasn't the man she needed to tangle with. He needed to be on their side.

Jake's brow shot high. A corner of his mouth quirked.

The guard bristled. "You two need to leave immediately."

"I apologize"—Libby gestured toward the motorcycle and the man's arm—"for everything, but we need to get to my friend Marlis McCain's unit right away."

The guard sized them up one at a time. He turned his back on them and stalked to a counter, barring entry into the back. When he met her gaze again, his scowl was gone. In its place was a go-fuck-yourself grin. "I'm sorry, I can't let you up without express permission from Ms. McCain."

"Check her admittance log," Libby ordered.

Ken doll's already rigid posture puffed another inch. "How about you leave and come back another day when you haven't assaulted me."

"Assault?" Libby coiled. If he thought that was assault, wait until she'd finished with him.

Jake's fingers wrapped around her bicep, barring her from springing across the counter and pummeling the pretty off the man's face.

"Ms. McCain is missing. We will not leave without checking her home." Jake's voice was even and unwavering.

"Are you cops?" Ken lifted his chin.

If only she had her badge, she'd show him exactly who she was. But she didn't. And she wasn't.

"No, we're concerned friends," Jake explained.

The man scoffed. "If you were her friends, you'd know that she was out of town, not missing."

"Who told you she was out of town?" Libby demanded.

"She did." Ken looked down his too straight nose at her.

"When she was leaving?" Libby gasped. Hope bloomed.

"No."

"Then how did she tell you?" Libby gripped the edge of the counter and squeezed.

"How?" Jake barked.

"It was in the log," Ken huffed. "It was called down …" He accessed the computer. "Thursday evening."

"By who?" Jake asked.

"An unknown caller," Ken admitted.

Libby released the counter and the shred of hope she'd been clinging to. Jake's chest steadied her.

"We need to get up there now," Jake said.

"I can't let you up there." Ken shook his head, and his perfectly coiffed hair stayed in place. "Besides, this facility is very secure."

"I'll be right back." Jake turned and marched out the front door.

Libby didn't have time to worry about what he was doing. She needed to get up to Mar's condo. "Why can't you let me up there? I'm on Ms. McCain's visitor log."

"She's not home."

"How do you know for sure?" Libby braced her forearms on the counter.

"It's my job to know."

"Do you know the whereabouts of every tenant in your building? Or just Marlis?" She leaned in. "Do you like her?"

"No. I mean, yes," he stammered. "Not like that."

"Not how?"

"Not inappropriately."

"You don't watch her on the monitors when she's walking through the building? You don't pay special attention to her? You don't make sure she's greeted with a smile and a kind word? You don't want to have a more intimate relationship with her?"

"Look, lady—"

"Libby." Jake called to her from behind the counter. He pressed a button on the desk and the waist-high door opened. "Let's go."

"Hey!" Ken took one step toward Libby.

"Don't," Jake warned.

"You're not supposed to be back here," Ken whined.

"And this is supposed to be a secure facility." Jake reached out his hand for her.

"I already called the cops," Ken boasted. "They'll be here any minute."

"Good." Jake tugged on Libby's hand.

As if on cue, sirens wailed in the distance. Jake didn't let up on his strides toward the elevator.

"Freeze." They turned to see Ken doll holding a TAS-ER and pointing it toward Libby.

"Turn that thing this way unless you want to lose the ability to piss without pain." Jake released her hand and took one step forward.

Ken swung the Taser his way and stepped back until his ass hit the counter. "Stay there."

Jake stepped forward once more. "Why won't you let us up? Did you hurt Miss McCain?"

"No. I never hurt her." A bead of sweat rolled down Ken doll's perfect face.

"If we find her and she's hurt in any way, you'll be the first one we look at," Jake promised.

"I didn't. I swear."

"What did you do?" Jake took another step toward the man. "You're hiding something. I can tell."

The sirens grew louder.

"No. I ... I just. No."

Jake moved so quickly, Libby couldn't catalogue all the moves. In a blink, Ken's own Taser was turned on him. He was wedged against the desk with Jake's body, and the projectile electrodes were pointed at Ken's throat.

"What did you do?"

"I took some money." Ken's arms flailed.

"Who from?"

"A guy. I don't know. I never saw him. It was over the phone."

"What did he pay you to do?"

"Keep people out of the apartment over the weekend. He said he was working on a surprise, and he didn't want it spoiled."

Libby reached for the wall to keep herself upright. This was real. There was no overreaction. This was no nightmare. Bile choked her.

The sirens bled through the front door as Owen ran through. His gaze locked on Jake. Owen reached for his sidearm. "Police. Hands in the air."

"No!" Libby threw her hands into the air. "He's with me."

Owen's shoulder relaxed.

Jake righted the Ken doll and then shoved him down into a chair. "You have cuffs?" he asked Owen.

"Of course." Gen's boyfriend grabbed the counter that separated the lobby and the elevator access, flung his legs high, and landed gracefully on their side. He pulled cuffs from a leather pouch near the small of his back and handed them to Jake. "What's the deal with this guy?"

"He took money from someone who wanted people kept out of Marlis's apartment. Said he never met the guy. I have more questions, but we've gotta move." Jake cinched the metal bracelets around one of Ken doll's wrists, clicking the metal as tightly as it would go. The other end he latched to the base of the counter, which pulled the guy low to one side.

Breaths wheezed in and out of Libby's chest. Every bad feeling she'd ever had in her life coalesced. Hair on the back of her neck stood on end. Cold sweat coated her skin. Knots formed well-knitted nests with her innards. Her knees shook, and her eyes watered.

"You can't leave me like this," Ken doll said from the awkward angle.

Jake ignored him and rushed toward her. His jaw was set. His eyes were narrow. He didn't try to comfort her with false promises but simply wrapped an arm around her back, pulled her to his side, and urged her ahead. Despite her wobbly steps, they moved through the corridor at a frantic pace to the bank of elevators.

Owen stabbed the call button.

Seconds stretched to an eternity.

She didn't dare look at the gaunt, ghostly expression on her face reflected in the sleek silver elevator doors. It told too much truth.

No one spoke. Every ear in there perked in tune with the elevator car's lumbering descent. Libby did her best to swallow the sickness stinging her throat. She averted her gaze to the ceiling, pressed her nails into her right palm, and squeezed the leather of Jake's jacket in her left.

Jake's dark gaze moved up and down the lobby meant exclusively for guests and deliveries. In fact, Libby had never come in this way. She'd always been with Mar and come in through the key-pass automated security entrance. "Stairs?"

"Her apartment is on the eleventh floor," Libby explained.

"Might be faster at this rate." Owen rocked on to the balls of his feet.

Jake squeezed her side. The gesture was simple, yet it focused Libby for the task ahead. Find Mar at all costs. She nodded.

Owen lifted his radio and said something into the static line. It was a code. She didn't know police codes.

Goddammit.

Someone on the other end gave him a 10-4.

Behind the shiny doors, metal screeched on metal. Slowly, the doors parted, and they rushed inside. The ride was just as silent, just as tense. More so with each passing floor. She hung her head in hopes the floors would pass more quickly. Fat tears she hadn't realized she was crying plopped onto the sealed concrete floor.

She could get through this. She would get through this. For Marlis.

Libby released Jake and straightened. She drew a deep

breath, rolled her shoulders, and stared the passing floors down like demons.

Beside her, Jake nodded. He pulled his gun from his shoulder holster, cocked it, and held it to his side. Owen's gaze narrowed on Jake, as though really studying him for the first time. The elevator dinged their arrival. Owen, the New York City Police detective, removed his sidearm and prepared for who knew what.

Why the hell didn't she have her gun? There was a madman tormenting her and now her friend. If tormenting was the only thing he'd done …

She hurried out of the car, taking the lead down the hallway to Mar's condo door. 1102. By design, there were only two condos per floor. They were stunningly modern and surrounded you with the best part of the city—the view—and minimized the worst parts—the crowds. The thing had cost her a mint.

"Shit. I don't have a key." Libby banged on the door. "Marlis!" She didn't like the full-fledged panic in her voice. She banged again. "It's Libby! Mar, open the door! Please!"

"I'll go get one from downstairs," Owen said before giving her knocks a second to garner a response. It was clear he didn't expect one.

Without a word, Jake holstered his weapon, pulled latex gloves from the inside pocket of his coat, and pulled them on. He crouched in front of the door and used a small tool to reach inside the lock.

"Who is this guy?" Owen asked.

"My neighbor."

With another thin tool, Jake pushed farther into the mechanism. He slipped it just so, then he turned the lock.

Libby pushed the handle and moved to enter.

Jake grabbed her arm and shook his head just once.

"Let us go first," Owen begged.

They had the guns. Jake had the killer instinct. Owen had the ability to heal. All Libby had was a cracking heart.

She motioned them ahead.

Jake stowed his tools, kept on his gloves, and grabbed his weapon.

The moment they opened the door, the scent of death crawled its unholy legs over her body like an army of spiders. They marched up her nose and descended her throat. She turned and retched but held back her fluids. This was a crime scene. Rage and fear mingled until she could take no more.

Owen's arm lifted back as though telling her to stay.

Libby surged forward.

Morning light poured in through the condominium made of windows.

Not a strand of linen was creased on the gray entry carpet. Not a pillow was out of place on the long, wide couch. Not a wet bar glass smudged. Not a paper edge of a coffee table book was dogeared. Not a fingerprint marred the walls of glass. Not a dish or envelop cluttered the kitchen counter at the far end of the room.

Yet something was horrifyingly wrong.

Marlis lay face down in the center of the living room.

The sallow of her skin. The lack of movement. The smell. They all said … death.

Yet Libby ran to her friend as though she could bring her back, as though she could roll back the clock, and thought she could right this inconceivable wrong.

A taut arm hooked around her waist, stopping her in her tracks.

Libby clawed and kicked. She screamed and elbowed. Her arms reached for Marlis.

Owen took three measured steps forward.

"Don't!" she screamed.

He didn't look at her. Instead, he crouched and placed two fingers at Marlis's carotid artery. His head dipped low. His shoulders dropped. Someone deflated the stoic man.

"No!" Libby's head thrashed. Her heart disintegrated.

She was pulled from the condo. She tried to fight. She tried to run.

Jake easily overpowered her, turning her and wrapping

her in his arms. He pinned her to him as though she were a child. Her fight turned inward, taunting her, hating her, ripping her apart. Marlis was dead because of her.

TWENTY-SIX

FLORESCENT LIGHTS BORE INTO LIBBY'S raw eyes, yet she couldn't block out their serrated reflection from the metal table. It burrowed deep, twisting the blade of pain that radiated from the bridge of her nose to the center of her brain. The burning sting was a welcome relief from the broken misery that started in her chest and radiated through her to the points of her fingers and the tips of her toes. Waves of its acute detonation still rippled out into the universe. The damage. Catastrophic. After what seemed like a lifetime of raging at the anguish, it won, taking even her ability to fight it. A gouged-out hollowness remained. The shell of who she'd been.

"Libby?" Jake's stalwart voice registered somewhere on the outskirts of her blinding headache. It was the first time he'd spoken since their gruesome discovery. Other people, so many other people had said things. They added letters together, combined consonant and vowel sounds, and formed garbled words and muffled sentences. The meanings she hadn't cared to discern.

Her head turned slightly to the right. His dark narrowed gaze was a foot away. Of course she'd known he was close. The width of his shoulders and the bulk of his muscle had gotten her from the 11th floor to this one. Whether it was the first or second, she didn't know.

"As your lawyer, I suggest you answer no questions at this time."

Libby saw the words form on Jake's full lips. She saw his tight jaw work. The rumble of his vehemence vibrated her eardrum, but not a single word made sense.

Questions? Whose?

His gaze shifted across the room and rose. Slowly, hers followed.

On the other side of the table, Owen sat with a notepad in front of him. Pages were splayed, and indecipherable symbols that might have been angry letters slashed about the lines filled half of the visible sheet. Next to him sat a man she didn't recognize. He wore a cheap suit and a gray-browed scowl that jumped up from behind the laptop on which he'd been clacking away. The man looked near to sixty, and either retirement or a heart attack.

How long had they been in the room? What had they asked her?

Trying to answer anyone's questions would be fruitless. Futility in trying to answer the thousand in her own head had shut down her system until this surreal moment.

Her gaze jumped back to Jake in search of something, but she didn't know what.

"You're a lawyer?" Disbelief filled Owen's voice. It brought her back around to the two men sitting across from her and Jake, as though they were suspects or something.

Her stomach quaked. She'd thought it had abandoned her along with her heart. No, it was very much still with her and very much about to erupt. She drew in a deep breath.

"If you're an attorney, then I'm the archbishop of the Catholic Church." The other man patted his chest. "And I'm Methodist ... on my good days."

"Who are you?" Libby was surprised her voice worked without releasing the bile churning inside her. It sounded reedy and thinner than one of Owen's notebook papers.

The strange man's brows shot high. His gaze slid to Owen's. The two exchanged a look. Libby shifted in her seat and straightened a little so that her back was no longer a crooked question mark.

"Like I said before, I'm Detective Rich Davies of the NYPD, Ms. Irish."

Special Agent Irish. When had he introduced himself?

But then, she wasn't an agent, was she? She hadn't even registered an introduction that had apparently already happened. Of course, she wasn't equipped to be an agent. At least, not now.

Jake pulled a wallet from an inside pocket of his leather jacket, taking the attention off her. He extricated a card from the leather billfold and handed it to Davies with one hand. It seemed an odd thing to do. The man typed something into the computer, and the room grew silent. Heartbeats passed. But none for Marlis. Her head dropped forward. It was then that she noticed Jake's left hand in her lap knotted in the center of her pale hands. She should feel something, but everything she felt hurt. Maybe that was why she didn't feel his touch. The absence of pain, even if in a small insignificant area, helped.

"It looks like I need to start the conversion process and find a big sparkly hat." Davies handed Jake back his credentials.

"Whether you check out or not," Owen said, "a man being a lawyer doesn't amount to much in my book."

Libby knew that to be true because of Perry Carter, but Jake was nothing like that conscienceless murderer.

"I'd like a moment alone with my client," Jake said.

Owen directed his somber gaze expectantly to Libby. She nodded. The two men stood and turned to leave.

"Take your computer with you, Davies." Jake's demand was complete.

The older man shuffled back and snatched the laptop off the table as though indignant that his integrity had been questioned. An angry hobble later, the door closed behind them.

Libby's breaths came in a rush as if waiting for the right moment to ambush her again. She pulled from Jake's hold and covered her mouth with both hands, limiting the amount of oxygen she ingested. With all the guilt and misery inside, there wasn't room for much else. When her breathing regulated, she found Jake's steady gaze on her.

"I have to tell them everything. I have to help catch Mar's …" She slapped her hand over her mouth, once more unable to complete the thought. Her head shook away the images—the horrible, haunting images. "I have to catch this monster."

Jake braced her face in his hands and shifted hers away from her lips.

"I need you to listen, Libby, and I need you to trust me."

Trust was such an extravagant commodity on a regular day. This day was anything but ordinary. A fourth of her cracked apart and slid into the abyss today.

"Please," he begged. Jake wasn't the type to speak, much less plead for a single thing.

"Okay."

"I will find whoever is doing this, and I will stop them." She searched his gaze for hesitation and found only certainty. "My ways are much faster than the cops or even the Bureau's." Jake's lips brushed her temple. His hands brushed back her wild hair, and then he stood.

"Are your ways legal?" She stared up at him.

"I'm a lawyer." He winked.

"That's not an answer." Every cell in her body felt world worn. The simple statement took all her focus.

"I know exactly which laws I'm breaking. There have been a lot of them. There will be more." He extended his hand to her. "That's my burden to carry, and I do it well. Let me take as much of it as I can now."

Libby stared at the calloused skin across his palms. She catalogued a series of thin scars that peppered the inside of his hand. The largest of them ran across the meaty part opposite his thumb. They looked like knife wounds or, maybe, glass. Whatever it was, it seemed not to ping on his radar. It was the hand of a warrior. His gaze was that of a warrior. A warrior was exactly what she needed.

She placed her hand in his and stood on weak legs. He caught her bobble and tucked her into the crook of his arm. After he steadied her, they headed out the door. Owen was nowhere in sight, but his new sidekick, Davies, jumped up from the wall on which he'd been leaning.

"We're done here." Jake ushered her to the right.

"Now just wait a—"

"Are you ready to charge me or my client with a crime?" Jake asked without slowing their steady pace.

"How about obstruction of justice?"

"Try again."

The hallway was lined with doors. Most were closed, but one down on the left was open. Beyond it, the hallway opened up into what looked like the atrium, the place they'd entered what seemed like a lifetime ago. In reality, she had no idea how long they'd been there. An hour? Three?

Behind them, Davies cursed.

Jake's strides didn't falter. He propelled them on toward the exit now in sight. They passed the open door. The security guard was cuffed to a chair in front of a computer screen divided into four grainy security feeds. Owen stood over him with his arms crossed over his chest. He barked a question she didn't catch. They marched on, at least Jake did. She moved only by his strength.

"Hey?" Owen's voice cut through the hallway.

Davies called something to Owen. She didn't know if they were in the slowest foot race ever or if the police were letting them go for now. Her gaze centered on the path to freedom. If only she could be free from her mind for just a few minutes.

They were ten feet from the lobby when Douglas and Beckett rounded the corner. Libby's eyes shut. It was her only form of defense against the ugly truth she was about to confront. Soon, they would know that Marlis was dead because of her.

Jake stopped, and she stopped too. Next to her, his muscles tensed. Her eyes popped open.

"We're not about to let you take Libby anywhere," Douglas announced. "We don't know who you are. From what I understand, all this began when you came into the picture."

Her eyes blinked open.

Beckett stood like a dark specter. His scarred face studied Jake without moving. He was dressed in regular clothes, but Libby noted the bulge at his hip.

"That's not true." Libby's voice boomed as if she hadn't been crushed; mind and spirit. She took a half step in front of Jake, blocking him from their line of sight. Part of him, anyway. "It all started after the picture."

Douglas's hand extended to her. "You'll be safe with us."

Jake's back blocked her view of the men. She chanced a look behind and found Owen reaching for his sidearm. In front of her, Jake relaxed, as though he was ready to strike.

"No!" Libby threw her arms around Jake's middle. "You, none of you can hurt anyone in here without hurting me more than I already hurt." Tears she thought were all wrung out spilled over her lids and rolled down her cheeks. A sob shook her.

He pulled her to his front and held her to his chest. One hand smoothed back her hair while the other caressed her back. A heavy breath hissed from his lips.

"I'm a contractor for The Trust." Jake's voice was low, but she'd heard every word. Though, once again, they made no sense.

She looked at Douglas and Beckett. The older man's shoulders relaxed. Beckett's dark brow rose.

"What the fuck does that mean?" Libby and Jake both turned to find Owen's hands plowing through his hair. His stance was wide and expression indignant.

She'd like to know herself.

"That he's trusted with things so critical to the country's success that even the president and the head of the CIA don't know about it," Douglas offered. "It also means that if he'd wanted Libby dead, she would've been dead already with zero suspicion on him."

"I've never heard of The Trust," Owen scoffed.

"I thought it was urban legend," Beckett countered.

"Says the Base Branch Agent." Jake shook his head. "Suffice it to say when we leave this circle, we'll never hear of it again."

Owen huffed an exaggerated breath. "And I thought my NYPD poker club was top secret."

Libby still didn't know exactly what being a contractor for The Trust meant except danger and secrets.

"We can all go to The Ashford," Douglas suggested. "We can talk, there's room for everyone, and after the fiasco last year, its security is tighter than The Metropolitan Museum of Art's."

TWENTY-SEVEN

THE IDEA OF THE ASHFORD and the reality of it were two different things. If she'd had the energy to fight the herd of men propelling her into the building she loved, then she would have run to New Jersey. She didn't know many people in Jersey, and that would be the whole point.

Libby sagged against the wall of the elevator as it rose into the sky. Gravity compounded, tugging her toward the ground harder and harder the higher they went. If only it were gravity. She could handle that. It was regret that crushed her lungs and compacted her spine. The knowledge that if she'd just told the girls the whole truth and given over to their overprotective ways, Marlis would still be alive. A wave of full-body chills rolled over her. Sweat clung to her cheeks.

The burn started in her throat and crept up her nostrils. She collapsed to her hands and knees. Her hair curtained her shame as bile thrashed its way from her stomach like demon spawn. She gagged. The eager warriors leaped to the far side of the elevator car. Not all. Someone gathered the hair from her face, exposing her. She longed to hide her face, but there was nowhere to go and nothing she could do to stop the onslaught.

Libby retched. Sickness spewed onto the floor, splashing her hands. Tears blurred her vision. The moving car stopped. The doors opened, and still she was helpless to stop her body's assault on itself. Jake's boots shifted in front of her, blocking her from the outside world. A hint of relief in the mire. With each retch, her intestines knotted tighter until they formed a painful ball. Then as quickly as it came, the convulsions ceased. Her entire body trembled.

Strong, insistent arms pulled her up and around the mess she'd made. There was no potential with which she could flee. All of her lay bare before him. Weakness. Vulnerability. Guilt. Disarray.

Jake turned her in his arms and braced her against his chest. The car was empty save for the two of them. Douglas and Beckett must have run at the first chance. She closed her eyes, desperate for some reprieve. He adjusted her, and she let him, though she had no choice. A cloth brushed across her lips and chin. She blinked to focus while he used a handkerchief to wipe down her arms. Douglas must have left it before he bolted.

Over his shoulder, she caught a glimpse of the girls. Well, of Gen and Larkin. All that ever would be of the girls. They clung to one another in the hallway outside Larkin's penthouse home.

She looked at Jake. He threw the spent cloth onto the floor and met her gaze. She wanted to bury herself in the crook of his neck and never come out. Her body shivered.

He held her tight and stepped toward the exit.

"No," she whimpered.

Jake stopped. He looked a question at her, but then it fell away. His fingers smoothed her hair back, and he cupped her face. "You have to face them."

Why did the truth always hurt so much?

"Libby, they love you. Let them."

Had he ever let anyone love him? If he said or did one more caring thing, he wouldn't have a choice. She'd love him, no matter.

"Wise words ... for a mute," she hedged.

The hint of a smile crooked his lips. "Let's go."

She hoped she could. He straightened her on her feet, but the weight seemed too great. Determination alone kept her upright. When she didn't hit the ground, he turned, grabbed her arm, and guided her forward.

Larkin clung to her father. Her sobs echoed in the pedestrian corridor. Beckett hung back, giving the pair space. Owen, who'd left Davies in charge for the time being, hugged Genevieve to his chest. The most stalwart of them, she held back the tears threatening to fall.

Jake's hold doubled on her arm, and he wrapped the other around her waist. Humiliation heated her cheeks. Shame drained her dry.

Douglas stepped away. Beckett and Larkin shared a look before he stepped forward and wrapped her in his arms for a quick hug. He'd been with Larkin when she'd found out, and he'd gone to get Gen and bring her to The Ashford before going to the apartments with Douglas.

Larkin's gaze met Libby's. Her friend smiled through tears and stepped forward. She beckoned Libby to her with frantic hands. Libby's grip cemented on Jake's arm. If he let her go, she might collapse. There was still the barest hint of a bruise on Gen's forehead where a madman had tried to kill her several short weeks ago. The girls didn't deserve this. They'd been through so much in the past six months. And … they would hate her once they knew everything she'd been keeping from them.

Gen stepped around Owen and joined Larkin in urging her forward.

"I'm so sorry, Libby. If I'd known what you would find." Larkin's head shook. "I'd have never suggested you go. I'm so s—"

"Stop." Libby lifted her free hand. "Just stop. Marlis is dead, and it's my fault."

Larkin's brow scrunched.

Gen pursed her lips and turned her head ever so slightly. "Did you stab her or strangle her?"

"Gen," Larkin scolded.

"Did you shoot her or do whatever it was that stopped Mar's heart from beating?" Gen persisted.

"No," Libby growled.

"Then it's not your fault," Gen whispered.

If only that were true. Libby shook her head.

"Yes, it is. Someone had been screwing with me for two weeks now. Ever since that fucking picture came out. I didn't say anything." Libby covered her sour mouth to block a sob. "I didn't say anything because I didn't want you guys involved. I didn't want you to get hurt."

Emotion choked her, and she gave over to it. She buried her face in her hands.

Jake slipped his hold from her back. As well he should. She deserved to be on her own in the sea of torment. Thin, nimble arms wrapped around her. Four of them. The scent of Gen's perfume overtook the vile burn in her lungs. Larkin's soft hair brushed her cheek, and the girls shored her up on her left and right. But something was missing. Someone was missing. They sobbed together in the center of the hallway for what seemed like forever, and then slowly, their sobs turned to hiccups which turned to shaky breaths.

Larkin kissed her head. She grabbed her hand and squeezed. "There's only one person responsible for this."

"Whoever it is, we're going to catch them and make sure they spend the rest of their life behind bars," Gen promised.

"No, we're not." Jake stepped into their little circle. He pulled her from the girls and pressed a chaste kiss to her lips. His gaze hung on her a beat. "I'll be back as soon as I can." He turned to the guys. "Take care of her."

Libby's instincts screamed that she could take care of herself, but that wasn't exactly true right now. Jake stepped onto the soiled, smelly elevator. He didn't flinch as the doors closed him inside and took him away from her and toward Lord knew what.

"That's your neighbor," Gen whispered.

He was her something.

TWENTY-EIGHT

TINY PAWS MASSAGED THE SKIN covering Libby's sternum until she rubbed puffy lids and blinked the dim room into focus. Her fingertips grazed silken soft fur and the tiny, delicate skull under thin skin. The kitten offered a mew. She settled it with a long, "Shhhhhhh." Her hands cupped the small animal to her chest. Its hair was damp at the ends. Libby's gaze roamed the room. A shadowy cityscape loomed through the wall of windows to her right. It was only then that she remembered where she was … and why she was in one of the condos Larkin was renovating in The Ashford.

Her face hurt. Her heart, well, it was inaccessible at the moment. She pulled the plush comforter up over her bare breasts and shoulders, tucking the kitten into a protective cocoon. Larkin had left her a large suitcase full of clothes last night, but she hadn't the energy to sort through them. It had taken her all to brush her teeth, strip, shower, and fall into the bed. Not for a second had she expected sleep to come, yet here she was, groggy in the early morning hours that capped the worst day of her life.

The mussiness in her brain cleared a step further. Libby grabbed the kitten and lifted him to her face. Sure enough, it was the same fluffy gray kitten Jake had pulled from beneath her home, the home that was terrorized by a psychopath. Confusion crowded close.

A light poured into the room from under the bathroom door. She lowered the kitten to her chest. Worry didn't have time to fully form before the door opened and Jake stepped from the steamy room with a towel wrapped around his waist. His hair was damp. Shaggy ends curled this way and that. His gaze found hers. The breadth of his chest spread on a deep inhale. He let it out slowly and then reached back. The light flicked off, allowing the ambient light pouring in from the city to bathe him in a hallowed glow.

His steps were silent, incongruous for such a large man. He strode to the side of the bed, dropped his towel, and slid under the covers. No missing him there. The bed dipped under his weight. Heat almost instantly radiated from him, warming the temperature several degrees.

Libby rolled to her side to face him. He did the same, bringing their bodies to within touching distance. The kitten, who'd been nuzzled between her breasts, curled under the edge of a pillow between them.

"Did you give him a bath?"

His large shoulder bobbed. "The grubby little guy needed one."

"How'd that go?" She'd never tried to give Killer a bath, but the mental images of how that would've gone made her shiver.

"He's pretty chill."

Yes, he was. The kitten snored lightly. Not at all concerned with another change of scenery.

"I brought you some clothes, but it seems your friends have that covered." He gestured to the massive suitcase near the closet.

"Thank you. I'd rather have my own things."

"No promises that I did any good."

"I'm sure it's fine." Unable to entertain their small talk a second longer, she blurted, "Where have you been?"

His chin lifted slightly, and his gaze measured her for several seconds.

"Hunting." His voice was quiet, but there was such strength in it.

She swallowed. There were plenty of times she'd been on stakeouts and tactical operations, but no one had ever referred to them in such a way. "Any luck?"

"Just eliminating."

"People or possibilities?" she whispered.

"People as possibilities."

Libby nodded. Disappointment and relief warred inside her.

"If I'd said people, how would you feel?"

Good question. She'd been about to ask herself the same thing.

"I don't know." She licked her lips and rubbed them together. "I guess it would depend."

"On?" He watched her as though her answer really mattered.

"Their culpability."

"Killing is killing, Libby."

What was he trying to say? He was a killer? Without a doubt, she knew he hadn't hurt Marlis. But others? Ones who deserved it. Libby knew there were people in this world who needed killing. If Jake was one who made that happen ...

"Killing is killing, if you live in a world of black and white."

"In what kind of world do you live?" His timbre rumbled.

"Gray."

Jake looked at her. His throat worked. He scooped a single hand under the kitten and moved him to the other side of her, tucking him under the edge of the pillow. The little guy didn't stir.

The same large, hot hand wrapped around her middle and pulled her under him. Every part of him was large and hot and hard. His thighs and forearms bracketed her, shielding her from sorrow and pain. The heavy length of his cock nuzzled her mound. His chest plumped her breasts, and their bellies connected. He pressed his forehead to hers while his entire body hugged her.

He stared into her eyes as though he wanted to say something. Surely, it wasn't the same thing she wanted to say, but would not.

I love you, Jake Ronin.

There was no surprise in her revelation. She'd obsessed over him for a year. He'd ignored her that entire time. But the moment he chose to let her in was the time she needed him most, and she'd never needed anyone. Needing meant vulnerability. Neither of them was the type to appreciate that core emotion.

She arched into him and pressed her mouth to his. He opened for her, letting her set the pace. Desperation, did it have a pace? She ate at his mouth and reached low. Her hands grabbed two handfuls of his taut ass and pulled him closer. His length strummed her clit. What was closer than skin to skin? She needed him inside her.

Jake's hands plowed through her hair, and his fingers bit hard into her locks. He pulled her head back, exposing her neck. His open mouth roamed her flesh, tasting and biting. Libby undulated against him. Her clit throbbed deeper, longer with each graze. Need slicked her thighs. She tried to part them, but his weight barred her movement.

"Please, Jake, I need you." She could have tempered her words by adding more; inside me, to take me. It was as close to the truth as she dared come.

The impetus in her voice must have worked. He lifted just enough that she was able to free her legs. She spread her thighs wide.

He captured her mouth a moment before he pressed the head of his erection at her opening and filled her completely with one weighted thrust. Libby grabbed his shoulders, held tight, and gasped against his lips. His gaze met hers and held. Their hips thrust and rocked in a frantic tempo.

In defiance of death, they grabbed hold of life and rode it into oblivion.

TWENTY-NINE

BEFORE THE SUN ROSE, SHE'D WOKEN. found an oversized FBI sweatshirt and its matching pants in the bag Jake had brought from her house, and dressed. If she hadn't already loved him, that was enough to seal the deal. There was no room for frills or cutesy when grief was so fresh. She hadn't even bothered to brush her hair but gathered it into a messy bun atop her head. The man she loved—wild and wildly—lay sprawled across the king-size bed with the gray ball of fur cuddled at the crook of his neck. Despite everything or maybe because of it, she stayed far longer than she normally would have, appreciating the simplicity and complexity of the scene before her.

She wiped her tired eyes with the backs of her sleeves and headed for the kitchen, pulling the door closed behind her. The space was freshly remodeled in gray and gold tones similar to Larkin's penthouse apartment. However, this space had a homier feel, where Lar's space was coolly modern. This one had greenery. Actual plants. It was large, taking up nearly half of whatever floor they were on. That bit was still fuzzy. The condo boasted four rooms, one at each corner with their own bathrooms. At the heart of it was a kitchen and living space out of a magazine. A home and garden kind. Not her friend's usual jam. She'd always been a Vogue type, whereas Libby didn't give a shit about any of them.

The scent of coffee and the hypnotic drip, drip, drip of brew greeted her before she stepped into the warm space.

"Couldn't sleep either?" Gen sat at a thick wooden table painted a country white in a large wicker chair that nearly swallowed her whole. She clung to a clay coffee mug as though it were her life raft.

"How long have you been up?" Libby pulled out another of the four chairs and sat.

"Three hours."

"How many cups have you had?" She pointed at the mug Gen drew to her mouth.

"Toooo many. Want one? I'm brewing a third pot and don't need to drink it all by myself."

Libby eyed the carafe. "No thanks." She crossed her arms over her belly. "I don't know if it'll stay."

"You have to have something," Gen said, unusually motherly.

"It's not even six a.m. I will … eventually."

"Libby?" Gen set her mug on the table and straightened.

"Gen," she breathed.

"You are not to blame."

She nodded, unable to speak without crying, and she was too exhausted to shed another tear.

"Dark roast. You know the way to my heart, woman."

Owen breezed into the kitchen, cinching the Windsor on his tie, and headed straight for Gen. He pressed two kisses to the top of her head and hugged her face against his chest.

On any ordinary day, her friend would have made a joke about a vigorous hand-job. Today was no ordinary day. Today, Gen's lip pursed, and she bit the inside of her cheek. Moisture gathered in her stunning green eyes. Libby averted her gaze to an oddly shaped light fixture and the naked bulb at its center.

"You're leaving already?" Gen sniffed. "You didn't get back until midnight."

"Lots to do, but not before I share a cup with you." The gentle smacking of a chaste kiss echoed in the space.

"Take mine. I don't need any more." Gen shoved the cup to the next empty chair.

"I thought your hands looked a little shaky." Owen sat and took a deep gulp. "And here I was prepared to deal with early onset Parkinson's."

He lifted her hand and pressed it to his cheek.

The condo door opened. Owen turned and reached for his sidearm in time to see Larkin round the foyer. She carried two paper bags from one of their favorite brunch spots. Douglas followed her with another bag. Beckett trailed him with yet another.

"I hope you're hungry." Larkin set the bags on the massive marble island, pulled paperboard takeout boxes from them, and separated them into stacks. "We have pancakes, waffles, bacon, eggs—sunny-side-up, scrambled, poached, Benedict—scones, hash browns, and orange juice." Her head swiveled up. "Dad, you have the orange juice, right?"

"Yes, I have the orange juice." He extricated it from the bag and set it next to her breakfast buffet.

"Beckett?" Larkin gasped.

"I have the rest here." He handed over the bag as though giving her something to do would help.

"We have syrup, jelly, jam." Larkin unpacked condiments and utensils from the bag. "There are napkins too. Knives. Forks. I didn't get spoons. I didn't think we would need them, but if we do, I can run upstairs and grab some."

The rest of them watched, stunned. She'd hardly taken a breath since she entered the room. Larkin was a woman about business. She was a calculated person not one prone to prattle.

She finally looked up and found them staring at her. "What?"

"Lar, pancakes? Syrup?" Gen squeezed. "You haven't eaten a simple carb in a decade."

"I know." Larkin slapped at a tear. She drew in a deep breath and let it out while shaking her head. "I didn't know what else to do."

"Then you're in the right place." Gen waved her over. "Bring those pancakes with you, and the bacon, and the eggs."

Beckett handed over the utensils and napkins.

"Thank you." Libby offered him a sedate smile. He winked, and then headed for the coffeepot. Only when he'd winked had she registered the scar that ran from the edge of his eyebrow down to the hinge of his jaw. When they'd first met him, it was all she could do to keep from looking at it. Now she only saw the non-perfect perfect fit he was for her friend.

Larkin stacked three boxes, lifted them, but then stopped halfway around the island. A high-pitched squeal eked from her throat. She dropped the boxes onto the counter and extended her arms toward something Libby couldn't see. A moment later, Jake entered the kitchen with the kitten in the crook of his arm.

"Oh, sorry. We couldn't leave him at the house alone."

She hadn't thought about Larkin's reaction to having a hairy animal in the newly remodeled condo. Hair. Litter. The occasional accident, if he had them. He was learning, after all.

"Of course you couldn't." Her friend didn't ask or acknowledge Jake's existence as she plucked the tiny animal from his grasp and pressed his cheek to her cheek. "Hello, precious."

Gen leaned over, pressing her mouth to the shell of Libby's ear. "You two have a cat together. When did all this happen?"

"It's complicated." Libby shrugged.

"You're welcome here forever and ever." Larkin hugged the cat to her chest and turned toward the group who watched her as if she'd lost her mind once more. She averted her gaze back to the kitten.

"I didn't know you liked animals," Libby offered.

"I didn't know I did either. I never had one growing up, and it never occurred to me to get one when I became an adult." She ran her hand over the puffy gray fur.

Beckett eased to Larkin's side, wrapped an arm around her shoulders, and rubbed the animal's head. "He's a scrawny thing."

"Can't be more than six weeks old. Freshly weaned," Jake informed.

"Where'd he come from?" Larkin asked.

"It's a long story," Libby hedged.

Gen perked up next to her. "We have some time."

Libby didn't want to tell them the kitten had come from the psycho who'd killed their friend. She didn't want to tell them about finding Killer in her fridge or nearly being taken. Jake's gaze met hers. He wore his standard jeans and a T-shirt, sans shoes. Still, his height surpassed Owen's and rivaled Beckett's who wore boots. Jake nodded, urging her on. For the next twenty minutes, Libby told them the horror story she'd been living, and the one she'd inadvertently spilled into their lives.

Larkin hugged the kitten close. Gen leaned forward so far that Libby feared she'd fall from her seat and catch her chin on the table during her descent. To their credit, they listened intently, not interrupting for any of the millions of questions that animated their faces throughout the awful tale.

A shrill ring echoed in the shocked silence that followed. Owen reached into his pocket and pulled out a cell phone. "I have to take this." He stood, but Gen grabbed his arm and pulled him back into his seat.

"We can handle it," she assured.

Could they? How much more?

Jake's gaze remained on her as he moved through the room. He grabbed a stool from the island, came closer, and set it next to her chair. After he sat, his fingers intertwined with hers at her shoulder. He didn't say a word, but then he didn't have to. His presence was enough to settle the worst of her jitters.

The collective held their breath and listened closely. Only Owen didn't say much. He listened like the rest of them. His upper lip curled.

"What about the other rooms?" he finally asked.

His head dipped. "Okay. Thank you, D." There was a pause. "Yeah, in about an hour." He added an affirmative before ending the call and facing the firing squad with a firm jaw and angry eyes.

"I spent last night calling in favors. Not that it'll prove to be much help. There was zero DNA on the body," Owen stated.

"On Marlis," Larkin corrected.

He dipped his head. "No disrespect. I was creating distance."

"We don't need distance," Larkin insisted. "Like Gen

said, we can handle it."

"Understood." He drew a deep breath. "Marlis had been cleaned postmortem. White fibers were found on her and through her home."

"White fibers?" Gen's nose scrunched.

"We found a match for them." Owen made an epic statement but didn't look pleased about it. Not at all. His jaw worked on a ball of irritation.

"Already?" Beckett asked.

"Yes," Owen offered with a grimace. "Most law enforcement and forensic agencies use the same brand of coveralls and booties to keep crime scenes from being contaminated."

Libby's brain fried.

"Do they believe it was from your crime scene techs or the killer?" Gen asked. At least one of them had firing synapses.

"Based on the amount of fibers collected, the killer. They were under her nails and in abrasions on her elbows and knees." He said the last softly as though it would alleviate the blow.

It caught Libby in the gut.

"She fought." Douglas's soft, respectful timbre bolstered the room.

Libby wiped away silent tears. "I'd hoped she hadn't seen it coming."

No one said anything to comfort her or any of them. They couldn't because they were in the middle of a real-life horror film.

"I'm going to question Ross Quinn today." Owen placed the phone in his pocket.

"Libby's boss," Larkin gasped.

"Yes," Owen said.

"He's not involved."

Every gaze in the room turned to Jake, including Libby's. How in the world could he make such a bold statement?

"Wait, what's your name?" Gen demanded. "I can't keep calling you The Neighbor. If you're going to say things like that, I need to know your name at the very least."

"Ronin." Jake offered his last name, not his first, and nothing more.

"How do you know Quinn isn't involved?" Beckett demanded.

"A man with his nuts in a vise will tell you anything you want to know." Jake's words were so cool, unaffected.

"He's kidding, right?" Larkin chuckled.

Douglas stepped around his daughter, coming close to the island. "What did he tell you?"

"To look at Joel Ornby."

The female collective groaned. They knew him well. Tales of him anyway.

This was what Jake had been doing last night.

"Quinn said that Ornby maneuvered to take Libby out in the academy, but she outperformed him in all areas. He's also been the most vocal during the viral picture fiasco and is the person who took the photo."

"And?" Owen pressed.

"He's a limp dick," Jake stated. "Sorry, ladies."

"Are you fucking kidding me," Gen swore. "We don't give a shit about foul language."

"Nope," Douglas assured.

"We want to know about that rat bastard, Ornby." Gen smacked a hand to the table.

"He cried the whole time." Jake's lips pursed on one side. "At least Quinn had a little fight in him." His head shook. "He admitted to taking the picture and circulating it in the inner-office newsletter but swears on his mom's life that he had nothing to do with posting them in the break room. He thought that was the only thing I was there about."

"And you believed him?" Libby asked.

"No, so I made him bleed." Jake rubbed a hand down his jeans. "After a few hours of mind games, he didn't break. Then I had a look at his records. High school. College. Entrance exams. He took five before he passed."

"That's not permitted," Libby protested.

"It is when your aunt is Senator Leslie Perro," Jake countered.

Libby's mouth gaped. Several gasps and groans littered the air.

"You, better than anyone, know that he can't tie his own shoes without help. He's not smart enough to carry out this elaborate of a scheme." Jake released her hand and cupped the back of her neck.

She leaned into his touch.

"Now what?" Larkin begged.

"Now we cross-reference the two scenes and analyze them to see what we missed," Owen said. "I'd also like to finger-print your house, Libby."

"My people did it," Jake offered before she could agree with Owen. "I'll get you the full report within the hour."

"Who are your people?" Larkin stepped forward with a hint of threat in her stance.

Beckett laid a hand on her shoulder. "He can't say."

She whirled on Beckett. "No." Her soft locks shook about her shoulder blades. "I can't handle another one of your kind."

"Is my kind so bad?" He pressed a kiss to her lips, barring her answer.

His kind. Libby stood and wrapped Jake in her arms. His kind was the best she'd ever known.

THIRTY

THE UNFORGIVING POINTS OF THE THORNS dug into Libby's palm and the meat of her fingers. Fat tears blurred the lines of the silver casket and the heaps of red roses atop it. Libby knew she had to release the flower she'd clung to at the viewing. The viewing. What a simple name for such an emotion-riddled event. Marlis's older sister procured the best makeup artists and hair stylists to care for Mar's body. She'd looked so pretty. Too pretty to be dead. They'd obscured the bruising around her neck and fabricated a sunny glow into her cheeks. Their work had done little to erase the images haunting Libby or her culpability in them.

Mar's voice echoed in her mind.

When will you girls learn to spill the beans before things get so bad?

"Too late," she whispered.

Her head hung, but she choked back her sobs. No one needed to see them. They were each dealing with their own grief. They didn't need hers.

"Libby. Babe." Larkin's arm looped through Libby's right arm. Her head settled in the crook of Libby's neck.

Another, softer form hugged her left. Gen nuzzled her head to the side of Libby's shoulder.

Libby held tight to the rose. "I don't want to tell her goodbye."

"We have to." Gen never held back, and for that, Libby was grateful.

She released the flower and grabbed her two remaining friends. They clung to one another in front of Marlis's grave and said their final farewells to the person they'd still want to call the next day, and the day after, and the one after that, until they joined her. In the depths of that sadness, Libby had hope. Hope they'd find the man responsible. Hope they'd one day not hurt so much. Hope that they'd grow stronger through this hellacious journey. It'd be what Marlis would want for them.

"Most of the family and friends have headed to The Ashford for the celebration of life." Larkin straightened. "We should join them."

All Libby could do was nod as she blinked back tears. The three of them turned away from the shell of their friend, held hands, and headed for the car. Douglas stood at the mausoleum's double doors. His smile was kind and knowing. It was just what they needed to lift their chins. He grabbed his daughter's hand, wrapped it in the crook of his arm, and walked with them out of the opulent structure.

Janney, Gen's assistant, waited with her husband at the marble edge of the entryway. Libby released her, and Gen rushed forward, greeting the sassy Irish woman with a huge hug. She, Larkin, and Douglas continued toward the limo at the bottom of the hill.

Owen stood beside the car with his hands clasped in front of his body. His eyes roamed the mourners who'd attended Marlis's service and now searched for or visited other loved one's graves.

The three of them quickly came to a plot of weather-worn headstones, some of the earliest in the cemetery's long history. Leaves rustled in the trees overhead, and a chill tickled Libby's neck. It was the first feeling besides sorrow. She welcomed it, and the first winter storm threatening the horizon.

"Go ahead." Libby released Larkin's hand and waved her and Douglas forward. No way was she walking on someone's grave.

They preceded her past some of the most ornate 19th century grave markers in Green-Wood Cemetery. She eyed the life-sized stone carving of an angel looking down upon a grave. Its massive wings arched toward heaven. Her feet slowed, and she read the name. Bagely. How long had it been since someone had read the name? How long had that person been forgotten? Judging by the smooth edges of the once sharp stone, it'd been decades. Would any of them be remembered?

She looked back to the large domed structure that boasted the name McCain. Marlis would be remembered. As long as Libby lived and breathed.

"I'm so sorry for your loss."

Surprise choked Libby. She'd been alone. Her gaze jerked left. Alec shoved off a tree trunk. He clutched a bouquet of wildflowers by his thigh.

"Oh …" Libby gulped a breath and blinked him into focus. She'd been jumpy since the discovery. It didn't suit her disposition or her social acumen. "Alec, hi."

"I didn't mean to startle you." He stepped over a root

toward her. "I didn't want to intrude earlier. There were so many people."

"Yes, Marlis was well loved." Hundreds of people had filled the church and spilled out onto the streets. Beckett, who'd insisted on running point for the event's security, had called the turnout a nightmare. Libby had thought the number fitting for a life well lived.

A life taken too soon.

"I can't believe it." His gaze slid past her toward the place where her friend would be entombed. "She was so young. Our age."

"I can't quite believe it myself."

"She looked beautiful."

Alec's words struck her like a glove across the cheek. Libby blinked at him. She hadn't seen him until he'd surprised her. Of course, she hadn't seen anyone but Jake and the girls through the ceremony. Looking at Mar's mother, sister, and brothers had been too much.

"I mean, they did a good job on her." He grimaced and smiled simultaneously. "That's what people say at funerals, isn't it?" His head shook. "I'm a moron. I don't know. I went to my grandmother's, and someone said it. I was seven, maybe." He hitched a shoulder. "As an adult, I've been to two now." His lips turned inward. "I didn't say much at the other one. I'm sorry."

"It's fine." She waved it off. "How are we supposed to act? What are we supposed to say? I don't know."

"You're kind." He stepped awkwardly forward. She hoped he wasn't going to give her the flowers. After today, she didn't want to see another flower except on her runs in the garden. If she would ever be free to run again. It was as if sorrow trapped her feet to the ground.

She must have been staring at the bouquet. He lifted it between them. "Oh, these. They're for Olivia." His chin jutted, gesturing toward the distance.

Libby hadn't been at the top of her game for the past few days. Thoughts came to her through a molasses drip. Words came even slower still. When she searched her memory bank for the name, she came up empty. Completely empty. She hadn't even gone to school K-12 with a person of the name. "Olivia?"

"Kate's mother." His gaze shifted to the right. "She's buried a little ways over."

"Kate, your ex-girlfriend, Kate?" Alec hadn't breathed her name since they split.

Alec nodded. His kind blue eyes narrowed and hardened so briefly had she not been studying him she would have missed it completely. It shouldn't have struck her as odd. Hell, when she thought about the first boy who ever broke her heart, she could still light a string of curses about it.

And that was the thing. His emotions were so even-keeled they were almost nonexistent. Emotions were made to be freed. If they weren't, they carved out your insides. Even when you released them, they often did damage.

That brief look into his angry heart startled her more than it should.

"I had no idea her mother died," she offered.

"A little while after we ..." He paused. "After she did what she did."

"Oh." How had he known her mother had died, if they'd broken up? Facebook was the logical answer. Not everyone severed ties. Though she'd expected Alec to, the way he never mentioned her again, as though she'd died. Through mutual friends was another completely valid option.

"She was such a nice woman." His knuckles whitened around the flowers, and his fingertips turned red. "It was such a tragedy. Kate wouldn't let me say a proper goodbye."

The anger in his eyes returned more acute than before.

Libby had no idea what to say. She shifted in her toe-pinching shoes, and for the first time since their conversation started, she searched the horizon. The crowd had thinned even more considerably. Only a few mourners hung around their vehicles, but they were so far away they looked like ants. Larkin's car still sat at the bottom of the hill only Douglas, his daughter, Gen and Owen were nowhere to be seen. Surely, they were in the car. Not that it mattered. Alec was her friend. She'd been alone with him plenty of times before. Though, not completely alone. They had always been at work or in public. They were in public now, and Libby's pulse really needed to remember that.

She forced a deep breath in through her nose and held it for a four count before letting it out.

"Oh." Alec took a half step back and half shrugged one shoulder. "I'm sorry. I didn't mean to make you think about Marlis." He blubbered a breath. "Not that you can help it."

"Family and friends are gathering at The Ashford." Libby pointed toward the car. Movement in the distance caught her eye.

"Thank you. I'd love to swing by after I pay my respects to Olivia." Alec smiled.

She'd meant the statement as an exit strategy, not an invitation, though one more person didn't matter one way or the other. He was a friend. She'd just run out of energy to entertain the simplest of conversations. That was it.

"Great." Libby bowed her head. "I'll see you later then."

Alec stepped closer and extended his arms.

Surprise held her ramrod straight.

They'd never hugged before. They'd never shown any affection before. They were friends … work friends.

His fingers grazed the side of her shoulders for the briefest of seconds before Alec's face contorted. He bent at the waist. His arm was wrenched high, where his head had been … and Jake's meaty hand was knotted around Alec's wrist. Jake's other hand torqued his hand in such a way she thought the thing would break off. He towered over the other man, dwarfing him in breadth and girth, and height too even if he wasn't hinged.

Alec held tight to the flowers. Not a sound squeaked out between his pinched lips. His knees hit the ground.

"Jake, this is Alec Keith. He's a friend." Libby flailed her hands in surrender.

Her lover glared down at the man in front of him. His gaze slowly took Alec's measure. "From?"

"Work," Libby gasped.

Jake's thick brow arched at her.

A sheet of ice formed over her skin.

Jake jerked Alec to his feet. "What are you doing here?"

Alec rolled his wrist at his side and glared at Jake, who placed himself between her and Alec. "Paying my respects."

"You could have done that earlier, like everyone else," Jake countered.

"There were a thousand people earlier." Alec shook the flowers so hard a few petals and a leaf fell onto the grass.

"And you're special?" Jake asked.

The line of Alec's jaw sharpened. His kind eyes turned cold, and then shifted to Libby. "I see you got yourself a guard dog."

"You see nothing," Jake whispered.

Alec's head canted. "Is he more than that?"

What business was it of Alec's? How dare he ask her?

Libby drew taut. "Thank you for your condolences, Alec. Have a good day." She turned and stalked toward the limo as much as she could without pitching herself down the hill. She could feel Jake behind her, blocking her from Alec's view.

Did he really think that sweet Alec could be behind any of this? Did she? Her head shook even as she walked.

When she crested the hill, she saw that Douglas, Larkin, Gen, and Owen sat on benches across the road under the shade of a tree that nearly leaned over its leaves were so gathered to one side. Beckett had joined the group. He stood guard behind Larkin. Or maybe he simply offered comfort. His hand entwined in her hair and rested atop her collarbone.

Libby reached for the limo's handle.

"Just a minute." Jake held out his hand, ushering her around to the other side of the car.

"What?"

"Wait with the others please."

"Why?" Libby was sad and angry and confused.

Jake's warm fingers pressed to her cheeks. He lifted her chin and pressed their mouths together. With that simple touch, the world stepped back, and her problem melted away. It was just him and her. She wrapped her hands around his middle and pressed their bodies together. His heat bolstered her. His touch lit her from the inside.

Too soon, he pushed her to arm's length and nodded toward her friends. She shuffled over; love drunk and bone weary. Gen pulled Libby onto her lap, hugged her tight, and pressed her head to her bosom.

"As soon as it's appropriate to ask for details, I'm going to need every last one of them between you and your hot, hot, hot neighbor," Gen purred loudly enough for the entire group to hear.

"Genevieve," Libby scolded.

"What? I didn't ask." Gen winked.

"He's hot, if you like that dark and mysterious look." Owen screwed up his perfectly angelic face.

The corners of Libby's mouth turned up. She patted both of their cheeks. "You two. Thank you."

Owen patted Libby's back, then draped an arm around Gen's shoulder and pulled her close, which in turn pulled Libby close too. Her gaze lifted to see Jake sliding under the edge of the limo in his full black suit. "What's he doing?"

"Checking for bombs," Beckett said.

Libby's head jerked toward the big guy. Her eyes bloated to the size of her head. "You're kidding, right?"

Beckett didn't bother to respond. He just looked at her.

"Wouldn't be the first, would it?" Douglas asked.

She bit her lips. Nope, it wouldn't be the first physical or metaphorical bomb this psycho had dealt them.

"I'm going to check under the hood." Douglas stood and headed for the car.

"Dad." Larkin reached for him.

He kissed the top of her hand. "I'll be fine."

"You better be," she warned as he walked away.

Jake better be too. If she lost him … She was ready for all this to be over, but she wasn't ready to lose Jake.

Owen's phone vibrated, and in an instant, all eyes were on him. He answered, stood, and eased to the far side of the benches, away from the limo. Larkin turned toward him. Gen did as well, shifting Libby. She stood and eased toward the limo. Whether good or bad, she couldn't handle any information on the case right this minute. The last they'd heard hadn't been great. No prints on Mar, nor in her home. No prints in Libby's house. Plus, they'd confirmed that her beautiful, warm, loving friend had been strangled to death after quite the struggle. The kicker had been that her building's security recordings had been erased by the stupid guard for a thousand dollars. Of course, he hadn't met the deal maker. It had shown up on the front desk in an envelope with the word favor written on the front.

They'd sent the envelope for testing. Not that they expected it to produce a lead. Libby didn't, anyway. Owen walked farther away, toward a clump of gravestones, pressing the phone to his ear and grabbing his hip as if it hurt a little. Before a minute had passed, both girls had stood and crept in his direction. Beckett hung back but followed the girls.

Libby watched Jake pop up from the ground and brush himself off. She met him near the rear of the car, expecting that if he'd found anything, he would have stopped her sooner. He offered her a heavy stare.

She'd wanted to know the answer to a question since she'd realized that she loved him. For better or worse, she needed to know if he helped her because he felt something in return.

"Why are you helping me?"

"Because I can." Jake leaned in and brushed his lips across her temple. "You all good?" he called to Douglas. The older man's hand popped up from behind the lifted hood with an OK signal. "The car is clear." Jake turned toward the rear door.

Never before had she been the pushy female. Actually, she'd always been the opposite. Never before had it truly mattered. Her hand shot out, and she grabbed his forearm.

"Why, Jake?"

He stopped. "Because I don't want to see you hurt." His large chest expanded. He huffed a breath.

"Why?"

She wanted him to say something about feelings and emotions, which was preposterous. They enjoyed the physical connection again and again, but wanting more was outrageous. He didn't do feelings and emotions. Neither did she … until him.

His arm dropped to his side. He shrugged off her hold and opened the car door.

Libby's feet rooted to the ground.

"All clear." Douglas gently dropped the hood and waved the others over.

Beckett and Larkin. Owen and Gen. The couples walked hand in hand from the benches and trees. Judging by the set of their heads, the news hadn't been strong one way or the other. It suited her today. There was only one thing she wanted to go one way or the other today. And it hadn't gone in her favor.

One at a time, the four slipped into the limo.

Still Libby's feet refused to move. Jake rounded the door, grabbed her hand, and pulled her along with him inside the car. He settled them on the rear seat and closed the door. The interior was darker and gloomier than it had been on the ride from the church.

Larkin and Beckett leaned into the open partition and spoke to Douglas. Owen held Gen's head to his chest, wrapped his arm around her, and whispered into her ear. Libby did not want to know what that conversation was about. It could have been about the case, but just as likely they were talking about butt plugs or handcuffs. So she stared out the window at the hundreds and hundreds of marked graves.

Jake slid his palm over her left cheek and pulled her to face him. His mouth met hers for a brief second, and then he pulled away. He was what she wanted. She stared at his dark eyes, long lashes, and haunted face, stricken by the mixture of joy and grief.

"What's wrong?" he breathed.

"You're weird and mysterious and stubborn."

His lips parted.

"And I love you," she added.

Any slack that'd been in his mouth screwed tight with the flexing of his jaw. A breath hissed out of his nose, and his head shook. He grabbed a handful of hair near his nape, and his feet shifted on the floorboard. After a second, he rocked forward, jamming both elbows against his knees. Still, his feet shimmied back and forth. The squirming bobbed his head.

Libby stared at him. If she could've laughed, she would've. It was ridiculous. The badass glared danger and death square in the eyes, but love rattled him. She turned back to the dead outside the window, hugged her arms across her chest, and embraced the emptiness inside.

THIRTY-ONE

JAKE PULLED BACK THE EDGE OF THE FLUFFY throw Libby had been hiding under since they'd left the reception. When Marlis's sister had revealed the Marlis McCain Foundation, her heart had been knocked clear out of her chest. Just kidding. It'd been missing for nearly a week now. Had it been there, the man with the dark eyes searching hers would have sent it packing.

"I'm going to question Alec."

All the sleepy sadness that had been pinning her to the sofa evaporated.

He replaced the cover over her cheek and straightened.

"No!" Libby threw off the small blanket and shoved off her side.

Gen jerked upright on the sofa across from Libby. Owen blinked the world into view and slowly sat up next to his lover. Larkin and Beckett rounded the corner from the kitchen. Douglas sat in the chair at the head of the seating area nearest the fireplace. He continued reading the newspaper in his hands, but his attention wasn't on it.

Jake stopped his retreat and turned in the middle of the living room.

"You can't hurt him," Libby commanded.

"I won't, unless I need to," Jake said.

"Who?" Gen demanded.

The man she loved reverted to a mute. Every gaze in the room landed on her. Especially Jake's.

"Alec Keith," she huffed.

"Alec, from work, Alec?" Larkin asked.

Libby nodded.

"He's a sweetie." Larkin walked farther into the living room, and Beckett followed.

"He's a suspect," Jake countered.

"Based on?" Beckett demanded.

Again, Jake locked down and waited for Libby to fill in the gaps.

Libby slipped her feet from the cushion, pressing them to the cold floor. She eased to the edge of the sofa and grabbed the edge to keep herself grounded.

"He showed up at the funeral to pay his respects," she explained.

"Did you see him at the funeral?" Jake asked.

"No."

"No, neither did I, and I was looking for him." Jake had changed out of his suit and into his usual jeans, boots, and leather jacket. He braced his hands on his hips. "He showed up at the cemetery and cornered her when none of us were around." His gaze sliced around the room before settling back on her.

Larkin's hand flew to her mouth.

Gen's gaze bloated. "When?"

"He didn't corner me," Libby defended.

A wrinkle furrowed Jake's brow.

"He startled me." Libby rolled her shoulders. Her traps were suddenly tight. "It was after we placed our roses on the casket."

"After everyone had left?" Gen asked.

"Yeah," Libby admitted. "He … was acting a little weird. Though he's never been the definition of social skills." The comment he'd made about Mar looking good had crawled all over her. She didn't dare share that tidbit. Jake would have him trussed up within the hour.

"What was he doing with the flowers?" Jake asked.

"You saw him?" Gen asked.

"I did more than that." Jake's jaw worked. "The crazy fuck tried to put his hands on her."

"He tried to hurt you?" Gen shoved to the edge of her seat.

"He tried to hug me. Jake brought him to his knees." Libby wrinkled her brow at Jake.

"Hmm?" Gen tapped manicured fingers to her lips as her gaze slid back to Jake. "You sure this isn't just jealousy talking, big boy?"

Libby was fairly certain it wasn't, but she wasn't about to get into the nitty-gritty of their non-relationship.

"What was he doing with the flowers?" Jake repeated.

"He didn't bring them for me." Libby brushed a hand over her shins and nearly hugged her legs to her chest but stopped herself. "He said they were for Olivia, the mother of a woman he dated last year."

"They're no longer together?" Douglas asked.

She shook her head.

Gray brows pinched, along with nearly every brow in the place.

"He said the mother was nice to him. She died shortly after they split, and he wasn't welcome at the funeral,"

Libby pressed.

"Jake should question him," Larkin declared.

"I hate to say it, but he's sounding more and more suspect." Gen sighed. "Who brings flowers to their ex's parent's grave?" Her hand tilted with the question. "Even if they'd been married," she added.

If they were right … "Owen should go. If he's the one, which he's not, it needs to be official."

"If he's the one, the only thing official about him will be his disappearance," Jake promised.

"I second that." They all turned to Larkin. Tears hung in her eyes, but her jaw was set. "Someone stole Mar from us. We'll never get her back, and they deserve no better. She was the best of humanity. They are the worst."

Gen stood. "If we allow this, then we're no better than that monster."

"I'm tired of being better," Larkin growled. "Look at what good it did for Marlis." Her tears fell in earnest, and she choked on a sob.

Beckett pulled her into his arms and nestled her face in the crook of his neck.

Jake turned to Owen. "Question him. Bring backup in case he's the one."

Douglas's mouth dropped open. Libby's would have too if she could have moved an inch.

Owen sealed a kiss on Gen's lips, stood, and grabbed his phone. His fingers were moving across the screen before he rounded the sofa. He grabbed his badge and sidearm and was barking orders on his way out the door.

"What do we do now?" Gen blinked up at Jake.

"We wait," Jake grimaced.

Gen stood and marched to the wet bar. Crystal clanked. Liquid poured. "Who wants one?"

Douglas's hand went up first. Jake nodded. Beckett did too.

Libby waved her off, while Larkin dried her tears, scooped the kitten into her arms, and collapsed onto the cushioned seat opposite her father. One hand cupped the small animal to her chest while the other stroked its puffy fur head to tail. With each pass, the worry lines in her face eased and the high draw of her shoulders fell.

Fiery red hair, voluptuous legs, a full rack, and four glasses of bourbon sailed past Libby and stopped momentarily at each of the men in the room. Without preamble or salute, they tossed back the fingers of liquor in turn. Gen followed suit, and then headed back toward the bar.

"Who wants another?" She wasted no time pouring herself another finger. After a pause, she added another to her glass.

"Want?" Douglas looked back and forth between the men. "I'm certain we all want another. Whether we need it is another thing entirely." He swatted the air and lifted his glass. "I'll have just one more."

Gen brought her glass and the crystal decanter half full with a dark ginger-colored liquid to the center of the room. She filled Douglas's glass with two more fingers and then stepped to Jake who still stood in the middle of the room.

"No. Thank you." He set the glass on the stone coffee table and walked to the wall of windows.

Coldness crept over Libby once more. She shifted to the back of the sofa, tucked her legs under her, and pulled the comforter over her shoulder.

"Half." Beckett's voice pulled Libby's sorrowful gaze up to him and Gen.

After adding the liquid he requested, Gen plopped on the sofa next to Libby and scooted close. "Sure you don't want one?"

"If I start, I might not stop." Libby rested her head on her friend's shoulder, drawing on her unwavering strength. Of all of them, she was the littlest and the mightiest.

"What's wrong with that?" Gen sipped her drink.

Libby just threw a grimace in Gen's direction.

Gen poked her tongue out at Libby. "Spoilsport."

"What's this precious guy's name?" Larkin hugged the kitten close and centered Libby in her gaze.

Again, Libby just stared. No, she bobbed a shoulder and possibly gave a shake of her head.

"Jake?" Larkin swung her gaze behind Libby. "Does the kitten have a name?"

There was a beat of silence before his deep voice rumbled. "Nope."

Larkin held the kitten in the air in front of her and studied him. A smile lifted her cheeks, and she hummed. Then she nodded. Her smile grew.

"What's his name?" Gen begged.

"Xanax." Larkin beamed.

Libby shrugged.

"If the cat is that calming, I might need one." Gen sipped her bourbon. "Or twenty," she added. "Is that why crazy cat ladies have so many cats?"

"More than four cats and I'm pretty sure it has more to do with the lack of an actual Xanax prescription or something stronger," Libby chimed. She hadn't expected to add to that conversation, but just like that, life continued no matter how you hurt.

"It seems a fitting name." Beckett scooped Larkin up from the seat, took her spot, and settled her onto his lap. He kissed her forehead and then scratched behind Xanax's ear. The kitten mewed at the big guy. A sweet smile stretched Larkin's lips.

"How did Kate's mother die?"

The question came from behind Libby, also known as left field.

Once more, Jake turned each pair of eyes in the room

toward him. Silhouetted by the low-leaning sun and the cityscape, dressed for covert battle, he'd never looked more delicious. The question that'd come from his lips shackled and caged her libido.

"The ex-girlfriend's mother?" Gen asked.

Jake nodded. His keen gaze narrowed on Libby. Discomfort clung to her like a bad outfit. Not from his gaze but from his question. She hated where answering it might lead. He patiently waited.

"I don't know." Suddenly burning hot, she shrugged off the throw. "I didn't know she'd died until he told me this afternoon. He never mentioned it, which I thought was odd. Then again, he never mentioned Kate. One day, he turned the Kate switch off, and he never said her name again."

"She cheated on him?" Larkin slipped the heels from her feet, letting them fall haphazardly to the floor.

"Yes, for a few months before they broke up, with a guy she dated in high school," Libby explained.

"How'd you find out?" Gen inquired.

"Alec went from saying, 'Kate this or Kate that. Kate. Kate. Kate,' with every breath to not saying it at all. I noticed immediately but didn't say anything, thinking things would go back to normal. They didn't. After a couple of weeks, I asked what was going on, and he told me."

Jake walked from the living room down the hallway toward the bedroom they'd shared for the past two nights. Libby stared after him, listening for any noise that would give her a hint as to what he was doing.

"He's not going after Alec, is he?" Gen grabbed Libby's arm and tugged. "He told Owen to go. He can't show up and put Owen in that position. Owen is a lawman, first and foremost."

Beckett stood, lifting Larkin up with him, and set her back in her spot.

Libby's intestines dropped into her feet. If Beckett confronted him … If the two giants got into a fight … She swallowed, but nothing moved inside her throat.

The heavy tread of boots heralded Jake's return. He stopped short of the wet bar. His gaze cut to Beckett and then to the girls' faces.

"Chill, I'm not leaving. Not yet, anyway." He lifted a thin laptop that she hadn't noticed into the air and gave it a shake before he headed to the sofa across from her.

Love … a man repellant.

She kept from rolling her eyes but just barely.

He opened the matte black machine and typed and typed some more. Beckett sat on the arm of the sofa near Jake. His eyes bulged.

"Eyes on your own paper." Jake turned the computer screen away from Beckett.

"How do you have access to that database?" Beckett's mouth hinged. His chin jutted. "I have to go through an ocean of requests and red tape just to get narrowed, mostly redacted reports."

"It's safer that way." Jake offered him a wink.

Safer. Was he in danger?

She gripped the hem of the throw and twisted it in her hand until her finger went numb.

He typed some more and then finally looked at her. "What's Kate's last name?"

Did he have nothing else to say?

I like you, Libby. I'm fond of the time we spend together, Libby. I really am feeling things I've never felt for anyone else, Libby. I love you, Libby.

Gen's elbow met her ribs in a sharp jab that had nothing on the pain she felt for so many other reasons. "Libby!" Gen hissed.

"What?" she growled.

"Kate's last name." Gen pointed at Jake.

Since when was she on his side?

"Archer," Libby barked.

Gen grabbed her hand and pulled it into her lap. Her friend smoothed her soft fingers over her knuckles. "Hey," she whispered.

Libby met her gaze.

"What's wrong?" Gen mouthed.

She pursed her lips.

"Beyond the obvious." Gen's lips created the words without a hint of sound.

Libby almost denied that anything was wrong, and then she thought about the reason they were all together. She let her gaze slide to Jake.

Gen caught her face and lifted it to meet her gaze once more. "Give it time," she breathed. "He obviously cares deeply for you."

"Obviously?" Libby scoffed.

"Very obviously." Gen smiled.

"Gen." Jake's voice jerked them to attention.

"Yes?" Gen coughed.

"You might want to grab that bourbon and get pouring." Jake slid the computer across the sofa toward Beckett.

"Why?" Larkin scooted to the edge of her seat.

"Fuck me." Beckett's head shook.

Libby jumped to her feet. The throw dropped to the floor. "What is it?"

Jake stood and cleared the distance between them in one large step. His hands wrapped around her shoulders. "Olivia Archer was murdered."

THIRTY-TWO

"HOW?" LARKIN'S VOICE CAME FROM FAR AWAY.
"No." Libby couldn't stop the shake of her head. "Please, no." Back and forth. Back and forth. Back and forth. If Alec was the one who'd taken Marlis away, Jake wouldn't have to kill him because Libby would do it herself.

Jake pulled her to his chest. Through his thin cotton shirt, heat burned her cheek. The strength of his grip kept her upright. And she thought she could kill someone.

Ha. You can't even stand on your own two feet.

"Beckett, how?" Larkin repeated.

"Strangled to death in an apparent robbery." The man's deep voice burrowed into her brain and ripped it apart.

Aside from the robbery, it was the same manner of death Marlis had suffered.

"Suspects?" Gen demanded.

"No prints or suspects in the crime. The investigation is still open." Libby closed her eyes against Beckett's voice. As if that would help stem the flow of information.

"Owen needs to know." Jake's voice vibrated his chest and her cheek in turn.

"I'm on it." Gen sounded so strong, so sure.

The only thing Libby was sure of … well, he wasn't sure of her. Why should he be? For all her badge and badassery, she was frightened and dependent. She'd pushed herself through high school, college, and the academy when a minimum wage job and teen pregnancy was all that'd been expected of her. She'd dominated at work when every man expected her to crumple and quit. She had a home and friends who loved and supported her. What did any of it matter? She was the same scared little girl she'd always been. Fear of losing her friends' approval, her parents' shock, and her career held her prisoner.

Jake turned them and sat, pulling her into his arms. He settled the throw over her. She burrowed deeper into his protective hold, deeper into oblivion. It wasn't sleep as much as it was a complete system shut down. As if in defense, her body flipped the switch to auxiliary power. It only ran the most vital of functions. Voice. Vision. Thought. They vanished, and darkness took hold.

For how long?

No idea.

Something shifted. The air? The tension? Jake? The next thing Libby knew, she rubbed her face against the soft cotton of Jake's soft T-shirt, brushing the hair back from her face, and blinked Owen into view. Gen wrapped her arms around his neck and pulled his face down for a kiss that went on so long that Libby averted her gaze. Douglas had vanished, but Larkin curled into a ball on the same chair she'd been sitting. Her eyes were closed, and her chest moved in the slow, steady cadence of sleep. Xanax nestled himself in the crook of her neck, joined in slumber. Beckett was passed out at the end of the sofa nearest Larkin. His thick arms were crossed over his chest. Long legs stretched out farther than the coffee table, and his mouth gaped at the ceiling.

Her gaze rose. Jake's dark, content gaze settled on hers. How long had he been awake, holding her, watching over her? More than ten minutes seemed like a level above duty. She stole her gaze away and found Owen and Gen still by the door. The hot display of tongue-on-tongue action subsided.

"So?" Libby tried the word, but it came out more like a croak. She coughed and tried again, more successfully.

Beckett jackknifed on the sofa. He perched on the edge, his back ramrod straight and his gaze searching for an enemy that was absent.

Everyone saw, save for Larkin and Douglas. No one said a word.

A few breaths later, Beckett scrubbed a hand over his face. He slipped from the cushion onto his knees in front of Larkin. His hand gently cupped her face. She bloomed to wakefulness like a daisy to the sun; smiling and bright. Her blue gaze blinked her lover into view. Her smile brightened to a beam until her eyes shifted, taking in the whole room. Realization dimmed her. She jabbed an elbow into the arm of the chair and straightened.

All of them gave the detective their attention.

Owen's head shook. "His apartment was empty."

Hope died nearly as brutally as her friend had.

"He wasn't there?" Gen asked.

"Nothing was." Owen pulled the tie loose around his neck and unfastened the button below his Adam's apple. "I spoke with the landlord, who said he turned in his key yesterday."

"Any forwarding address?" Larkin's question was hopeful, but didn't she know they lost hope like a severed artery lost blood?

Owen yanked the tie from his collar and tossed it onto the back of the sofa. His head shook.

"What about the office?" It wasn't hope but practicality that made Libby ask. Damn her, she was hopeful in spite of everything.

"Quinn was more than eager to answer my questions." Owen eyed Jake. "Thank you."

Jake didn't bother with a response.

"I expect it would have taken a court order and a decree from the Almighty to get him to speak otherwise." Owen slipped his hand into Gen's. "Alec took off half a day Friday and hasn't been back since. He said after two days and two no-shows, he would have called the police to report it, but that he received a call from Alec Keith this morning, stating that he was deathly sick and would be out the rest of the week."

"Sick in the head," Larkin hissed.

"What is he up to? What's his endgame?" Beckett asked the question everyone had been thinking. The question to which no one knew the answer, save for Alec himself.

"I've submitted a warrant to Judge Weir. As soon as it's approved, we'll pore through his records to see if we can track his movements. Plus, his image will go out to all state and local jurisdictions." Owen scrubbed his free hand down his face. "Until then, we're hamstrung. Unless you have an idea of where he might be."

Owen sized up Libby.

"No." She grabbed her head and racked her brain for any ideas as to Alec's location and came up blank. "I don't know. If I did, I'd go myself."

Jake's grip around her waist tightened.

"Not a chance." Gen glared.

"Until further notice"—Owen motioned between Beckett and Jake—"if you see him, detain him, by force, if necessary. Ladies, if you see him … run."

Gen nodded.

Larkin's gaze narrowed, and her upper lip curled.

Beckett's neck snapped in Larkin's direction. "Run."

His low-growled demand left no room for rebuttal. After a moment's reluctance, she nodded.

"I suggest we try to get some sleep. It'll take at least three hours to get the warrant and then it'll be more waiting." Owen tugged Gen toward their bedroom. Her friend didn't bother looking back. She simply followed.

Larkin scooted to the edge of the seat with the kitten in the crook of her right arm. Beckett stood and offered her a hand. She took it, stood, and smiled wanly at Libby. "If he knows what's good for him, he'll be halfway to Mexico by morning. But it won't matter. We'll catch him and put him away for the rest of his life with a man named Bruce as his cellmate."

"Night, Larkin." Libby's fingers flicked in a makeshift wave.

"Night." Larkin and Beckett and the kitten left the condo and locked the door behind them.

The sealed door made Libby doubly aware of Jake. Heat, his heat, formed a protective barrier around her. His breaths whispered past her neck. The thunk, thunk, thunk of his heartbeat echoed the beat thrumming between her legs. She didn't dare look at him, nor ease her cheek back to his chest.

"Where's Douglas?" Libby eased off Jake's lap and onto the cushion.

Her back faced him. She placed a hand over her mouth to keep from asking him to join her in bed. The touch of his skin to hers made everything else fade away. No matter how horrible or ugly. Sure, she wanted to embrace the void, but more than that, she wanted Jake.

"In his bed." Jake's voice was closer than she'd expected. His breath caressed the highest point of her shoulder, where her black dress scooped. "He knew Owen wouldn't find Alec tonight. He knew what to expect." The end of her long hair tickled across her shoulder and neck as it fell down her back. He settled her hair to the right side. "I didn't."

The wet press of his lips sizzled at her nape.

Her head dropped forward.

"I never expected ..." Jake's lips rubbed down her spine.

Libby's fingers couldn't stop the question from slipping through, no matter how hard they pushed.

"What?" she gasped.

"You." He kissed each vertebra until his lips were stopped by the fabric of her dress.

Libby held still. If she moved, if she breathed, if she allowed her mind to process his words, they would only hurt that much more in the morning.

"I should have trusted you." She dropped her hand from her mouth and gripped the hem of her dress. "I should have let you get Alec."

If he'd gone, he wouldn't be here right now, burning her skin with his lips.

"I don't want to hurt you, Libby."

Then love me.

Everything inside her wanted to scream it, but she wouldn't. "I know." Really, she knew he didn't intend her any harm. He'd saved her life. He'd supported her so much. "You tried to stay away."

"Libby." Her name was a moan. The flats of his hands spread over her traps. His forehead centered on her nape, and his head rolled slowly back and forth. He sighed.

She stood, grabbed his hand, and led him to the bedroom. The fallen night filtered in through the windows, casting haunted hues in the space. Her bare feet stopped near the end of the bed. Behind her, the door clicked closed. She gripped the zipper of her dress and pulled. It gently scraped from her shoulder blades to the dip above her butt. Cool air breezed over her skin, drawing gooseflesh to the surface. After shrugging it off her shoulders, the sturdy material dropped, baring her breasts to the chill. She shoved the dress and skimpy panties over her hips. The material pooled at her feet. She kicked it away and turned, completely stripped of everything; clothing, ego, expectation.

The spark of need she'd sensed in Jake on the sofa burned like a ceremonial pyre behind his eyes. His nostrils flared. The dark centers of his black-brown gaze dilated, making him look more demon than man. His hands hung loose at his sides as though he were ready for anything.

When he looked at her, it made her feel invincible in a way she never did before. What a discord. Because he could and would hurt her unlike anyone before. A smile tickled her lips. The entire situation was absurd.

How ironic. He was fully clothed, ready for battle, while she stood before him more vulnerable than ever before. She loved him, and he wasn't about to allow himself to be defenseless.

"Strip." She couldn't demand that he love her, but she could insist upon this. "Everything off."

She expected him to comply at warp speed. Of course, he worked on his own schedule, removing clothing as though she were his executioner and not his lover. In his mind, maybe they were one and the same. Once again, her lips curved when they had no right. His resilience, his independence, his tenacity; they were the things she loved most about him. They were the things she'd miss most about him. When he grabbed his shirt in one hand and yanked it over his head, she second-guessed what she loved most.

The delineation of his abdomen, the swell of his pecs, the slopes and ridges in his shoulders all vied for first place. His hand gripped the wide belt, jerking the end back through the buckle. Leather snapped. Libby's mouth watered. He unzipped the jeans and shoved them down with his boxers, freeing himself from the last stitch of clothing. He stood proud and hungry.

Libby stood her ground. For a long time, they studied one another. With each passing second, her desire multiplied until it slicked her folds and reddened the eager points of her nipples.

Jake gulped the distance between them with one step. He grabbed both hands and lifted them high. His tongue slicked over the pad of her middle fingers. Teeth nipped from her sensitive skin between her index fingers and thumbs. Wet heat enveloped her right index finger and weakened her knees. Libby slicked her lips. She eased forward, grazing his abdomen with her breasts.

He sucked her digit to the tip until it popped out of his mouth. His eager lips framed her pinky. The sting of his tongue lashed at her palm. Sexy noises of raw desire ricochet off her, showered around her, and somersaulted inside her. When he slipped it between her fingers, the arches of her feet tingled.

"Jake," she gasped.

As though she'd said nothing at all, he continued tuning and strumming her to his whims. With each movement of his mouth, she performed like a well-tuned instrument, rubbing against him, keening. And he was the first chair. The only chair.

Each stroke of his tongue forced her to wiggle and writhe. Why women wanted a thigh gap, she'd never know. Her full thighs abraded her clit with each jive and thrust of her hips. Moisture slicked the inside of her legs, coating her swollen lips and aching folds. Her head thrashed. Her core shook. She quivered on the edge of coming stroke after stroke. Then obliteration. Pleasure popped like a sky of firecrackers behind her lids. Each explosion rippled through her entire body. Her breaths grew heavy and spiked in pace until they ceased altogether.

He buried his face in her hands and held her up with his grip.

She felt as if she held his soul in her hands. It was dark, troubled, and stunningly gorgeous. Emotion stung her throat.

Libby pulled his head low and burrowed her forehead against Jake's. Something fragile and profound passed between them for what seemed like forever. Even forever with this man would be tragically short.

His fingers gripped her hips. Her feet left the ground, and she wrapped her legs around his waist. He drove into her without preamble, locking their bodies together in the most perfectly solved puzzle ever known. She kissed his lips, sucking his breath into her lungs and holding on tight.

A tear slipped down her cheek. It hit her fingers and slid lower, dripping onto his face. He growled. His arms coiled around her middle, and he hugged her close.

She felt him in her belly. She felt him in her heart. She felt him in every cell, tainting her, ruining her for the world.

Libby arched and bowed. Jake matched her move for move, and then every muscle in his body went rigid. His heat spilled into her, filling her. She rocked on his wet length and cried her orgasm against his lips.

"Lib." He sighed.

His mouth slanted over hers. She sucked his lower lip into her mouth and tangled their tongues. He secured an arm around her waist and grabbed the back of her neck, as if possessing her. He did. No question. She was gone. Owned. Every part of her belonged to him whether he wanted it or not.

He walked them toward the bed. The world tilted; not that it'd been on a proper axis since Jake Ronin had come into her life. His weight pinned her to the mattress. Their mouths knotted, but his hands, his gentle hands mapped her face. She savored each kiss and every touch, cataloguing them in her brain to analyze and enjoy later.

Jake shifted his hips in a leisurely in and out.

She slid her fingers along his jaw, down his neck, and over his traps. They settled in the groove of his spine. The puckered skin tickled her fingertips. She'd seen the scar that ran from his nape to the base of his dimpled ass several times but had never touched it. Now, the temptation was too great. It was the most mysterious part of him that she had the possibility of ever accessing. Libby rubbed her fingertips over the traumatized skin as though she were reading Braille. As with the raised text, Jake's spine told a story of pain and fear. Beneath the knurled scar, a metal structure made of bridges and screws lined a small portion of his spinal column near the top. Another set of manmade frameworks bordered two more sections of his spine.

What have you been through, Jake?

Her arms wrapped around him. He was so strong, and he'd clearly been through so much. She'd been so willing to lean on him, but who did he have to lean on?

"I love you, Jake."

It hadn't slipped out. She'd meant for him to hear it. Whether it ruined the mood or not, she wanted him to know that if he wanted her, she was his, here for him forever.

The tempo of his thrusts ramped to a high point that stole her breath. His body slammed against her nearly to the point of pain. He buried his face under her neck and pumped furiously.

"Let me in," she begged. Libby wasn't one to beg, but he deserved it. He deserved someone to fight for him. After all, he'd fought for her.

His teeth sank onto her clavicle, and hot moisture slicked over her neck. For a moment, she thought blood, but there was no pain. He growled, but emotion chopped off the edge.

Tears?

She couldn't imagine it.

Libby held him tight and rode the heinous waves of his emotion and lust. His body scuffed hers. Hot breaths shot over her breasts. Frantic strokes of his cock drove her toward an orgasm she hadn't expected. She grabbed it as boldly as she grabbed Jake and screamed her pleasure and misery.

Jake gnashed a stream of curses. He thrust into her one last time and filled her completely. He collapsed atop her. Breaths heaved in and out of his chest. They rocked her. He'd rocked her. And now what?

THIRTY-THREE

"COFFEE?" LARKIN EXTENDED A RECYCLED paper cup with a re-cycled bamboo lid to Douglas.

He stopped midway out the door of what had become their home base over the past few days. His feet remained, but he canted his head and stared at his daughter. Thick salt and pepper brows pinched. His gaze scanned her up and down.

"What?" Larkin laughed. "It's just coffee."

The corner of his mouth hitched. His gaze slid to Beckett and narrowed.

"I don't have anything for you." Beckett sat across from Libby. He laid muscled forearms on either side of his breakfast, blocking the older man's view of half-eaten waffles, crispy chicken, and drizzled syrup.

Libby's stomach turned at the combo, that and the distance Jake had kept between them this morning.

"There's plenty more." Jake, who stood behind the island, shoved a paper bag toward Douglas.

"Thank you." Larkin grabbed the bag by the handles. "Yes, take it with you."

"No." Douglas smiled at his daughter. "I've already eaten and had plenty of coffee." He blew her a kiss, then his gaze slid back to Beckett. "Don't let her out of your sight."

Beckett dropped all pretense of a joke and turned to Douglas. "Never."

"Good." His smart gaze turned to everyone else in the room. "We've doubled our security staff. Everyone's seen his picture, and it's been scanned into the computer. If Alec shows his face on the security cameras in or around this building, we'll go on lockdown. You're safe in The Ashford. I'm going to make sure of it."

They all knew this. He'd told them in their don't-leave-the-building speech earlier, but Douglas was nothing if not thorough.

"Thank you, Dad," Larkin beamed.

Douglas blew her a kiss and closed the door behind him.

"I don't think my own father ever forbid me from leaving the house." Gen stabbed a quarter of a strawberry with a fork and placed it between her painted red lips.

"Maybe he should've." Libby shoved the leg of her friend's stunning blue pantsuit.

Gen's leg slipped off her knee and fell to the ground, jarring her.

"No maybe to it." Gen forked a grape, the last of her breakfast, and launched it at Libby.

Snapping a hand up, she caught the purple fruit in midair and popped it into her mouth.

"How'd you do that?" Gen tossed her fork into the

tray and dabbed the corners of her mouth.

"Cat-like reflexes." Libby winked.

"Meeeow." Her friend leaned over, kissed her cheek, and then grabbed her container and stood. She sashayed past the island to the garbage can. Owen's gaze tracked the progress of her ass.

"Who else hasn't eaten?" Larkin harped over the bag of unused food.

"Did you eat?" Libby asked.

Dress-clad shoulders perked. "I will." The pale pink fabric of the simple shell looked especially pretty against Larkin's skin today. She was usually pale and had been especially so lately, but a fresh glow warmed her cheeks to a natural rose. "With everything, I haven't felt like eating until lunch lately."

"And all I want to do is eat." Gen booty bumped her.

"That's not all." Jake chuckled under his breath.

Libby covered her mouth to pin back laughter. It wouldn't be stopped. After their own soul crushingly, beautifully, awkward lovemaking, they had listened to Gen scream and moan for quite a while before being able to fall asleep.

Owen's cheeks burned bright red. He stared at his coffee cup with a callow grin he tried to hide between clenched lips. It didn't work.

Larkin joined in with a chuckle of her own.

They were only missing Marlis's laugh.

Libby straightened and tugged the edge of her over-sized sweater over her knees.

"No, that's not all." Gen puffed her chest and lifted her chin. "Which is why I can still fit into my work clothes." She grinned. "For the record." Gen swung her luscious gaze to Jake but pointed back and forth between herself and Owen. "We may have gone longer, but you two are the loudest people I've ever heard fucking." Gen might have swung a finger between her and Jake, but Libby wouldn't know. It was her turn to stare at a coffee cup with burning cheeks.

A knock sounded at the condo door. Libby jumped, shifting from embarrassment to fear in an instant. Jake's hand moved to his sidearm. Beckett jumped to his feet.

"Stand down, militia." Gen raised both hands palm out. "It's Janney. She's escorting me to work." When Larkin's mouth opened to speak, Gen gave her the shush gesture. "Along with Owen, who'll head to the precinct only after I'm safely locked in my office."

Owen stood, leaving Libby at the breakfast table by herself.

Jake stepped around Gen, blocking her way to the door.

"Hey." Her fiery friend shoved at his large back.

He looked down over his shoulder at her. "Better safe than sorry."

Gen nodded sheepishly and motioned him ahead.

Jake stepped to the center of the door and opened it, blocking the rest of them from whatever was on the other side; a bad guy, a bullet. Libby jumped to her feet. He didn't need to do that for her. No one did.

"Oh Lordy." Janney's familiar Irish lilt filled the room, even with her still in the corridor. Jake stepped to the side, and Janney clutched her chest. "I'll never get used to you. So big. So hot."

"Janney," Gen scolded.

"What? He is." The short woman fanned herself.

"What about Owen?" Gen popped a hand on her hip. "You don't ever fan yourself around him."

Jake walked backward out of the huddle, putting himself a foot away from her for the first time since they'd left the bedroom two hours ago.

"He's gorgeous, for sure, but he's too goody-goody."

Janney smacked Owen's cheek. "Look at that face." Her head shook. "I'll never know how she worked her magic on you. She's the devil, you know?"

"Out." Gen stabbed the air, ordering her assistant out the door. "We've got to put that loudmouth to work before I decide to fire you."

"Bye." Janney blew a kiss to the men in the room, winked at Libby and Larkin, and then marched out the door she'd hardly entered.

Gen kissed her fingers and waved at Larkin and repeated the gesture for Libby. "I love you."

"I love you too." Larkin waved.

"I love you." Libby kissed her fingers and blew it to Gen.

Her friend caught the kiss and then lowered her hand toward her crotch for a split second. She lifted it to her breasts, debating right or left. Finally she smacked it onto her cheek.

A sense of joy filled her. They would be forever changed, and forever beautifully the same. She rolled her eyes at Gen.

Owen corralled them out the door, and Larkin closed it. A deafening silence settled over the room until Larkin sighed. She looked at her watch and then at Beckett's container.

"I'm finished." He grabbed the demolished meal's container and threw it away.

"I guess we're off." Larkin pursed her lips.

Libby crossed her arms over her chest and huffed. "Why do you two get to work?"

"Because we both work in the building." Larkin bobbed a shoulder.

Even before Gen had gotten out of the hospital from her ordeal, Janney had handled the paperwork and begun moving things to the new office in The Ashford in preparation for Gen's own firm, Holst & Co. So far, she hadn't figured the Co. part, but she already had a client list she couldn't keep pace with. Almost all of her clients transferred with her and droves more came. Janney complained about fielding their phone calls so much that Gen hired another assistant.

"Technicality." Libby kept her arms knotted.

"You could lease an office from Gen and start your own private detective business." Larkin smiled.

"Just get." Libby shooed her toward the door. "You could hardly keep a straight face while saying it."

"I was just thinking of the epic fights you two would have." Larkin grabbed her purse and the bag of food off the counter. "And you'd only be a few floors away."

Larkin's smile faded. "On second thought—"

"Nope." Libby stepped forward and opened the door. "Go." She motioned them out the door.

"I love you." Larkin stopped inches from Libby and kissed her cheek.

"I love you too." Libby kissed her friend's cheek. "Be safe."

"I will be." Larkin hiked a thumb at Beckett, who eased out the door behind Lar. "You too."

"Always," she promised.

For the first time since Larkin had shown up with breakfast and introduced a little noise to her and Jake's silent stare off, Libby realized that she hadn't brought back the kitten.

"Wait." Libby flagged her friend. "Where's Xanax?"

Larkin's bright gaze jumped from Libby to Beckett and back several times. Libby's heart sank. If she'd lost the kitten, Libby might be sick.

Beckett threw his palms into the air and shook his head. "This is all you." He backed farther down the hallway.

"Just tell me," Libby barked.

"He's in my office." Larkin grimaced. "I kind of went out this morning and bought everything a cat needs for my condo, house, and office. I set it all up before grabbing breakfast." Her grimace turned into a forced smile. "Don't hate me." She looped the bags over her arms and pressed her hands together in prayer form. "I just love him so much. I'll give him back, if you're really, really upset, and serve me with papers."

Libby drew a deep breath and shoved the door closed.

"Thank you so much!" Larkin hollered through the door. "I love you, and I'll give him the best home ever, ever, ever."

She turned away from the door.

"I love you," Larkin called once more.

"Yeah, yeah." Libby braced both her hands on the polished stone island.

Finally, the retreat of stilettos echoed through the door and slowly faded.

Why were people always stealing her animals? Was she unfit or what? Tension clawed at her neck. She stretched it this way and that. The feeling of imprisonment grabbed her by the wrists. Even though this condo was nicer than her home ever thought about being, it was still a proverbial prison until Alec was caught. Everyone was certain he was behind it, and Libby should have been. If he was at all responsible, what did that say about her judgment? She'd been friends with him, worked with him daily for years, and had never seen the dead-eyed monster capable of such horror.

Douglas had found surveillance cameras from the surrounding areas in and out of a white van. Owen had found record of Alec renting the van just before Marlis's disappearance. He'd dug further and figured out that Alec had rented a van during the timeframe of Olivia Archer's murder. Both vehicles were impounded for forensic testing.

Alec was the killer. Jake didn't love her.

There were certain things she needed to face.

She'd fallen apart last night. Stress and shock had filled the cracks and expanded, but she wasn't broken. She would put herself back together. No matter. She was independent. She wasn't her job. She wasn't her friends. She was Libby Irish with or without any of those things. She could change her life on her own whims. Not based on the work of a madman. Her life was hers to mold and change how she saw fit. And it had no room for those who didn't love her and believe in her.

Libby shoved off the island and straightened. Jake hadn't moved, not much. She met his gaze.

"You don't need to babysit me. I have friends who can pay people to do that, Ronin."

His shoulder's straightened. His gaze narrowed. "Don't be like that, Libby."

"Don't be like that, Ronin." She pointed at him as if something was wrong with him. There wasn't. He didn't love her. Simple as that. There was nothing wrong with her. It was them together. As good as they were, they weren't meant to be. Simple, yet so painful.

"I am who I am." His hand spread wide. "There's nothing I can do about it." He hit his chest. "Believe me. I've tried."

"Well, that makes two of us. Only I haven't tried." Her head shook. "Not until you." Tears threatened, but she blinked them back and stepped around the island. "I'm not asking for rings and babies, Jake."

His hands came up as though to ward her off. She stopped a couple of feet away from him.

"I can't let myself love you."

"And I can't make myself stop loving you." Libby laughed, but there was no joy in it. "Thank you for saving my life. Truly. But your services are no longer necessary." She grabbed the door handle and yanked. The door nearly collided with her body, but she stopped it.

"Don't shove me away, Libby. Not now." He stepped close

to the door and put a hand on it.

"I can't be your phone-a-fuck. I'm not made like Reece. I don't work that way."

"You're not, Libby. You're ..."

"I'm what?" She didn't mean to scream, but she couldn't hold it together for much longer. The edges were crumbling under the weight of his intense gaze.

"You're everything." The gruffness with which his words came made her want to believe them, but it only twisted the knife.

Emotion streamed down her face. She didn't turn away but bore her gaze into his. "I'm everything you can't love."

Libby waited for a rebuttal, but there was none. Facts were facts. She shifted her gaze toward the hallway. His hands balled into fists. Fear didn't cross her mind. He wouldn't hurt her, not more than he already had.

Jake turned and walked out of her life just as quickly as he'd entered it.

Her weight sagged against the door, closing it sharply. She sank to her hands and knees and gasped for air, knowing that one day it wouldn't hurt this much.

THIRTY-FOUR

"TODAY IS NOT THE DAY." Libby glared at her bedraggled reflection in the foggy mirror. As much as she'd wanted to crawl into bed and cry the day away, it had smelled like Jake. She'd smelled like him too.

She'd stripped the sheets off the bed, tossed them into the wash, and set about scrubbing his scent from her body. If only she could scrub her brain and erase all the wonderful memories with him. There's no way she would, but it'd be nice to at least have the option.

Libby rubbed her swollen lips and rosy cheeks. Her hair dripped water droplets onto her chest and arms. They reminded her of tears. She blinked wildly. If she cried any more, her green eyes would turn as red as the point of Rudolph's nose. Already a halo of vibrant pink rimmed her lids. She pushed her cheeks into a smile.

"One day."

After wrapping her hair in a towel, Libby fired up her favorite streaming channel and cranked the music as loudly as her phone would allow. She grabbed her toiletry bag from the room and tossed it onto the counter. What else was a girl to do after a non-breakup except get dressed and go blab to her friends? After all, they were both in the building. Both. Not all. She unzipped the bag, unfurled her options, and chose a simple moisturizer.

The music died. A phone call cut in. Her phone vibrated.

Alec Keith's name brightened the screen.

Libby recoiled from the phone. The tube of moisturizer slipped from her hand, bounced off the counter, and then skittered across the floor.

Her gaze jumped back to the phone. It wasn't as if he could see her.

Actually, she'd suggested calling him the first time he'd come under suspicion. Everyone—even Beckett, who seldom voiced his opinion—forbid her to call him. Later, Owen had found out that his cell phone stopped pinging the day before Marlis's murder. But now it was on, and he was calling her.

If he was making calls, they could ping his location.

She lifted the phone to dismiss the call and dial Owen.

A shrieking siren filled the condo. Piercing lights strobed.

"Fire alarm?"

Everything inside Libby shook, even her voice. Alec's name vanished from the screen. The shrill tones and flashing lights continued … and she was in a towel.

She stumbled on wobbly feet into the bedroom she and Jake had shared. The jeans and sweater she'd worn for a couple of hours this morning were strewn on the floor.

She grabbed them and tossed them onto the bare mattress and moved to chuck the phone too … but it vibrated in her palm.

Alec Keith.

Libby jerked open a drawer, yanked a pair of underwear from inside, and hiked them up her legs under the towel and over her ass. The phone continued to vibrate.

"No. No. No." She didn't want to hear his voice. Not after Mar. But instinct told her he was closer than she expected. Instinct told her he was the cause of the siren and flashing lights.

Her finger slid across the screen. She grabbed a bra from the drawer, put the phone to her ear, and listened. On the other end, the rumble of a crowd filled the line punctuated by shouts and the wail of sirens.

Libby's insides twisted, but before they could tighten, rage took hold. She knew this man. He wanted her. She wanted him. Not in the same way, but she could end this. Her gaze jumped to the nightstand and her gun and the two ready magazines.

"Alec?" Libby yanked the towel from her body and wiggled the bra into place.

"Listen carefully." Alec's voice was stern and harder than she remembered.

"I'm listening."

"You have five minutes to get to the east exit of The Ashford, alone, without a weapon."

Five minutes. She could hardly get out of the building in five minutes on a good day. She needed to stall him.

"Alec, we're friends. Why are you ordering me aro—"

"We're more than friends, Libby. You're mine. Mine! Ever since Kate betrayed me, you were there for me. You've been there for me, with me, getting me through the days. You showed me what life could be like with you, and then you betrayed me. Flaunting yourself to the world. Really, did you think I wouldn't see the picture, see the way you begged for attention from everyone?" He huffed and puffed as though he were transforming into the Hulk. Maybe he was. From the unhinged, unrealistic words flowing out of his mouth, he'd done a 180 degree personality switch.

The sirens and voices faded from the background. They were there but farther away. Was he in a car? If he was near the east entrance, it made sense.

"I placed three bombs around The Ashford."

Rage urged her to spew hatred all over him, but her training kicked in. Too bad it was the same training he had. Then again, he wasn't operating on the same plane as he normally did.

"I saw the bomb you put under my house. It wouldn't have done much to hurt it." Not much more than start a fire. She pulled on the jeans. "What makes you think these will hurt The Ashford?"

"The bombs. They won't do anything. The ammonium nitrate next to them, well, they'll blow a crater into the Earth. And I have three vans full of it surrounding Larkin's building. Now do I have your undivided attention?"

Ammonium nitrate.

She clutched the sweater to her chest.

Four thousand pounds of it gutted the Alfred P. Murrah Federal Building, killing one hundred and sixty-eight people and injuring hundreds more. They were statistics she'd learned in the academy, but the weight of her duties cemented when they'd visited the memorial before graduation. The victims had shifted from numbers to people, people with families and lives crushed.

Alec had been on that trip before her. They hadn't had the same takeaway.

"You do."

Libby ripped the towels from her hair, pulled the

sweater over her head, and shoved her feet into suede boots.

"If you bring a gun, knife, mace, pepper spray, or any kind of weapon, I'll detonate."

"You're close. If you detonate, it'll kill you too." Libby ran to the kitchen, trying her best to keep the heavy heels from clacking on the floor.

"You think I care about that?" Alec chuckled.

She snarled at the phone.

"If you alert the police, your friends, or their lovers, their security detail, anyone at all, I'll detonate."

Libby snatched a paper bag out of the recycling and grabbed the black marker Mother Hen Larkin had used to correct the improper labels on their food that morning.

"How am I supposed to get past my bodyguard?"

"You mean the man you betrayed me with?" There was a bite to Alec's voice that stole Libby's breath. "I killed him."

"No." Her head shook. "No, you can't."

Jake was invincible. Nothing and no one could hurt him. Not even a broken back kept him down for long. Not even her love could touch him. Alec was lying.

"I did, Libby. I can do whatever I want. I will do whatever I want. Do you understand that you're one click away from death?"

Tears dropped onto the paper bag, staining oddly shaped circles, raising uneven texture on the once smooth surface.

"I could start shooting the people leaving the building, just like I did your lover." He hissed.

"No." Her hands clenched.

A sense of calm washed over her. Jake would handle the situation. He wouldn't let it handle him.

Libby wrote.

(For Larkin Ashford)

Alec
3 vans w / Ammonium nitrate bombs around building
kidnapped east exit
I love you ALL
"I will," Alec threatened.

"Please don't. I'll do whatever you want. Tell me what you want me to do, Alec."

"Put your phone on speaker, now."

She clicked the speaker before he completed his sentence. "Done. What next?"

"Leave it that way. I want to hear what you're doing."

"Okay. Can you hear me?" Libby wiped the tears from her cheeks, grabbed the bag off the counter, and ran for the door. It flopped at her side.

"Yes." He released a shaky breath. "Good." His breaths heaved.

Libby didn't dare breathe. She didn't know what would set him off. The wailing sirens gave some background with which to buffer her movements. She ran for the service elevators. If she was by herself, she used them. Mar and Larkin always thought they were dirty. They weren't posh, but they were clean and way faster than the main set that every uppity asshole in the joint used.

"Don't make me grab the detonator again," he begged. "I don't want to kill everyone, just those close to you."

"Alec, you're close to me."

"No. I thought I was."

"You are." She rounded the corner and pressed the call button.

"Stop lying," he snapped.

"I'm not."

"Bring the phone with you so I can hear what you're doing."

"What if I lose you in the elevator or stairs?"

"Just hope you don't."

"What if I do? That's not something I can control."

"You're wasting time, Libby." Indeed, she was. Since Larkin had security install cell boosters in all the elevators, she hadn't lost a call, but he didn't need to know that.

"Where am I going, Alec? How do I get to you?" She knew exactly where the east entrance was, but if she kept him talking, it gave him less time to think about how long it was taking her to get to him.

He explained to her the two main routes she could take. Main elevator. Stairs.

The white doors opened, revealing an empty interior. She dived inside and stabbed the lobby button. The east exit was on the sub level, but Douglas or one of the heads of security would be on the first floor.

"What are you doing?"

"I'm waiting for the elevator."

"Why aren't you taking the stairs? They'll be faster."

"I'm on the seventy-fifth floor. There's no way that'll be faster. Especially with all the people." She hedged. The doors closed, sealing her in with a deafening siren.

Libby shielded the phone with her hand. "Alec?"

"What?"

"I'm glad you called."

"Stop lying, Libby."

"You know me. I don't lie." Her skin crawled. "I am glad you called."

"Why?"

She watched the numbers tick lower and lower on the readout above the double doors, drew a deep breath, and lied her ass off.

"I know if we can just talk, face-to-face, then you'll see how that picture was a cry for help. It was me trying to get your attention, not the world's, Alec. Yours."

"What are you saying?"

"You were so caught up with Kate. Everything was

Kate to you. It was Kate this, Kate that. I knew you loved her. Even after she was gone, I knew you didn't even see me because you loved her so much." Her mouth burned from the lies.

"No." Alec growled.

"Yes." Libby breathed. "I tried not to let it bother me, but it hurt. I tried to tell you, but I knew you wouldn't hear it."

"No. Every time I asked you out, you—"

"Thought you just wanted to be my friend. Friends, when Kate had your heart."

"Kate is nothing to me."

"She was your everything." Libby's thoughts wrapped around images of Jake. She covered the sob that ruptured from her throat. He'd said she was everything.

Wasn't everything enough? Why had she needed a stupid word? What was love anyway?

Still, she'd sent him away. To his death? No. There was no way. He was too strong for that. She was too strong to let him die.

The elevator slowed. No. Red LED lights read the number 11. She needed 1.

"The elevator's here, Alec. I'm coming down. I'm on my way to you."

"Hurry, Libby."

"As fast as I can."

Libby held her breath. The doors opened. Two workers in navy coveralls lumbered onto the elevator car. She mentally rushed them into the space. One of the men lifted a beefy arm across the doors. His friend shuffled on and leaned so hard against the back wall that it jarred the car. But the first man didn't remove his arm.

She stared daggers into the side of the man's head.

He ignored her.

"Move your arm," Libby ordered.

The man's thick head jerked back. Slowly, double jowls turned his bulging gaze in her direction. He barked a single laugh and readjusted his gaze.

"Now," Libby pressed.

"You're on the service elevator, our elevator." He tapped the pocket of his coveralls with The Ashford's embroidered logo and his name, Samuel. "We're waiting for two more."

Libby could tell him that she would have him fired if he didn't move his arm. She could tell him that she was in service to the FBI and that she would have him arrested when they hit the lobby. She could tell him about the three bombs and the madman waiting for her downstairs.

Lumbering idiot number one motioned her toward the open doors. "You're welcome to take the stairs, but you won't get far. So stand there, shut your mouth, and look pretty."

"Libby," Alec's voice sounded shrill and angry at the same time. "Show them your badge."

"I don't have it, remember? But I'm fine," she assured him.

"Wait a minute. I know you," the second man started.

She cocked her foot back at the man blocking her path and launched her knee high, sinking into dangling flesh and ramming it up into his throat.

He dropped to his knees. A reed of air hissed through his clenched teeth.

Libby grabbed his head, shoved him into the corner, and slapped the close door button. She sliced a glare at his buddy in the corner. He bent at the knees and cupped his balls in apparent sympathy.

"Would you like to wait or say anything?"

His head shook wildly. The doors closed.

"Good. I have to meet my boyfriend." Bile crawled up Libby's throat, but she hoped the public admission would help cement her place in Alec's trust.

"Lucky guy," the second worker croaked.

Lucky he was still breathing. He wouldn't be for long.

The next five floors sailed past. At the sixth, her big friend picked himself off the floor and glared at her.

"Are we going to have a problem?" She hitched her knee, testing him.

His oversized Adam's apple bobbed. Both his hands dropped to his crotch, and he muffled a curse.

"Libby, where are you?" Alec demanded.

"On my way to you."

"Where, exactly?" he barked.

"Forty-fifth floor, Alec." She glared from one man to the other, daring them to contradict her.

"Hurry," he urged. In the background, the sirens had shifted from building alarms to police and first responder units. The level of the crowd had multiplied.

"I'm going as fast as I can." She smiled at the two men.

"Pushy," the second guy mouthed.

"You have no idea," she promised.

The elevator stopped on the fourth floor. Seriously, at that point, it would've been simpler for the person to take the stairs. The doors parted. A woman with eyes nearly as large as her pregnant belly stood outside. She wrangled two toddlers, holding them by the wrists, one in each hand.

"Come on." Libby signaled them onboard.

The woman surged forward, dragging the flailing children with her.

"Door close, please," she tossed to her ball-busted buddy.

His fat thumb jabbed the button without a word.

They descended the rest of the floors without incident. She didn't count the spilled sippy cup or the tantrum an incident even though the children's mother did.

The doors opened, and Libby hit the first floor running, before anyone could give away her location. She rounded two corners and hit a wall of people, flowing slowly toward the main exit.

"Libby? Libby? Libby!"

She lifted the phone to her ear, having barely heard his pitched scream.

"I'm having to use the stairs. The elevator wasn't going anywhere. I'm in a sea of people."

"Make it work, Libby."

"I am, Alec. I am." She shifted toward the wall, pressed her breasts to it, and shimmied.

Elbows jabbed into her back. Someone stepped on her toe. After only ten feet, the crowd came to a complete halt. Slowly, the jostling sea parted, diverting around a waist-high table she couldn't think of the name for. Larkin would know, if it mattered, which it didn't. Libby climbed atop it, sending a lamp crashing to the ground in her haste.

From the vantage point, she saw the security desk and Douglas standing at it, barking orders into a phone close to his ear. He faced away from her.

Libby used the paper bag as a flag and flapped it high back and forth. She caught the eye of a large African American security guard. His face drew into a scowl, probably because she was standing on a table that cost more than her house. He stepped in her direction.

She stopped flagging, held both hands up, and pointed at Douglas. It took several tries, but he finally turned toward Douglas and tapped his shoulder. Her friend's father turned, saw her, and dropped the phone. Libby pointed at hers and mouthed, "Alec." Douglas shrugged and plowed through the crowd. She placed her index finger to her lips and waited for him to fight the flowing river of people.

When he was five feet away, his eyes bulged. Libby nodded, and mouthed, "Alec speaker." She tossed him the bag.

The more he read, the more his jaw tightened.

"I'm making my way through the crowd, Alec. A few minutes more and we'll be together." She spoke loud enough for both men to hear her.

"Good job, Libby. Good job. Hurry to me," Alec urged.

"I am." Libby teared up but blinked away the emotion. She set the phone on the table and rushed to Douglas.

"I have to go," she whispered.

He gripped her arms.

"It's the only way to keep everyone safe," Libby insisted. His grip loosened.

She grabbed him into a bear hug. "He said he killed Jake. That he shot him when he was leaving the building."

"He wasn't supposed to leave you!" Douglas bellowed.

She covered his mouth. "It was me. I sent him away. You have to find him. He's somewhere close."

"We will. Here, take this." Douglas pulled a tie pin from his sedate blue tie and clipped it to the collar of her sweater.

"Thanks?" She smiled, despite it all.

"Tracker."

Libby nodded, feeling a little stupid, but she was FBI, not CIA. She kissed his cheek, turned away, and ran. Her shoulders rocked people out of her way. She grabbed the phone and continued to plow through the relentless crowd.

Finally, it thinned, and she zipped through the back hallways and hidden corridors to the east exit. Before she could second-guess herself, she burst through the door and onto an asphalt alley. Cold wind slapped her face and bled through the knit of her sweater. She looked left and right but didn't see him anywhere. Not Alec. Not Jake, who she really sought.

It was all for the best. The sight of his body would be her undoing, and therefore her friends' undoing.

"I'm here," Libby nearly sobbed into the phone. "Where are you?"

"I see you. Walk toward the crowd."

She turned toward the main street and put one foot in front of the other. Two-thirds of the way, a black sedan was backed into one of the security parking spots outside of the small parking garage. He couldn't have been there long. There weren't many people in the area, and surely, security would have noticed the car sooner. Though they did have their hands full at the moment.

The front door opened, and a tall, lean man with a prosthetic nose, as well as a gray wig, brows, and false beard got out.

"Alec?"

"It took you more than five minutes." The unfamiliar man with the very familiar voice smiled and held up a switch.

Libby slowly lifted the phone. "But I kept you with me the whole time, and I fought a huge man to get to you."

Alec's phone echoed her words inside the car.

"So you did." He slipped the switch into the breast pocket of his charcoal suit. His hand extended toward her. "Your phone."

She handed it over, hoping beyond reason that Douglas's little contraption worked. Alec took the phone, dropped it onto the ground, and stomped it with the heel of his wingtips. The screen went black and shattered, but the body of the phone seemed no worse for wear. He opened the back door.

"Let's go someplace. Let's go away from Kate and work, all of it." Libby stepped forward and slipped her hand into Alec's. She expected it to be cold and broken, like his heart, but irritatingly, it was warm to the touch. His face shifted toward her. Surprise lifted his cheeks. "Just you and me." She forced a smile.

"You've been crying."

Libby shrugged. "I thought I wouldn't make it to you in time."

THIRTY-FIVE

COLD METAL SLIPPED OVER HER WRIST. Libby recognized the feel of handcuffs before she heard the click-click-click of the restraint. Alec cinched it to the point of it biting into her skin. Everything inside her wanted to fight him, to punch and kick and wail until he was unconscious. Then she could find Jake herself. Thoughts jumped from his imagined bloody body to the detonator in his pocket and her friends in the building and the thousands of people in there as well. She had to get Alec as far away from the bombs as quickly as possible.

"Do you want them in front or in back?" She lifted her left hand toward the already cuffed one, praying he'd choose the front.

Alec leaned close. "I want to trust you, Libby."

His head lowered, bringing his lips within inches of

hers. It was as if he was giving her the option to prove herself.

She could fake a smile. She could restrain the urge to gouge out his eyes. But she could not make herself kiss the man who murdered Marlis, said he killed Jake, and threatened to kill thousands more.

Libby looked at Alec through her lashes as though she were bashful and not absolutely revolted.

"But you've given me no choice." He gripped her left hand and wrenched it behind her back.

Her feet pivoted just in time to keep her arm from snapping in two. A yelp slipped from her lips, but she kept it from morphing into an all-out shriek. The last thing she needed was to draw attention to their situation.

The other handcuff tightened around her arm. Moisture coated her eyes in reaction to the pinching of her skin. She blinked it away and drew a deep breath. Alec jerked her forward, ramming her chest into the side of the car like an unsub. He opened the back door and shoved her inside. Her face and chest skidded along the leather seat. The slamming door rammed the toe of her shoes and jarred her knees.

Before Libby could use her pretzeled legs and core to right herself, Alec was behind the wheel. They moved through the city away from The Ashford at a reasonable speed. Nothing to cause alarm. She shifted and worked, and finally sat, leaning forward to keep pressure off her hands and wrists.

He angled the rearview mirror, allowing Libby to see his sinister gaze and him to see her. "If you make any attempt to alert a passing vehicle, I'll detonate."

What was the remote distance on a bomb? How far away did they have to get before the remote would no longer set off the explosives?

"I won't, Alec. I want to be with you."

The lie tasted sour on her tongue.

If she was with him, her friends were no longer in danger, and she had some chance of stopping him. Just as easily, she had a chance of dying. She didn't want to die. She didn't want to spend a minute more with this psychopath than she had to.

"Stop," Alec warned.

"No," she challenged. "I won't stop telling you what I'm thinking. Not now that I know how you feel."

"Felt," he corrected.

"I don't believe that." Libby scooted to the edge of the seat. She set her lips near the shell of his ear. "You can't change your feelings about me before I've even had a chance to reciprocate them."

Alec's breath caught. His knuckles whitened on the steering wheel. His speed rose, not in excess, but enough that Libby realized she wasn't buckled. She never buckled in the back of limos. However, every time she drove or rode in a regular car, she used a seat belt. There was no way for her to fasten the belt around herself. Not with her hands behind her back.

In front of them, the traffic gathered.

Libby eased back onto the seat.

Alec shook his head from side to side so forcefully that she half expected them to careen into the cars ahead of them. Finally, he pumped the brakes.

"If you knew what I did, you wouldn't say that." His laugh was low and quiet, almost as if he was laughing to himself.

The sound shot chills up her legs. They traveled high and fast. If Libby could, she'd clamp her hands over her ears to keep from hearing what he was sure to tell her. Fuck, if she had her hands free, she'd wrap an arm around his throat and block his carotid.

"If you knew half of the things I've done, you wouldn't

say that."

They were far enough away from the building that there was no way for the remote to trigger the bombs. Her gaze drifted toward the door nearest her. If she could manage a tuck and roll from the vehicle, there was nothing to keep him from turning around and heading right back to The Ashford.

"We've all done questionable things. It's human nature."

"You've done bad things." Alec smacked the steering wheel with his fist.

Libby tried her best not to jump. Her eyes blinked. She swallowed a lump of fear that clogged her throat. Alec rubbed a hand over the place he'd struck. Whispered words filtered from his lips. It sounded like apologetic garble. She leaned her shoulders back onto the seat, leaving room for her hands behind her.

The car motored west out of the center of the city. Pedestrians speckled every sidewalk and street corner, making her most far-off and desperate thought yet impossible. She wouldn't risk more innocent lives in this drama.

The farther away they drove, the more erratic his behavior became.

In the last twenty minutes of mumbled silence, Libby's anger fled, having been overtaken by utter fear. She'd saved her friends, but she was Alec's prisoner, and she had no idea where he planned to take her nor what he planned to do to her.

They'd nearly run to the end of 42nd Street. In less than three blocks, he'd turn one way or the other. She had to do something before he took her off the island. Off the island, there were so many places he could take her. Too many places where she'd never be found.

"I know you killed Olivia Archer."

In the rearview mirror, his glazed-gazed ramblings

ceased. His brows arched.

It had taken everything for her to launch that declaration into the air. In doing it, she regained some level of control … or enough of the illusion to fortify her.

Libby lifted her chin. "Why kill her?"

He looked at her with dead eyes, as though he'd forgotten the road. "For the same reason I killed Marlis."

The words punctured her chest like bullets.

Each one struck a nerve. Rage sparked. Fury burned from the inside out.

"If Kate was in danger, she should have come to me." Red flushed Alec's cheeks. The small lines at the corners of his eyes squinted so hard they turned white.

"Danger?"

"Someone was sending her ugly letters and stole mementos from her house. They even broke in and watched her sleep." A horn blared. The car drifted across broken white lines. Alec flipped off the driver behind them. "Fuck you, I'm driving here."

Her heart beat its fists against her sternum in an effort to escape this madness.

"But did she come to me for help? Did she tell me about her trouble? No!" His scream echoed in the car, slapping her eardrums.

"She should have come to me. I thought if something drastic happened, she'd come to me. When she didn't, well, I took her mother from her."

The car accelerated, zipping past pedestrians and store fronts.

"You should have come to me, Libby. When you love someone, you confide in them. You turn to them in your time of need."

Love? No. That wasn't right. Love had never been a part of their casual friendship. Had Kate and Alec ever been a couple? Had the woman even known Alec outside of a casual acquaintance?

The possibility became less and less likely the faster they went.

Kate hadn't cheated on Alec. The woman probably hadn't been aware of the psychosis blooming in the man's brain that'd centered on her. Libby certainly hadn't been. Not for her own sake or Mar's.

Tires squealed. Libby's gaze jerked to the street. Only a light and four lanes of cross traffic stood between their careening car and the Hudson River. The yellow taxi leading the turning lane full of vehicles into their path lurched to a stop but remained in their trajectory, since Alec had drifted farther and farther to the right.

With each passing second, Alec drove them closer to the taxi with a running meter and a back seat full of passengers.

Libby grabbed the edge of the seat with her cuffed hands. The metal pinched and pushed. She raised her knees to her chest, aimed her heels at Alec's head, and launched.

A roar ripped from between her lips, pouring out all her anger and sadness and fear. Impact radiated up her calves and through her quads. Alec's head snapped to the left. The car lurched.

Her ass slipped off the edge of the seat. The floorboard hump rammed into her ribs. Sharp pain stole her breath while the rest of her wedged between the front and back seats. She tried to push up, to see what was happening.

The crash of metal on metal turned the car into a top. All her weight poured into her skull. Her face mashed against the scratchy carpet. The crown of her head drove into the speaker on the back passenger door.

Around and around they went.

She was helpless to move. Helpless to stop physics. Wham!

The car stopped cold. Her body did not.

Libby's feet tried to touch her cheeks. Her neck tweaked. The organs filling her insides threatened to come out through her mouth.

As fast as it crunched her into a pretzel, the momentum died and the accordion she'd become unfurled. Her ears rang. The edges of her vision clouded. Darkness threatened to take hold. She blinked furiously. Each flap of her lashes felt like a crashing cymbal inside her head. The taste of copper stung the tip of her tongue.

She needed to get up. She had to see Alec.

What state was he in? Where was the detonator? Where was his gun?

Muffled horns blared in the distance, beyond the nagging and persistent ringing.

Libby bent her knees and wedged them under the driver's seat. She tightened her aching core, used her right elbow on the floor panel, gritted her teeth through it, and heaved herself upright.

The top of the seat was just out of view. She tried to block out all other sounds and listen for Alec, but the ringing continued. Since she was upright, it seemed to grow louder. With each pump of her heart, a whoosh, whoosh compounded the problem. A surprising sob slipped between her swollen lips. She bit it back and stiffened her body, pushing herself up the leather.

Alec's bloody head slumped forward between the driver's door and the steering wheel. Breaths shifted his chest, but they were sporadic and shallow. The seat belt that should have been strapped across his chest hung near the top of the car, awaiting use. Glass littered the interior like confetti. The jagged remains of the driver's side window poked up from the door. A massive crack ran the length of the windshield.

Crinkled metal changed the shape of the hood. To her right, gloomy concrete barriers butted against the car from the headlight to the taillight on the passenger side. Tons of metal and aggregate trapped inside the shrunken space with a monster.

Sudden suffocating need overtook Libby. Her gaze found the door handle. She needed out as much as she needed her next breath. Forget the detonator. Forget the gun. She needed out.

Out. Now.

She scooted to the driver's side rear door. Leaning over stabbed her between the ribs. Still, she wrenched her hands high behind her back and frantically felt for the handle.

After two near triumphs, Libby's fingers wrapped around the cool metal handle. Tears of relief filled her eyes. She pulled. The latch gave as though it were attached to thin air. She pulled again and again, but nothing happened.

"Excuse me?" A thirty-something Asian man in a peach-colored trench coat approached the shattered window. "Hey man, are you okay?"

"Please." Libby reached for him, but her arms only jerked her off balance. She landed with her right cheek against the headrest.

"Oh, shit. Hey." The man grabbed the door handle and pulled. Nothing happened. He grimaced, leaned closer, and pulled again. Once more the door didn't budge. But his gaze lit on the handcuffs, trapping her arms behind her back.

His hand slipped off the handle. He backpedaled.

"Wait. No. He kidnapped me," Libby screamed.

The man's eyes bugged. His retreat quickened.

"No, please. Come back." Libby shoved herself off the headrest and pled through the window. "Please."

"I'm calling the cops!" the Asian man hollered.

"No. Come back."

He joined a growing number of bystanders, creating a distant semi-circle around the scene. Apparently, their car had glanced off another vehicle in the distance before clipping the front left of the car on a metal median protector. The African American man in an Armani suit stood in front of his scuffed Mercedes, grabbing his head and staring at the damage.

Libby leaned onto the seat, ratcheted her legs to her chest

once more, aimed at the window, closed her eyes, and released them. An immovable surface met her heels, vibrating the bones and ligaments in her legs.

"Motherfucker." Her side radiated.

The only way out was over Alec and through the window. She could wait until the police arrived, but the need to be free trumped ease. Libby hiked a knee onto the center console. Her left shoulder pressed against the side of Alec's seat. With all the core strength she possessed, she dragged her left knee up onto the console and shoved up off the seat. If she stayed upright, she could keep from falling on her face.

She extended her right leg toward the window. At such an awkward angle, the toe of her boot just reached the remnants. She banked her shoulder on the front of the headrest and scraped at the tiny mountains of glass. Tinny sounds rained. Sweat collected on her brow, slipping into her eyes. After one more drag of the boot, she'd cleared out as much of the broken window as she could reach.

Libby drew several deep breaths. Blood trickled onto the back of Alec's jacket from her split lip, or ripped gums, or broken nose. She blinked away the stinging sweat. Hell, she had no idea what was wrong. Only that she needed out.

She pulled in one more breath, held it, and moved the boot of her extended leg onto Alec's back. The warm, bony, shifting surface made her stomach clench. Without too much thought, she pressed her throbbing head against the ceiling and heaved her other knee forward.

A groan rumbled from under her knees.

Fear knotted Libby's esophagus.

He grumbled and mumbled something more.

Libby tucked her chin to her chest and threw herself through the open window. Cool air swished over her body. The cloud-filled sky tilted. Asphalt and impact came fast squarely between the shoulder blades. Blood sprayed from her mouth. Her wrists felt like they shattered beneath her. Wind sailed from her lungs as though it were on a circumnavigation of the Earth. Her abs cramped. Her chest burned.

It took a solid slice of a minute for her chest to grab even the smallest amount of air. Instead of distributing it, they held tight. She rolled to her side in an effort to take pressure off her hands, wrists, and arms.

Finally, she sucked in several greedy breaths.

A shard of glass fell from above, landing on her cheek. Libby's eyes grew two sizes. Her head jerked up. There was no sign of Alec, but she wasn't about to wait for the crosshairs to find her forehead. She shoved up onto her knees and pushed herself off the ground.

Alec's blood-soaked eyelids blinked. Then his sick gaze focused on her.

With no other thought than survival, Libby turned and ran. She rushed past the crumpled rear end of the car. Her gaze assessed the surroundings. To the right, cars with honking horns had cramped the intersection, and people gathered in groups. To the left was a dock. Knowing Alec wouldn't hesitate to harm bystanders, she hurried toward the usually bustling riverside. The summertime umbrellas and tables, vendor booths, food and delivery trucks were gone. Great for the innocent. Terrible for her.

There was no place to take cover.

A siren screamed behind her, but it was too far away to help.

Libby hiked a leg over the thick boat chain limiting vehicle access. Pain knifed between her ribs, stealing her breath. Her arms moved to cover her side, to protect from the pain, even though she knew they were cuffed behind her back. There was no helping instinct. It was all she had. It pushed her past the sting and propelled her forward.

With her arms pinned, everything was off balance. She couldn't pull and churn or counter the movement of her legs. It didn't matter. There was no way she could fall. If she fell, she was dead.

Libby shoved her legs and lungs harder than she ever had before. The edge of the water was fifty yards away.

But she couldn't swim without arms.

She looked for an alternate escape. The boats that docked here and took people for rides up and down the Hudson were gone for the impending winter.

A shot echoed from behind her.

Numbness spread across her left shoulder. It lasted several strides. Then it vanished, taking over by pain that hit so swiftly it made the horizon rock and her body shake.

Her steps teetered. Tears filled her eyes.

Another shot rang out.

Small hunks of concrete exploded to her right. The debris pelted her leg. A shriek escaped her lips.

There were twenty yards between her and the river.

The quickest path between two points was a straight line, only she couldn't outrun bullets.

Warmth trickled down her arm. It reached her fingertips, and she was oddly grateful not to be able to see the blood.

Libby zagged to the right, and then zagged right some more before jerking left. Moving targets were more difficult to hit. It was all she had.

She was an animal hunted in an open field.

A shot, louder than the others, split the day.

THIRTY-SIX

SHE EXPECTED TO HEAR THE BULLET WHIZ past her head or nothing at all. In the distance, she heard the screams of the crowd. Maybe that was the welcome at the entrance to hell.

The water was still fifteen yards away. If she could still see it and still run, she wasn't dead yet, and there was no way in hell she was about to give up. She bit back a sob, the burning pain in her side and shoulder, zigged once more, and propelled herself toward the edge of the concrete.

"Libby! Libby!"

Though she hadn't heard it all that much, her heart knew that voice.

"Libby!"

It came closer with each bellowed cry.

Jake!

He was alive!

Wait!

Did he not see the madman with a gun? Was he trying

to get himself killed?

She turned to warn him, but it was too late.

Alec sprawled across the heavy chain at the dock's pedestrian entrance. His body was slumped in an unnatural bend brought only by death. Brain matter splattered the sidewalk. The gun that he'd been shooting lay at his side, next to his useless hand. The crowd that had gathered around the crash fled in disorganized panic.

One man stood apart from the rest.

He ran toward her at full tilt. A tactical vest covered his wide chest, and a high-powered rifle was slung across his body. Blood soaked the bottom of his shirt and the left side of his pants.

"Jake."

Her legs turned to rubber, and she dropped to her knees. Whether from relief, terror, or blood loss, she couldn't be sure.

"Jake." Tears flowed freely over her cheeks.

He skidded to a stop on his knees in front of her and extended his hands.

Libby buried her face in them. The warmth of his hands on her cheeks was everything. She sobbed and breathed him in. He was alive.

Her body shook. Her mind reeled. Alec, her torturer and Marlis's murderer, was dead. Jake was alive. But what about everyone else?

She jerked upright. "Larkin and Gen? The people in The Ashford?"

"All good." He smiled and drew their faces together. "You drew him away. Damn you."

Their mouths melded. Joy she hadn't felt maybe ever washed away every horrible and unimaginable thought. At that moment, nothing else mattered beyond their bond. Not its timetable. Not its durability. Its mere existence was enough.

When he released her and settled back onto his heels, a grimace knitted his lips and his teeth gnashed. Fresh blood seeped through his already stained shirt.

"You're hurt!" Libby's heart lurched. The mania of the day

returned in a crushing blow.

"Ah." He waved off her concern and shifted to her side. "There's more QuikClot in the cruiser I jacked."

"He said he killed you." She blinked. "Wait, you stole a police car?"

"He tried to kill both of us. I just borrowed the cruiser." His fingers slid down her arm. Metal clicked and the tension at her wrists eased.

"Oh, thank—" The sweet relief of freedom lasted a fraction of a second before it was bombarded, bowled over, trampled, crushed by scorching pain. "Motherfucker!"

"Easy." Strong hands braced the center of her chest and back. "The increased blood flow unleashed the pain. Breathe deep. In through your nose. Out through your mouth. Again. It'll fade."

"Ha." Tears slipped out of the corners of her eyes.

Jake's lips brushed the edge of her brow. He hissed a breath over her ear and eased his head to hers. "Thank fucking Christ he was a terrible shot over distance."

"Yeah." Libby leaned into his strength.

Sirens that had been wailing in the distance drew closer with each second that passed.

Libby turned her face to Jake. Sweat clung to his brow and slipped down his cheek. A smear of blood stained his neck. His gaze searched hers.

"I'm sorry," she breathed.

"Why?"

"I'm sorry you had to kill him because of me."

The hand steeling her back lifted to her nape and tightened ever so slightly. Jake smiled, but it lacked even a hint of mirth. His head shook.

"Listen closely, Libby. I killed him because of him. I've killed many men in my line of work. A few women too. The world is a better place because they're no longer in it. I never dwelled on my job. I was paid to kill; an assassin. This is the first time I've killed without being paid to do so, and my only regret is that I can't kill him again."

So many words and thoughts swirled in her mind. It all made sense. The secrets. The distance. His quiet. One million questions jockeyed for position on the tip of her tongue.

"NYPD! Hands in the air!" The barking order came from a black female officer twenty yards away with her weapon drawn on them.

Libby's jaw dropped. The ramifications of what had just transpired crammed down her throat.

"It's fine. Lift your hands slowly," Jake instructed.

"What about you?" Libby squeaked.

"What about me?" His arms were already in the air.

"Miss! Hands in the air!" The officer advanced. Her partner came into view. He was no taller than his female counterpart but was as tall as he was wide. Like a bulldog.

Her gaze jumped to Jake. He gave her a look that she'd seen before. Its meaning was deeper than the deepest crevasse on earth and as unreachable. He was withdrawing.

"Don't do that," Libby warned. "Don't you dare disappear on me. We're not finished. I'm just getting started with you."

"Lift your hands, Libby." Jake's expression warmed with concern.

Libby gritted her teeth and lifted her hands into the air. Pain swelled her shoulder to the point of bursting with every heartbeat. A growl rumbled her chest.

"Libby?"

"Huh?"

"I fucking love you."

She stared at Jake, at the eyes that said so much, at the mouth that usually said nothing at all. Her mind whipped and whirled around those four words.

The bulldog of an officer rattled off orders that all summed up to move and my partner will shoot you. He removed the rifle from Jake's body, cuffed his hands behind his back, and lowered him chest first to the ground.

"He's been shot," Libby cautioned. "He needs an ambulance."

"They're on the way," the female officer assured. "Do you

have any weapons on you?"

"No." Libby answered but didn't take her gaze off Jake.

"Looks like you need an ambulance too." The bulldog cuffed her hands behind her back, an irony that wasn't lost on her, but the pain was. When she looked at Jake, everything else faded away.

The officer pressed her forward onto her belly, closer to Jake.

"I think I've loved you since the first time you accused me of stealing your cat." Jake's lips quirked and then fell.

Dread gathered around Libby like a funeral shroud. "But?"

A precinct's worth of officers rushed onto the dock. One of them pulled Jake to his feet.

"Wait," Libby begged.

They didn't pause. Jake didn't speak.

It was the worst kind of goodbye. The feeling of finality required flowers and a headstone.

THIRTY-SEVEN

"EXCUSE ME!" LIBBY HOLLERED from inside the emergency room ... that was an actual room with four solid walls and a door. Out of all the times she'd been to the emergency room, she or the unlucky person she accompanied only ever received a gurney surrounded by cloth curtains in earshot of all kinds of horrors. Her bellow echoed off the walls and the one lonely glass at the upper middle of the door. Through it, she couldn't see much except the top of the NYPD officer's hat and the edge of his brow and the crook of his jaw.

Her terribly polite demand for attention from the officer guarding her room went unnoticed. Maybe not unnoticed. She couldn't see enough of the big man's face to gauge his reaction. Her plea was most certainly ignored, just as it had been with every other attempt. The only difference was this time she didn't flail her one good arm about. Jerking against her now two pairs of handcuffs and the all too durable plastic of the hospital bed rails only caused a spike in her irritation and a dip in her ability to deal with the pain.

Because he wasn't actually guarding her room so much as he was guarding her, as in making certain she didn't escape, as though she were a criminal, as though she was to blame for the bombs and crash and dead man. Sure, the crash might have been her fault, but the rest? No. Not even a little bit. But no one seemed at all interested in her side of the story.

They'd tossed her onto the bed from the stretcher, hand-cuffed her, stabbed her to the bone with a needle of antibiot-ics, shoved an IV in her hand, and left. At least the EMT had stopped the bleeding and wrapped her shoulder. Could some-one answer a question or ten?

Did she have a bullet in her arm? Had it hit anything important? Would she need surgery? Where were the girls? Where was Jake? And, uh, could she get something for the pain?

Now that the adrenaline had worn off ...

"Holy shit!" She breathed deeply in and out like the man who'd upended her world had told her. Then again in and out.

A deep sting pulsed with each second. It radiated through her shoulder, down her arms, and across her chest and back. It had been an hour since she'd lost sight of Jake. Her attempts to garner information indicated that she'd be stuck in this room for hours more. Her cell was in pieces on the asphalt outside of The Ashford. The officer had taken the phone out of the room, not that she could have reached it anyway.

Libby slung herself back on the bed and immediately re-gretted it. She gritted her teeth, closed her eyes, and cursed a string of epithets in her mind that would make Genevieve blush.

The door burst open as though she'd screamed them aloud.

Had she?

She blinked the scene into focus.

A woman in a crisp doctor's coat brandished a chart. She

used big medical words that pertained to tests that needed to be run immediately. Her long dark hair draped down her back. A heavy accent weighed her words. Latin America. Chile, maybe.

"Fine, but I'll need to escort the suspect."

"Of course." The doctor turned and entered the room.

Libby's heart stuttered. It was called AFIB, wasn't it?

She stared into the face of Jake's friend-a-fuck, Reece Foster.

"Hello, Misssss," Foster assessed the chart, "Irish. How are you feeling this afternoon?"

"Uhh. Confused." Libby puffed her cheeks, and then slowly released the breath.

"That's understandable. You've been through a lot." The doctor or whoever the hell she was slipped the chart onto the foot of the bed, adjusted the height of the rod holding the IV, and depressed something that made a large popping sound from under the bed. "We're going to run some tests and get you some answers. How does that sound?"

"Answers sound great." She wanted to cross her arms over her chest, but the cuffs wouldn't allow it. There was absolutely no way to regain any pride in her current situation.

Libby ignored the burning in her cheeks and went for a ride out the door, through the emergency room, and down a long corridor with her handcuffs, police escort, and bloody shoulder on display. She gathered the tiniest scraps of self-respect she could find and lifted her chin, looking each of the gawkers in the eyes. The corner of the bed hit the wall. It jarred every bone in Libby's already battered body. She pinched an insult between her lips.

Reece Foster didn't apologize. She redirected the bed down the hall and left onto another corridor as though she'd done it a thousand times. They slowed at a door with a sign, announcing Radiology.

"I'm sorry." Reece lifted her hand to the officer. "Only medical staff beyond this point."

351

"I have to—" the officer started.

"HIPPA laws prevent even law enforcement from entering," she explained, while waving a card across a pad on the wall. A light on the pad turned green. With one swift heave, they pushed through the double doors. "We'll meet you right back here in twenty to thirty minutes. If anything goes wrong, I'll call security." She pointed to the right. "There's coffee in the break room. Help yourself."

They carried on past several rooms and several medical professionals. One didn't seem to notice them while the other smiled and nodded, and then saw the cuffs. Reece nodded back and shoved her past several more doors until they reached another hallway. She maneuvered the bed through a set of double doors and into a room with what seemed to be medical supplies.

Libby was cataloguing their surroundings when a sharp sting lit the top of her hand on fire.

"What the he—"

"Quiet." Reece's accent had vanished. She threw the IV line to the side, slipped a key from her pocket, and removed the handcuffs.

Blood pooled on the back of Libby's hand. She couldn't concentrate on it because the pressure from holding her arm up for the cuff finally released. Sweet Christ it hurt, but it felt good at the same time.

Reece moved to the other cuff and freed her good arm.

"What's going on?" Libby demand in a whisper.

"I'm getting you out of here." The mysterious woman moved to a nearby shelf, pulled clothes from a bag, and chucked them at Libby. "Strip and put these on."

"Why?"

"We're trying to be inconspicuous."

"Not the clothes." Libby didn't hesitate. She'd already pulled the gown from her naked body and slipped her legs to the side of the bed. When she stood, the world jittered.

Warm hands bracketed her waist. Maybe they should grab an X-ray before she set out into the wild. Forget about the bullet wound to the shoulder, she had at minimum one broken rib. Judging by the sheen of sweat coating her skin and the electric jolt to her nervous system from simply standing, she was looking at more like two or three fractured, splintered, shattered, in some way broken bones that moved every time she did.

"The moment police moved in on Ronin's position, they began extraction on Ronin."

Libby shoved her extreme discomfort to the side of her brain and blinked Reece into view, trying her best to make sense of what the woman was saying. Even with the lack of distance between them, nothing computed.

They who?

Extraction?

Where?

"They've erased all trace of him from the system. They're going to make him disappear."

"They're going to kill him?" Libby bellowed the question so loudly that Reece pressed the flat of her hand over Libby's mouth and narrowed her gaze so sharply that she felt it like a jab to her broken side.

"No. They're trying to fully reinstate Ronin. In which case, he might as well be dead to you. You'll never see him again."

Libby's head shook.

"I didn't think you'd be in favor of it. Get dressed. If we move, we might be able to stop it."

The sweet drug, adrenaline shot through Libby's veins like jet fuel. She elbowed Reece off her, grabbed the clothes from the bed, and shoved her legs and arms into nurse's scrubs. The pain hadn't left. She banked several curses behind her lips, but a singular goal overrode it.

Get to Jake. Get to Jake. Get to Jake.

Reece brushed Libby's hair while Libby tried to get her shaking fingers to knot the drawstring at her waist. The woman pinned a nurse's badge to her pocket that had Libby's picture on it and looked legitimate enough to get them through employee-only access areas. A thousand questions swirled in

Libby's mind, but none of them mattered. Asking them would only slow them down.

Next, Reece dropped a pair of sneakers in front of Libby's feet and squatted down.

"Here." The woman who'd banged Jake for the last six months pulled the first shoe's tongue wide.

Libby shoved her feet into the most comfortable shoes she hadn't known existed. They had high arch support and pillows under her heels. Reece tied them and stood, putting them nose to nose.

"Don't limp or grimace. Stay by my side, Nurse Williams. I'll take care of the rest."

"Got it." Libby shuffled to the end of the bed, grabbed the patient chart, and held it out to Reece. "Let's go."

The woman's head canted. Her steely brow hiked. "You call that walking without a limp?"

"We're not in the hallway yet."

Reece snatched the chart from Libby's hand, turned, shoved out of the double doors. Libby gritted her teeth and hurried behind her fast enough that she didn't have to catch their side of the heavy, swinging obstacles. Safely on the other side, she plastered a tired smile on her face and matched the operative's quick strides.

They didn't head down the hall toward the guard but turned away, heading in the opposite direction. Still, sweat rolled down her arms. The "good doctor" had given her long-sleeve scrubs. At this pace, they'd be soaked by the time they made it wherever they were headed. Each step she took pushed back at her wave of adrenaline until it was a sloshy puddle. Determination carried her past two hospital transport staffers and their patients, through another secured door, and out ... to the hospital's main hall.

"Come on." Reece hurried past the gift shop and the front desk.

Outside, the cool air stole what breath she'd managed to maintain. Her grimace was back. It was all she could do to stave off the limp.

"Not much farther."

Libby followed the woman to a sleek black sports car parked in a handicapped space. When she slipped inside a moment after Reece, a blue sign complete with a white stick figure in a wheelchair and registration number hung from the rearview mirror.

"You don't look handicapped," Libby hissed through her teeth while struggling to pull the seat belt across her chest.

"I'm not." Reece started the car and whipped it out of the parking space and out onto the street so quickly it pinned Libby to the seat. "Jake was."

"I've seen his scar and the slow disappearance of his limp. What happened?"

They careened through light traffic, slowing only long enough to jerk and weave around sluggish drivers. Libby clipped the seat belt into place. She scanned the horizon, not for safety purposes, but in an effort to figure out where they were going.

"At first, he couldn't walk." Reece's voice startled Libby. It'd been two minutes since she'd asked the question, so she never expected to be answered. "He went through two surgeries and three months of physical therapy before he was released to the outside world."

They took a hard turn right. Libby gripped the door handle for dear life. The back wheels squealed for purchase. A car behind them honked. They didn't slow.

"You remember Slade?"

"How could I forget him?" He'd made her home a fortress at Jake's request. Not that it'd helped because she was a sucker for a suffering animal.

"He and Ronin were on assignment. They'd done the job and met the extraction team on the roof." Reece juked a car and slowed slightly as she sailed through a yellow light. "Ronin was back providing cover when a guy popped up from the stairwell at the side of the building. He drew and took aim at the back of Slade's head. Ronin's gun jammed. So naturally, he launched himself at the man and tackled him right off the side of the building.

"The structure was eight stories. He should have been dead. Slade shouldn't have even looked back, much less hooked repel gear onto the Helo to recover the body."

"What?" Libby gasped.

"Protocol." Reece didn't bother with a shrug or frown. She just pushed the gas pedal. "Slade risked the bigger picture. It's why he's out on his own."

"It must be an ugly picture." Her head shook just thinking about Jake being left behind.

"It usually is," Reece agreed. "Slade found Ronin draped over the railing of a concrete balcony three stories down. The bad guy had broken his fall, but not enough that the fall hadn't broken Ronin. Somehow, the son of a bitch was still alive."

"He's too stubborn to die." Images of Jake barreling toward her with no concern for his own injuries bombarded her.

"He's also too stubborn to live."

"What do you mean?" Libby cast her gaze at Reece.

Reece slid her gaze to Libby.

"Eyes on the road!"

The woman smirked but did as instructed. "He doesn't want to be reinstated but doesn't think he can stay."

"He can do anything. Anything at all." For Christ's sake, the man had battled back from a broken spine and tamed the wildest cat on Earth. He'd even made a hardened woman fall in love with him.

The car slowed and turned into a narrow parking lot of one of the city's heliports. Reece grabbed Libby's hand. "He can do anything. He just needs someone to tell him so. Someone he'll listen to. Someone he loves."

Libby blinked back tears.

"Take this and go through the side gate. Don't stop for anyone. Don't stop until he sees you." Reece shoved a plastic card into Libby's hand, and then reached across and opened the passenger door. "Last pad on the dock. Hurry, they're due to take off in two minutes."

"Thank you."

"Thank me by saving him. He deserves it."

"You do too."

"No. I really don't." A grimness clouded the woman's beautiful face, but Libby didn't have time to contemplate it. She pointed toward the heliport. "Now go!"

With one hand on the frame and the other on the seat, Libby hoisted herself out of the car. She didn't bother closing the door. Reece had the full use of all her limbs and mad driving skills, so she could close it. Libby gripped the key card, focused her strength and energy, and ran. Each step radiated oxygen-burning pain throughout her torso. It charred her shoulder and crackled in her arms. It sizzled in her fingertips.

She reached the gate in three strides and whipped the card across the scanner. The chain-link pedestrian-sized entryway rolled slower than her current running pace. Each fraction of a second passed by like an eternity, an eternity where she'd never see Jake again.

Finally, it opened enough that she shimmied through and ran past the small building that housed crew and a handful of waiting passengers, judging by experience and the number of cars in the parking lot. She didn't want to see any of them.

Get to Jake. Get to Jake. Get to Jake.

The words became a chant to drown out the pain and fear.

When she rounded the corner, two helicopters sat on a tarmac that would support four of the machines. One was closest to her. The rotors on it slowed, and a member of the crew stood in front of it, signaling the pilot. At the far end of the landing pad, a crew member stood at the front of a fully black Helo. Even the windows were darker than Alec's soul.

"Hey!"

The call came from over her shoulder. Whipping wind sliced through the cry, making it easier to ignore.

Libby pushed forward, running along the edge to keep from getting sliced herself. Her hair crowded around her face, whipped by the wind caused by the deadly blades. The first Helo was large and carried around ten passengers. The one she sought was built for speed and maneuvering. It carried only two.

At the front of the far helicopter, the crewman didn't see her. His gaze remained on the pilot. He gave a hand signal and the long blades began to whir. In two strides, they were spinning so quickly she couldn't make out how many blades the aircraft had. They blurred into a freaking gray nightmare.

"No! Stop!" Libby sprinted toward the middle of the tarmac and barreled for Jake. Even though she couldn't see him. "Hey! Stop! Don't go!" She waved her arms high and didn't feel a thing beyond determination.

If only he saw her. It would be enough, wouldn't it?

The crewman did. He frantically shooed the Helo into the sky and ran to intercept her. "Miss. Stop!" He yelled something about danger, but Libby didn't care. The landing skids left the asphalt, pulling twenty feet into the air in seconds.

"No! Stop!" Her arms flailed, but her footsteps faltered. She watched the Helo rise to the nonexistent treetops. The machine's nose pivoted away from her.

She ran into something hard. Still her eyes remained locked on the aircraft hovering above her hopes, ready to scatter them in the wind.

"Miss. You can't be out here." The crewman hooked a hand around her waist. It hurt. At least it should have, but everything was numb. "Christ, you're bleeding." Indeed, warmth trickled down her arm. It did little to help the tingling cold taking over.

"Stop them," Libby begged.

"Are you hurt?"

More than she'd ever been before.

"Miss?"

When she didn't answer, the crewman turned her away from Jake. He waved his co-worker over, who'd already cleared most of the distance.

"What the hell is going on?" the co-worker asked.

Libby checked out. They ushered her closer and closer to the heliport. The wind kicked up, forcing her hair into her face. She hid there.

"Fucking hell!" The man holding her up shoved her off and ran.

The crewman in front of her turned to his co-worker and jumped up and down. He waved his hands as frantically as she had moments ago. "No! Not that close!"

Libby hugged her middle in an effort to stay upright. Slowly, she turned to see the polished black helicopter landing on the second helipad, just fifteen feet away. The side door opened, and a bloody boot perched on the edge of the frame. His hand came into view, and Jake jumped from the bird's belly. He looked back into the beast, nodded to someone inside, and then slammed the door.

His back remained to her while he watched the helicopter lift into the sky and zip toward the horizon.

When he turned, a new layer of expression was etched in his features. She'd caught a glimpse of it during their lovemaking, but this was different, reverent. It warmed her from the inside out and banished her pain.

He cleared the distance to her slowly. He limped and grimaced and would fool no one into thinking he was a nurse. The two crew members gave him ample space to pass.

A grin caught Libby's lips, turning them toward the sky.

"What's so funny?" He stopped a foot away.

"I never pegged you for a coward."

His chin lifted. "Good. I'm not."

"Then why were you running away from me?"

Jake drew a deep breath. It hissed out his nose. His jaw worked. For a moment, they stood there on the windy tarmac, cataloguing one another.

"Libby, there are broken pieces of my vertebra still imbedded in the tissue surrounding my spine. If I move the wrong way, I could become paralyzed. It could happen at any moment." He rocked onto his heels. "I'm not going to do that to you. Always wondering when it'll happen. It's like someone handing you a grenade, pulling the pin, and then telling you to go live your life."

A tear slipped down Libby's cheek. "Don't you realize.

It could happen at any moment for anyone. You never know what life is going to throw at you. One day, you're vibrant and full of life. The next, you're dead." She shrugged her right shoulder. "But you're not dead. Neither am I."

With one step, she brought them toe to toe.

"If you move and become paralyzed, you'll be you. Stubborn. Non-communicative. Heroic. Caring. Kind. Deadly. All with or without the use of your legs. And I'll be me. A crazy broad." She smiled. "And I'll love you all the same."

Jake bent his head forward and pressed his forehead to Libby's.

"What is it about fucking crazy animals that gets to me?" He grazed his lips across hers.

"I don't know. But I'm glad we do."

EPILOGUE

"THROUGH HEARTACHE AND FRIENDSHIP to plans finally coming together." Larkin lifted her foam headed beer into the air.

"Dinner?" Gen hoisted her half empty—or half full, if you were one of those assholes—mug to join their friend in celebration.

Libby swiped foam from her upper lip and set her drink on the table with a little too much gusto. It shook the thick oak high top. Her mild outburst faded quickly among the shouts and curses that surrounded them. The Rangers were playing the Blackhawks and trying to give away the game.

"I knew it," she huffed.

"Knew what?" Gen and Larkin parroted one another. The only difference was Gen set to finishing her beer while Larkin set hers on the table with much more class than Libby had. They both looked guilty as hell, and they should, shouldn't they?

"That you two have been planning our move for months." Libby pointed at Gen. "Since before you and Owen moved into The Ashford." She threw her hands into the air. "And that was months ago."

"Three," Larkin offered.

Libby shifted her sharp index finger at her friend. "How long have you been scheming?"

"Over a year." Larkin crossed her arms over her chest and smiled. The thick sleeves of the knitted sweater she wore made the diabolical expression she gave almost comical.

Gen's mouth fell open.

"Yep, you were bamboozled." Libby nodded.

"I thought moving in was my idea," Gen gasped. Her gaze shifted toward Larkin.

"Hey, I don't have a Fortune 500 company off my looks alone." Their friend shrugged. "Don't look at me that way, either of you. You are both grown ass women with the ability to make your own decisions. You said yes. So did your lovers."

A huge, stupid grin stretched Libby's cheeks to the point of pain. Why was she getting pissy? The dream of having her mysterious, mystical neighbor had come true, and it was better than she could have ever imagined. He'd stayed. He'd healed and helped her heal by her side. He'd sold his house and moved in with her at The Ashford on the same floor as Gen and Owen into one of the condos Larkin had commissioned for them.

"We can't complain about the maintenance or security." Gen finished off her beer.

"No, we can't." The boys had pooled their expertise and created an even more foolproof network of security for the building, including those that surrounded it.

That pooling of expertise and resources sparked the idea for a business venture between Beckett, Douglas, Owen, and Jake. In fact, while the girls celebrated, the men worked on their mission statement for their own private securities firm.

"Now that you have your job back—" Gen began.

"With a promotion," Larkin interjected.

"And Ross Quinn fired." Libby didn't know where Gen was headed with her original thought, but if high points were being hit, that was a spectacular one not to be forgotten.

"Yes, with all of that"—Gen flipped her red hair over her shoulder and gestured widely, circling all the high points— "in The Ashford, your commute is shorter."

"Not as short as either of yours," Libby pointed out.

"True," they agreed.

Gen grabbed the extra mug of beer they always put in Marlis's symbolic place and pulled it next to her empty one.

"Christ, Gen. We haven't been here for ten minutes," Larkin gasped.

"Mar wouldn't mind," the fiery redhead countered.

The wound wasn't fresh, but it still hurt every hour of every day. Libby longed for the time when it would only hurt a few times a day. They all did.

"No, she wouldn't." A tear slipped from Larkin's cheek. "I'm sorry. I just …"

"We know." Libby grabbed Larkin's hand with her left, which was a feat in itself. Months ago, her range of motion had been limited. She grabbed Gen's hand in her right. Something stabbed her thumb. "Ow!" With a jerk and a flip of Gen's wrist the culprit blinded her in the dim bar light. "Holy shit!"

Larkin gasped and covered her mouth with her free hand.

"Is that what I think it is?" Libby shrieked.

Gen, the woman who joked about giving Douglas—Larkin's father—the best night of his life in front of Larkin without blinking, blushed the same shade as her hair.

"Oh my God!" Larkin muttered beneath her hand.

"Owen is nothing if not traditional." Gen grinned like she'd just made good on her threat with Douglas.

"How did I miss this?" Libby released Larkin's hand, grabbed Gen's in both of hers, and shook the rock that glittered … and most likely left a bleeding gash on her thumb.

"He asked me last weekend, and I wanted to wait to share it until we were all together." Gen swiped at a tear that snuck from the corner of her eye.

Larkin finally dropped her hand from her mouth and shoved Marlis's symbolic beer closer to Gen. "How are you holding up?"

"I'm so in love my heart hurts when we're away from each other, which makes me want to roll my eyes at myself. I never thought I'd get married. I never thought I'd want to, but I'm so ready to make him mine that I suggested Vegas." Gen grinned.

"He already is yours," Libby assured her.

"I know." Gen nodded, and then rolled her eyes. "He's traditional, remember? So, it's going to be an obnoxiously large wedding."

"You're about to close your first case as a solo attorney, taking down Beena Carter. Now a wedding. I can't wait." Libby lifted her mug. "To our journey, the ups and downs and inside outs, may we make it together."

The girls raised their glasses. They clanked and cheered, overwhelming the boos being tossed at the screens.

Gen and Libby drank deeply, but Larkin very ceremoniously set her glass on the table without taking a sip.

"You didn't drink," Libby whispered.

Gen slammed her mug onto the table. "What!"

Larkin smiled slowly. Her hands went to her belly in a protective hug.

"Oh my God!" Libby echoed Larkin's words from a moment ago. "Does Beckett know?"

"Of course he knows." Larkin laughed. "It was his idea."

"How far along are you?" Gen straightened. "I've never asked anyone that question before." She giggled.

"Twelve weeks," Larkin breathed.

"Douglas is going to be a grandfather. That's hot." Gen fanned herself.

"Don't upset her. She's with child," Libby warned.

"You two." Larkin shook her head and then grabbed their

hands. "If it's a girl, we're going to name her Mara Elise."

"That's perfect." Libby sighed.

"And if it's a boy?" Gen asked.

"Then Lord save us all." Larkin laughed.

If you enjoyed *Who*, please consider leaving a
review on Goodreads and your
favorite book vendor.
If you enjoyed *Who*, check out *Why* …

BOOKS BY
MEGAN MITCHAM

BUREAU SERIES

FOR ALL TO SEE

PAINTED WALLS

STALKER SERIES

WHO

WHY

HOW

ABOUT THE AUTHOR

Megan Mitcham is a USA Today bestselling author who has penned more than 15 sizzling suspense novels. Her work is said to whisk you across the globe, wedge your heart in your throat, make your hands sweat and your skin tingle. Check out Megan's special forces heroes in the Base Branch Series. If you like the darker side of suspense, try her Bureau Series or her Stalker Series. She is a Mississippi native, living and loving it in the natural state.

Megan was born and raised among the live oaks and shrimp boats of the Mississippi Gulf Coast, where her enormous family still calls home. She attended college at the University of Southern Mississippi where she received a bachelor's degree in curriculum, instruction, and special education. For several years Megan worked as a teacher in Mississippi. She married and moved to South Carolina and began working for an international non-profit organization as an instructor and co-director. In 2009 Megan fell in love with books. Until then, books had been a source for research or the topic of tests. But one day she read Mercy by Julie Garwood. And Oh Mercy, she was hooked! For information on new releases and giveaways sign up for her

Readers' Group at **meganmitcham.com!**
Goodreads: **Megan_Mitcham**
Pinterest: **MeganMitcham5**
Website: **www.meganmitcham.com**
Facebook.com/**AuthorMeganMitcham**
Twitter.com/**MeganMMMitcham**

www.ingramcontent.com/pod-product-compliance
Lightning Source LLC
Chambersburg PA
CBHW072113250626
47159CB00007B/2428